Beth Slocum was the most perfect thing Joshua Kendall had ever seen.

She met his eyes, then turned to the fridge and stretched up onto her tiptoes, reaching for something.

He frowned then, because her top stretched up, revealing her back, and he saw the long, linear scar that didn't belong with her smooth, taut skin. He'd never noticed it before—and as he thought about that, he knew why and said, "I just noticed the scar on your back."

She dropped what was in her hands, paused for a moment, then came closer to him and pulled up her shirt to reveal a tiny mark. "This is where it went in. It really isn't very deadly looking, is it?"

He put his hands on her hips, drew her closer and pressed his lips to the spot. His heart was breaking as he relived the moment, pulling the trigger, sending a searing-hot piece of lead into this woman's abdomen. Why had he pulled the damn trigger?

"God, Beth, I'm so sorry."

She shrugged. "Don't be silly. It's not like you had anything to do with it."

But he had, and he knew that the truth had finally caught up with him.

Also by MAGGIE SHAYNE

EDGE OF TWILIGHT
THICKER THAN WATER
EMBRACE THE TWILIGHT
TWILIGHT HUNGER

*Watch for Maggie Shayne's
next vampire romance*

BLUE TWILIGHT

Coming March 2005

MAGGIE SHAYNE

COLDER THAN ICE

MIRA®

ISBN 0-7783-2094-4

COLDER THAN ICE

www.MIRABooks.com

Printed in U.S.A.

COLDER THAN ICE

Prologue

— ◆ —

Arthur Stanton stood in the middle of the narrow, deserted road while the rain poured down on him. In the distance, sirens wailed. Bloodhounds bayed, their unmistakable yowk-yowk-yowks rubbing his nerves raw. Every few seconds a helicopter passed overhead, its searchlight sweeping the ground. Men's voices rose from far away. Too far away, though. Right now, it was just the two of them: Arthur Stanton and the man in prison grays who'd come stumbling out of the tree line only to stop in his tracks, thirty feet away.

The convict met his eyes; then his glance slid lower, toward the gun Arthur held. He didn't move, just held his breath, waiting.

Arthur's hand trembled, not with fear, nor with the symptoms of his age, but with the weight of the decision tearing at his soul. David Quentin Gray, Jr., white-collar criminal and former attorney to a madman, wasn't the offender Arthur lived to apprehend. But he *could be* the key to that criminal. If he were free. Imprisoned, he was useless.

Swallowing against the bile that rose in his throat, Arthur lowered his weapon.

The convict frowned at him, jerking convulsively in an almost-lunge, before going motionless again.

He thinks I'll shoot him in the back if he runs. Hell, maybe I should.

But Arthur didn't. Instead, he turned and trudged back to his car. It waited on the muddy shoulder, where he'd skidded to a halt when he'd spotted the scarecrow silhouette among the trees, picked out by his headlights as he rounded a curve.

After three steps, Arthur stopped and squeezed his eyes tight. *I can't, I can't just let him walk. He's a criminal. I've spent the past forty years working against his kind.*

He raised his gun as he turned again, unable, unwilling, to do something so contrary to everything he believed.

But David Quentin Gray, Jr. was gone. The decision was made.

Headlights found Arthur, as if to illuminate this newest stain on his soul. Tires skidded, and a car door slammed. It was done. He couldn't undo it. And now, he thought, the lies begin.

"Stanton? What's going on? Did you see something?"

Arthur recognized the voice and turned. "Thought I did. It was just a deer, though."

Assistant Warden Martin Phillips sighed deeply, came closer and clapped a hand to Arthur's shoulder. "Dammit, I'm sorry. I know what this prisoner meant to you, Stanton."

"We'll get him. He can't get far."

"Still…" Phillips sighed, looked around just in case, lowered his voice. "You'll probably have to move her now, right?"

Arthur lifted his head.

"Hell, only a handful of people even know she's alive," the assistant warden went on. "Much less where she's hiding out."

"*You* shouldn't even know."

"I wouldn't—if Gray's cellmate hadn't been so eager to earn a few brownie points. He was coming up for parole and thought telling me what he knew would help his case." He grinned. "By running his mouth, all he really did was force us to keep him inside, where he couldn't spread what he knew about Elizabeth Marcum. Poor stupid shit."

Arthur reacted instantly, gripping the man by his lapels and drawing him up onto his toes. "She's dead. As far as the world is concerned, she's dead. I hear you say her name again, I'll have to put *you* someplace where you can't spread it around."

"All right, all right. Damn." Arthur released the man, and Phillips smoothed his lapels. "You act like it's my fault Gray saw that news clipping of some small-town Blackberry Festival with her in the background. Hell, if it were up to me, they wouldn't have access to television, newspapers or anything else from the outside."

Arthur unclenched his fists. He was angry with himself, not Phillips. He'd fucked up. Again.

"So will you move her?" Phillips asked, apparently too stupid to know when to let it drop.

"No." He'd come this far, Arthur thought. He might as well see this through.

"But—"

"But nothing. You've been keeping the prisoner under surveillance since you found out what he knew. Haven't you?"

"Well, yeah. We've watched him like a striptease."

"And he hasn't tried to get word out to anyone about the woman's whereabouts, has he?"

"No. But…all due respect, Arthur, that doesn't mean he won't run straight to Mordecai Young now that he's free."

I'm counting on it, Arthur thought. But aloud, he only said, "How about you do your own job, Phillips, and let me worry about mine?"

"Jesus, Arthur, if Young finds her, he'll kill her."

"I'm not going to let that happen." He couldn't let that happen. He couldn't have the blood of one more innocent staining his hands. He would see to it that Elizabeth Marcum—Beth Slocum, as she was currently known—remained safe. Not by moving her, but by being ready for the madman to strike. And then he could finally catch Mordecai Young and redeem himself. God knew he didn't have a lot more time to make amends. He was on the far side of sixty, and facing mandatory retirement.

He was using an innocent woman as bait to capture a madman. He knew that. And it was wrong. He knew that, too. He'd had to make a snap decision, and he'd made the wrong one. But it was made. Now he had to follow through. He could make it work out right; he knew he could. The key was in seeing to it that "Beth Slocum" had the best protection he could give her. Someone who would lay down his life before letting any more harm come to the woman.

And he knew there was only one man he could count on to do that.

A man who, like the rest of the world, believed she was dead. A man who had spent the past eighteen years convinced he was the one who had killed her.

Mordecai Young sat in his car with the wipers set on intermittent and the headlights turned off. An observer, had there been one, would have said he was alone in the car, yet Mordecai was never truly alone. He waited right where he had said he would. He could wait all night. But he wouldn't have to. He had it on pretty good authority that his old friend and former attorney, David Quentin Gray, Jr., would make it here unscathed.

It would be good to see David again. It had been a long time.

He really had picked the perfect spot—or rather, his guides had: a pull-off near a railroad crossing where no trains ran anymore. Back roads, no one around.

Oh, there would be roadblocks, but that didn't matter. He didn't know why yet, but he knew they were not going to be a problem. He knew it with a certainty that told him it was "given" knowledge. It came from beyond him.

Mordecai sat a little straighter in his seat when he spotted the man, hunched and shivering, near the edge of the woods. Gray was peering through the rain at the car, as if too wary to come any closer. Smiling to himself, Mordecai flashed his headlights on, then off, then on again. He left them on, because he couldn't believe his one-time attorney looked the way he did. Prison had apparently forced him to overcome his obsession with Italian suits and flawless grooming. David could have passed for a scrawny, half-drowned alley cat.

When he drew closer, Mordecai reached across the car and opened the passenger door.

David peered in at him, his face drawn and pinched, even when he smiled—a smile that never reached his eyes. "Mordecai. Damn, it's good to see you." He started to get in.

"Wait." Mordecai reached into the back seat for the red flannel blanket that lay folded there, pulled it into the front and draped it as best he could over the upholstery. "You're a mess, David. What did you do? Crawl out through the prison sewers?"

David scowled at him but got in. As soon as he'd closed the door, he pulled the loose ends of the blanket around him. "I'm frozen half to death."

"No wonder. You're skin and bone. You don't look well, David."

"Prison will do that to you." He glanced at Mordecai. "You look good, though. You never change."

It was true. Mordecai hadn't changed. His head was still clean shaven, his eyes still his most distinctive feature. He would have to change, though, once he found out where Lizzie was hiding. It wouldn't do to have her recognize him too soon.

He started the engine and turned up the heat. "I was glad to receive your letter, David. I have to say, it surprised me."

"It should have," David said, using a corner of the blanket to wipe the rain water from his face. "They've been watching everything I do—listening in on every conversation, every phone call, reading my mail both coming and going. My own fault, blabbing to my cellmate about what I knew. I know the little bastard ratted me out."

"It wasn't smart to tell him anything. It's never smart to give away too much. You taught me that yourself."

David frowned, but didn't ask what Mordecai meant by that. Maybe because he knew where the conversation was going. Or maybe the reference to his disloyalty of a year ago had sailed right over his head.

"I had to smuggle your letter out with another prisoner on work release."

"I didn't mean I was surprised you could get a letter out. What I meant, David, was that I was surprised your *loyalty* to me had lasted so long." He tipped his head slightly.

Bull. He wanted you to get him out of prison, and that's the only reason he told you a damn thing.

Don't trust him. He could be trying to trick you, the way she did.

Ask him where she is. Stop wasting time!

Mordecai closed his eyes briefly, slowly. The voices had multiplied. Where there used to be one or two, there were now too many to count. Though it had occurred to him that there were likely twelve. That would make the most sense, wouldn't it? Twelve.

And perhaps, he thought, one of them might be his Judas.

He didn't know them all. Some were more accurate than others, and he'd been struggling to learn which ones he should heed and which he would do better to ignore, or whether it was the flaw of his own human condition that twisted their messages so that they were not always quite right—a far more likely possibility. The voices came from Spirit. Spirit couldn't be wrong. His guides had taught him many things over the years. A deeper understanding of scripture. The importance of faith without question. The intricacies of poisons, and everything there was to know about explosives. The true depth of his twofold mission: to bring Lizzie to her knees, and to find his rightful heir.

He lifted his chin, tried to will the voices to be quiet. They chose to obey this time. They didn't always.

"I'd still like to know how you managed to get me out," David said. "I know some of the guards had to look the other way, let it happen."

Mordecai smiled softly. "It wasn't hard. My guides told me which guards would be open to bribery. Most men have their price, David."

David lowered his eyes. "Still with the voices, huh?"

"Of course. They're spirit guides. They don't just go away."

He could tell David would have liked to argue with that, but he had the good sense not to.

"So how are you going to get us out of here without being caught? Did your guides tell you that?"

"They will, when the time comes. But first, David, you have to keep your promise. Tell me what you know about my Lizzie. Where is she hiding?"

David licked his lips, looked out the rain-streaked windows into the darkness. Then he shook his head. "Not here. It's not safe, sitting here like this. How about you get me out of here, past the roadblocks and shit first? Then I'll fulfill my end of the bargain."

Mordecai didn't like that.

He's an ungrateful bastard, this one.

Put him in the trunk!

Mordecai nodded, rubbing his forehead a little. "All right. You're going to have to ride in the trunk, David. In case they do stop us."

"The trunk?" David looked horrified at the thought.

The man's soaking wet and frozen to the bone. Have mercy for God's sake.

God, how he hated it, Mordecai thought, when the voices disagreed.

He was your friend once.

That much was true. David *had* been his friend. Once. "Just get in the back, then. Lie on the floor and keep yourself hidden under the blanket. All right?"

David nodded, smiling a little. "Thanks, Mordecai." Then he climbed into the back seat and curled up on the floor, a skinny, wet blanket-bundle.

Mordecai drove the car. He drove where the voices told him to drive, even though he didn't understand why. Faith, he reminded himself, wasn't about understanding why. It was about believing, about acting without hesitation to obey the dictates of Spirit. He drove for ten minutes, then twenty. And then he pulled off and stopped the car.

He leaned over the back seat. "We're clear, David. All clear."

"God, you didn't even get stopped," David said, pulling the blanket from over his head and staring up at Mordecai from the floor. "Are you sure?"

"I'm sure. You know how ineffective the police can be."
David smiled and started to get up.

"Wait," Mordecai said. "I've been very patient with you, David. Very patient. But my patience is wearing thin. Tell me what you know about Lizzie."

David was sitting up now, but still on the floor. He nodded, sighing. "There was this picture in the newspaper, some kind of festival, late last fall. She was in the background of the shot, standing in the crowd watching a parade go by." He shook his head. "I couldn't believe the coincidence."

"Oh, it was no coincidence. It was the hand of Spirit. You were meant to see that photo, and I was meant to find my Lizzie."

David nodded, licking his lips and looking a little nervous. "The town was some rural place in Vermont. Blackberry."

"Blackberry, Vermont. God, it's almost too quaint." He pictured her, the way she had been, long ago. Lost and alone, and so very needy. He'd been her hero, her savior, then. "I presume she's using an alias."

"I don't know. I would imagine so. The government probably set her up with a whole new identity after—after what happened last year." He shook his head. "I can't believe she actually shot you. If it wasn't for that vest—"

"We don't discuss that, David."

David's eyes shot to Mordecai's, then lowered. "All right."

"That's all you know? You've told me everything?"

He nodded. "That's all. I don't know if she's living in that town or was only there visiting. But I know it was her. I'm sure it was her. I saved the clipping for you." He dug into a pocket as he spoke, tugged out a folded scrap of paper and held it up.

Mordecai took it. It was damp and worn. He unfolded it carefully, then turned on the overhead light so he could see it. The headline read "Harvest Time in Smalltown, USA." The photo was three columns wide, and in color. Floats with giant pumpkins and small children. A high school marching band. A crowd of spectators. A backdrop of crimson and gold foliage. Despite the wet blotches and creased folds, Mordecai spotted her right away. She stood in the crowd, and yet alone. She wore blue jeans and a suede jacket. Her long blond hair was pulled back in a ponytail. He was irrationally glad she hadn't cut it.

"You're right," he said to David. "It's her. It's Lizzie."

"I knew it. Anyway, the article doesn't say anything about her. But it's something. It's more than you had before."

Mordecai nodded. "Then I guess I'm finished with you now. You can get out."

Blinking, frowning in confusion, David said, "You… want me to just…go? You're just going to leave me out here like a stray dog? Mordecai, I need a place to crash, some dry clothes, maybe a few dollars in my pocket. I've got to survive. After what I've done for you, I thought—"

Mordecai sighed. "You're right. I mustn't forget what I owe you, after all. I'm going to take care of you, David, the way you took care of me. Come on, get up now. Come with me."

Mordecai opened his door and got out; then he opened the back door and took David's arm to help him out of the car. "You have taken good care of me, after all, haven't you, David?"

"I knew you'd want to know."

"Oh, I don't mean this," Mordecai said, shoving the clipping into his pocket. "This…this was good, David, but we both know it was self-serving. You did this for yourself, not for me."

"No—"

"Yes. You wanted me to get you out of prison. You knew this information would ensure I did so. After all, you could have just enclosed the clipping with the letter."

David broke the hold of Mordecai's eyes to look around. He was getting very nervous. "I could have. But I didn't want to risk losing it. It could have been found."

Mordecai shrugged. "And what about last year, when you told them where to find me after I'd reclaimed my daughter from that bitch Julie Jones? Was that all for me, as well?"

David's gaze snapped back to Mordecai's. "I didn't—"

"David, David, don't lie to me. I know it was you. You were the only one, besides Lizzie and I, who knew about the mansion in Virginia. And even if you weren't, my guides told me who played Judas to my Christ."

"Jesus, the guides again. Mordecai, you can't always trust those voices in your head. They aren't—"

"Aren't what? Aren't real? How have I survived, then? I could have been killed at the raid on my compound eighteen years ago. I could have been killed in Virginia last year, when the woman who claimed to love me fired a bullet into my chest. Or later, when the police descended on me. But I wasn't. My daughter could have been killed, as well, by those bastards claiming to have come to rescue her. From her own father. They called it a kidnapping. Can you imagine?" He shook his head. "I survived. I always survive. The guides see to that. And they tell me all I need to know. Admit it, David. You betrayed me."

David blinked. He was shaking again, but not from the cold this time. "You're right, I did tell someone about the Virginia house. Not the authorities. Another prisoner. I had no choice in that, Mordecai. He had clout, a lot of respect. You don't know what it's like in prison. They would have killed me if I hadn't talked."

"So again, your self-interests outweighed your concern for me." Mordecai shrugged. "I suppose it's part of the human condition. Selfishness. Disloyalty."

David couldn't hold his eyes, so he looked past him. And then the worry returned. "Mordecai, this looks like the same place where you picked me up. Isn't this right where we started?"

"Right where *you* started, perhaps. I'm miles ahead of where I was a short while ago. Goodbye, David."

Mordecai lifted the gun, as the voices had been screaming at him to do for countless minutes now. It had come to him very clearly why the roadblocks would not be a problem tonight. It was because David wouldn't be cowering in the back seat when Mordecai's car was searched. David wasn't going anywhere—nowhere on this plane, at least. He pointed the gun's barrel at David's head, and even as the man flinched and cried out, Mordecai calmly squeezed the trigger.

David's body collapsed downward like a building when well-placed demolition charges go off. He sank fast, landing in a heap at Mordecai's feet.

"I promised to free you from your prison, David. And now I have."

Mordecai left the blanket where it was, twisted around David's body. It was wet, muddy now, and tainted with blood. He got back into the car, sliding the gun into the holder he had mounted under the driver's seat, and drove away.

It was time to find Lizzie. It was time to right the wrongs she had done, wash clean the sins she had committed—against him, against their daughter.

Against God.

1

— ◆ —

Thursday

Elizabeth Marcum was running again.

She was always running, it seemed.

One after the other, her powder-blue Nike cross trainers hit the winding road's soft shoulder, her steps cushioned by a thick, fragrant carpet of leaves. She sucked in the aroma of them with every harsh breath she drew. Sugar maples lined the roadsides, arching overhead like a vivid circus canopy of scarlet and purple and pumpkin orange. It crossed her mind that she loved it here, but she brushed the thought aside. There were a hundred other small towns with country lanes and breathtaking foliage where she could be just as comfortable. Comfort wasn't love. She could take Blackberry, Vermont, or leave it.

She hit the three-mile mark just as she rounded the curve that brought the old Bickham place into view. The once stately Victorian's white paint was peeling. A few of the black shutters were crooked, others missing, like neglected teeth in an old man's mouth. On the porch, Maude waved from her wicker rocking chair. Elizabeth slowed to a walk, her heart rate slowing naturally as she veered off the road and onto the overgrown flagstone path. She preferred it to the driveway, despite its cracks and weeds.

The sidewalk started at the tilting signpost, with its weather-worn sign and fading letters—you could hardly make out "The Blackberry Inn" anymore—and wound its way to the porch, forking off in one spot to twist around the old house to what had once been a garden in the back.

At the bottom of the porch steps, Beth leaned over, braced her hands on her knees and took a few breaths.

"Gettin' older, girl," Maude called. "You might better walk, like you used to."

Beth smiled. Every day, Maude began their morning visit with the same remarks. When Beth had first come here—God, had it really been a year ago?—she had started this ritual with a daily walk. It had scared the hell out of her to even leave her house, but that daily walk had been an act of defiance, a way of thumbing her nose at her own fears. It had evolved into a run.

"I like to run, Maude. It makes me strong."

"And what does a thirty-five-year-old woman need with muscles, anyway?"

Beth grinned and trotted up the steps. "Thirty-six. And I need 'em to fight off all my suitors."

Maude slapped her knee, chuckling to herself, and rose from the chair. "Tea is just off the burner. Still piping hot. You made good time this morning." She leaned over the rickety tray table to pour from a china teapot into two matching cups. Antiques, white with pink rosebuds and gold edges. There was an old silver tray with a cover, and an empty hypodermic needle beside it.

"God, Maude, why don't you get an insulin pump so you can stop sticking yourself three times a day like your body's a pin cushion?"

Maude waved a hand at her. "I don't trust machines. And if you could see what they charge for one of those gadgets…"

"You have insurance."

"That's no reason to throw good money away on nonsense. 'The frivolous can waste more by the teaspoon than the frugal can bring home by the wheelbarrow.'"

"Is that one of your originals?"

She shrugged. "You'd have called the original sexist. So I put my own twist on it, just for you."

"And I'll bet you've been waiting for the opportunity to use it."

Maude sent her a wink. Then she reached to the tray table and poured from a dewy pitcher into a tall glass. "Here's a nice glass of cold water. Cool you down after all that ridiculous running."

"Perfect." Beth took the glass from the table and tipped it up, drinking half the refreshing, sweet water down before lowering herself into her customary seat, a second wicker chair that matched the first in age and wear, if not color or design.

"Cookie?" Maude offered.

"Chocolate chip?" Beth asked, leaning over the table to lift the tarnished silver lid from its platter.

"How did you know before you even looked?"

"I could smell them baking in my dreams last night."

Maude chuckled, but then her smile died, and she shook her head. "A young woman ought to have something to dream about besides cookies."

Taking a big bite, Beth said, "What else is there?"

But Maude didn't join her in her teasing. "I'm serious, Beth. Life without friends is like pie without ice cream. You've lived in Blackberry for a year now, and yet you've barely made any friends at all."

Beth tipped her head to one side, reminding herself that the old woman needed something to occupy her mind, and if worrying about her was the thing to do it, then fine.

She would indulge her. Reaching across the table, she patted Maude's hand. "I've made one friend, Maude. One very good friend."

That got a smile out of Maude. She actually had to blink a little moisture from her eyes. "Oh, you. Now you've gone and made me misty."

"Well, I mean it. I'm so glad you called me over here that first time."

"Saw you walking by, then running by, day after day. Any fool could see you were lonely. Besides, I was curious to ask what it was you were running away from." She took a sip of her tea. "Not that I've managed to get an answer to that question."

"'A woman without secrets has led far too boring a life,'" Beth said, repeating one of Maude's own pearls of wisdom back to her.

"Score one for you." Maude sighed, settling back in her chair. "You know, there are some nice people in Blackberry. You're missing out on a lot by keeping so much to yourself."

Here it comes, Beth thought.

"Take Jeffrey Manheim. Owns the coffee shop down on Main Street. Nicest unmarried man you could ever want to—"

She broke off there, looking up as a shiny white pickup truck pulled into her driveway. Beth shielded her eyes to try to make out who was inside, but already she was on guard. She didn't recognize the man who got out of the truck and glanced their way. A younger man—maybe eighteen—got out from the passenger side and came around the truck to join him. Strangers. New in town.

This couldn't be good.

Maude rose to her feet and stumbled a little as she started forward, so Beth got up as well, and grabbed hold of her forearm to steady her.

"Joshua?"

The man flashed a smile. "It's me, Gram. It's been way too long." By the time he finished the sentence, he was mounting the steps, and then he swept Maude into his arms for a hug. Maude hesitated only slightly before returning it.

The man released her and stood back just a little to look her over. "You look wonderful, Gram. Just as pretty as ever."

She smiled at him, and Beth could have sworn her cheeks went pink. "Well, I don't know about that."

"Bryan, get up here and say hello to your great-grandma."

The boy joined them on the porch. It was obvious now he was the man's son. He had the same milk-chocolate hair and the same jawline—as if it were etched in stone. But there was a brooding quality about him. He didn't stand quite straight, didn't meet his father's eyes—or Maude's, either, for that matter—and he didn't look happy to be there. He kept slanting sideways glances at Beth.

She really should leave, she thought, as the boy took his hands from his jeans pockets long enough to give the old woman a halfhearted hug. "Hello, Grandma."

"My, my," Maude said. "What a fine young man you have here, Joshua."

"He sure is," Joshua said. "Gram, aren't you going to introduce us to your friend?"

"Oh, of course. Where are my manners? Beth, this is my grandson, Joshua, and his boy Bryan. Boys, this is Beth Slocum. She's a good, good friend to me. You be sure you treat her right."

Joshua turned to face her fully for the first time, extending a hand to close it around hers. He met her eyes, and then something changed in his face. The smile seemed to freeze in place, and he looked into her eyes so intently it made her squirm. He looked stunned, shocked, and maybe there was a hint of recognition amid all the other things swimming in his eyes. It worried her.

Swallowing hard, she tugged her hand, but he didn't let it go. "Um… It's nice to meet you," she said, wishing like hell that she could read his mind as she tugged her hand a little harder.

He blinked, glanced down at their hands, and let go quickly. "Sorry about that. You…remind me of someone."

"Really? Who?"

His eyes were still dancing over her face. My God, she thought they might even be dampening. What the hell was with this guy? "Never mind," he said. "It's not important." He tore his gaze from hers and looked at his son. "Bryan, say hello to Miss Slocum."

Bryan looked at her. "Hi." Then he turned to his father. "I'm going to get my MP3 player out of the truck." He turned on his heel and marched back down the steps to the truck, where he took a few suitcases and duffels from the back.

"He's not happy to be here," Beth said.

"He's had a tough year," the stranger explained. "His mother and stepfather were killed over the summer. Plane crash. Then I had to uproot him from the West Coast and move him to Manhattan. He's not dealing well."

Those words wrapped themselves around Beth's heart and squeezed. "His entire life has been stripped away from him," she said, her throat tightening. "There's no way to deal well with something like that."

Josh was looking at her again. "Sounds like the voice of experience."

She shrugged and lowered her eyes. His were too intense. Too filled with something she couldn't name, and too intent on probing, on digging into her soul.

To change the subject, she said, "Maude, I always assumed you and Sam didn't have any children."

"Now why would you assume that?" Maude asked, fussing with the sleeve of her blouse.

"I don't know. You never mentioned any kids, and there were no pictures around the house."

"I really do need to get some photos put up," she said, as if that explained everything perfectly.

Beth glanced at Josh, saw the way he was watching Maude, watching her responses to Maude's explanations. He looked a little nervous.

"There was a death in your family over the summer, and you never said a word?" Beth asked.

Maude blinked. "Well, the family's so estranged, you know, I never even heard about Bryan's mother until a week ago, when Josh phoned me."

"Kathy kind of cut my side of the family off after the divorce," Joshua said.

Beth nodded as if it made perfect sense, when in fact it made none.

"Honestly, none of that matters," Maude said. "All that matters is that they're here now. Come from Manhattan to spend some time with me."

"That's nice, Maude." Beth watched the boy, felt the pain coming off him in waves. She loved kids and felt an empathy for this one. Maybe because she, too, had been stripped of everything in her life. "Is he still in high school?" she asked.

"This is his senior year." Joshua looked guilty now. "But I could barely get him to go when the semester started. He hated everything about Manhattan, but especially going to school there."

"So what are you going to do?"

He shrugged, then faced her. "This parenting thing is

like rocket science to me. I'm damned if I know what to do with him."

"Beth can help with that," Maude said. "She's a teacher. You two sit down and chat. I'm going to get more cookies." She went through the door and into the house without another word. The screen door banged.

Josh said, "So you're a teacher?"

"I used to be."

Josh sat in one of the wicker chairs, waving her to the other one. She glanced toward the young man, but he was sitting on the tailgate now, with headphones on.

"So why did you stop?"

She sent him a quick look. Was he a little too interested in her past? Or just being polite? "Needed a break. I still tutor, though."

"Really?"

She nodded. "So how long are you going to be here?" she asked, turning the tables by asking questions rather than answering them. It was a skill she'd perfected over the past year.

"To be honest, I don't know. It depends on a lot of things."

He had a way of answering a question without revealing a thing. She recognized the tactic, because it was another one she'd grown deft at employing.

"Why is it Maude's never mentioned you?"

He shrugged. "There's been a rift in the family." Then he met her eyes. "It's kind of personal."

"Sorry."

"It's not a problem." He looked toward his son again. "I wish I knew what to do about Bryan."

"I could talk to him…if you want."

He looked at her as if surprised. "Do you have kids, Beth?"

Jesus. The innocent question knocked the wind out of her. She tried not to let it show in her face, turning away quickly, just as Maude called for Joshua to come help her for a minute.

"Did I say something wrong?"

"Why don't you go help Maude with those cookies? And tell her I'll see her in the morning."

Beth walked down the steps, but she didn't take the flagstone path. She went out the driveway, pausing by the pickup to tie her shoe and pull herself together. It wasn't Joshua's fault, she told herself. He couldn't possibly know her chance to raise her only child had been stolen from her because of some toy soldier with an itchy trigger finger eighteen years ago.

When she rose it was to see Bryan staring at her. She glanced back toward the porch. Joshua had gone inside. The porch was empty.

Bryan had stacked suitcases on the pickup's tailgate, though it was completely unnecessary. "Don't worry, my father has that effect on a lot of people," he said.

She looked at him, then allowed a smile as she realized he'd witnessed her reaction to Joshua's question, though he probably hadn't heard the dialogue. "Then it's not just me?" she asked.

"Nope."

"That's good to know." She rolled her eyes and saw Bryan's smile turn from polite to amused. "Your dad tells me you're in your senior year."

"Yeah. But I'm taking a semester off."

She nodded. "What do you still need to graduate?"

"History, Spanish Four, English Twelve."

Beth smiled a little. "I used to teach English Eleven and Twelve."

"Used to? What, you don't anymore?"

"I'm taking a semester off."

He smiled at her, his eyes, and interest, sincere.

"Actually, more like a few semesters. I still tutor, though. Let me know if you want to get those English credits out of the way while you're in town. Give me an hour a day and I'll have you ready for the final by Christmas."

"I doubt we'll be here that long."

"Then give me two hours a day and make it Thanksgiving."

He looked at her. "You know, it's actually not all that bad an idea."

She liked Bryan, she decided. She liked him a lot. Dawn would like him, too, if she were here. "Well, it's up to you. I'm not pushing. And it would be tough on limited time. You'd have to be up for a challenge."

"English is my best subject. How much do you charge?"

"What are you, kidding? You're Maude's great-grand-son."

"I don't want a free ride."

"Well, we can work something out, then. Maybe you could help me with a few chores?"

He nodded. "Okay. Sounds good."

She smiled, pleasantly surprised. "You mean we're on?"

"We're on," he said, extending a hand.

She shook on it, feeling buoyant and knowing why. She could help this kid. And he was going to let her. "We can start tomorrow. My place at noon. Maude can tell you where."

"Great. See you then."

"You'll see me sooner." She jogged down the driveway, turned left onto the lane, and fell into an easy rhythm.

She didn't think she liked the man. Then again, she didn't like any man. She didn't trust them. But she liked his son. Maybe that was because looking at all the grief and loss in the boy's eyes was like looking into a mirror. Or maybe it was because she knew that no matter how much the people in his life would like him to "get over it" there was no such thing. He could deny it, defy it, or learn to live with it. But he couldn't get over it.

God knew she never had.

Mordecai had set himself up in one of the seven perfect Victorian homes situated in a neighborhood halfway between the towns of Blackberry and Pinedale. The houses had been purchased by some brilliant entrepreneur twenty-odd years ago, according to Mordecai's research—he didn't believe in going anywhere without all the information. The houses were rented out to wealthy families as vacation homes in the summer and to foliage-seeking tourists in the fall. In the winter, the skiing enthusiasts took over, and from February through March, they were inhabited by folks in town for the maple syrup season, and all the festivals and events it brought. In April the houses were closed for upkeep.

The others were all occupied. This one should have been, too—by Oliver Abercrombie, who'd made his reservations six months in advance. Unfortunately for the late Mr. Abercrombie, he was the only tenant without an immediate family, or anyone else close enough to miss him right away.

Mordecai had also learned that the school districts of the two tiny towns had merged a decade back, when the population of students had outgrown their buildings and the cost of educating them had outgrown the towns' respective tax bases. Now the Pinedale-Blackberry Central School System had its elementary building in Pinedale and its high school in Blackberry. The towns were eight miles apart, and this hamlet—which wasn't a town at all, but was called Bonnie Brook by the locals—was halfway between the two.

Lizzie was a teacher. He expected to find her working in one of the schools. So getting into the school system would be his first order of business.

This town was too quiet, he thought as he drove. It gave the voices too much silence in which to operate. When Mordecai was surrounded by noise and activity and people, they mostly kept quiet. But here, where the only sounds at night were the creaking of the old house and the gentle rustling of the October wind in the drying leaves... here they almost never went silent.

They were whispering now, in the background of his thoughts as he drove slowly along the winding, narrow roads, among the Day-Glo yellow of the poplar trees. Whispering...

She's here, somewhere.

You're close, Mordecai. You're very close.

She was supposed to burn in the fire, you know. Eighteen years ago, when the government raided your compound and all those young women died. She was supposed to die with them.

He frowned, and said aloud, "Maybe I was supposed to die with them, too."

You know you can't die without leaving an heir, Mordecai.

You need a child, someone to carry on your gifts, your work.

He sighed, disappointed anew that his own biological daughter, his and Lizzie's, had not turned out to be the one. Spirit had rejected her. Still, he loved her, in his way. He set her free because of that love. But he yearned for another, his heir. Perhaps he would find that heir here.

He turned the car's steering wheel, leaving the poplar-lined lane for one that wound and twisted between rolling meadows, dotted by fat, slow-chewing Holsteins with swollen udders and huge eyes.

He saw a woman running, jogging, along the road's shoulder.

She wore maroon warmup pants with a thin white stripe up the sides, and a white tank top that fit her like a second skin. The jacket that matched the pants was knotted around her waist, and her blond ponytail bounced with every step she took.

That hair…

"Lizzie?" he whispered, slowing the car to a crawl so he could get a good look at her when he drove by. But there was something decidedly un-Lizzie-like about this woman. The squared shoulders. The pumping of her clenched fists. The way she held her head, chin high. Her stride was powerful, almost aggressive.

Slowly, he eased the car past her, then looked into the side mirror so he could see her face. But she'd stopped, was bending now, tying her shoe.

Go on, Mordecai. Keep driving. You have a date to keep. This one can wait.

The guides were right, he thought with a sigh. Besides, this wasn't his Lizzie. His Lizzie was insecure, cowering and needy. And he was here for more than just Lizzie. He was here, he suspected, because this was where the heir would be found.

He drove the rest of the way to the high school, and waved to the woman who was waiting outside as he pulled into a vacant parking slot. Then he tipped the rearview mirror down to check his appearance.

Coke-bottle-thick glasses made his eyes appear huge, and emphasized the green of the colored contacts. The toupee looked real enough, mostly because few people would wear a hairpiece that was thick, black and mussed. He'd had it custom made. His new jet-black goatee was trimmed to a point at his chin and accompanied by a matching moustache that connected to it, bracketing his mouth. The new Oliver Abercrombie didn't resemble the Mordecai Young of eighteen years ago, with his long mink hair and thin layer of stubble. Back then he had looked the way most westerners imagined Jesus Christ had looked. He didn't resemble his more recent persona, Nathan Z, who'd been utterly bald, with striking brown eyes and a clean shaven face, either. He didn't think Beth herself would have recognized him today, even had she bumped into him on the streets of Blackberry.

That was the way he wanted it. For now. She mustn't know he had found her, not until he was ready.

He got out of his car, and Nancy Stillwater came limping toward him from the school's main entrance, smiling. The smile put creases into her plump face. "Hello, Oliver," she said, pushing dull brown hair, with a few gray strands, behind her ears.

"Ahh, Nancy. You are a vision. How is your day going?"

"Not too badly, so far. The new textbooks I've been waiting for finally came in."

"Wonderful. Are they as good as you'd expected them to be?"

"Better. Even my students approve. So where are we having lunch?" she asked, lifting the basket she had, no doubt, taken great pains to fill.

"Anywhere you like," he said, taking the basket from her. "It's such a nice day for a picnic."

"It really is. We won't have too many more like this."

"No, we won't."

"There are picnic tables this way." She actually took his arm as she led him around the building, either because she was attracted to him and wanted to touch him, or because her bad leg was bothering her. The limp was considerably worse today than it had been yesterday, when he'd met her while applying for a job as a substitute teacher at the high school.

His false credentials had impressed the office staff, and by the time they got around to checking them out, his work here would be done. After all, his claims put him far above what was required of substitute teachers.

His résumé ought to put him at the top of the list, if they even had a list.

List or no list, you will be the one they call. We'll see to that. You have to stop doubting us, Mordecai.

Yes, stop doubting us. All is in place. All we need now is for one of the regular teachers to get too sick to come in to work.

"Here we are," Nancy said, as they walked into a court-yard with round concrete tables, benches and planters situated everywhere. "This spot's reserved for staff and seniors. And the staff know when the seniors have their lunch period," she added with a smile. "It's nice, don't you think?"

"Particularly without the seniors present." He laughed softly, setting her picnic basket on the nearest table, lifting the lid and beginning to unload dishes.

She sat down beside him. "I was surprised when you asked me to join you for lunch today, Oliver."

"Now why should that surprise you?" He pulled out the bottle of sparkling grape juice, removed the cork with a flourish and poured juice into stemmed, plastic wine-glasses.

"Well, I'm not exactly used to the attention of men."

"Then the men around here must be stupider than I imagined." He handed her a glass. "To the beginning of a lovely friendship, and the promise that, next time, the wine will be real." He held his glass toward her.

She tapped hers against it, took a sip and smiled.

Mordecai smiled back, glancing down at the sectioned

plates with their air-lock plastic lids, specially designed for packing picnic lunches. He removed the lid from the first one, and with his hands still hidden inside the basket, twisted the cap off the vial he'd palmed and emptied its contents onto the salad. Then he picked up the plate and set it gently in front of her. "Ah, this looks wonderful, my dear."

"It's my special ambrosia salad, chicken coq au vin— albeit cold—antipasto, and a homemade double chocolate brownie for dessert."

"My goodness! You're a goddess."

She smiled as he passed her a napkin-wrapped set of silverware. "I don't eat like this every day, mind you. But I thought today it would be all right to forget about my diet."

"Diet? Please, you're perfect. A Botticelli nude."

"Oh, my." She averted her eyes as her cheeks went pink.

Mordecai pocketed the empty vial and casually cleaned his hands with an antibacterial wipe he'd brought along. Then he removed the lid from his own plate, set the basket on the ground and dug into his meal with relish.

She dug into hers, as well. Poor stupid woman.

2

—▶◀—

Joshua Kendall walked into Maude Bickham's house in a state of shock. The woman, Beth Slocum, the resemblance… No, no, it was more than a resemblance. She was identical to the girl his bullet had torn apart eighteen years ago. The girl who'd lain in a deep coma as he sat by her bed, wishing he could change places with her. The girl he'd been told had no chance of surviving.

She was older, of course. The eyes he'd only seen closed in mindless slumber had a few lines at their corners that hadn't been there before. God, how he'd longed to see them open, to know their color.

He knew it now. Emerald green, like the Gulf of Mexico at midsummer.

The round cheeks of youth had been replaced by sharper angles, but there was no question she was the same person.

He stumbled into the house, barely seeing where he was going, so many questions were whirling through his mind.

"Well, there you are. My goodness, I almost lost it out there. I have to tell you, son, I'm not used to telling lies."

"You, uh…you did fine, Maude."

"Well, it's well worth it, if it's to help protect Beth from whatever shadows she's been running from. Like I always say, 'You have to crush some tomatoes to get any sauce.'

This won't wash for long, though. There are folks in this town have known me far longer than Beth has. Oh, I can put 'em off for a while. Sam and I were old enough when we bought this place that any kids we might have had would have been grown. Most folks don't know we never had any. All but Frankie, anyway. She won't be so easily— what is it, Joshua? You look as if you've seen a ghost."

"I…" He gave his head a shake and forced himself to pay attention to the woman. "It was a long drive. I guess I'm tired out."

"Well, then, go on up to your room. I've put you in the blue room, and your boy in the one beside you. Go left at the top of the stairs. It's the second door on the right."

"Thanks."

He took her advice and sought out the privacy of his bedroom. And the first thing he did was to make a phone call to Arthur Stanton, his longtime mentor, former superior officer, and the man who'd hired him for this job. Arthur was out. His machine told Josh to leave a message.

Josh held the phone to his ear, staring out the bedroom window. Down there on the scraggly lawn, a ghost was talking to his son. A woman who was supposed to be dead. He should know, he thought. He'd killed her himself.

"Arthur, it's Joshua. Call me back and tell me what the hell is going on. Is this woman—is she—Jesus, Art, what are you doing to me here?"

He couldn't take his eyes off her. Not even when the image of the girl she had been when he'd seen her last overlaid the scene below in his mind. He saw her as she had been: pale, far too thin, barely seventeen. Wires taped to her temples and forehead, and running from underneath her clothes. Tubes in her wrists and mouth. White sheets, white hospital gown, white skin. The damned incessant beeping of the heart monitor that sounded sluggish and slow.

A lot of kids had been caught in the cross fire when federal agents raided the Young Believers' Compound eighteen years ago. But most of the bodies burned in the holocaust that followed.

Hers hadn't.

Josh had been an ATF agent then, overzealous and eager to be a hero. And maybe a little too quick to fire back at the muzzle flashes coming from the compound. Ballistics matched the bullet that took her out with Joshua's own rifle. When Josh had gone to the hospital to see her, they'd told him she wouldn't live out the week.

She'd been haunting him ever since.

It couldn't be her. It couldn't be. Not like this, strong, older...alive, running now down the tree-lined lane, her strides powerful and confident. It couldn't be her.

There was a knock on his door. "Dad?"

He shook himself, opened it. Bryan stood there with a large red-white-and-blue envelope in his hands. "Mailman was just here. Left this for you. It came express, so I figured it was important."

He took it, eyed the return address.

"It's from that guy who hired you—Arthur Stanton."

The man who was like a father to him. The man he trusted, had always trusted, even after the raid.

"He was your boss when you were in the ATF, you said."

Josh nodded. He'd been fired, because the nation needed a scapegoat. Not that he hadn't been guilty—just no guiltier than every other man on the strike team that day. Art had been too well respected to be fired; he'd been moved, instead. Lost his command, gotten stuck behind a desk pushing papers for the rest of his career. Put to work for the Federal Witness Protection Program. If she was who Josh thought she was, she must have been one of Arthur's first cases.

Jesus.

"So what was really going on down there?" Bryan asked.

Josh tried to focus on his son. "What do you mean?"

"With that woman. First you looked at her like you were seeing a ghost, and then you tried to cover—lamely."

Josh pursed his lips. "I wasn't trying to cover. She really does remind me of someone."

"Yeah, so much you nearly lost your lunch."

He averted his eyes.

"I mean it, Dad. I thought you were going to blow it out there. I mean, you're the one who's supposed to know what you're doing here, the one who spent three straight days lecturing me on not blowing our cover. So I figure this is something major."

He forced himself to meet his son's gaze. "You might be right."

"Then you know Beth Slocum from somewhere?"

"I don't know yet."

"But you think you might?"

He didn't say anything, his gaze dragged as if by force to the envelope again.

"Right," Bryan said. "It's none of my damn business, anyway. You should have just said so. I'm going out."

The tone jerked Josh back to the present. "Going out where?"

"Hell, Dad, I don't know. I'm not sure what my options are around here, so I can hardly answer that one. Around, I guess. I'm taking the pickup."

"Just be careful. And call if you're going to be late."

Bryan didn't answer, just headed out of the bedroom.

He didn't quite slam the door, but he didn't shut it any too gently, either.

Josh sighed, wishing to hell he knew how to be a decent father to his son. He probably shouldn't have let him go, but hell, the boy was almost eighteen. It wasn't like he needed baby-sitting.

He didn't know what to do. He knew his son was in pain and acting out in anger, but he didn't have the first clue what to do about it. And frankly, given the shock he'd just suffered, he was in no state to figure out the answer today.

He sat down on his bed and tore open the envelope. It contained a complete dossier on Elizabeth Marcum, aka Beth Slocum, beginning when she'd awakened from a coma eighteen years ago. When he read the hell she'd been through because of his bullet, he wondered if it might have been better if he had killed her after all.

She'd awakened with no memory, no life, facing years of rehabilitation and physical therapy. She'd lost all of it…because of him.

He was sure of only one thing: he owed her. And this assignment hadn't come out of the blue. Arthur had chosen him deliberately, knowing he would protect Beth Slocum better than anyone else ever could, because of that debt.

Bryan thought he probably shouldn't hate his father for keeping secrets from him when secrets were a part of his job. He *did* hate it, though. He hated just about everything his old man did these days. Every word out of his mouth seemed unreasonably irritating and made Bryan want to snap back, even when it wasn't altogether warranted.

Bryan wasn't stupid. It made sense to resent his father for not giving a damn about his mother's death. Josh hadn't shed a single tear. And it made sense to hate him for dragging Bryan out of his school, away from his friends, his home, and making him live in an apartment the size of a closet in Manhattan.

He thought maybe Joshua was starting to get that. He thought maybe that was why, when his dad's former boss from his days in the ATF, days before Bryan was even born, contacted him about this job, he'd accepted so fast. He knew Bryan detested the city. He probably thought this middle-of-nowhere town in Vermont would be better for him.

But Bryan didn't want to be here, either. He just wanted to go home.

He drove the pickup, which he secretly loved, into the tiny town of Blackberry, which was all of two miles from the old woman's run-down house. He spent the entire drive trying to locate an alternative or punk station on the radio, with no luck at all. Nothing out here but easy listening, country and talk radio.

God, he was going to die of boredom inside a week. He pulled off when he found a park, walked the entire thing, and found a fountain, a basketball court, a hot-dog stand. He bought a dog and continued on. The town was packed, way more people than could possibly live in a place this small. Must be the tourists his dad had told him were liable to be around. God, there were a lot of them, walking around with cameras, or driving with their heads sticking out the windows, pointing at the trees.

It was pretty here. He had to give it that.

Just at the edge of town there was a library, and he spent a couple of hours there, using their Internet connection and playing video games.

He'd killed the rest of the morning and was working on the afternoon when he pulled into the blacktop square beyond the ornate little sign that read Blackberry Public Parking. It was smack in the middle of a strip of road that was lined on either side with businesses. They all had awnings, and all the awnings were color coordinated— green or white, or green-and-white stripes. The stores— shops, really—had old-fashioned lettering on the windows, and they all looked like something out of one of the Norman Rockwell prints his mother used to have hanging all over their house. If not for the tourists, Bryan would have felt as if he'd walked right into one of them. The barbershop had an actual barber pole.

He pocketed his keys and took to the sidewalk. It was clean, unbroken, no weeds springing up in between the blocks. Oak trees grew from circular holes in the concrete, with red mulch covering their bases. Almost every building had a flag on display—not all of them American flags, though. Some were Canadian, some Italian, and some bore peace signs or rainbows.

He scanned the shop windows. Drugstore, grocery, ice cream "shoppe," hardware, electronics… "Now we're getting somewhere," he said.

He went through the swinging doors of the tiny electronics store, nodded hello to the woman behind the counter and started perusing the shelves. There was only one other customer in the place, an absentminded professor type in a baggy suit.

The woman behind the counter said, "Can I help you find something, young man?"

"Yeah, I'm looking for a set of headphones for my MP3 player." He pulled the tiny device out of his pocket as he spoke and held it up, but as he did, the other customer placed his purchases—a video camera and several tapes— on the counter.

"They're right over there, son," she said, pointing at a

pegboard right beside the counter, where about twenty different sets of headphones hung.

Bryan went over and began looking for one that would fit his player.

He noticed the guy at the counter taking his purchases and turning to go. A twenty lay on the floor at his feet. As the man walked toward the door, Bryan hurried to grab it. "Excuse me, mister, I think you dropped this."

The man turned as if surprised, saw Bryan holding out the twenty and smiled. He had thick, unevenly cut black hair that looked as if he'd combed it with an egg beater, thick-lensed glasses with black plastic frames, and the kind of pointy beard you'd expect to see on the villain in an old movie.

His smile was warm, though. He quickly pulled out his wallet and checked his cash. "You're right, I did drop it. Thank you, young man. That was very thoughtful of you."

"No prob."

The guy took the twenty, tucked it into his wallet and tugged out a five. "Here, for your honesty."

"No, really. It's okay," Bryan said, holding up a hand.

"You're sure?"

He nodded. "My mother was always telling me if you can't be honest for the sake of honesty, you're not really being honest at all."

The man tipped his head to one side. "Your mother sounds like a very wise woman."

"She was," Bryan said. He turned back to the rack of headphones beside the counter.

The stranger cleared his throat, and Bryan turned again, surprised to see him still there. "I don't mean to pry, but, uh…do you go to school around here?"

Bryan shook his head. "I'm taking a semester off, but I have a private tutor so I won't fall behind."

"Ah. A private tutor, is it? That's very wise. One of the teachers, I assume?"

"No, she's not teaching right—" He bit back the rest of the sentence, as his father's coaching and warnings came whispering through his brain. He was talking about Beth Slocum, the woman they were here to protect. A woman in hiding. "I mean, I don't really know what else she might do. I'm brand-new in town."

"I only ask because I'm a teacher myself." The man dug a card from his pocket and handed it to Bryan.

"You teach here in Blackberry?" Bryan asked.

"Well, it's not official yet, but I expect to be hired any day now. What subjects are you taking with this tutor? Maybe I can offer to cover the ones she doesn't?"

"No, thanks," Bryan said, deciding to err on the side of caution. "I don't want to take on too much at once. But, uh, I'll keep you in mind if I need another tutor."

"You do that. And thank you again for your honesty. Your mother would be proud."

Bryan had to swallow past the lump in his throat as he watched the man go. Then he looked at the card. Oliver Abercrombie. There was a telephone number, but no address. What an odd man.

Mordecai got into his car—a car far below his standards, but one that would stand out far less than his former one would have done. It was a nondescript brown sedan, five years old and nothing fancy. Nothing noticeable or memorable. He was dying to get back to searching for Lizzie.

No, not yet. You have to stay.

You have to watch the boy. We sent you into that shop for a reason, Mordecai. When will you learn to trust us?

"But Lizzie—"

She's not going anywhere, Mordecai. And finding the heir to your powers and your gifts is just as important as finding Lizzie.

He blinked. "The boy is the heir?"

He could be. Only you can decide that, Mordecai, and that is the primary mission right now.

Maybe it should be, he thought. It wasn't, though. To him, nothing was more important than finding Lizzie, reclaiming her, purifying and redeeming her. He supposed that was yet another symptom of his flawed human form. It was selfish. The will of Spirit must always come first.

That's right, Mordecai. You're a tool. A messenger. A servant. So stay and watch the boy.

He bowed his head. "I'm sorry. Forgive me my sins. I surrender all, Father. Not my will, but thine, be done. I'm sorry. Forgive me." His throat felt tight, and his eyes hot and damp.

Here he comes!

Mordecai looked up, brushing the moisture from his eyes so he could see as the boy came out of the shop. He went into a couple of others but didn't stay long anywhere, and finally, with a few bags in his hands, headed to a white pickup truck in the town parking lot. He started it up. Mordecai started his own vehicle, as well, and followed the boy home.

He lived, apparently, in a Victorian house two miles past Blackberry. The style of the place was similar to the one Mordecai was renting in Bonnie Brook, six miles in the other direction, except that it wasn't as well kept. It showed signs of neglect, needed paint, and the lawn was a weed patch.

Mordecai did everything he could to ensure he wouldn't lose track of the boy. He pulled over and memorized the address, the directions, the license plate number of the pickup truck. It was nearly noon. He whispered, "Can I go and search for Lizzie now?"

No.

He swallowed, lowering his head. "The school might have phoned for me. God knows Nancy Stillwater has to be quite ill by now."

You have your cell phone.

"They may have left a message on the machine. If I don't return the call, they'll hire someone else."

Your lack of faith will be punished, Mordecai!

Pain—splitting, racking, blinding pain—blazed through his skull. Mordecai slammed his palms to either side of his head, squeezed his eyes shut tight and grated his teeth. Pressure built inside his head as if it were being inflated, until finally it felt as if it would surely burst.

And then it was gone.

He lay limp against the seat of the car, panting, trembling, his cheeks damp with tears. "All right. All right. I'll stay."'

Use the cell to check your messages, and keep your eyes on the boy.

"Yes, yes. I'll obey."

3

—→——

Friday

"No, Bryan, you cannot stay home. I let you slide in the city, but that's over. You're going to school. You're going to register, and you're going to take classes. This is your senior year. It's important."

Beth couldn't help but hear Joshua's raised voice as she stepped up onto the porch to join Maude for their morning tea. The front door was open. The screen door was closed, but sound traveled right through that. Maude looked up, shaking her head sadly. She was in the middle of her morning injection—one before every meal was the routine—and she pulled the hypodermic from her arm and set it on the tray table.

"Important to you, maybe," Bryan said. He wasn't shouting, but he wasn't quiet, either.

"No, Bry, it's important to you. To your future. I told you before we left Manhattan, you'd have to register at the high school here."

"And I told you to forget about it."

"If you keep letting school slide, Bryan, you'll never get into a good college."

"I don't give a damn about college."

"Since when?"

"Just leave me alone, okay?"

Beth went slowly to her chair as Maude poured their tea. "Doesn't sound like they're doing too well, Maude."

"They aren't. But it will get better."

"Maybe we should, uh, close the door. Give 'em a little privacy?" Beth suggested, with a nod toward the still-open front door.

"Well now, if I close the door, how are we gonna know how to help those two?"

"What do you mean, 'we'?"

Maude just shushed her as the voices rose again.

"Bryan, you had a ninety-eight average your junior year. You were talking about applying to Ivy League schools, for God's sake. What happened to that?"

"Gee, I don't know, Dad. I can't imagine what could have happened between then and now, can you?"

Beth winced. "Ouch. That was a bull's-eye."

For a moment, Josh didn't reply. Probably reeling from the blow his son had just landed. Then, his tone gentler than before, he said, "All right, I know what happened. Your mom died. And that's the most horrible thing that could ever happen to a kid. But, Bryan, you can't die with her. She wouldn't want that, and you know it. If she were here right now, she'd be telling you to knock it the hell off. You have to find a way to pick up the pieces and move on with your life."

"Like you have, you mean?"

"What is that supposed to mean?"

No reply.

"Bry, don't think for one minute that I didn't care about your mother. I loved her once. We created a son together."

"You wouldn't know it to look at you, though. Her dying hasn't made one ripple in your life, has it, Dad?"

There was a loud bang, the slamming of a door, and it

made Beth jerk in reaction. Moments later, footsteps came down the stairs. Through the open door, Beth saw Joshua stop at the bottom of the stairway, push a hand through his hair and close his eyes briefly. He looked haggard. She felt sorry for him. Not as much as she did for his son, though.

"Good morning, Josh," Maude called.

Josh looked their way, his glance sliding from Maude to land on Beth. Sighing, he came out to join them on the porch.

"I'm sorry about all that," he said. "Not a very pleasant way to start the day for you."

"For you, either," Maude said.

"Or for Bryan," Beth said. Josh shot her a look, his lips thin.

"Join us for a cup of tea, Joshua. One of my homemade medicinals. Just the right blend to sooth your nerves." Maude was pouring before she finished speaking, and Beth noticed for the first time that she had set three cups on the tray table, where there were usually only two. And there was a white plastic lawn chair against the wall.

Josh sank into it and accepted the cup Maude handed him. "If I can't even get the kid to go to school…" He sighed, sipping the tea, not finishing the thought. "This is good, Maude. How did you know I'd need my nerves soothed this morning?"

"Made it for Beth—chamomile and honey. I thought she seemed a little edgy yesterday."

"I was not edgy."

Maude shrugged. "You're always edgy when there's a male of the species within twenty feet of you, girl." She winked at Josh. "Thinks you're all up to no good, I guess."

"Most of us are." He smiled a little, his eyes actually teasing her as he took another sip of his tea. "This is really hitting the spot."

"Maude has a tea and a platitude for just about every imaginable occasion," Beth said. "But I imagine you already knew that."

"You'd be surprised how little I know about her," he said.

"No, I wouldn't." She dropped the statement, then let it hang there while he tried to figure out what it meant. Bryan's footsteps came tromping down the stairs, across the floor and into the kitchen. Joshua sighed, his eyes clouding with real worry, and Beth took pity. "I do some private tutoring, you know."

"Do you?" He looked her in the eyes, and she got the feeling he had already known that. Probably Maude had filled him in. "If that's an offer, Beth, I accept. Assuming I can convince Bryan to go along with it."

"He seemed willing enough yesterday, when I spoke to him about it."

His brows bent together. "He talked to you about tutoring him?"

She nodded. "Yeah. Agreed to start at noon today."

"Well, why the hell didn't he just say so, instead of arguing with me?"

Beth tipped her head to one side. "Maybe because you didn't ask."

His face darkened. "So this is all my fault?"

"Not all, Joshua. But of the two of you, he's the one who just lost his mother. And you're the adult. The only one in the world who can swoop in and pick up the pieces of his broken life for him."

"Don't you think that's what I've been trying to do?"

He stopped himself there, literally seemed to bite off the rest of his tirade before it could spill out, held up a hand, closed his eyes. "I'm sorry. It's stress, and I've got no business taking it out on you. Are you all right?"

He was searching her face now, his expression remorseful and almost…tender. As if he thought she were so fragile an angry word or two from him could reduce her to tears. "Of course I'm all right. Why wouldn't I be?"

"I don't know." He dragged his gaze away from hers. "Listen, if you have suggestions, advice, I'd be more than happy to hear it."

"I don't know a damn thing about being a parent." She looked away, thinking of Dawny, the hole in her heart yawning wider. "But I know a little about teenagers. I taught in a public school for seven years."

"I didn't know that," he said.

She frowned at him. "Funny, I had the feeling you did."

"No. I don't think Maude mentioned it. What did you teach?"

"English Eleven and Twelve, mostly. I offered to tutor Bryan in English Twelve, so he would only have History and Spanish to catch up on. He'll be fine, if he does the work."

Josh settled back into his chair, seeming to relax a little. "So you think I should let him take the semester off, so long as he sticks with the tutoring?"

"I think you should consider agreeing to that, yes." She sipped her tea. "But don't count on it lasting. Once he meets some of the local kids, makes a few friends and has time to get bored out of his mind, he's going to decide to go back to school. If you let me tutor him until then, he won't be behind when he does."

He nodded slowly. "For someone who doesn't know much about parenting, you're pretty good." She shrugged, and he went on. "Seriously, you're light-years ahead of me. Okay. Let's do it—the tutoring thing, I mean."

"Okay."

The screen door creaked open, and Bryan stepped out onto the porch with a toaster pastry in one hand and a glass of chocolate milk in the other. Both had to have been in the pickup, because neither would have been within a mile of Maude's kitchen.

"Good morning, Bryan," Maude called, sounding as cheerful as if she hadn't noticed a thing out of the ordinary this morning, much less overheard his fight with his father. "Did you sleep well?"

He offered her a halfhearted smile, his dark hair falling over his forehead before he pushed it back. It was so much like the way Josh had pushed his hand through his hair earlier that Beth almost smiled.

Bryan avoided his father's eyes. "Slept better than I do in the city, that's for sure."

"Well, now that you're up, I'll get your breakfast out of the oven."

"Oh, that's okay, I made my own."

Maude looked at his pastry and rolled her eyes. "*That* is not a breakfast. It's a future health crisis. Now, I've had a real meal staying warm in the oven for you for the past hour." She glanced at Beth. "Join us, dear?"

"No way, Maude. I eat one of your meals, I'll be crawling home instead of running."

"Oh…you're going home?" Bryan asked. He sounded a little…off.

"That's the plan, Bry."

He shot his father a look, and Beth got the feeling their earlier argument was suddenly the furthest thing from the young man's mind. "Well, why don't you stay? You can, uh, talk to my dad about that tutoring thing."

Something had certainly snapped Bryan out of his petulant state. "I already did that," she said. "Was kind of surprised you hadn't done it yourself by now."

He nodded, all but admitting he probably should have clued his old man in.

"I gotta go. See you at noon, Bryan?" She reached for her tea to finish the cup.

"Uh, yeah, about that..." Bryan began. He sent his father another quick look, as if uncertain whether to speak.

"What is it, Bry?" Josh asked.

"It's probably nothing. I mean, one summer in the city and all of the sudden, I'm paranoid, you know?" He offered a half smile and shrugged. "Can't help it, though."

Beth frowned at him. "Paranoid about what?"

"It's just...there's been a car parked up the road a little ways for a while now. I can just see it from my bedroom window."

Beth's hand jerked, and the still-hot tea sloshed onto her bare legs. She sucked air through her teeth and wiped it away with her hand.

Maude handed her a napkin. "Oh, it's probably someone bird-watching or checking on the progress of the foliage," she said. "We have a lot of nature lovers living in these parts, and this time of year every leaf-peeper in the country seems to show up. Was it a red Blazer, Bryan? That would be my nearest neighbor Frankie Parker. Loves to watch the birds, that one."

"No, it's a brown sedan. Chrysler, I think."

"Brown Chrysler," Maude repeated to herself. "Maybe I should give Frankie a call."

When they all looked at her oddly, Beth clarified for them. "Frankie's the police chief."

"Oh." Bryan nodded. "Right next door, that's handy."

"Well, right next door is a half mile, but still..." Maude said.

Beth dabbed the tea from her thighs and tried not to notice Josh's scrutiny, until he forced it. "Call me a paranoid city slicker, if you want, but, um...why don't you let me take you home, Beth? Just to be on the safe side."

She looked up at him, crushed the damp napkin in her hand and shook her head. "I may not look like much, Joshua, but trust me, I can handle myself." She glanced at Bryan. "Oh, and I almost forgot." She dug into her shorts pocket and pulled out a folded sheet of paper. "You'll need these books for our session today. You can pick them up at Books Ink, in town."

"Cool. I can pick them up right now and drop you off on my way," Bryan said.

What was with these two? You'd think she was made of glass, the way they were acting. "And miss out on the great breakfast your grandmother made you?" Beth asked. "No, I don't think so. Besides, I live in the opposite direction. And I run for a reason. I'm not messing up my daily routine by taking the lazy way home."

Bryan looked at his father. Joshua sighed and glanced at Maude.

Maude frowned. Then she lifted her chin. "Joshua, go change your clothes. She won't let you drive her, so you can run with her. And, Beth, don't even begin to argue with me. I'll worry myself sick if you go off alone."

"Since when is there anything in Blackberry scary enough to worry *you*, Maude Bickham?"

"Since you got so scared you spilled tea on yourself at the mention of a strange car, young lady. Now, my word is law, and I have spoken. Finish your tea while Josh changes his clothes."

"Fine. Fine, he can run with me." She looked at Josh as he rushed into the house and added, "If he can keep up!"

Beth was running faster than her normal pace in honor of his presence; Josh was sure of it. He broke a sweat ten minutes in, but he wasn't complaining. It felt good to run. It had been too long. He watched the lengthening and flexing of her calf muscles and her thighs with every stride, and he thought it was too damn cold to wear shorts, and yet he was irrationally glad she had. She was probably as strong as she claimed she was. She certainly ran like she meant it. Not that it would matter much if some maniac came after her.

She wasn't happy about Maude's insistence that he come along. Her jaw was tight, her eyes serious. She hadn't spoken a word or cracked a smile since they left. God, it was difficult for him to believe this was the same pale, weak, comatose girl he'd visited in the hospital so long ago. She wasn't pale. Her skin was sun-kissed, and her cheeks pink right now with exertion. Steady, powerful breaths rushed in and out of her lungs, not the steady mechanical rasp of a respirator. Heat rose from her body in spite of the autumn chill.

When she slowed to a walk for the final quarter mile and he caught his breath again, he wanted to talk to her, ask her what her life had been like since coming out of that coma eighteen years ago. He wanted to hear every detail, in her own words, rather than the dry accounts in the typed pages Arthur had sent him. He'd been up most of the night reading those. They'd given him nightmares.

But he couldn't very well ask about her past, and even if he did, she wouldn't tell him. So he made conversation about the one topic he thought would interest her in talking to him: Bryan.

"I think Bryan must like you already," he said.

"He doesn't even know me. But yeah, the way he reacted to seeing a strange car—I suppose after losing his mom, it makes sense he might feel a little protective of me. I'm probably around her age. Maybe I remind him of her in some way."

It made perfect sense, except that she was nothing like

his ex-wife, Josh thought. Kathy had been confident, demanding, had known exactly what she wanted and would settle for nothing less. Beth was…nervous. Skittish. Strong, but he got the feeling she was never quite sure which path she would choose at the crossroads of Fight and Flight.

"He likes you better than he seems to like me, at the moment," he said. "That's worth something."

"He thinks you don't care about his mother's death."

"He acts as if I caused it."

"Did you?"

He looked at her sharply.

"I mean, in his mind? Is there any way he might blame you?"

"I don't see how. It was a weekend getaway with her second husband. The plane went down in the mountains." He shook his head. "Bryan would have been with them, but he got sick at the last minute. Some stomach bug."

"Oh. Well, no wonder."

He lifted his brows.

"He feels guilty," she explained. "Wishes he had been with them, wonders why they had to die when he was spared. Survivor's guilt. Surely you've heard of it."

"You don't know the half." She looked at him, a question in her eyes. "Yeah," he said. "I've heard of it."

"So that's part of it, then. I mean, it might be." She shrugged. "Maybe I can get him talking."

He looked up as a car passed. A brown sedan. The windows were tinted, so he couldn't see inside. Only one person, though, he thought. The driver. The license plates were too coated in dirt to read.

"I suppose you've tried that already, though."

He glanced her way again. "Tried what?"

"To get him to talk to you. About his feelings."

"I've asked him to talk to me. It hasn't worked."

She licked her lips, then pressed them tight.

"What?"

"Nothing."

"No, you were going to say something just now."

"I'm butting in, and that's not my way. It's none of my business."

"If I'm asking, you aren't butting in." He waited. Then, "Please, Beth. I need all the help I can get here."

She sighed. "I don't know Bryan very well, so this could be way off base. But what I've found in other kids his age is that the best way to get them to open up to you is to open up to them first. Maybe he needs to see your feelings before he'll feel safe showing you his own. It's hard to admit to weakness and confusion to a man you see as always strong, in control, perfect."

"You were right in the first place. You don't know Bryan very well. He doesn't think I'm anything close to perfect."

"You're his dad. You might be surprised. Even my…"

He studied her face. "Even your what?"

She shrugged and stopped walking. "This is my place."

Her place was a little square cottage with siding designed to make it look like a log cabin, though it wasn't. "Thanks for seeing me home, even though it was far from necessary."

He looked beyond her, seeing no sign of the car that had driven past them. Not at the moment, anyway. But her house was in the middle of a stretch of empty road. A thorny hedgerow marked the boundaries of the open field behind it. A stream meandered through. The water caught the morning sun and changed it into diamonds. Across the street there was a woodlot bordered by scrub brush. Cover. Not another house in sight in either direction.

"I don't suppose I could hit you up for a glass of water before I head back? I'm not as used to running as you are. Out of shape."

"Liar." She led the way to her front door.

He followed her inside, even though she hadn't really invited him, and took everything in. The front door led into a small living room, where a settee and overstuffed chair sat on a brown area rug in front of a television set. A large punching bag dangled from a hook in the ceiling, near one corner.

"I'll get your water." She walked through, into what he presumed was the kitchen. He heard ice rattling into a glass, took a few steps farther inside and peeked into the only other room he saw—her bedroom. There were a twin bed with rumpled covers and a weight bench with a bar balanced in its holder. He thought it had fifty pounds on each end.

"Snoop much?"

He spun around fast, almost bumping into her. "Sorry."

"So what are you looking for?" She shoved the icy, dewy glass into his hand.

He took a long pull, mostly to give himself time to come up with a convincing answer. Then he lowered the glass, licked his lips. "Just looking. You spend a lot of time with my grandmother, after all."

"Oh. And you think I might be some sort of a con-artist, out to fleece her? Maybe offer to reshingle her roof and then vanish with her money, something like that?"

"I didn't say that. I'm just…curious about a woman who lives in a small town like this for a whole year and only makes one friend. One elderly, vulnerable friend."

"Maude Bickham is far from vulnerable. And who said she was my only friend?"

"She did."

She lowered her head. "You done with that water or what?"

"No." He took another drink, a slow one. He could see

it was pissing her off. She wanted him out of there—now. When he swallowed, he nodded toward the punching bag. "So you box?"

"You want a demonstration?"

He blinked in surprise.

"Look, I know what you're doing. I saw that brown car go by. It was nothing, okay? I'm fine. Perfectly safe all by myself. Have been for over a year now. No bogeymen have come calling. And if you knew your grandmother at all you'd know what she was up to with all this make-believe worry about me walking the streets alone."

"She's up to something?"

"Of course she's up to something. You're single, I'm single. She's probably hoping you won't even come back home tonight."

"Oh," he said. Then he lifted his brows. "*Oh*. Well, there's no danger of that happening."

She blinked, clearly not sure whether she'd just been insulted.

He let it hang there for a moment, then added, "Your bed is way too small for both of us."

She snatched the water glass from his hand, turned and marched to the front door. "Very funny. Tell your son I'll see him at noon."

"I will," he said following her. "And, Beth?"

She stood there, holding the door open, his glass in one hand. He was glad he'd drained it, or he thought he might be wearing it.

"What?"

"Thanks. For offering to tutor Bryan, and for the advice. I mean it."

Her bristles softened almost visibly. "Like I said, Josh, I'm no expert."

"That's ten times the expert I am."

Smiling just slightly, she nodded, and he thought he was forgiven for intruding and even for snooping. She didn't like people looking out for her. He'd been warned about that, he thought, studying her eyes, how green they were, and the stubborn set of her jaw. Arthur had sent federal agents to protect her, but she always spotted them and sent them packing. That was why, he'd said, he wanted someone else, a civilian, and Josh had been the logical choice. Josh and his former partner had a very successful private security firm; they'd gone into business together after leaving the ATF. After the raid. After he'd shot Beth.

A wave of nausea rose and receded with the thought as he stared at her, the curve of her neck, the little pulse he could see beating there after their run. Alive. God, it was a miracle.

In truth, he thought, Arthur Stanton must have had a whole other set of reasons for sending Josh, of all people, on this mission—reasons Josh still wasn't certain he understood.

"Do I pass inspection?"

He shook free of his thoughts and realized he'd been staring at her. Her cheeks were a little pinker than they had been just from the run. Embarrassed? Flattered, maybe?

"Sorry. You're…you're a beautiful woman, Beth. I got distracted there for a minute." And he still was. Did she look this good to him because she really was as beautiful as she seemed? Or did she only look that way to him because he was so God damn glad to see her alive?

"Thanks," she said. "I think. Goodbye, Josh."

It was his cue to leave. Sighing, he stepped outside, and Beth closed the door.

He didn't leave right away, though. He walked down the road a short distance, then stopped and looked back. He wasn't used to cases where the client didn't want to be protected, much less those where she wasn't even supposed to be aware of her bodyguard's presence.

Much less those where you don't particularly want to leave the client's side, his inner voice scolded.

He ignored it. He liked being able to have someone watching his clients 24/7. And though it was doubtful, there was always a chance that brown car might come back. Its driver could just be waiting for him to leave.

So he would spend a few minutes doing surveillance, just in case.

The brown car didn't return. But Beth did step out onto the porch. She looked around carefully, up and down the road. And he thought maybe she was looking for the brown car, too, but he couldn't be sure.

He could be sure, though, of the item she held in her hands. He figured any man who'd worked in law enforcement could spot a gun from three hundred yards away, just by the way a person held it, the shape of the thing, its weight. Identifying firearms in the hands of suspects was something he'd had drilled into him during his training. You didn't want your agents shooting people for pulling out wallets or cell phones, after all.

He hadn't lost the skill.

Beth had a gun in her hands. A large caliber semiautomatic handgun. Black, not silver. From here it looked like a .45; a damn big gun, and the scope on the top made it look even bigger. You didn't see scopes on handguns very often. Avid hunters seldom had them, because avid hunters had much better luck with shotguns. Militarily trained snipers rarely used them, because rifles were so much more accurate. Professional killers used them, because, though huge, they were easier to conceal than a shotgun or rifle would be.

Beth Slocum meant business. She could probably take down a small elephant with that thing.

She held the gun two-fisted, in front of her body, muzzle to the ground, arms extended. She handled the weapon as if she knew how to use it.

She was nervous, he thought. But she was ready, too. Or thought she was.

Whether that readiness would make her safer or put her at greater risk remained to be seen.

Beth looked up and down the street, waiting, watching, listening. She didn't see anyone. Probably, she told herself, the brown car had been nothing more than a sightseer or nature lover. Probably her blood pressure was going through the roof over nothing.

After several minutes she went back inside, hit the release and let the fully loaded clip drop from the hollow butt into her waiting palm. Then she locked the gun in its assigned drawer, next to the tiny derringer. The key was on a chain around her ankle. She returned the clip to the top of a bookshelf, where she could grab it fast but no one else would ever notice it.

Her telephone was ringing. She snatched it up and whispered hello, half-afraid the man she'd been thinking about—Mordecai, not Joshua—would somehow start whispering to her from the other end.

"Hey, Beth. It's Julie."

"And Dawn!" Dawn called from somewhere in the background. Not on an extension, though.

Beth closed her eyes against the rush of sheer pleasure hearing her daughter's voice brought welling up inside her. God, it was heaven to hear her voice. Warm, sweet heaven. The night of that horrible raid, Dawn had been only a baby. Beth had been shot, certain she was dying, when she'd given her daughter to her best friend, begged her to take Dawn out of that place. And Jewel—Julie now—had done it. She'd raised Dawn as her own, believing, as the rest of the world had, that Beth had died in the raid. By the time Beth found them again, Dawn had been happy, thriving, and calling Julie "Mom."

And yet…. "Are we private?"

"Yeah. Pay phone, outside a convenience store. Nowhere near us. It's clean, don't worry. I'll put Dawn on after we talk." Her next words were muffled. "Dawny, go grab us a couple of Diet Vanilla Cokes, will you?"

"Sure, Mom. Be right back. Don't you *dare* hang up."

Beth sighed, ignoring the blade she felt twisting in her heart every time she heard her daughter call her best friend "Mom." She swallowed the pain, kept it hidden from her voice. "It's not like it matters. Sooner or later, he's going to find me."

"Not necessarily," Julie told her, just as she always did. "Beth, you have a new name, new town—"

"It won't matter. His gift is genuine, Jewel. Even if his mind is broken, his gift is for real. He'll track me down."

"You have some reason to feel like he's getting close? You sound…shaky."

Beth swallowed. "I don't know. It's probably nothing. I'm probably overreacting."

"I have never known you to overreact. Maybe it's time you accept some of the help the government is always offering—the bodyguards, I mean."

Beth shook her head. "I don't trust anyone who works for the government. Hell, it was a government man who shot me." Her and thirty other teenagers, she thought silently, in a riot that should have been avoided. She'd lost everything because of it. Her soul, for a time, as she lingered in a coma. Her memory for years afterward. Her daughter, the only one she would ever have. Her identity, her entire life. Gone, all of it, because of one gung ho soldier with an itchy trigger finger and a lousy aim. "I don't want another one like him *protecting* me."

"Then maybe you should get out of there."

She pursed her lips. "No, Jewel. Like I said, it's probably nothing. I'm just paranoid. Besides, I'm sick of running and hiding."

"Yeah, and when did you decide that?"

"I don't know. It's been a long time coming." She licked her lips. "When he comes, I'll be ready. Maybe I should just face him. Only one of us would walk away, but at least the running would be over."

"You're scaring me, Beth."

Beth swallowed hard. "I'm being melodramatic. I'm lonesome. I miss you guys. I miss Dawny."

"I know. She misses you, too. She's been begging me to let her come up there for a visit."

Beth closed her eyes. It was strictly against the government's rules for her to see her daughter. Then again, according to Arthur Stanton, she wasn't supposed to communicate with Dawn by phone or e-mail, either. It hadn't stopped her from doing so. Still…

"It may not be the best time to risk it, Jewel. Try to put her off until I can be sure it's safe." She didn't think Mordecai would harm Dawn, and he probably wouldn't try to abduct her again now that he'd surrendered his parental rights to her. But given his state of mind, there was no point putting her within his reach.

"Will do. Listen, Beth, I got wind of something at the newsroom. I don't know if it means anything. In fact it probably doesn't, but…David Quentin Gray—Mordecai's ex-lawyer—escaped from Attica last week. They found him dead, shot once in the head, the next day."

Beth got a chill that didn't make a hell of a lot of sense. "Who shot him?"

"They don't know."

Beth sighed. "It's probably nothing," she said. "He didn't know anything about me. I mean, how could he?"

"No. It's nothing. I'm sure of it. I just thought you should know."

"Thanks, Julie."

"Here's your drink," Dawn said. "Can I talk now?"

"Just a sec, hon. Beth, if you need us, let us know. Sean and I can be there in no time. We love you, you know. And we owe you a hell of a lot."

"I'm the one who owes you, Jewel. Now put the brat on the phone before she has a fit."

She heard the telephone move, then Dawn's voice came on the line, and Beth let it wash over her like rain over a dying flower. Dawn talked about her senior year of high school, her teachers, her classes, her plans for graduation and where she might go to college. She was driving now. Her Jeep had gotten a dent from a kid in the school parking lot, and she was mortified about it, and so on and on and on.

Beth listened, commenting in all the right places, and she somehow managed to keep the tears that were sliding down her cheeks from being evident in her voice.

4

—◆—

It *was* Lizzie. This was *her!*

Mordecai's heart had pounded, and he'd barely been able to catch his breath as he watched her running along the winding country lane. Running. Hands clenched into fists pumping at her sides. As if she were fighting.

And then she slowed and walked right up to the front porch of the very house he'd been watching: the fading, former Blackberry Inn. All night, he'd been parked in his car, keeping the boy under surveillance, just as the guides had told him to do. It had made no sense. He'd been frustrated, thinking it stupid and senseless to sit there, cold and uncomfortable, overnight. He knew where the boy lived now, so what was the point? Even if he was to be Mordecai's heir...

Now he understood. *This* was the point. The boy was a beacon, pointing the way to Lizzie. Already he was connected to Mordecai, already aiding him in his work. He had led Mordecai to Lizzie. Obviously he was the one. The boy, Bryan, was the one he'd been waiting for. He should have trusted, had more faith. The guides always had a reason for everything they told him to do.

Mordecai took out his binoculars and watched every move Lizzie made. He watched her sit on the porch, sipping tea with an old woman, watched the looks, the smiles, they exchanged.

They were close. The old woman was important to her.

Then the man came out to join them, and Mordecai's body went stiff and his nerve endings prickled. The man had to be Bryan's father—the resemblance between the two had told him that much. But what was he doing with Lizzie?

A short while later, she was running again. But this time the man ran with her. The bastard had no business there, Mordecai thought. Lizzie was *his*. Always had been, always would be. Dead or alive, she belonged to Mordecai.

He let them get a good distance away before starting his car and driving a little closer. He was careful not to get too close, and he never let them spot him.

God, how different she seemed…felt. The energy he sensed surrounding her was not the same as it had been before.

She'd changed.

She thinks she's escaped you, Mordecai. Thinks she's above you now.

Look at her, running. Trying to grow strong. She'll fight you this time.

"She fought me last time," he muttered. "Isn't shooting me in the chest fighting me?" His chest ached a little at the memory, even though the Kevlar vest had ensured he only suffered a pair of broken ribs from the bullet she had fired at his heart…even as she kissed his lips.

She was weak, back then. And she still loved you, in some desperate, dependent way. She wept when she thought she had killed you.

But she's not weak anymore. She won't shed a tear for you now.

Mordecai decided to ignore the voices for a while, just the way he was ignoring the presence of the man, the interloper, and simply bask in Lizzie's presence. In being able to see her, watch her. In being this close to her. God, how he'd loved her once. Still. As he should.

Jesus had loved Judas, even after his kiss of betrayal.

Mordecai followed her to where she lived, in a cottage just at the edge of Blackberry. He knew it when they slowed to a walk, entered the house. He even saw her opening the door with her set of keys.

They've seen the car, Mordecai.

"Yes. I know."

You know now. You know where to find her. You can come back.

Nodding slowly, Mordecai drove past the two this time. He had to return to his rented home away from home, because there were things that needed doing. He'd begun the preparations, but he had to finish them. So he went to his temporary home. He took time to shower, to change clothes, to get a bite to eat, take his messages off the machine. The school had called. He phoned back and agreed to come in on Monday. Then he rechecked the cord he had run throughout every room of the house, along the baseboards, and the batteries in his remote control. Finally he drove out of town and got himself a different car.

A few hours later he was back at Lizzie's house, in a dark blue, late model sedan almost as unremarkable as the first car had been. He'd transferred all his supplies into this one. The trunk was filled with various controlled substances, some of them too powerful even to be carried by the average pharmacy—like the vial of salmonella, a bit of which he'd used on poor Nancy Stillwater's picnic lunch. Cruel, but effective. It wouldn't kill her, though she would be terribly sick for a week, maybe longer. That was all he needed.

Mordecai didn't kill unless Spirit dictated it. He wasn't a murderer. He was a tool of God. Besides, Nancy wasn't an evil woman. She'd even phoned him to see if he, too, had become sick. When he said he hadn't, she ruled out her picnic lunch as the source of the food poisoning and wondered aloud where she could have picked it up.

He parked the car in a pull-off, where autumn foliage concealed it from view. Then he walked back to Lizzie's house and took up a position on a tree stump just inside the edge of the woods across the street. This time he had a video camera, a digital camera and a pair of high-powered binoculars.

He never let her out of his sight for the rest of the day.

A woman delivered groceries around eleven. Beth ate an early lunch, alone at a small table in her kitchen. Yogurt and a banana. After lunch, a teenage boy showed up, and Mordecai recognized him even before he raised the binoculars for a closer look. It was young Bryan.

He and Lizzie worked over textbooks in the living room.

I have a private tutor. The boy's voice repeated the words in Mordecai's memory. He closed his eyes, thanked his guides for putting the boy into his path, apologizing again for doubting them earlier. The boy was more than just an honest young man and heir to Mordecai's gift. And more than a signpost, pointing the way to Lizzie. He was connected to her in some way. Connected to *him*, too. He marveled anew at the intricate web of the universe and the complex machinations of almighty God. The brilliance of linking Mordecai to Lizzie through this new child. The son.

"No wonder I couldn't find her right away," he whispered. "She barely goes out. She's entirely self-contained. Except for that run in the morning."

When Bryan left, Lizzie worked out with a punching bag that hung from the ceiling in a corner of her living room, shocking him with the power and fury of her blows. Then she showered. Later she made herself a solitary dinner and went to bed. Alone.

Always alone, Mordecai. She's changed. Like a lone wolf now, she thinks she's independent, thinks she's strong.

And you know why, don't you, Mordecai? She's waiting. She knows you'll come for her, and she thinks she's preparing. Thinks she's going to be ready.

Thinks she can defeat you.

Defeat God.

Mordecai lowered his binoculars and closed his eyes. "Oh, Lizzie, Lizzie. Don't you know you've only made matters worse by adding the sin of pride to the list of things for which you must be punished?"

He drew a breath. He didn't want her proud and independent and strong. Before he revealed himself, Mordecai wanted Lizzie reduced to the needy child she had been once; the lost, confused runaway who saw him as a savior.

She has to die, Mordecai. It's her fate. You need to correct a terrible flaw in history. She's supposed to be dead.

He tightened his jaw. "She has to be taught. She has to be stripped of every ounce of pride and rebelliousness, and returned to a state of purity and humility. She'll come to me on her knees then. She'll beg me to take her back."

Are you questioning us yet again? Haven't you learned better? She has to die!

"Stop!" Mordecai pressed his hands to his ears, awaiting the pain that inevitably came when he questioned his guides.

The voices went silent, and the pain didn't come. Not this time. But he was worried. If Spirit insisted, he would have no choice but to obey. Oh, if only there could be another way. Maybe, if Lizzie suffered enough, Spirit would be satisfied that she had found redemption. Maybe, if he could bring her down low enough, she could still be saved.

Impossible.

"I have to try." He licked his dry lips and wondered why he hadn't thought to bring along some food or water. But he knew why. The voices hadn't told him to get those things. Maybe it was fitting that he fast while he watched Lizzie. Maybe there was a reason for it.

Lifting the binoculars again, he resumed watching her. He could see her clearly through the sheer curtains, from her blond hair spread on the pillows to the outline of her body beneath the sheets of her small bed.

She slept with the light on.

He knew now where Beth went when she went running in the morning. To that house, where the boy was living, with an old woman and a handsome man. The man who had accompanied Lizzie back to her house.

A dark flame burned in his belly. He didn't like the man.

It's the old woman she's closest to, Mordecai. It was obvious from their interactions this morning.

Again he nodded. He was making progress, he thought. He was identifying the underpinnings that supported her in her fraudulent new life. She had students. She had friends. A home and a job. All of those would have to go. One by one, they would have to go.

"Whatever happens, from here on, Lizzie, it's your own fault. And everything I do is for your own good."

You've watched her enough for now, Mordecai. Tonight you've got other work to do.

Bryan sank down onto the sofa, took up the remote control and began flipping channels on the television. Josh came in from the kitchen, a coffee mug in one hand.

"I'm glad you came down," Josh said. "I was going to come up."

"To lecture me about school again?"

"No. Just to talk."

Bryan shot him a skeptical look. Then he dropped the remote and leaned back. "Why not? There's nothing better to do."

"Beth predicted you'd get bored out here in short order."

Bryan nodded. "I've listened to every music file I've ever downloaded, ten times each."

"What would make it better?" Joshua asked.

His son looked surprised. "An Internet connection would help. My laptop's set up for cable, but Maude says there's no cable here."

"Done. I'll get on it tomorrow."

"Really?"

Josh flinched inwardly. Had he been so self-absorbed that his son was surprised he would want to do something nice for him? "Sure. I'll find out what the local dial-up service is and get you signed up. I'll have to clear it with Maude first—it's her phone."

"I should have wireless."

"We're not going to be here that long, Bry. Dial-up will do."

Bryan nodded. "Where is Maude, anyway? Gone to bed?"

"Out at the movies with her next-door neighbor."

"Frankie the cop?"

"Frankie Parker." Josh smiled. "I know, a police chief named Frankie doesn't inspire much confidence."

Bryan looked at him more closely. "You're...different today."

"How so?"

"I don't know. Less tense. More laid-back."

Josh nodded. "It's a laid-back kind of a town. Hell, I don't know, Bryan, maybe I've needed to take some time off for a while now. Or maybe it's…that I've been sitting behind a desk too long. You know, when Kevin and I first started our own private security business, we did all the work ourselves."

"Bodyguards-R-Us," Bryan quipped.

"Yeah. Now, I don't know. We've got three offices, dozens of men working for us, high-profile clients, and it's all about paperwork."

"It's not fun anymore," Bryan said.

Josh looked him in the eye. "You know what? You're right. You nailed it. It's not fun anymore."

Bryan nodded. "So quit."

"It's not that simple, Bryan."

"Sure it is. You don't like what you're doing, so stop doing it."

Josh sighed, sensed himself getting impatient with Bryan, and Bryan getting impatient with him, and decided to change the subject. "How'd the tutoring go?"

"Fine." Bryan reached to the coffee table for a magazine and began flipping pages. It was a copy of *Vermont Dairy Monthly*—a field full of fat cows on the cover.

"Any sign of that brown car lurking around?" Joshua asked.

"Nope, not that I saw."

Josh sat down on the sofa beside his son. "Meant to tell you, that was a good call this morning. Spotting the strange car, telling me about it."

Bryan shrugged, but at least he looked up from the magazine he wasn't really reading. "I wasn't sure whether to say something in front of Beth or not. It made her nervous, didn't it?"

"Seemed to."

"Guess she has reason to be."

Josh nodded. "Yeah. I wanted to talk to you about that."

"About what?"

"About me. About…Beth Slocum. And why I reacted the way I did when I first saw her."

Bryan lifted his brows. They disappeared beneath the shock of brown hair that slanted across his forehead. "I thought that was none of my business."

"You said that, Bry. I didn't. I just…had to make sure she was who I thought she was before I said anything."

"And now you're sure?"

"Yeah." Josh took a breath, telling himself that Beth's advice had sounded great at the time. Carrying it out was another matter. "This goes back a ways, so bear with me. Before you were born, I worked for the ATF. It was one of the things that came between your mother and me. She hated it."

"I know all about that."

Josh blinked. "You do?"

"Yeah. Mom told me." Bryan set his magazine back on the coffee table.

Josh nodded. "Okay. But she probably didn't tell you why I was fired from that job. There was a cult leader, keeping underage kids, mostly girls, on a fenced compound, with armed guards and dogs. He was dealing drugs and stockpiling weapons, and no one was sure the girls who were there were free to leave."

"The Young Believers," Bryan said.

Josh lost his entire train of thought. "You know about them, too?"

"Sure I know. Mom told me about the raid that went bad. She told me about the girl you accidentally shot, how you lost your job over it. And she told me never to bring it up with you. She said it was the worst time of your life and probably the main reason you two broke up. She said the guilt ruined you."

Josh just sat there for a moment, absorbing his son's words. "I had no idea she'd told you all that."

Bryan tipped his head to one side. "Doesn't mean I don't want to hear your version of it. Besides, what does all that have to do with Beth Slocum?"

"Everything," Joshua said softly. He looked his son in the eyes. "It turns out she's the girl I shot."

Bryan bobbed his head forward, eyes widening. "But I thought the girl you shot was dead."

"So did everyone else. Nearly everyone, I mean. For all these years, I believed it. When I went to see her in the hospital after the raid, she was in a coma. They told me she wouldn't live, and the way she looked, I had no trouble believing it. She was…hell, she was your age."

"And they let you think you'd killed her? I can't believe no one ever told you. You recognized her when we first saw her, didn't you?"

"I did. It had been a while—she was eighteen years younger and at death's door when I last saw her, after all. But yeah, it's not like that face hasn't haunted me ever since. I just couldn't believe it could really be her."

Bryan nodded slowly, his eyes holding his father's, almost probing them. "That's what's different, then."

Josh looked at him, unsure what his son meant.

"The guilt you've been carrying around, Dad. Jeez, finding out you didn't kill her after all must have been like having a lead weight taken off your shoulders."

He nodded slowly. "You know, that's probably it." Then he frowned. "You ought to look into a future as a shrink, you know that?"

"Doesn't take a shrink to nail that one." He paused, studying his father's face so closely that Josh wondered what his son saw there. Then he said, "Tell me the rest, Dad."

He really wanted to know, Josh realized. He organized his thoughts and continued his story. "The cult leader, Mordecai Young, didn't die in the raid, either, though for a long while everyone believed he had."

"So that's who they think might come after Beth?"

Josh nodded. "A year ago they crossed paths. She was a teacher—he'd kidnapped one of her students. She bluffed her way into the house were Mordecai was holding the girl, and then she tried to kill him."

"No way."

Josh nodded. "Shot him point-blank, right in the chest. But he'd vested up ahead of time. The Feds figured the most she'd done was piss him off, and that if he could ever find her, he'd return the favor. So she was relocated."

"You think it might have been him—Mordecai Young—in that brown car earlier?"

"I don't know. We should probably err on the side of caution, though." He closed his eyes. "I don't like her being in that cottage alone. It makes protecting her nearly impossible."

Bryan opened his mouth, then closed it again and leaned back on the couch, looking stunned by all his father had revealed.

"What?" Josh asked.

"Nothing. Hell, I'm blown away by this. I can imagine how you must feel, but—no. Nothing."

"Bry, come on. I wouldn't have told you all this if I didn't trust you. So if there's something you want to say, spit it out."

Bryan shrugged. "Just…I don't know. Lying to her to protect her was one thing. Not telling her you're the guy who shot her… It's way worse. It feels wrong."

"I know. But…she'd send us packing if she knew. And that would leave her unprotected."

"I guess. But shouldn't that be up to her? I mean, it's her life, Dad."

Josh sighed. "I know. And you're right. I hate this, Bry. But Jesus, if I make the wrong move and she ends up dead…"

"You figure this is your chance to make up for the past."

"It's more than that. This isn't about me. It's about protecting Beth."

"I don't blame you, Dad. I mean, I disagree with you, but I don't blame you. I guess I might do the same thing."

No anger, no accusations. Josh couldn't believe it. He hadn't told his son the worst of what he'd learned by reading Beth's dossier, though. That she'd had a child, a daughter who'd been adopted while she'd lingered in a coma, fighting for her life. And raised by someone else while she'd been putting that life back together again.

A daughter. A little girl she had lost because of him. And if there was one tragedy Joshua understood, it was the loss of a child.

Bryan didn't need to know all that. That was Beth's private hell—and his own.

"I just wish I could come up with an excuse to get into Beth's house long enough to check the place out, make sure her locks are secure, things like that."

The screen door creaked open, and Maude walked in, accompanied by another woman, one who wore baggy jeans and a sweatshirt with a one-horned moose on the front. Printed beneath the moose were the words, Is That Your Final Antler?

Bryan grinned at the sweatshirt as he got up, to relieve the women of the shopping bags they carried. "A movie and shopping in one night?" Bryan asked.

"It was a long movie. We got hungry," the newcomer said. She had short copper-red hair, in tight kinky curls, and was younger than Maude. Late fifties, Joshua guessed.

"Boys, this is my good friend, Frankie Parker."

Joshua was on his feet, as well. "Police Chief Frankie Parker?"

"The one and only," she said, extending a hand.

"Frankie, this is my grandson Joshua and his boy Bryan."

Frankie was smiling, but her smile died. "Don't play with me, Maude. You don't have any grandson."

"As far as you or anyone else in this town is concerned, Frankie, I most certainly do."

Frankie frowned at her.

"Trust me. It's important. And it's between us, Frankie. I knew you would hear about this and start snooping sooner or later. How much Josh does or does not want to tell you is up to him. All you need to know is that he's here for a good reason. And that I trust him."

"I don't like this, Maude."

"You don't have to, Frankie."

Frankie moved her gaze to Josh's. "Good to meet you."

"Same here," Josh said, but he wasn't happy about the situation. Clearly this woman knew more than she should.

"If you're up to no good, I'll find out."

"I've got no doubt about that. But I'm not."

Bryan looked worried, and when the old woman's eyes fell on him, he said, "I'll, uh, put these away for you." He carried the groceries into the kitchen.

"Leave the dry goods right in the bags, Bryan," Maude called. Then she turned to Frankie. "Thanks for helping me in with the bags, hon."

"Anytime, Maudie. You…give me a call if you need anything." She sent a lingering look at Josh, and he had no doubt she would be on the horn tomorrow, checking him out with every contact she had.

"Like I'm gonna need anything with these two strapping men around the house," Maude said. She walked her friend to the door, waved as the other woman left, then turned to face Josh. "Don't look like that," she said. "What else could I say? She's known me for thirty years. And unlike most folks in town, she knows I never had children." She shrugged. "Besides, I trust her. She's not going to blow your cover."

"Are you sure?"

"Of course I'm sure. I've know *her* for thirty years, too. And you might want to think about confiding in Frankie— God knows she's not going to let this go until one of us does. She's good at her job, even though she's far from your typical law enforcement type."

"You can say that again."

She smiled. "Now, did I hear you saying you needed a chance to snoop around Beth's house?"

He lifted his brows. "Why, you have an idea?"

"Well, since my range is on the fritz, I thought we could all have dinner at Beth's place tomorrow night."

"I didn't know there was anything wrong with your range."

She smiled, adding wrinkles to her wrinkles. "There's not."

"You oughtta work for the government, Maude."

"Isn't that what I'm doing?"

"I guess you are."

Maude knew nothing about his reasons for being there, other than what he had told her: that her good friend Beth had some enemies from her past who might be a threat to her, and that he needed her help to make sure Beth would be safe.

That was all he'd needed to tell her.

"I'll clear it all with Beth when she stops by on her run tomorrow morning," she said.

Josh got the feeling Beth wasn't going to have much choice in the matter. She was hosting them for dinner tomorrow night. Because what Maude Bickham wanted, Maude Bickham got.

5

———•———

Saturday (wee hours)

Beth was dreaming. She knew she was dreaming, and she wanted to wake up, but just like before, she was unable to.

Her dream self lay in a hospital bed. She could tell by the antiseptic smell, the steady beeping of her monitors and the tubes she could feel at her nostrils, gently blowing cool, ultradry oxygen, and the one in her throat that she kept thinking would choke her.

She was asleep in that hospital. She didn't think she was dead, but it wasn't a normal sleep. She couldn't wake up. She didn't know where she was, and when she tried to think about who she was, or what had happened to her, a yawning black hole opened up in her mind. She felt close to panic at that gaping hole in her mind. It felt as if she were teetering on its edge, as if she might fall in and be swallowed up by its darkness, so she chose not to look there anymore. Instead, she focused on the sensation of a warm, strong hand that surrounded one of hers.

And from that point her senses opened wider, to admit the soft, tormented voice that spoke to her.

I'm sorry. God, I'm so sorry.

She wondered what he was so sorry about. Was he

somehow responsible for whatever had happened to her? But he held her hand, and he sounded so kind....

I don't even know your name. No one does.

Not even me, she thought.

But believe me, I'd switch places with you if I could. I'd rather it were me in that bed than you.

She liked the man who held her hand. She wished she could find a way to tell him that it was all right. That *she* was all right. And then she realized—she wasn't. She couldn't wake up. Maybe she never would.

I'd give anything in the world if you would just open your eyes. I want to see them. Their color—I want to see that more than anything. He squeezed her hand a little tighter. *Come on. Open your eyes for me. Open them.*

Then there was a woman's voice. She told him he had to leave. And on the way out, she said, "It wasn't your fault, we all know that. She was in the line of fire. Any one of the agents could have been the one whose bullet hit her."

And then she went on. "There's really no point in your coming back here, you know. She doesn't know you're here. And besides, she's not going to last out the week."

Then I'm not sure how the hell I'm supposed to.

God, his voice was so familiar. And so filled with regret!

A telephone rang, shrill and sharp. It cut through the dream, and Beth sat up, looked at her bedroom around her and sagged in relief when knowledge filled her mind. She knew who she was. She knew where she was. She was all right after all.

But that dream—it had been a long time since she'd had that particular dream. She'd all but forgotten about the man who had come to sit with her while she wasted away, a comatose Jane Doe in a hospital bed.

The phone rang again. She turned toward the nightstand, reached out for the telephone, the night-light making it easier. Then she brought it to her ear.

"Hello?" No one was there. "Hello? Who is this?"

When no one answered, a chill slid up her spine like an icy finger. The memory of Mordecai crossed her mind, and she reminded herself that she had always known he would find her sooner or later. Maybe tonight was the night.

Then she frowned, because she could hear voices. She pressed the volume button on the side of her phone, clicking it up as many notches as it would go. It sounded like…it sounded like Maude, speaking to someone else. It was muted, distant.

Beth flung back her covers and got out of bed, going into the living room, where the caller ID box was, and looking at the digital readout. Maude's phone number showed on the screen. She listened, heard nothing more, then depressed the cutoff and dialed it back.

A harsh busy signal was her only reply.

"Hell." Something was wrong over there. She didn't know Joshua Kendall well at all—and the fact that he'd stirred some kind of insane attraction in her should probably be taken as a bad sign rather than a good one. The last man she'd been attracted to had turned out to be an insane mass murderer.

Beth shoved her feet into her running shoes, simply because they were near the door. She yanked a coat off one hook and her car keys off another as she went out the door and into the brisk chill of an autumn night in Vermont.

Joshua had been dreaming about hot, wet, frantic sex with Beth Slocum when something woke him up—and at the worst possible moment.

He groaned, wondering when the hell he'd started having dreams worthy of a seventeen-year-old, then rolled over and glanced at the clock. The time—5:06 a.m.— glowed at him in neon green. Then he heard footsteps and was on his feet and pulling his gun out of the holster on the bedpost before another thought had time to cross his mind.

He yanked a bathrobe—one Maude had laid out for him that was not his own—from the footboard and jerked it on, then headed barefoot into the hallway, the gun in his hand, his hand in the robe's pocket.

At Maude's room, he paused, because her door was opening. He stepped back a little. She poked her head out. "Is that you, Joshua?"

"Yeah, it's me. Something woke me."

"Me, too." She swung her door wider and turned around, shaking her head. "I could have sworn I heard someone in the kitchen."

"Why don't you stay right here and let me go check?"

"My goodness. Yet another benefit to having a young man around the house, I guess. All right, I'll force myself to let you wait on me. After all, 'A woman who says she dislikes chivalry is both dishonest and a fool.'"

"That's a good one. I'm gonna write that down." He gave her shoulder a squeeze, then took hold of her door and told her to get back inside. She did, and he pulled it closed. Then he closed his hand around the grips of his .38, tiptoed to the stairway and down it.

There was someone in the kitchen. Even now, he heard movement. Soft, barely audible, but there.

He crept through the house, through the dining room and into the kitchen. Reaching inside, he flipped the light switch and raised the gun.

A large black cat sat on the counter, glaring at him with eyes that seemed more irritated than startled.

Sighing, he lowered the gun.

"Well, I'll be…" Maude said from behind him.

He frowned, turning to face her. "I thought I told you to stay upstairs."

"Oh, Joshua, don't be silly. I've never obeyed a man's orders yet, and I don't intend to start now, chivalry or not." She nodded at the cat. "That's Frankie's beast. Comes in here any time I leave a window open more than a quarter inch, looking for a snack. I swear he's made of rubber. Aren't you, Siegfried?"

"Siegfried?" He shook his head. "Don't tell me— Frankie has another cat named Roy?"

"Dog. Bluetick. Dumb as a rock, but twice as friendly." She moved to the fridge, pulled it open and reached in to straighten the row of tiny brown vials of insulin before grabbing a small carton of cream. As she poured some into a bowl for the cat—who weighed fifteen pounds if he weighed an ounce—headlights invaded the house from the front, and then footsteps raced across the porch and someone pounded on the door.

Maude paid no attention. She was looking at the cordless phone that lay on the counter beside the feasting cat, bringing it to her ear and frowning at it.

Joshua went to the door and, after a cursory look outside, opened it.

"What is going on?" Beth asked. "Where's Maude?"

"Um…" His brain was not processing her questions, because she was standing there in an unbuttoned denim jacket with fake fur at the neck and sleeves, and a T-shirt. Aside from the sneakers on her feet and the goosebumps on her legs, he wasn't sure she was wearing anything else, and that idea sort of lodged in his brain and wouldn't let go. "Uh…"

She snapped her fingers in front of her chest, then raised

them to point at her eyes. "Up here, Josh. Hello? You with me now?"

He nodded. His gaze faltered, started to slide lower again. She had great legs. Kind of funny to see them with sockless feet and running shoes at the bottom and a T-shirt hem at the top, but still... Must be all that running that made them so slender and firm and—

She hooked a finger under his chin and lifted his head. "Hey, caveman. Me Beth, you Josh. Where Maude?"

"Kitchen."

"Ugh." She rolled her eyes and walked past him into the house. He followed as if she'd slipped a leash around his neck, barely remembering to close and lock the front door before he did.

"Beth! Well, my goodness, what are you doing out here at this hour?"

"My phone rang. When I answered, no one was there, but the call came from here."

Maude thinned her lips and sent the cat a glare. "Siegfried! Did you do that?"

"You think the cat called me?"

"I have you on speed dial, dear. Siggy had knocked the phone off the charger stand and more than likely stepped on a button or two while he was scavenging the kitchen for a free meal."

Beth heaved a sigh and sank into a kitchen chair. "Well, that's a relief. I thought something had happened."

"You don't need to worry about me, hon. Not with Joshua and Bryan here."

Beth slid a glance Josh's way, and he knew it had been his presence she'd been worried about. She didn't trust him.

He turned to Maude. "The question remains, though. How did Siggy here get into the house? I thought it was locked up tight."

"Oh, I probably left a window cracked. My bathroom, more than likely. I'm always leaving that one open. Or the basement, maybe."

He nodded slowly. "I'll check them. It's probably a good idea to try to break that habit."

"Hell, Josh, Maude's got nothing to worry about. Everyone in town adores her, and it's not like we get any random crime in Blackberry."

"Well, you never know," Maude said. "You feel free to check, Joshua, and I'll do my best not to forget again."

"Kiss-up," Beth accused.

Maude sent her a wink. "I'm goin' back to bed. You two put that cat outdoors when he finishes his cream. He'll go right on back to Frankie's. Always does." With that, Maude left them in the kitchen and headed up to bed.

Beth sighed. "You may as well go back to bed, too. I'll head home."

"Hell, it's heading for five-thirty. No point going back to bed now." He turned to the counter, started running water into a carafe. "I'm making coffee. Stay for a cup?"

"Sure. Why not?"

He measured ground roast, poured in the water, turned on the switch. "So you were worried I had done something to Maude and came rushing over here to save her."

She frowned at him. "I was afraid something had happened to her. She could have fallen, broken a hip or something."

"If she had, didn't you think I would have taken care of her?"

"She's in her seventies, Joshua. Almost eighty. She has to shoot insulin into her veins before every meal, and I know her balance is getting pretty shaky, though she'd rather be shot than admit it. I was worried. She's my friend."

He nodded. "And I'm a stranger."

She pursed her lips. "It wouldn't matter if you were a stranger or not. I...don't trust men."

"None of us?" He made his eyes wide and lifted his brows as he searched her face. "Not even the good ones?"

"You telling me you're one of the good ones?"

"Lady, I am the *best* one."

"You're full of yourself, too."

He let his teasing smile die. "You've been burned by my gender before, I take it."

She met his eyes, and he saw swirling depths of emotion—whirlpools that threatened to suck him right in. "Burned. Yeah. I've been burned. Fell for the bad guy, then was damn near destroyed by the rescuing heroes."

He winced inwardly at that, had to avert his eyes briefly.

"I've got horrible taste in men, Joshua."

"Then it's a good sign that you don't like me, right?"

"That's just it. I do like you." She slid out of her chair and got to her feet. "I'll take a rain check on that coffee, okay?"

Without waiting for an answer, she walked to the door. Without waiting for an invitation, he followed her. He reached past her for the door, opened it for her. She turned to look up at him, smiled just a little. "Don't try to kiss me, okay?"

He'd been thinking about doing just that, and her frankness surprised him. "How am I supposed to resist? Huh? You show up at the crack of dawn with your hair practically standing on end, wearing a baggy T-shirt and the most god-awful jacket I've ever seen—and sneakers. Damn, woman, I'd have to be a saint to resist that."

She smiled broadly and turned to step outside.

Then she stopped and turned back again. She gripped

the lapels of his bathrobe, jerked him forward and planted a brief, platonic kiss on his cheek. "Thanks for looking after Maude. It's sweet, the way you are with her. And with Bryan."

"That's me. Sweet as apple pie."

"See you later—on my run?"

He was suddenly looking forward to it. He glanced down at his own attire, a bathrobe over boxer shorts, and said, "I'll even wear clothes."

"Me, too."

"Crying shame."

She grinned at him and hurried to her car. Joshua watched until she was out of the driveway and out of sight down the road. Then he put the cat out, poured a cup of coffee and began checking the house for open windows.

Beth spent more time looking into the mirror than she usually did before a morning run, her hands a little too concerned about getting her higher than usual ponytail perfectly centered.

The moment she realized what she was doing, she scowled at her reflection. "What's the matter with you? He's a stranger."

She pursed her lips, shrugged. "Well, he's Maude's grandson. That's not exactly a stranger."

Sighing, she brushed her teeth, then rinsed her mouth with mouthwash. Twice. And she used a triple coat of roll-on, because God forbid she should run into Joshua Kendall smelling of sweat.

"You're pathetic," she told her reflection. Then she tucked her itty-bitty derringer into the pocket of her maroon-and-white warm-up jacket, zipped it up to keep it there, and stepped out her front door into the brilliant autumn sunshine.

She could see her breath this morning. It was getting awfully cold for running. She was a diehard, though. She would push it until the snowbanks along the roadside made it too dangerous. Then she would haul her treadmill out of the storage space under her rented cottage, assemble it, oil it up and plug it in.

She started out slowly, building up to a stronger pace as her body warmed and her muscles limbered. She felt good today. Not in the usual way that running made her feel good, but in a new way—a way she hadn't felt in a long time.

It was because of him. She wasn't so naive that she didn't know that. It was because a great-looking man with no apparent mental defects found her attractive. Imagine feeling so buoyant over something so juvenile.

Not that she was going to let it cloud her judgment or weaken her caution. If anything, the feeling made her even more wary. Not only didn't she trust him, she was going to have to be very careful about trusting herself.

Still, the closer she got to Maude's house, the more she had to fight to keep the smile from her face. And when she arrived there, and saw that both Maude and Joshua were waiting for her on the front porch, the smile was impossible to suppress.

She walked up the sidewalk, taking deep, lung-bursting breaths and blowing them out slowly, so she wouldn't be panting when she got to them.

Joshua was on his feet, glancing at his watch. "Ten minutes early."

"I didn't know anyone was keeping track," she said, mounting the steps.

He shrugged. "I was getting ready to worry in case you were late."

"Don't," she told him. "Worrying about me is a waste

of time." She noted his clothes. "And you're not running home with me again."

"I'm not?"

She shook her head firmly. "No, you're not."

"And why not?"

"Because I have the feeling you're trying to be protective of me for some reason. And I don't like that. I resent it, in fact."

"You do?"

She nodded. "Good morning, Maude." She leaned over Maude and planted a kiss on her cheek.

"Morning, dear. Don't be angry with Joshua for wanting to watch over you. I was the one who put him up to it."

"And since when do you think I need watching over?"

She shrugged. "That car yesterday spooked me, I guess." She reached for a pot and poured tea. "Today's brew is for energy and heat, er, warmth, I mean. It's going to be too cold for our outdoor tea parties soon," she said, setting the pot down and rubbing her arms. She wore a heavy fleece sweater and a knit hat.

Beth sank into her chair and lifted the beautiful china cup, bringing it to her nose and sniffing. "Mmm…cinnamon?"

"Yes. And ginseng and cloves, with just a hint of vanilla."

"It's really delicious," Joshua said.

Beth took a sip. "Mmm, it is. You're brilliant, Maude."

"You may not think so much longer," Maude said.

"Why's that?" Beth was curious, frowning from Maude to Joshua and back again.

"Well, my kitchen range is on the fritz. Now, I can get by with the hotplate and microwave for breakfast and lunch, but I had such a special dinner planned."

Beth set her cup down. "I'll take a look at it for you."

"Don't bother, Beth," Joshua said. "I already looked it over. I'm afraid it's gonna require professional help."

"Really?"

He nodded. Maude nodded, too, very enthusiastically. "I've got a call in to Milt Rogers, in town, but he's working on a furnace over in Pinedale today. Said he could come out first thing tomorrow. Which still brings me back to tonight's dinner." She smiled her sweetest smile. "I thought I'd just bring all the groceries over and cook dinner at your place," she said with a firm nod. "That wouldn't be any trouble for you, would it, Beth?"

Beth blinked and knew better than to argue. She couldn't say she had plans to go out, because she never went out and Maude knew it. She couldn't say she didn't feel well, because if she were ill, she wouldn't be running. And saying no for no reason at all would just be rude. So she smiled right back at Maude and said, "Of course it wouldn't be any trouble."

"I didn't think so," Maude told her. "Drink your tea, dear. It's getting cold."

The screen door creaked, and Bryan stepped out onto the porch. He wore sweatpants, a T-shirt, and his feet were bare. He wasn't skinny like a lot of boys his age, she thought. The tight T-shirt revealed a physique that probably drove the girls his age wild. Not quite as nice as his father's, but...

"Morning, Bryan," Beth called, dragging her unruly thoughts to a halt.

He frowned at her. "Are you all crazy? It's freezing out here."

"Oh, I like to enjoy the outdoors while I can," Maude said. "Soon enough it'll be winter, and I'll be cooped up in the house till spring. When I think about the snow to come, this autumn chill seems like nothing."

"Winters pretty bad up here, are they, Maude?" Joshua asked.

Bryan reached back through the door and reemerged with a jacket in hand, one he pulled on quickly.

"We get hammered with snow and frozen with cold," she said. "If you call that bad, then I guess they are. I think it keeps life interesting. Why, you never know when the first blizzard of the season is going to hit. It's happened as early as mid-October and as late as mid-December. But it always happens."

"Is there a betting pool?" Bryan asked with a grin.

"There are several," Maude told him with a sly wink.

He laughed softly and came out farther, reached for an empty cup and then the teapot.

"Oh, you don't want that, Bryan—" Maude began.

But he was already pouring. "Sure I do. I heard you say it makes you warm. I'm frozen."

"Well, the tea might help," Beth said, "but maybe some shoes and socks would help more."

He grinned at her, curling his toes and sipping his tea. He seemed better this morning than he had before, Beth thought. Definitely not as sulky and brooding as he had been. Then again, he hadn't been sulky or brooding at her place yesterday, either. Only around his father.

Maybe things were better between them today.

Beth finished her tea in a single gulp. It burned down her gullet.

"Well, I'd better go."

"Yeah, me, too." Josh drained his cup and put it down, getting to his feet.

Beth scowled at him. "Where are you going?"

"My morning jog."

"Josh, I told you, I don't want you coming back with me."

"I'm not running with you. I'm running by myself. It's a free country, and you don't own the road."

"But—"

"But nothing. If my morning jog happens to follow the same route as yours, that's hardly deliberate."

"You're really pushing it, you know that?"

He smiled and winked at her. Beth hugged Maude goodbye and jogged down the steps, along the sidewalk and out to the road. Josh came right behind her.

He'd followed her, single file, for about fifty yards, when she finally rolled her eyes and looked over her shoulder. "For God's sake, you might as well come up beside me."

He picked up the pace, drew up beside her. "If you insist. I was enjoying the view from back there, though."

"Very funny." She sighed, glanced sideways at him. "Why are you doing this, Josh?"

"Look, I care about Maude. And she cares about you. She's worried, Beth. I mean, it's not like her to hear noises in the middle of the night and get all nerved up like she did last night, is it?"

"No. At least, it's never happened since I've known her."

"It's because of that car yesterday. I know it doesn't make any sense, but that made her nervous. She's got it in her head that whoever it was, was up to no good, and you know how she is when she gets something in her head."

She nodded, her lips thinning. She did know. Arguing with Maude was about as practical as arguing with a bulldozer.

"So if it makes her feel a little better to have me watching out for you, then I'm willing to do it. Aren't you?"

She narrowed her eyes on him. "And that's all this is? You're humoring Maude?"

"If I say it's not, are you going to send me packing?"

She pursed her lips, thinking that over. "No. Not yet, anyway."

"Okay. Maude isn't the only reason I'm tagging along after you like a lonely pup. The truth is, I like you, Beth."

She nodded. "Okay."

"Okay? Just okay? Not even an 'I like you, too, Josh'?"

She looked sideways at him. "You can tag along until we get to my house. Then you turn right around and jog your butt right back to Maude's. Agreed?"

"Fine."

She nodded. "My place is around the next bend. You want to race?"

Before he could reply, she took off at a sprint.

6

Beth looked across her coffee table at Josh, who sat in an easy chair. Maude was in the kitchen, whipping up something that smelled wonderful. Beth caught glimpses of her beyond the archway in the kitchen and kept offering to help. Maude flat out refused. Bryan was at the small desk on the far side of the living room, using Beth's computer to catch up with his e-mail.

"Thanks for letting Bry use your PC," Joshua said. "He's been bored out of his mind."

"It's not a problem. I certainly don't mind him using my computer if he doesn't mind using my screen name. Did you ever get hold of the local ISP?"

"Phoned them today. They're 'processing our application.' But they said he should be able to log on by morning."

"That'll make him happy."

Josh shrugged. "He thinks I should have upgraded him to wireless service."

She smiled. "Typical teenager."

"How's he doing? With the tutoring, I mean?"

"We had a great session today. I assigned him *Hamlet* last night, and he's already halfway through it. He's smart, Josh. And he's a good kid."

"Thanks."

She was quiet for a moment. The silence stretched, and

it was awkward. She looked toward the kitchen. "I wish Maude would let us help."

"I think she's enjoying having people to take care of," he said.

Beth nodded, knowing he was right about that. "So is there really anything wrong with her stove?"

Joshua looked alarmed. "What do you mean?"

"Come on, Josh, isn't it obvious?" She shook her head at his puzzled look. "She's been trying to fix me up with some 'eligible young man' ever since I met her. I'm afraid I was right in my earlier assumption. You are the newest candidate."

"Oh, that." He smiled as if to cover it, but she didn't miss the look of relief that crossed his face. "So you still think she's matchmaking."

She shrugged. "I'm sure of it."

"Do you mind?"

She shrugged. "I keep telling her I'm not in the market for a man."

"Ouch."

She looked up quickly. "I didn't mean—"

He held up a hand, stopping her. "It's okay. I'm not easily offended. Or dissuaded."

She shrugged, not sure what to say to that. "Things seemed better between you and Bryan, this morning."

"Changing the subject, huh?"

She raised her eyebrows, waiting.

"Actually, yeah, I think things *are* better. And I have you to thank for it."

"Me? What did I do?"

"I tried what you suggested, talked to him about what was going on with me."

"And it worked?"

He shrugged. "He didn't respond in kind. Then again,

he didn't stomp away and slam a door on me, either. I call that progress."

"It's a start."

The dull bleat of a cell phone came from Beth's purse, which was hanging from a hook in the tiny foyer, near the door. She crossed the living room, dug it out and answered.

"Hey, Beth? It's me. Is everything okay there?"

She frowned, recognizing Dawn's voice instantly. "Fine, hon. Where are you calling from?"

"My cell. It's new, don't worry. And I'll only stay on a minute. I'm online with someone using your screen name. I thought it was you and sent an instant message. He says his name is Bryan. I thought I'd better check on you."

Beth glanced into the living room, where Bryan sat by her laptop, tapping his fingers on the desk as he watched the screen. Then she looked at Josh, who was several feet away, but still within earshot. She turned her back and walked as casually as she could closer to the front door. "Yeah. One of my students. He's cool," she said, keeping her voice low. "I like him a lot, actually."

"Okay."

"Just watch what you say, Dawny."

"I know that. I'll talk to you later."

"Bye, hon." She clicked the off button and carried the telephone with her back into the living room, setting it casually on the coffee table. Josh was still sitting where she'd left him, looking a little too disinterested.

"Everything all right?" he asked.

"Fine. Just a…former student, checking in on me."

The computer made a chiming tone, Bryan focused on the screen and began tapping keys again. It was a little too odd, Bryan chatting with her daughter online. It made her feel skittish. But Dawn was sharp. She wouldn't let anything slip.

"I see you moved your punching bag in our honor."

She smiled at him and nodded. "This place is too small as it is. No room for company *and* a punching bag." She took her spot on the settee, trying to look relaxed even though she was tense. It was odd, having a man in her house. Though she didn't think she would feel so tense if he were any other man. Not *this* tense, anyway. It was an odd sort of "quiet before the storm" kind of tension. Something was brewing between them, and as much as she'd vowed never to get involved with any man ever again, she was seriously considering making him an exception.

He must have read it in her eyes, because he leaned forward, reached across the coffee table and covered her hands with his. "It's sweet of you to indulge Maude like this. It means a lot to me, how good you are to her."

"She's important to me."

"I know."

She licked her lips, then noticed the look Bryan sent across the room, his eyes on their hands, his brow puckered in a disapproving frown. Guiltily, she pulled her hands from beneath Josh's.

"So what do you do? Back in Manhattan, I mean."

"I'm a businessman."

She lifted her brows. "That's a man for you. Sums up his entire life in one word."

"It really isn't all that interesting. Small consulting firm. My partner's running things while I'm away."

He had opened his mouth to say something more when a loud crash from the kitchen brought him to his feet. Beth leaped up and ran into the kitchen, and he was right behind her. Maude was lying on the floor beside a toppled chair and a broken china cup.

Beth fell to her knees beside her friend. "Maude? Honey, what happened?"

Maude moved her mouth as if to speak, but no words came out, only clipped, shallow breaths. Then she went still. Utterly, frighteningly still. Her eyes were open, wide-open, her face coloring pink, then red, then deepening to purple. "Maude!" Beth turned her head, "Josh, do something!"

Josh dropped to the floor beside her as Bryan burst into the kitchen. "Bryan, get help. Call 911." He barked the words, then leaned over Maude, a hand at her throat, his face intense.

Beth cradled Maude's head, holding it up just slightly. She looked into her friend's eyes and knew beyond any doubt that Maude could still hear her, see her. She still knew what was going on. There was an awareness in those wide, frozen eyes. A panic way down deep that couldn't seem to make its way out.

"She's not unconscious, Josh. God, look at her! Maude, honey, hold on. I'll make this okay, I swear."

Maude wasn't moving. No part of her was moving, not even her wide eyes, which seemed frozen in horror and were beginning to bulge.

"Hold on, Maude. Just hold on."

Beth glanced behind her, through the archway into the living room, and saw Bryan speaking rapidly on the cell phone, while he clicked keys on the computer, probably logging off.

Josh leaned closer. "Maude, what happened? Can you tell me what happened?"

The old woman's eyes never moved. They didn't close. Just locked there, frozen in horror.

"Josh, she's not breathing!" Beth shook Maude gently. "Breathe, Maude. Jesus, why isn't she breathing?"

Bryan came back into the kitchen, the phone still at his ear. He came all the way into the room this time, and Beth knew when he got his first look at the expressionless nightmare of Maude's face. It was as if she'd been flash frozen and dipped in blue dye.

Bryan's face paled. "Oh, God." He swallowed, seemed to shake himself. "They're on the way."

Josh laid his head against Maude's chest, his ear over her heart. He straightened again, looking grim. "Do you know CPR?" he asked Beth.

"Yes." But she had already seen it—she'd seen the moment when the awareness in Maude's eyes blinked out. They didn't close. But the horror vanished. And something, something…left.

Tears flowing, Beth gently tipped Maude's chin up. She leaned over her, fingers pinching her friend's nostrils, and blew gently into her mouth, two quick breaths.

When she stopped, Joshua started the chest compressions, five of them. And then it was Beth's turn again. They fell into a steady rhythm, while Bryan stayed on the phone, filling in the dispatcher as to what was happening.

Minutes ticked by like hours, but finally Beth heard sirens. Bryan disconnected, then ran to the front door to let the paramedics in. They were locals, though Beth barely knew them. She could probably have come up with some of their names, given a few minutes to think about it. Maude would have known them. She would have known who their parents were, how old their kids were, what their day jobs were and what they had been like as children.

But Maude wasn't talking.

Beth moved aside, shaking bodily as the medics took over. She was barely aware of it when Josh's arm slid around her shoulder. He pulled her against his side. "Hold on, Beth," he whispered. "Lean on me if you need to."

Bryan went over to where they stood, actually taking hold of her hand. It was as if they were trying to comfort her—when they were the ones who were Maude's family.

The door was still wide-open, but it banged the wall anyway when Frankie Parker charged in. She strode across the living room to where they stood in the archway, wearing her uniform and looking pissed at the world. "What the hell happened?"

"I don't know, Frankie," Beth said. "She was making us dinner. She just—collapsed."

The medics were jolting Maude now, sending bolts of electricity through her—two, then three, times.

"She's diabetic," Frankie snapped.

"Maybe that's it," Beth whispered. "She probably took her insulin already, and she hadn't eaten yet. Maybe her blood sugar dropped and—"

She stopped there as a medic lifted a huge needle in his fist and then stabbed it straight into Maude's heart. "God!" Beth spun around and crushed her face against Joshua's chest. His hands buried themselves in her hair and held her there, even as he moved her several steps away from the kitchen, farther into the living room.

She heard someone say to continue CPR, and a second later, the medics carried Maude out on a stretcher.

"We should go to the hospital," Bryan said softly.

Beth lifted her head from Josh's chest, turning to see Bryan; his eyes were wet. Whether it was for Maude or for the memories all this must be stirring up in him—he'd lost his mother only a few months ago after all—she didn't know. Probably some combination of the two. He put a hand on Beth's shoulder.

Beth's throat closed up, and she bit her lip, so the tears that rolled down her cheeks fell in silence.

* * *

Joshua watched, feeling helpless as the paramedics loaded Maude into an ambulance, resumed CPR even as the doors closed and took off for the nearest hospital, siren screaming. Beth and Bryan stood close together, looking shell-shocked as Josh unlocked his pickup and held the passenger door open.

Beth watched the ambulance go, distracted until Josh touched her face, drawing her attention back to him. He helped her get in. Bryan climbed in beside her, and Josh went around to the driver's side. He thought there was no real hurry. Maude was already gone; he felt it right to his bones. He kept a careful eye on Bryan. His son had seen too much of death lately. He didn't need this.

Maybe bringing him on this assignment had been yet another in Josh's long string of mistakes. Maybe he'd screwed up beyond fixing it this time.

Bryan said, "I think there were still burners on in the kitchen."

"I'll get them," Josh said.

Bryan nodded. "Let's you and I wait out here, okay, Beth?"

Josh watched his son as he leaned over her and fastened her seat belt, and a rush of pride surged through him. His son was a hell of a man. Not a kid, but a decent, honorable young man. A man, Josh realized for the first time, he would like and respect even if he wasn't his own son.

He was a little surprised that this was the first time that fact had occurred to him. He shook it off and went back into the house, taking a careful look around the kitchen as he turned off the burners and the oven. Then he glanced at the floor and saw the broken teacup. Hell, better safe than sorry. He opened drawers until he located the sandwich bags, then carefully placed the broken pieces of the teacup into one of them. He took a careful look around the entire room but found nothing out of the ordinary.

Maude was not a young woman, and he knew nothing about the state of her health, other than that she was a diabetic, though she'd certainly seemed fine. Still, there was nothing here to suggest...

He cut himself off with a shake of his head. He had to get Beth to the hospital. Though he was dreading it. God, he hoped Bryan was going to be all right with all this going on.

"I'm sorry," Dr. Granger said softly. He'd just come out of the treatment room into the E.R. waiting area. Beyond him, as the door swung slowly closed, Beth glimpsed a sheet-covered form in a hospital bed. "She's gone."

Beth closed her eyes as pain welled up in her chest. "I don't understand this. It doesn't make any sense. God, how? Why? She was fine."

"Her heart just gave out, Beth. There was nothing anyone could have done. Maude would have said it was just her time." He put a hand on her shoulder. "She didn't suffer. Small comfort, I know."

She looked up at him slowly. "You are so wrong about that, Dr. Granger. She suffered. I was there. I saw her. She suffered terribly."

He frowned at her. "Now, Beth, I know you're upset—"

"Her eyes were open. She was in there. She knew everything that was going on, I swear I—" She heard a gasp, realized Frankie Parker was nearby and bit her lip.

The doctor shook his head slowly. "Beth, she's at peace now. Please, take comfort in that." He turned to Joshua and Bryan, who were watching her closely. "I'm so sorry for your loss. But I'm glad you both were here for her. It's a blessing you got to spend some time with her."

"She really loved you, Beth," Bryan said. "She thought of you like a daughter."

"I know."

The doctor looked at Josh. "We'll need to know what you decide to do about the, uh…arrangements. Though I believe Maude had everything prearranged with Miller's."

Josh nodded, and glanced at Beth.

"Miller's is the only funeral home in town, Josh. It's okay, I'll make the call."

"I can have a nurse do that for you, Beth," Dr. Granger said.

"Wait." Josh glanced at Beth, then at the doctor. "Look, you were her doctor. Don't you find it odd that she would just suddenly… I'd like to know what happened. Not your best guess, but a definitive answer."

"Are you asking for an autopsy?" Dr. Granger asked.

Beth sucked in a sharp breath beside him. He looked at her, and she said, "God, please, Josh, don't. I know how horrifying this is, but I don't think Maude would have wanted that. If Dr. Granger thinks this was just her time…" She let her words trail off.

"Trust me, Joshua," Dr. Granger said. Beth thought his silver hair and gold-rimmed specs inspired as much confidence as his deep, comforting tone. "There's nothing unusual about a woman of her age dying suddenly. Even though it seems like an aberration to the bereaved, the death of a nearly eighty-year-old diabetic is natural. Even Maude knew she could pass away at any time." He patted Josh's shoulder. "She was lucky, Josh. She was healthy, and she had a wonderful, full life right up until the end."

Josh looked from one of them to the other and seemed

to be searching his mind for a reply. Finally he said, "Just make sure they don't do anything that would make it impossible. I'll give it some more thought and make a decision."

"Fair enough," the doctor said. "Do you want to see her?"

Beth glanced at the closed door of the treatment room. "I...don't. Maude wouldn't want me to. She'd have had a dozen platitudes to explain why." She stared at the door for a long moment. "No. She always said she wanted to be remembered at her best. It would dishonor her memory."

"Beth, why don't you come back to Maude's with us tonight?" Josh asked. "You don't want to go home to that empty cottage. Not tonight."

She licked her lips, wishing she had the strength to say no. But she didn't. And she couldn't imagine spending the night in the cottage where Maude had died, alone with yet another ghost. "You two don't need me hanging around tonight." It was a lame attempt at best.

"Yeah, we do," Bryan said. "We really do, Beth."

She met Bryan's eyes. "All right."

"Good," Josh said. "That's good."

Josh said he was going to bring the car around, but he used the time to place a call to Arthur Stanton, relieved when the man answered on the first ring.

"We've had an...event," he said quickly. "It's going to take some quick action, Art."

"What's happened?"

"Maude Bickham is dead. It looks like her heart gave out, but we're going to need to make sure. And it's got to be discreet. I can't think of a single believable argument for an official autopsy."

"Then it'll be an unofficial one. Where's the body?"

"It's being taken to Miller's Funeral Home here in Blackberry."

"We're on it. Anything else?"

"Yeah, Beth's cottage. That's where she was when it happened. I need the kitchen processed, just to be on the safe side. There's a broken teacup in a sandwich bag. I stuck it on top of the fridge. Check that, too."

"You can get Beth out of the house for this?"

"She'll be spending the night at Maude's place with Bryan and me."

"Perfect. I'll get a team in and out fast. Have a report for you, asap."

"Thanks, Art. It's probably nothing. I can't think of a reason in the world why she might be a target, but still…"

"It's necessary. You're not overreacting."

"What about the background checks on the people in town, Arthur? Any hits?"

Arthur sighed. "We've checked every hotel reservation, time share and rental unit. So far, nothing stands out. Reservations booked six months to a year in advance. No way Mordecai knew where Beth was that long ago. But we're still looking. I'll check back with you tomorrow."

He hung up, and Josh snapped his telephone off, pocketed it and drove the car around to the hospital's double doors.

Bryan and Beth were there waiting.

He felt a lump form in his throat when he looked at her, standing there beside his son in the hospital entrance. She didn't want to walk out and leave her old friend behind, lying there unattended. It felt wrong, he knew that. He'd felt the same way when he'd had to fly out to California to identify the bodies of his ex-wife and her new husband. Leaving them there, after the fact, had felt like abandoning them.

It wasn't easy.

He pulled the pickup truck to a stop, and Bryan opened the passenger side door and held it for Beth while she got inside. She slid across the seat until she was pressed to Josh's side, so there was room for Bryan, who climbed in and closed the door.

Josh drove and wished to God there was something he could do to ease her pain. He hated being in a position where he had to pretend his own grief even compared to hers, and he could tell by the looks he was getting from Bryan that his son hated it even more. He knew Bryan honestly mourned Maude's passing. He did, too. But they'd only known her a few days and were playing the part of devoted family members. For Beth, the grief was deeper, far, far deeper.

There was nothing to be done, though.

Nothing.

Josh drove Beth and his son back to Maude's house. And even to him it felt wrong that everything there should be the same, that there was no sign of the tragedy, the loss. They went inside, and the house *felt* the same—as if Maude would pop in from the kitchen any second, with her bright smile and her mischievous eyes and her pearls of wisdom.

"'Everything in life happens for a reason,'" Beth said softly. "'It's all part of the great plan. You can accept it with grace, or you can fight it like a wildcat, but what's meant to be is meant to be.'"

Her inward-turned gaze shifted outward again. It was as if, for just a moment, she'd forgotten he and Bryan were there. She shrugged and said, "It was one of Maude's favorite platitudes. The one she pulled out most often, at least. And the only one that never made a hell of a lot of sense to me." She shook her head. "She said it was the key to the universe. The secret of happiness. But this wasn't part of anyone's plan. There's no reason why Maude should have died. She wasn't sick or suffering. She enjoyed life more than most people half her age. More than I do, that's for sure."

Bryan came over to her, put a hand on her shoulder. He didn't say anything, just let his hand rest there for a moment. Then he turned and went upstairs to his room, telling his father with a look that he was done. Poor kid, he'd been through a lot today.

"Beth, sit down. You look ready to drop."

She stood there, shaking her head slowly. "I…can't sleep in Maude's room, Joshua."

"Of course not. There must be ten bedrooms in this place."

She nodded. "But they're not made up—"

"Sure they are," Josh said. "Maude kept them as clean as if she expected guests to show up at any time."

She closed her eyes, crossed the room slowly, sank onto the couch. "I didn't know that."

"I only know it from being here," he said. "Day to day, watching her routine." He cleared his throat. "We're here for you, Beth. Bryan and me. I know you don't trust men as a rule, but—you can lean on me. I mean it. I want to help you through this."

She met his eyes and shook her head slowly. "Listen to you. I'm pathetic. You're the one who just lost your grandmother."

"And you're the one who just lost your best friend. Your only friend."

She averted her eyes fast, but not in time to hide the tears. Josh slid his arms around her and drew her close to him, and she let him. She relaxed against his chest, lowered her head to his shoulder and let him hold her. God, he wanted to make things all right for this woman. So much pain in her life—most of it because of him. He wanted to take it away, to make everything good for her. He wanted to make her smile.

He drew back just a little and looked down at her tear-stained cheeks, lifting her face with a forefinger when she tried to hide it from him. And then something moved in him, something irresistible, and he bent closer and slowly covered her lips with his own.

It wasn't a passionate kiss. It was a tender one, slow and lingering and gentle. When he lifted his head away, she didn't look him in the eye. Instead she kept her gaze averted and said softly, "I'm exhausted. I'm going to try to get some sleep."

He nodded. "I'll walk you up." She looked at him, about to say something, but Josh held up a hand. "The heat isn't on in all the bedrooms. And I want to know where you are, in case you need anything. And *that's all*."

She nodded, her eyes expressing silent gratitude; then she turned and walked up the stairs as if her legs were made of lead. Josh walked behind her and tried to figure out what had just happened between them. The feelings that had been roiling inside him ever since he'd set eyes on her again were not real feelings. They were based on guilt, on the crushing responsibility that had been bearing down on him for nearly twenty years. He'd thought he'd killed her. He hadn't. But having destroyed her life left him compelled to repair the damage. And that was a powerful motivator.

He was going to have to be very careful, he realized, to keep his head on straight, and to keep his guilty feelings uninvolved in the job he had come here to do—and, more importantly, not to confuse them with anything else.

7

——▸——

Sunday (wee hours)

Maude was standing beside the bed, holding Beth's hand and talking to her as if she were still alive.

I know, Beth. I know what I always say; that when my time comes, I'll be more than happy to go. That I've had a happy, full life in the best town in the whole wide world, and that I haven't got a single regret. And all that holds true, Beth. Every last bit of it. And I'm fine. I really am. But I don't think it was my time. Something…something went wrong. I'm worried about you, Beth.

Beth opened her eyes, coming slowly awake. She smiled up at Maude, gave her hand a squeeze, then realized that there was no one there. Beth lay in the bed with her arm raised, hand closed around nothing but air, and the reality startled her so much that she sat up suddenly. God, it had been so real! She'd *felt* Maude's hand in her own, *heard* her voice.

She swallowed the dryness in her throat and looked around the strange bedroom. It wasn't one she'd ever been in before.

It was nice, though. Amazing that she hadn't realized Maude kept the inn's old guest rooms in a constant state of readiness, the beds made up, bedding fresh, the comforters smelling of the outdoors, as if she'd aired them on a regular basis. The room was free of dust, its furniture polished, its floor mopped and its bathroom sparkling. To save money, Maude had shut off the heat in most of the bedrooms simply by closing the valves on the old-fashioned radiators. Josh had ducked into his own room long enough to grab a T-shirt for her to wear to bed. Then he'd come into her room to bleed the air from the pipes and turn her heat on for her. He'd offered to bring her a glass of warm milk, but she'd turned it down. And then he'd left, without any hint he wanted anything more.

The man was treating her like a fragile, wounded dove. She wasn't. Far from it, she thought. But it was sweet, and he meant well. And maybe—maybe Josh was a man she could trust, one she could let herself care for. Maybe…

She tugged back the paisley print spread and slid out of the bed. She didn't have a robe or slippers here. She was wearing Josh's T-shirt as a nightgown, but she didn't think she would run into anyone downstairs. The clock on the nightstand told her it was 2:45 a.m. Bryan and his dad were sound asleep. Beth wasn't even close.

Not after that dream.

It kept replaying in her mind. Was Maude trying to tell her something? That it hadn't been her time?

"It was just a dream," she whispered. She padded out of the bedroom and down the stairs, not sure where she was going, just knowing she was too restless to sleep. Too lonely in this house without Maude. God, why did she have to die? It was selfish, Beth knew, to feel the way she did, but dammit, Maude was the only friend she had allowed herself to make here. She couldn't imagine life without her.

She crossed the dark living room, then paused as she heard the sound of an engine starting up. Frowning, she moved quickly to the front door and peered out into the night. Josh's pickup had come to life. Not in the driveway, but on the side of the road, as if he'd rolled it out there first, before starting the engine.

What in the world was he up to?

Every shield she'd built sprang up around her soul, and Beth went icy cold. He was obviously doing something he didn't want her to know about. It shook her. Up to now she'd accepted that Josh was exactly what he claimed to be, that he had no secrets. Now it seemed he had something to hide after all.

She should have known. God, when had she met any man worth trusting? Hadn't Mordecai taught her anything?

Beth decided it wouldn't be wise to just wait around to find out what Joshua Kendall was hiding. She held off until his pickup crept out of sight, then grabbed her coat and pulled it on over the T-shirt, shoved her feet into her sneakers and found Maude's car keys right where she had always left them. She dashed out to Maude's old station wagon, started it up and headed off in the same direction Josh had gone, driving slowly, headlights off. It didn't take long at all to catch up to him, either. He drove into town, pulled over along the side of the road, and shut off his engine and headlights.

She pulled over and shut Maude's car off as well, three blocks behind him. She didn't think he'd seen her. Carefully, she got out and walked quickly, quietly, ahead. It was cold. As she walked, she buttoned up her long coat, glad she'd had this one on today rather than the short jacket she'd worn on her last middle-of-the-night run. She could see her breath in the eerie silence of the night. A new chill raced up her spine when she realized Josh's truck was parked right in front of the funeral home. And he wasn't in it anymore.

Oh, God. What was this?

She looked toward the building. It stood there, tall and narrow, yellow clapboards, white shutters framing pitch-black windows, and a sign on the lawn that swung in the night breeze and creaked with every movement.

She swallowed hard and crept along the sidewalk toward the front entrance, but she didn't go up the steps. Instead she veered off the path and walked around to the rear. And there, from the seldom viewed back lawn of the town's only funeral home, she saw a light on in one of the windows.

She shivered and hugged her coat more tightly around her. Her bare legs were trembling with cold and with emotion. Still, she moved closer. The window was too high for her to see inside, but there was a water spigot mounted to the cinder block base of the house. She put one foot on that, dug her fingertips into the window frame and pulled herself up.

Beyond the glass was a scene from a nightmare. Maude's body, white as porcelain, and nude, lay on a table, and a woman in a white coat stood over it, a hypodermic in one hand.

Beth jerked backward so hard and so fast that she stumbled from her perch. Her foot turned the water valve as she fell, and icy spray shot from the spigot onto her legs.

From beyond the window she heard the woman's voice say, "What the hell was that?"

She scrambled to her feet and ran, splashing in the still-growing puddle as she did. She raced across back lawns, finally cutting between two houses and coming out near Maude's car. Without looking back, she jumped into it and made a U-turn, heading back the way she had come.

Dammit, she was freezing!

And frightened. Who the hell was messing with

Maude's body in the dead of night, in secret? And how was Josh involved?

She remembered him asking about an autopsy. Could he have brought in his own person to perform it? But how could he have the connections to do such a thing, and why the cloak-and-dagger nonsense? Why not just insist it be done? He was Maude's next of kin, after all. He had every right. She wondered about Josh. He was hiding something, that much was clear. But what? He couldn't be working for Mordecai—he seemed more interested in protecting her than doing her harm. Protecting her… God, could he be another one of Arthur Stanton's goons? Sent to protect her whether she liked it or not? But how could Maude's grandson be working for Stanton? That would be too much of a coincidence. What, then?

She was no longer so sure about Joshua, and nowhere near comfortable spending the night under the same roof with him—assuming he even came back from his late-night excursion. She headed back to her own cottage.

"What exactly did you observe after she collapsed?" Marcia Black, government-employed forensic pathologist, asked Josh the question even as she gathered various samples from Maude Bickham's corpse.

Arthur had phoned Josh on his cell to let him know things were underway. He'd sent Marcia Black to the funeral home and a recovery team to Beth's cottage. Both missions would be accomplished under cover of darkness, in complete secrecy. Josh felt compelled to oversee the postmortem—to see to it that Maude's body was treated with respect, that nothing was overlooked, and that no evidence was left behind. Black wouldn't do an autopsy; that would be too obvious. She would have to settle for a visual exam, and some blood and tissue samples.

He'd arrived at the funeral home shortly after Dr. Black had been scheduled to begin her work.

"It seemed like she couldn't breathe," he said, in answer to Black's question. "But she wasn't struggling to breathe, either. It was strange. She was incredibly still."

Marcia lifted her brows. "How still? Was she speaking? Gasping?"

"Utterly still. Her eyes were open but not moving. Her mouth wasn't moving, either. Nothing on her was moving, but she wasn't dead yet. I'm telling you, it was creepy."

"You're saying she appeared...paralyzed?"

Frowning, Josh sent her a look. "Yeah. Why, does that mean something to you?"

She shrugged. "It might."

"Well?"

She shrugged. "There are drugs that can have that effect. But it's highly unlikely that's what this is. They have to be injected."

Josh narrowed his eyes. "Injected," he said. "Like insulin is injected."

"She injected insulin?" Marcia's eyes told him they were on to something as he nodded. "How long before the collapse?"

"She was making dinner, always took a shot before eating. It couldn't have been more than five, ten minutes at the most." He reached out to pull a sheet over Maude. "Keep her covered, will you?"

"She's dead, Kendall."

"Her dignity's not. So will you be able to find this drug in her system?"

"If it's what I'm thinking, it's going to be tough to find any trace of it. Even if we did, we couldn't be sure. There's no definitive test. Only indications. Do you have the syringe? The vial?" She pulled the sheet back down as she continued her work.

"The team is going over Beth's cottage now. I'll make sure they—" He broke off at a sound from just outside the window.

"What the hell was that?" Marcia said, looking up fast, a needle in her latex-covered hand.

"I don't know." Josh moved across the room and looked out, just in time to see a flash of toned flesh and gray fabric darting around the corner. "Shit."

"What is it?"

"I don't know. I'll be back. If I'm not, contact me in the morning. And make sure you don't leave any evidence."

"It's not like it's my first clandestine postmortem, Mr. Kendall. I work for the government, same as you."

He didn't work for the government—not anymore—but he didn't take time to correct her. Instead, he raced to the front door, slipped out and ran down the steps to where his pickup waited—just in time to see Maude's old car, illuminated by moonlight, pulling a U-turn a few blocks away and taking off as if its tailpipe were on fire.

Great. So Beth had seen something. Had she seen him? At the very least, she'd seen his pickup. How the hell was he supposed to fix this screwup?

He must be losing his touch.

He drove after her, lights off, keeping far enough back so she couldn't see him. He rolled his eyes when he saw where she was heading: her place. Where a federal forensics team was, even now, searching for evidence. He yanked out his cell phone, glad Arthur had given him a contact number for the team. A male voice picked up immediately.

"It's Kendall. The client is on her way to the cottage. You've got one minute. Get out now."

"Got it."

He hung up the phone and hoped to God they got out in time.

By the time he pulled the pickup to a stop outside her place, Joshua thought he had his story ready. At least, he hoped so. Best defense, as they always said, was a good offense. It would work.

It *had* to work.

Beth crouched outside her cottage, afraid to move, her eyes squinting in the darkness. She'd sworn there had been movement from her place. But there was nothing now. Just silence and darkness.

And then she went utterly stiff when Josh's voice came from behind her. "Beth? What are you doing out here?"

She pressed her lips together, straightened slowly and turned to face him. "I could ask you the same thing."

"I was looking for you."

"At the funeral home?"

He blinked, seeming surprised. "How do you know I...ah, hell, it doesn't matter. I went to see Maude. I...I guess I just needed to say goodbye. To make sure she was being taken care of. To see she was okay, as little sense as that makes." He pushed a hand through his hair. "But when I got there..." He bit his lip, as if stopping himself from finishing.

"I was there, too," she whispered. "I heard you leaving the house and followed you."

He looked up quickly. The night breeze ruffled his hair. "Did you see anything...odd there?"

She nodded. "I saw some woman working over Maude's body. If I didn't know better, I'd swear she was about to perform an autopsy."

He held her gaze. "That's what I saw, too, and I reached

the same conclusion. I couldn't believe it." He shook his head. "What the hell is going on, Beth?"

She frowned deeply, searching his face. No sign of a lie there.

"I was getting ready to slip inside and confront her, whoever she was, when I heard something. I thought I saw you taking off in Maude's car." He shook his head. "My first instinct was that you were somehow involved in…I don't know, something. Some kind of cover-up involving my grandmother. So I followed you here."

She pressed her lips tight, told herself she was stupid to want so badly to believe him. "When I saw your truck there, I thought the same about you."

He rolled his eyes. "Right. Me." Shaking his head slowly, he glanced toward her cottage. "So you were too afraid of me to come home?"

"My home is this cottage, Josh, not Maude's house."

"I think she would disagree with you there, but I won't argue with you." He sighed. "So why haven't you gone inside? What are you doing crouching out here in the cold?"

She held his gaze for a long moment, wondering if she dared trust him. God, she wanted so badly to trust someone. She had allowed herself to think he might be the one. Now…now she wasn't so sure.

Maude had trusted him. That ought to be worth something. "Someone was in my house when I got here."

He lifted his brows. "Are you sure? You saw them?"

"I saw…a movement. And shadows. I think."

"I'll go check it out." Turning, he started toward the house, but she shot forward, gripping his arm. He might be hiding things from her, but he was still Maude's grandson.

"Josh, don't. Just…don't. Something could happen to you."

"Don't be ridiculous. What could happen? It's probably just some kids or—"

"No. Look, there are things in my past, things that...that might explain all of this."

He turned slowly, staring deeply into her eyes. "Maude said you were haunted. Said you had more ghosts than any woman she'd ever met."

"I have my share. But they're *my* ghosts, Josh. The last thing I want is for any of them to hurt you. Or Bryan. Or anyone."

He nodded slowly. "Something's scaring the hell out of you, though."

She lifted her brows, nodded, though it killed her to admit to such a weakness. "Yeah. Something is. But it's not your problem." She turned to stare at her cottage, wondering who had been there, and why.

She was still looking at it when it exploded.

The sound was deafening, the shock wave devastating, so powerful it knocked her off her feet and slammed her flat. She found herself lying on her back.

Her head was spinning, her ears ringing, her heart racing...and her body was pressed to the ground by the warm weight of Josh's. He lay on top of her, his arms around her protectively as debris rained down on them, his head turned toward her cottage. Beth looked that way, as well, but there was nothing there. The cozy little place had been blown to bits. There was no fire, no smoke. Just rubble, scattered everywhere. It was like looking at the impossible. It was surreal, and she couldn't quite wrap her mind around what had happened.

"Are you all right?" he asked.

She jerked her eyes back to Josh. He was looking at her now, his eyes concerned, his face very close to hers. "Yeah. I think so."

He nodded, taking a careful look around before easing his weight from her body. He got to his feet, extended a hand. She took it and let him pull her upright, as well; then he frowned and moved her hair away from her neck. "You're bleeding."

"God, my house. My...everything. Oh, God..."

"It's going to be all right, Beth."

"How?"

"Hold still." He slid his hand over her neck, fingertips gentle, then tugging and causing a painful stab. She winced. "Sorry." He showed her the spear of wood he'd pulled from her neck. Then he covered her hand with his and pressed her palm to the spot on her neck. "Keep pressure on that until we get home."

She frowned at him. "We can't just...leave. The police..."

"Frankie will know where to find us. I think the safest thing is to get you out of here until we find out what happened."

She pursed her lips. "I think I know what happened here. And you're probably right."

He searched her face, "Do you want to tell me about it?"

She pursed her lips. "No. I don't want to, Josh. But I think I have to."

"Then let's get out of here."

Nodding, she let him lead her. He held her to his side, supporting her as if she were weak, when she was anything but. Everything in her world was shattering. And she knew in her gut it was Mordecai. It had to be Mordecai.

He'd found her.

"What happened to Maude?"

The words Sent by Dawn-S9 popped onto Bryan's computer screen. He'd found the Internet hookup operational by the time they all got home from that disastrous dinner at Beth's. He'd tried to contact Dawn then, but she hadn't been online, so he'd sent her an e-mail—no details, just telling her that something had happened, and he would stay online that night, so she should log on if she could.

He hadn't chatted with Dawn very long earlier, but long enough to figure out that she was close to Beth. She'd told him she was a former student, but he thought it went deeper than that. And he liked her.

He'd looked up her profile, just to check her out. There was a photo. And he supposed learning that she was drop-dead gorgeous had helped convince him that she was on the side of the good guys.

He'd left the PC on when he went to bed, just in case, and he heard the chiming tones that told him someone was sending him an instant message. Now the cursor blinked at him as if demanding an answer. He sighed, searching for a way to make the news easier to take. He had no idea if Dawn were close to Maude, or even knew her. But he figured there was no point in not telling her the truth.

"Bry? I know you're online. Tell me what happened."

Bryan realized there was no easy way to share bad news, so it was pretty stupid wasting time trying to think of one. "Maude didn't make it," he typed. "I'm sorry." He studied the words, drew a breath and clicked Send.

"OMG!" appeared on his screen. He flinched, but another message followed immediately. "Is Beth okay?"

"She's taking it hard. Spending the night here at Maude's place, with my dad and me."

The cursor blinked, steadily, emptily. She didn't reply, so he typed some more. "Were you close to Maude?"

"No. You?"

"Not really."

"I thought she was your great-grandmother?"

He swallowed hard, licked his lips, hoped he hadn't blown it. "I hardly ever saw her."

"Oh." There was a long pause, then. "What about Beth?"

"She went out a while ago. I think my father did, too."

"Together?"

"I don't know. I'll check. BRB." He got up and went to the window, noting the empty driveway. Then he returned to the PC. "Both cars are gone."

"Do you trust your father?"

Bryan frowned. "That's an odd question. Why do you ask?"

"Cuz people are after Beth. Maybe he's helping them."

"He's not."

"You sure?"

"I swear."

She waited a long moment. Then she wrote, "You already knew she was in trouble, didn't you? You weren't even surprised."

Bryan pursed his lips. "I think they're back. Gotta go."

"Who are you, really, Bryan?"

"See you later." He quickly hit Send, then logged off before she could reply. He went to the window and looked outside, because he really had heard something. But the driveway remained empty.

Swallowing hard, Bryan went to the bedroom door, pulled it open and stepped slowly out into the hall. Something rattled. A doorknob? Were those footsteps he heard crossing the porch?

What the hell, was Maude back for a visit?

A shiver tiptoed along his spine. Bryan shook it off and crept down the stairs, wishing he had a baseball bat. Then, just before he reached the bottom of the stairs, headlights flashed through the windows as vehicles pulled into the driveway. He heard the engines shut off, and he heard his father's voice. Then he watched the door open, and his dad came in, his arm around Beth, holding her as if she couldn't walk on her own. She had one hand to her neck, and when his father snapped on the lights, Bryan saw blood there.

He shot into the living room. "What's going on? What happened?"

Beth lifted her head. Her eyes looked wide and slightly dazed.

"Bryan, grab a first aid kit, will you? I think there's one in our bathroom."

Bryan nodded at his father and ran back up the stairs to get the first aid kit from their shared bathroom. He was back in less than a minute. By then Beth was sitting on the sofa, and his dad was on one knee in front of her, dabbing at her neck with a clean, wet cloth.

Bryan set the first aid kit on the coffee table, flipped open the top, took out some premoistened antiseptic wipes, tore them free of their wrappings and handed them to his father one at a time. His dad cleaned the blood from the small cut on Beth's neck.

"So what happened? Where did you two go?"

Beth glanced down at his dad, then up at Bryan. "I couldn't sleep. I decided to drive back to my place, but when I got there…"

There was a knock on the door. Frowning, Bryan went to get it, and was surprised to see Frankie Parker, in full uniform, on the other side. Her dark-blue shirt was tucked into navy pants with a stripe up the outsides. She wasn't a small woman, and the belt on the pants changed her softly rounded shape from one bulge into two. The gun, handcuffs and nightstick hanging from that belt seemed

so out of place. Her face looked like someone's grandma—
the kind you'd picture baking cookies and wearing a flow-
ered apron.

"Is Beth here?" she asked.

Bryan opened the door wider, turning toward where
Beth sat on the sofa, and Chief Frankie, as Bryan was coming to think of the woman, stepped inside. "Beth, I'm
afraid I've got some bad news. Your cottage…exploded."

"Exploded?" Bryan repeated. He sent a wide-eyed look
at Beth.

She nodded at him. "That's what I was just about to tell
you, Bry." She looked at Frankie. "I was there. I was just
pulling in to get some things when it happened."

"Then you saw it?" Frankie asked.

She nodded. "I'd have stayed to wait for your arrival,
but a piece of it landed in my neck."

Chief Frankie crossed the living room and leaned closer.
Beth moved her hand so she could see. "Hell."

Josh laid a gauze pad on the spot and applied tape to
keep it there.

"Do you have any idea what happened, Beth?" the
chief asked.

Beth glanced at Josh. Something passed between
them—a message. Maybe a secret, Bryan thought, and he
wondered what was really going on. Then Beth shook her
head. "I was hoping you could tell me."

"Neighbors heard the blast and called 911. Must have
been some blast, since the nearest neighbors are quite a distance away. Fire department arrived before I did, but there
was nothing to put out. Russ Powell—he's the fire chief—
says he suspects a gas leak," Frankie said. "Of course, we
haven't confirmed that. Once it's daylight, we'll get a better look at things and probably call in the state fire investigator. But I can't think of anything else that would set a

house off like that." She frowned. "You might want to have a doctor take a look at that, Beth."

"In the morning. Maybe."

"Whatever you think is best. Did you see anything at the house, before it blew to kingdom come?"

Beth shook her head. "No. Nothing."

Bryan saw the look his father sent her. As if he knew better. But he didn't say anything out loud.

"Were you there, too?" Frankie asked, addressing Joshua.

"I was alone," Beth said before Joshua could even get a word out.

Josh licked his lips, lowered his eyes. "I arrived after it happened. I didn't see anything, either, other than Beth lying on the ground bleeding."

Bryan thought Frankie was looking at his father oddly. As if she suspected him of something. "This is a whole lot to be happening all at once," she said. "Maudie dying the way she did. No warning. And then Beth's house blowing to hell and gone."

And all right after he and his father showed up in town, Bryan thought, putting his own interpretation on the look in Chief Frankie's eyes.

Frankie sighed. "All right. I may want to talk to you again tomorrow. You both going to be here a while?"

"I'm not going anywhere," Joshua said. He said it with a look at Beth, as if there were more to the words than was apparent.

"I'll give you a call tomorrow, then."

"Thank you, Chief Parker," Beth said. To Bryan, her voice just didn't sound right.

"You best get used to calling me Frankie," the chief told her. She nodded goodbye, an act that made her tight copper curls bounce, and then she left.

Bryan closed up the first aid kit. "I think I'm going to brew some of that tea of Maude's—she's got all the jars labeled. I'm going for the one that says, Tranquil Sleep. Anyone else want a cup?"

"I'd love one," Beth said. "Thank you, Bryan."

He went into the kitchen, but he made sure he could overhear the conversation he sensed they were going to have the minute he was out of the room. Something major was going on here. And he wasn't sure his father would tell him if he asked. But he *was* sure he wanted to know.

8

➤━◆━

"You lied to the police chief," Joshua said, watching Beth's face. "You didn't tell her you thought you saw someone in your house just before the explosion."

She shrugged. "I don't trust the government."

"Frankie's not government. She's a cop. You don't trust cops, either?"

She shrugged. "Cop, ATF, they're all variations on the same theme, right? All working for the same system."

"Frankie was Maude's friend. You know that, so I don't follow."

She shook her head. "You don't need to. All you need to know is that I'm poison, Josh. You and Bryan should stay as far away from me as you can possibly get."

He frowned. "We're not going anywhere."

"Bryan's in danger just by standing too close to me."

"In danger from what?"

She shook her head. "You don't need to know that." Then she lifted her eyes slowly. "I'm sorry, Josh." She got to her feet, and went up the stairs, knowing that in the morning, she needed to think about getting the hell out of here. Hell, it was already morning. But later. Later.

She hadn't planned to run from Mordecai. Not again. She had decided she would face Mordecai down, end this thing once and for all. But now there was more than her own life at stake. There were Josh's and Bryan's. God, this was the very reason she'd avoided personal involvements all this time.

Beth went up to her corner room in Maude's house, washed up in the adjoining bathroom and wished she could change out of the T-shirt, but she knew she no longer owned any clothes other than the ones she'd been wearing today.

She crawled beneath the covers, but she couldn't sleep. She could only lie there, running through an endless litany of things she had lost. All her clothes and books. Her television and furniture. Every bit of makeup. One of her guns, leaving her with nothing but the tiny derringer, which held only two bullets at a time and wasn't nearly lethal enough for her peace of mind.

Especially not now.

He'd found her. She knew it deep down in her gut.

She thought about her photographs of Dawny. Gone, every one of them. She would have been devastated by that, if not for her certainty that Jewel would make new copies for her.

The soft tap on her bedroom door surprised her. "It's open."

Josh opened the door, a mug in hand. "Bryan thought you might still want the tea."

She nodded, and he came the rest of the way inside, closing the door behind him. He put the mug on the nightstand, then sat on the edge of her bed. "It might help you sleep."

"I suppose so."

"According to Maude, her teas are good for just about anything."

She smiled, slid upward until her back pressed to the headboard, then reached for the mug. "Maude only served it in her antique china cups."

"I guess Bry figured if a little was good, a lot would be better."

"Typical male reasoning, I guess." She took a sip, grimaced. Bryan had made the tea far stronger than Maude ever had, and he had neglected to add the honey, which was the only part that made the stuff bearable. Licking her lips, she set the mug aside. "So why are you really here?"

"Here in Blackberry?" Josh asked.

"That, too," she said. "But let's start with why you're here in my bedroom."

He had looked alarmed at her question, but only for an instant. He was good at covering his emotions, she thought. Maybe a little too good. It was almost as if he were used to doing it.

"I got the distinct feeling down there that I might just wake up tomorrow morning and find you gone, Beth. And I don't want that to happen."

"No? Why not? God knows you'd be safer. Your son would be safer. Hell, *I* might even be safer."

He shook his head. "There's nowhere on the planet where you would be safer."

"Oh, that makes sense, when my house just got blown to smithereens and my best friend died under unexplained circumstances, doesn't it?"

"The doctor said her heart stopped."

"That ghoul poking around Maude's corpse in the dead of night says otherwise."

He averted his eyes almost guiltily. "Who do you suppose she was?"

"Government," she said. "Don't ask."

He closed his eyes. "I'm asking."

She shook her head. "No. No, I'm not dragging anyone else into this. Sorry, Josh." She slid out of the bed, took his forearm and tugged him to his feet, then led him to the door. "You were right about one thing, though. I probably will be leaving later this morning. I'm not sure there's even any point in waiting. I'm not sleeping anyway."

She was reaching for the knob, intending to gently escort him into the hallway and then close the door on him, but he stopped as she tugged the door open, put one hand on it and pushed it shut again. "You can't leave."

"I can do whatever I want."

"Dammit, Beth—"

"What? What in the name of hell is there to keep me from walking out of Blackberry right now?"

"Me."

She stared at him for a moment, and then he suddenly clasped her head in his hands and kissed her. It startled her, shocked her right to her toes. At first it was little more than an act of will, but then things changed. The pressure of his mouth against hers eased; the pace slowed. He sucked her lips between his and kissed her for a long time. She felt herself go pliant, like a crayon in the sun, and the next thing she knew, his arms were around her, holding her to him, and she was loving the experience. He was leaning back against the door when she managed to twist her head to one side for air.

She rested it against his shoulder, breathless. And she whispered, "It's no great loss, my house being destroyed. Do you want to know why?"

"I want to know everything about you. Including that. Why, Beth?"

"Because I don't count on keeping anything. I don't invest in anything. I don't collect anything. I don't expect anything to last. I've lost everything so many times it doesn't even faze me anymore, Josh. I've fallen into the habit of not acquiring anything it would hurt me too much to lose. You understand?"

He nodded, his hands in her hair. "I understand. I don't buy it, though. Not entirely. I think it hurt you to lose Maude."

She felt a stabbing pain leap into her throat and swallowed it back down by sheer force. "It did. She got past all my defenses, in spite of my best efforts."

"Maybe you don't know it yet, Beth, but so will I."

She stepped back a little, speared him with her eyes. "It's been a long time since I've trusted any man enough to let him into my life, Joshua."

"Then maybe it's time you tried." She started to shake her head, but he caught her cheek with a gentle palm, turned her face toward him, held her eyes with his. "You can trust me, Beth. I swear to God you can."

She wanted to, she thought. She wanted to share this burden so much it was killing her. But dammit, she was afraid.

"Let me help you," he whispered.

She tried to resist, but her strength was waning so low that she didn't have it in her to withstand his persistence. Swallowing hard, she said, "All right."

He had never realized what an excellent liar he was until tonight, he thought, as he sat on Beth's bed, with her curled up in his arms, and listened to her tell him the story she had never told anyone else, the story he thought he had already known.

"I was sixteen when I ran away from home," she said. "My stepfather would have raped me eventually. His gropings were escalating, and I knew it was only a matter of time. My mother worshiped him, would never have believed me. And my birth father lost any chance with me when he signed away his parental rights. I said fuck them all and struck out on my own."

He listened, wincing a little at her language. He'd never heard her swear like that before. And yet he was riveted. This part of Beth's history hadn't been in her files. He realized as he listened that he was holding her gently, stroking her cheek and sometimes her hair as she spoke. The kiss he had intended as a means to keep her close to him, to gain her trust and keep her from running away, had gotten out of hand. Hell, he wasn't sure what the hell had happened to him, but for a few moments, it had been way more than an act. It had been real.

"I met this girl on the streets. Jewel. And we heard about a haven for runaway teens in upstate New York. It was run by a group calling itself the Young Believers."

This part he knew, but he feigned surprise. "The compound that was raided? Run by that guy Mordecai Young?"

She nodded. "The one and only. It didn't take Jewel and me long to realize we were prisoners, not guests. Slave labor for Mordecai's drug business. Our meals were doped to keep us complacent. So we made nice with him in hopes we could find a chance to escape."

"And did it work? Did you get out?"

"No. I got pregnant."

Joshua went stiff. He'd had no clue she'd become pregnant while at the compound. Apparently neither had the government. Or if they had, they were keeping very quiet about it. It hadn't been in her file.

"There was something about Mordecai," she told him, her voice soft, trembling. "Charisma, I guess. He has... there's a real power to the man. And I was young and naive and half-brainwashed by then. I thought I loved him. Once the baby was born—"

"Wait a minute, wait a minute. You had *Mordecai Young's* child?"

She nodded. "He named her Sunshine, called her Sunny. Just before the raid, Jewel and I had decided to try to escape with her, but then…well, then hell erupted on earth. The ATF surrounded the compound. Came to rescue us, I suppose. The truth was, they were a gang of badly trained boys who shouldn't have been set loose with BB guns, much less rifles."

Joshua closed his eyes, pain stabbing deep. She couldn't see him, the way she was leaning on his chest, but she must have heard the hitch in his breathing. She was dead wrong, of course. His comrades had been far from badly trained boys. They'd been brave young men, highly trained, dedicated. Some of the best men he'd ever known. But he couldn't blame her for harboring bitterness. "Don't you think that's a little harsh? I mean…do you think they'd have fired if no one had been shooting at them?"

"*I* wasn't shooting at them," she whispered. "But that didn't stop one of the gung ho bastards from ripping my insides apart with a white-hot bullet." She lifted her head, and her eyes were fierce when they met his. "I swear, if I knew who he was—"

"What about Mordecai? Shouldn't your anger be directed at him?"

"You think it's not?" She lowered her head again, resting it against him. "We made it to the tunnel in the basement. Mordecai was down there, trying to escape with the baby. But Jewel and I got her away from him just before the floor above us collapsed, all but burying him. I took his key and left him there to die. But I couldn't make it. I thought I was dying—I very nearly did. So I gave the baby to Jewel, begged her to raise my daughter for me."

"And she did?"

"She did. She did a far better job than I ever could have done, I know that. Dawn—that's the name Jewel gave her…she's incredible."

He frowned, trying to place the name. Dawn. Hadn't there been mention of a teenage girl named Dawn in Beth's dossier?

"I was found in the rubble, barely alive. I spent months in a coma, and when I emerged, I had no memory. It was years before I remembered my past, and more before I was healthy enough to live on my own."

"The medical bills must have been astronomical."

She shook her head, as if it didn't matter. "The government shot me by accident and robbed me of my entire life, including my child. The only child I'll ever have."

"The only—"

She nodded. "The bullet did a lot of damage."

"God." His voice was tight. Choked. Maybe revealing too much. "I'm so sorry, Beth."

"Don't be. It has nothing to do with you."

But it had everything to do with him, he thought. And it was far worse than he had ever known.

"As soon as I was able to, I started trying to find Jewel and my daughter. By the time I did, quite by accident, Dawn was in sixth grade and thriving. I couldn't bear to butt into their lives and mess things up. So I settled for getting a job as a substitute teacher in Dawny's school district, so I could see her sometimes. I worked nights on my degree, until I earned it, and by the time Dawn hit high school, I was one of her teachers."

That was where he'd read the name. In the report of the incident last year. Dawn was the "student" who had been kidnapped by Mordecai Young. He hadn't chosen a random girl; he'd abducted his daughter. And Beth hadn't risked her life to save just any student but her own child.

"Then Mordecai resurfaced, a year ago," Beth went on. "Up until then, we all thought he had died in that raid, but he was still alive. He kidnapped Dawn. And I remembered how he used to talk about raising her in this mansion in Virginia. So I went there to get her out."

"How?" he asked, staring down at her with a brand-new kind of awe.

"Walked right up to the front door."

"And he let you in?"

"He thought I'd been killed in the raid, too," she said. "I convinced him I was still in love with him. Told him I'd thought he was dead and was so glad to see him alive, and that I wanted to pick up where we'd left off, with our plan to raise our baby girl together there in that mansion in the sky."

"And he bought it?"

She nodded. "He bought it. The police arrived, surrounded the place. I talked Mordecai into giving me a gun so we could go down fighting together, the way it was supposed to have been the first time. Then I threw myself into his arms for one last kiss, and I pressed the barrel to his chest. And I pulled the trigger."

Josh lowered his head, closed his eyes, a full body shudder working through him.

"The cops came in about then, Lieutenant Jackson—Jax, to her friends—leading the way. Julie's husband Sean at her side, wounded and ready to fight. They were all so heroic. So brave."

She was the brave one, Joshua thought.

"Jewel and Dawn and I went back outside with the police. I thought the nightmare was over. But when the cops went back inside for his body, Mordecai was gone. He'd been wearing a bulletproof vest. I didn't kill him after all. Just made him angry."

"I'll bet you did. So then what happened? You changed your name and moved away?"

"The government changed my name and moved me

away. I'd have stayed, except my presence put Dawn at risk. Mordecai has given up on her. When Julie and Sean got married, one of their gifts was a document, signed by Mordecai, surrendering his parental rights. No one knew how it got there." She shivered a little. Josh rubbed her arms. "I signed away my parental rights, as well, so Jewel and her husband Sean could adopt her. She's legally theirs now. But I knew Mordecai would still come after me, and she could get caught in the cross fire, so I agreed to the re-location."

"And to do that, you had to give up all contact with your daughter."

"Those were my orders." She shrugged. "But I've never been big on following orders. Dawn and I keep in touch. She knows who I am. We've become...close. Well, as close as two people who live miles apart can be."

"I understand that part of it, believe me."

"I know you do."

"But couldn't Mordecai track you down through your contact with Dawn?"

"Maybe he could." She shrugged. "The thing is, he's going to track me down anyway, sooner or later. I'm not willing to cut her out of my life just to put off the inevitable." She drew a breath, sighed. "That's all of it, Joshua. I've been living here in Blackberry for a year, preparing for the day he would find me. I had just about decided that I wasn't going to run again. This time, I was going to face him, end this thing, one way or another. But I can't stay here and confront my past if it's going to put you or your son at risk. So I'll go. And I'll wait for Mordecai in some other town, using some other name."

He shook his head slowly. "You don't know that he's found you. You can't be sure of anything. All of this might be coincidence. Maude's death could have been a simple heart attack. The explosion could have been caused by a gas leak."

"And the tooth fairy could pay me a visit before sunrise, Josh, but I'm not counting on it." She sighed, softened her tone. "I wish I could believe you. I wish I could—but it's just not worth the risk."

He nodded. "I wouldn't put Bryan at risk for the world," he said. "But I don't want to lose you. At least, not without a reason. Just let me do some checking into things. The cause of Maude's death, the fire inspector's report on your house. Let's make sure, just in case."

"But, Josh, even if he hasn't found me yet, that doesn't mean he won't. He will. Sooner or later, he will." She leaned against him to hide her face.

"And we'll deal with that when the time comes. I don't want you to leave. Not yet, Beth. Bryan and I were a mess until you came into our lives. He's finally starting to come alive again, and I know it's largely because of you. Jesus, I won't make it through Maude's funeral, and I doubt Bryan will, either. Not without your help. Please…"

She lifted her head from where it rested on his chest, searched his eyes.

"Please," he whispered again, and this time, he added a gentle kiss to the word.

He felt her shiver, then respond, then capitulate. "All right," she breathed. "I'll stay…for the funeral. But I can't promise anything beyond that."

"That's good, Beth. That's very good." He turned her in his arms, pulled her closer, stared into her eyes.

"I said I would stay for now, Josh. Nothing else."

He blinked, nodded once. "I guess that's my cue to get my ass out of your bed, huh?"

She smiled just a little. "I'm afraid so. I'm just…not

ready for anything more. But it feels good to have finally gotten all that stuff off my chest. Thank you, Josh."

He stroked a hand over her hair. "Don't thank me. I'm the one who should be thanking you."

"Good night, Josh."

"Night." He left the bedroom, closed the door behind him, wiped the dazed expression off his face and scrunched it up instead. "What the hell am I doing with her?"

"Now there's a question for you," Bryan said.

Josh looked up fast. His son stood in his open bedroom doorway, arms crossed over his chest, looking for all the world as if *he* were the parent.

"What *are* you doing, Dad? You can't put the moves on this woman. Come on, after what you did to her? And with her not even knowing?"

He held up a hand for silence and strode forward, nudging Bryan back into his room and closing the door behind them both. "You wanna keep it down to a dull roar, son?"

"Hell, no. I'm beginning to think it might be better all around to just tell her the truth. I mean, better than messing with her feelings like that."

"How the hell do you know that's what I was doing?"

"What, you gonna tell me you're really falling for her? That all that chivalrous bullshit and whatever else happened in that bedroom wasn't just part of your precious cover, Dad?"

Josh lowered his head. "Nothing happened in that bedroom."

"Nothing? Not even a few kisses?"

"Look, Bryan, whether or not I kissed her isn't relevant here."

"You did. You kissed her. I knew it! And it was part of your act. Part of your job."

"It wasn't—" Josh blurted. Then he cut himself off and pushed a hand through his hair.

Bryan said, "What do you mean, it wasn't?"

"Maybe not...one hundred percent."

Bryan gaped at him. He gave his head a shake and stared hard at his father. "Then it's even *more* important to tell her the truth!"

"No. No, Bry, I don't want to hear one more word about it. She's in danger, and I can't protect her if you blow my cover. I mean it. You keep your promise to me and keep our job to yourself."

Bryan rolled his eyes and turned away from his father. "Fine. Just freaking fine. You're one cold SOB, you know that?"

"I have to be. And one more thing."

"What?" Bryan turned to face him again, his eyes hostile.

Josh took a breath. "I've been thinking, and...I made a mistake, yanking you out of your home the way I did."

"Gee, you think?"

"Give me a break, Bryan. I'm new at this fatherhood game. It's gonna take some time to pick up all the nuances, okay?"

Bryan frowned, tipped his head a little to one side. "So what are you saying?"

"I'm saying that when this case is over and Beth is safe, we'll go back to California, if that's what you still want. I'll find us a place—in Marin County, even—and we'll live there at least six months out of the year. And you can go to college out there if you want, and still have a home off campus and a connection to your old neighborhood. Okay?"

Bryan blinked as if Josh had started speaking in tongues. "But your job, the business—"

"We'll find a way to make it work."

Nodding slowly, Bryan seemed to be probing his father's soul. "Are you just bribing me to keep me quiet?"

"Do I need to?"

Bryan shrugged.

"Take it however you want, Bry. I'm just trying to fix what I screwed up. Now I'm going to go try to get some sleep, and I suggest you do the same. Okay?"

His son held his gaze for a long moment, then finally nodded once. "Okay."

Bryan took his father's advice and got some sleep. A good solid two hours of it—before something woke him. Frowning, he opened his eyes, blinking in the dim bedroom. Then he went rigid when something hit the window from the outside. Even as he scrambled out of bed, the sound was repeated. Rapid-fire taps, as if someone were throwing pebbles.

His heart jumped, and he thought about everything that had happened. Maude's death, the cottage blowing up. Was the bad guy here? Was this the beginning of the big showdown?

He went to the window, standing to one side of it and peeking out. The sun wasn't up yet, or if it was it was hiding behind the overcast sky, which was a dull, cold, predawn gray. He spotted a girl standing on the back lawn. She wore a brown corduroy jacket with white fleece at the collar and cuffs, and had long blond hair that hung perfectly straight from beneath a knitted cap.

"Bryan?" she called in a stage whisper.

He opened his window, leaned out. "Depends who's asking." He couldn't see her face in the darkness.

"Duh. It's Dawn. Let me in, will you? It's freezing out,

and I have to pee. I've been driving like five hours—ever since we got offline."

Dawn? What the hell was she doing here?

"I'll be right down," he told her. "Back door." He closed the window and looked down at himself. Jockey shorts and a T-shirt were probably not going to cut it. He yanked his jeans off the back of a chair, pulled them on and was fastening them up even as he slipped out of his bedroom. He paused in the hall, listening, but didn't hear a thing from his father's room, or from Beth's. It occurred to him that this whole thing might be some kind of a trick to get him to unlock the house. Still, he didn't see how he would ever know that until he did it.

He'd told her to go to the back door because it was farthest from the bedrooms. It opened from the kitchen onto the back lawn, and he took a moment to look out the window before unlocking it.

The face looking back at him was so beautiful it sort of knocked the wind out of him. She was way better looking in person than in her photograph. He had to force himself to look beyond her, to see if anyone else was waiting to jump out. Not that he cared—he was going to let her in either way.

He opened the door.

"Are you alone?" she whispered.

He waited until she was all the way inside to close the door behind her and reengage the locks. "My father and Beth are sleeping upstairs."

Her brows went up. "Together?"

"No. Not yet, anyway, but I wouldn't rule it out." She smiled a little at that, and it made her even prettier. He had to fight to keep his mind on the million and one questions circling around it. "What are you doing here, Dawn?"

"I think Beth's in trouble," she whispered. "And I think you and your dad might be, too—at least, if you don't know what to look out for. I *do* know what to look out for, so I came to help. Where's the bathroom?"

"This way." He led her through the old house, wincing with every creak of a floorboard, to the downstairs bathroom. He hoped to God the flush wouldn't be audible upstairs.

He didn't hear anyone stir, so he assumed it hadn't been.

"Where can we talk?" she asked. "Where we won't wake them, I mean."

"Why don't we want to wake them?"

She frowned. "You don't think I have my parents' permission to be here, do you?"

Oh, hell, he didn't like the sound of this. "Won't they notice you're missing when they wake up?"

"They got sent out of town on assignment yesterday. They're press."

"Oh."

"And we can't let Beth know I'm here, either. She'd rat me out so fast it would make your head spin."

"Sounds like you could be in big trouble if you get caught."

She shrugged. "Doesn't matter. Beth saved my life once. And my mother's, and probably my dad's, too. I owe her. And I love her."

He nodded, more sure than ever that there was something more than a typical student-teacher relationship happening between her and Beth. "They'll be getting up soon. We can hole up in my room until they do. Once they're downstairs, we'll be able to talk without giving you away."

"Okay."

"Walk softly. The stairs creak," he warned her.

She nodded and followed him up the stairs.

9

Later Sunday Morning

Beth was stretching when Joshua came down the stairs in jeans and a sweatshirt. He paused at the bottom, eyeing her garb—those sweats looked slightly familiar—and then grimacing. "Honey, you're not up for this today."

"If I don't do something my head's going to explode." She didn't meet his eyes. They were too full of concern and that new level of tenderness he seemed to have reached last night—the one that was a little more than friendship. It scared her to death. "Besides, it's more important now than ever to stay strong." She pulled her heel to her backside, still stretching.

He studied her, shook his head. "It's okay to mourn her, you know."

"Wouldn't do any good. And it's not what she would have wanted. I won't be long."

"*We* won't be long. Give me two minutes to change."

"Josh, you don't have to—"

"Hey, Bry? You up?" he called, even as he headed up the stairs.

"Yeah?" Bryan's door opened a mere crack, and the boy peered through it at his father in the hall.

"I'm going on a run with Beth. Keep the place locked. I'm taking the cell if you need me. Okay?"

"Got it." The door closed again.

The boy wasn't exactly talkative this morning.

Josh went to his own room, then returned a minute later wearing a pair of black warm-up pants with his sweatshirt. When he joined her at the bottom of the stairs, she said, "I thought things were getting better between you and Bryan?"

"I thought so, too. But he wasn't very friendly just now, was he?"

She shrugged. "He was friendly enough when I asked him if I could borrow some sweats earlier. Delivered these right to my door." She tipped her head to one side, seeing the worry in Josh's eyes. She didn't know much about this man, but she knew he loved his son. And she admired and respected that about him. "Bear with him, Josh. He lost someone last night—the third person he's lost in the past few months. I don't suppose we can blame him for being moody. We all put in a hellish night."

"I know. I just hope he's going to be okay."

"He will."

He nodded and led the way out the door at a quick walk, increasing the pace to a slow jog by the time they reached the road.

Beth could see her breath emerging in puffs of steam. It was chilly.

"So do you quit when the snow flies?" Josh asked.

She sighed. "I did last winter. I had a treadmill at the cottage, used that instead. I don't imagine there's anything left of it, though. Don't know what I'll do this year."

"Join a gym?"

"The nearest one is twenty miles away. The cold didn't used to bother me when I was only walking."

"Hey, I'm all for going back to walking."

She smiled at him, knew he was trying to lighten her mood, though she also knew—as he must—that nothing could do that. Not today. "Running is good for you."

"So's liver, but you don't see me eating it." He glanced sideways at her as she rolled her eyes. His were intense, looking her over carefully with every glimpse, checking to be sure she was all right.

She had to avert her eyes from that kind of caring scrutiny.

"If you want," he said, "I could teach you some self-defense moves you could practice instead."

"You know about that stuff?" Her eyes shot back to him.

"Nothing special. Just some basics."

"Really?" She tipped her head to one side. "You any good?"

"I'm okay."

She had the feeling he was understating it. Could almost see it in his eyes, which were busily avoiding hers. That was odd. She frowned at him. "Why does a humble businessman feel the need to be familiar with self-defense moves?"

He looked at her sharply. "It's just a hobby." Then his expression eased. "Besides, it's no odder than a woman with a punching bag hanging in her living room."

"My former living room, you mean." She shrugged. "It's not so odd, really. Considering my situation," she said.

"Same here," he said, and when she raised her brows in question he added, "I live in New York City."

"Ahh." She nodded and kept on running.

"So are *you* any good? At boxing, I mean?" he asked.

"I can kick the stuffing out of an inanimate object. That's all I really know for sure."

"It's good to see you're still able to smile a little bit," he told her. "You're beautiful when you smile. You should do it more often."

"I really haven't had much to smile about lately, Josh."

"No, not lately. Hell, not ever."

They jogged a little farther. He commented on the brilliant leaves, and she told him they were at their peak, and it would go downhill fast from there. They jogged and talked like two ordinary people, two friends, and she wished she could pretend, even for just this hour, that was really what they were, and that when they got back from their run, Maude would be there waiting with a pot of her tea and a lecture on living life to its fullest. And maybe a chocolate chip cookie or two. She wished she could pretend that she wasn't being hunted by a tortured, spiritual genius who would kill anyone who got in his way.

She couldn't pretend those things, though. They lingered just beneath the surface of every make-believe smile, every attempt at "normal" conversation, and every footfall on the road's leaf-cushioned shoulder.

When they reached the spot where her cottage had been, Beth came to an abrupt and unplanned stop, struck anew by the devastation. Seen by the cold light of day, it was even worse than she had realized last night. She couldn't identify a single object. Nothing was left intact, but debris was spread everywhere.

Sensing her anguish, Josh put a hand on her shoulder.

A police car was there, the town's only one, as far as she knew.

Chief Parker sat inside, her door open. She was making notes on a pad, but she looked up when Josh called, "Good morning, Frankie."

"Ah, just the folks I need to see." She followed their eyes

to the wreckage, shook her head. "Cryin' shame. I'm real sorry for you, Beth."

"I know. It's all right. There's nothing I can't replace."

"Well, there is some good news, at least. I've had the whole force out here working since sunup."

"The whole force?" Josh asked.

Frankie sent him a frown. "That's right, all four of them. They've gone through a lot of the debris, managed to gather up several boxes of things. Clothes, mostly, some shoes, a few books, couple of photos, though the frames were demolished. Odds and ends like that. Wound up with four or five boxes full of undamaged belongings."

Beth got teary eyed as she listened to the woman. "I can't believe you did that for me, Frankie."

"Nonsense, what else was I gonna do? Besides, it's what Maude would have wanted. We've hauled the boxes back to the station. Except the clothes. Those Michael's wife took home to wash for you."

"She didn't have to do that." Beth wondered what had survived. Jeans, probably. Jeans could take anything. Had they found her handgun? If they had, Chief Frankie probably would have mentioned it by now. Asked if it was legal.

"Oh, there's more," Frankie went on. "But, uh—listen, would you two mind riding back with me? I need to get your statements on the record anyway, and there are some things we really need to talk about." She said that with a sideways look at Joshua.

"You are aware we haven't had breakfast yet, right?" Josh said. Trying to keep it light, Beth thought.

Frankie smiled, though it was tinged with sadness. "I have a dozen fresh doughnuts from the bakery sitting right on my desk. I'll brew us a pot of coffee, and you can eat all you want." Then she shook her head. "Maude loved those doughnuts."

"She would have said they had just enough calories to counteract this infernal jogging nonsense," Josh said.

"Will Bryan be all right home alone?" Beth asked.

"Oh, this won't take long." Frankie started back to the car. "Heck, I'll have you back in your dooryard before you would have made it home on foot from here anyway."

She opened the rear door, they slid inside, and she closed it, then got behind the wheel and drove toward town. On the way, Frankie used her cell phone to call someone and ask him to meet them at the station.

Beth sent Josh a quick, puzzled look. He only shrugged and patted her hand comfortingly, then, almost as an afterthought, closed his own around it.

She loved it—and yet it frightened her, having him nudging her ever closer to…something.

Within a few minutes, Frankie was pulling her cruiser into the small parking lot behind the redbrick building. The back half of the place housed the Blackberry Police Department, while the front half held the post office. She shut the car off and opened the door.

Beth went to open hers, but it wouldn't budge. For just an instant, that gave her a jolt. Josh's hand moved quickly to her shoulder. "They're always locked from the inside, Beth."

Then Frankie was opening the door for her. "Sorry about that," she said. "Should've warned you."

"I should've known. It's…apparently common knowledge."

Frankie cocked her head a little, confused by the comment, no doubt. But she let it slide, turning to lead them to the green metal door with its wire-mesh-lined glass window.

"Right in here."

The Blackberry Police Department consisted of two

rooms. The one they entered was a reception area with a cluttered desk, a computer on top and a thirtysomething brunette in the chair behind it, tapping dutifully on her keyboard. She looked up when they came in, smiled and went right back to typing. Along the walls there were file cabinets, a table holding a coffeepot and condiments alongside a doughnut box, a sofa, and several cluttered desks and chairs. A man rose from the sofa. He had thick white hair, a body like a barrel and a suit that included a bolo tie, of all things.

"Chief Parker," he said, nodding once to Frankie. Then he offered a hand to Beth. "Hello, Beth."

She blinked. "I'm sorry, do we know each other?"

"Ah, I'd know you anywhere. I'm Bert Hammond, hon. I know how close you were to Maude. I'm so sorry for your loss."

She took the hand he offered, just briefly. The chief said, "Bert here was Maude's attorney. Bert, this fellow with Beth is Joshua Kendall. Maude introduced him to me as her…grandson." She accompanied the words with a meaning-filled look at Joshua.

Bert had started to offer his hand to Josh, but he stopped it in midair and shot a sharp look at Frankie. She nodded once, and he looked back at Josh again, his eyes suspicious now.

"Well now, that's mighty interesting, considering Maude and Sam never had children."

"Same thing I said to Maude myself," Frankie said.

Beth felt a hammer slug her squarely in the chest. She shot Josh a searching look, but he didn't even seem thrown by the lawyer's suspicion. He only nodded and said, "It's more an honorary title than an official one. Maude liked us to refer to her that way, and we honored that." And he looked at Frankie. She pursed her lips but didn't say more.

"Us?" Bert asked.

"My son Bryan and I," Josh said. "My family had been estranged from Maude's for a long time now. I came back here to mend fences with her, and—I'm glad I did it in time."

Joshua seemed perfectly composed. But Beth was stunned. Never once had he mentioned to her that he wasn't *really* Maude's grandson. He'd never even hinted that they were less than blood relatives. Nor had Maude, for that matter.

"Why, uh…why don't we take this into my office?" Frankie said. "Grab yourselves a doughnut and a cuppa Joe, and follow me."

Josh went to the table, flipped open the doughnut box and helped himself to a large, frosted, cream-filled number that probably held enough calories to sustain him for a full day, Beth thought. He poured two mugs full of coffee, added sugar to one, a little creamer to the other, and handed her the light one.

She tilted her head to one side, wondering when he'd had time to notice how she took her coffee, then vowed not to let that minute detail distract her from the fact that he had lied to her. What did it mean? She'd quelled her suspicions of him largely due to the fact that he was Maude's grandson. But that had been a lie. And she was left to wonder who he really was and what he was doing here. Could she really trust him at all?

He picked up his own cup. Bert fetched his from the arm of the chair where he'd been sitting, and the four of them trooped into the chief's office. Three chairs were waiting in front of the desk. Ready for them, Beth thought. The men took the ones on either side so she got stuck in the middle. Frankie closed the door and went behind her desk.

Beth looked to her left, to the lawyer. "If you don't mind my asking, Mr...." She lowered her head, pinching the bridge of her nose. "I'm sorry."

"Hammond, hon. But you just call me Bert."

"Bert. Fine. If you don't mind my asking—"

"You want to know what all this is about, I'm sure. Well now, it's a relatively simple matter. Maude wanted you to have her house."

"She…what?"

He pulled a thick white envelope from an inner pocket, handed it to her. "Here's the deed, with your name on it. It's all legal, done and over with. There's a letter from Maude in there, too, along with other documents. Insurance, property tax statements and what not."

"She left me her house?" She was stunned, breathless, shocked right to her core. "But…but…she only just died yesterday. Surely there's probate or…something."

He smiled. "She was cagey, old Maude Bickham was. Came to me asking me to put you into her will two months ago, but when I told her about the inheritance taxes, she threw a fit. Actually put the place in your name then and there for the sum of ten dollars, just to save you some money."

She blinked, recalling Maude's uncharacteristic request to borrow ten bucks from her one day last summer, and how she'd seemed to forget about ever paying it back. Now she understood. "That sneaky little…" She lifted her head to meet Josh's eyes. "This isn't right. She should have left it to you and Bryan." She watched him to gauge his reaction.

"We haven't been in her life in years, Beth. Besides, we're not blood."

"I've only been in her life for a year, and I'm not blood, either."

"She loved you," he said.

"Don't think she didn't have her reasons," Bert added. "But you'll know all that when you read her letter. Anything else she left behind will be transferred to you as her will stipulates. There are some bonds, a small savings account, nothing major."

"The timing certainly couldn't be better," Frankie said. "With your own place being blown to bits."

"It wasn't really mine," Beth said. "It belonged to Gil Cranby. I was only renting."

Bert nodded. "Gil's insured, don't you worry," he said. "I just thank the Lord you were out at the time." He got to his feet, nodding goodbye, and left the room.

"What about the cottage?" Beth asked, looking at Frankie. "Have they determined what caused the explosion?"

"Haven't got the final report in yet, so it's not official. But the state fire investigator says it has all the signs of a gas leak. Looks to him like gas leaked into the basement for several hours. Eventually there was enough in there that when the furnace kicked on, it ignited the gas. There you have it."

"Do you think that's all it was?" she asked.

"I do. I expect his report verifying that by week's end. The explosion will be ruled accidental. You have renter's insurance, to cover your belongings?"

She nodded. She didn't believe for one minute that the explosion had been an accident, though. She told Josh so with her eyes, and he acknowledged her with his.

"Then...are we finished here?" Joshua asked.

"Uh, no. Actually, there's something else. It's...a little odd. Stu from the funeral home thinks he may have had a break-in last night."

Beth looked at Josh. He held her eyes until she looked away again. "What makes him think that?"

"Nothing obvious. A few things out of place. A big wet patch, as if his outdoor spigot had been turned on. Just…well, he felt whoever was there had been with Maude."

"With her how?"

"She wasn't exactly where he'd left her in the cold room—uh, that's what he calls the morgue. He said he was certain she'd been moved. I thought I'd check with you two, see if either of you felt moved to pay her a visit last night."

They both shook their heads slowly.

"Well, it's probably nothing. It's something about the fall, you know. Stu gets jumpy this time of year, and kids get crazy. If it was anything at all, it was probably some local teens on a dare or some such nonsense. That's Stu's theory, anyway."

"He's probably right," Beth said. "But I don't like the idea of anyone tampering with Maude's body that way. Did they…deface her or anything like that?"

"No, no. Believe me, if I thought anyone had disrespected Maudie, I'd have their hide nailed to my wall by now."

Beth nodded slowly. "Maybe Stu should change the locks, just in case."

"I've already suggested it, Beth. I just thought you two ought to know."

She nodded, getting to her feet slowly.

"Are you all right, Beth?" Frankie asked, her brows bending in concern. "You're not looking so good."

"It's been…a hell of a night, Frankie."

"I'll give you a ride home," she said.

Beth turned, looking out the window. The sun was shining brightly from a clear blue sky. "It's only two miles. I think I'll walk. Okay, Josh?"

"Yeah, as long as I can give Bryan a call first, just to check in."

She nodded.

"Go get yourself a refill on that coffee, hon. Joshua can make the call from my desk here," Frankie said. She opened her door and ushered Beth through it, then closed it behind her.

Josh lowered his head, knowing what was coming even before the woman in the uniform looked at him with iron in her eyes and said, "I think if you want to spend another night anywhere besides a cell, you'd better tell me who you are and what you're really doing here, son."

He met her eyes. "I didn't have anything to do with Maude's death. Or the explosion."

"Not good enough. Maude said you were here for good reason, and I couldn't pry more than that out of her with a crowbar. But now I'm done waiting. So you best start talking, Mr. Kendall."

He tightened his lips. "I work for the government." He walked to her desk, leaned over it and scrawled a number with a pen. "The man at this number can verify that for you. Beth had a…scary past, and I'm here to make sure no one from that past catches up to her. If she finds that out, she'll show me the road in a hurry, and that will leave her without protection."

"Protection from who?"

"I can't tell you that."

She stared at him. He stared back. "And none of this has anything to do with what happened to Maude?"

"Not that I know of. If I find out otherwise I'll tell you."

"I'm not sure I believe that."

"I'm sorry, Frankie. You call that number. My employer will verify all I've said."

She looked down at the piece of paper. "He'd better. Now phone your boy."

Josh took his cell phone from his pocket and quickly punched in the number.

Bryan ran down the stairs to answer the phone and made a mental note to remind his dad to pick up an extension for his bedroom. There was a jack in there—the PC was plugged into it. But no phone. He snatched up the old-fashioned, heavy phone receiver from its rotary base atop a doily-covered pedestal table at the bottom of the stairs, because it was closer than the cordless in the kitchen, and said hello.

"Hey, Bry. It's me."

"What's up, Dad?"

"Just checking in. Everything all right?"

"Yeah." Bryan frowned when he heard voices in the background. "Where the heck are you calling from? I thought you went for a run."

"Ran into Chief Frankie. She needed us to come to her office. We're walking back. I hope. Anyway, we'll be there in a half hour, tops. Okay?"

"Sure."

"Nothing unusual going on?"

"Not a thing," Bryan said, glancing up the stairs to where Dawn was peering out his bedroom door at him. He was glad she'd finally gotten out of the shower. They'd agreed that this morning's run would be the best opportunity for her to freshen up, but he hadn't anticipated it taking her so damn long.

He said goodbye and put the phone down, eyes on the girl, and walked back up the stairs.

She was worth the wait, he decided. She smelled good. Her hair was still damp. She'd dried it a little, not all the way. She'd put on fresh jeans and a baby-tee from the little backpack she'd brought with her.

"That was my dad," he told her. "They'll be back here in a half hour."

"That's just time enough to grab some breakfast."

He nodded. "Yeah, if we hurry. Damn, you should have seen the meals Maude made us. Enough to feed an army."

"Beth said she was always trying to stuff people with food. I wish I'd had the chance to meet her. I didn't know her at all, but I feel like I did, just by the way Beth was always talking about her."

"I didn't know her very well, either, but I kind of miss her."

She nodded. "That's the second time you've said you barely knew your own grandmother," she said, following him down the stairs.

"Great-grandmother." He glanced over his shoulder at her, trying not to show nervousness. "Not all families are close, you know."

"Sure. I know."

He led the way into the kitchen, started opening cupboards in search of food. "Maude wasn't big on cold cereal. I've got some toaster pastries and frozen waffles and—" he opened the breadbox "—fresh bagels. You want one?"

"Sure." She got up and opened the fridge. "Cream cheese, too. She wasn't worried about cholesterol, was she?"

"Guess not." He sliced two bagels and popped them into the toaster oven.

"So where are you from, Bry?"

"California. Little town in Marin County, not all that far from San Francisco."

"Hey, cool. My favorite band is from Marin."

He glanced at her. "Which one?"

"Stroke 9."

He nodded in approval. "I like them. Met Luke Ester-kyn once at a street fair."

"You didn't!"

"Did."

"What was he like?"

"Just like anyone else. Friendly, down-to-earth. I said hi, you know, not expecting much, and we wound up standing there talking for like ten minutes."

"I'd have died."

"No, you wouldn't."

"So why did you leave California?"

The toaster oven was done. He grabbed two small plates from the cupboard and set two bagel halves on each one. Then he snatched two butter knives from the drawer and carried everything to the table.

She took her plate and knife and began applying margarine and cream cheese.

"My mom and stepfather were killed in a plane crash."

"Oh, my God." She paused with her knife in the middle of reaching for more cream cheese. "God, Bryan, I didn't know. I'm sorry."

He shrugged.

"When was this? Not too long ago, I'll bet."

"June. How could you tell?"

She drew a breath, sighed, spread the cheese slowly over her bagel. "You have sad eyes."

"I do?" He frowned, tipping his butter knife in front of his eyes for a glimpse of his own reflection.

She batted at him. "Stop joking. It's okay to be sad."

"It has to be. I don't seem to have much choice about it."

"So then you went to live with your father, I guess."

He nodded. "In Manhattan at first, but then we came out here."

"That's lousy." She covered his hand with one of her own, and it surprised him so much he almost jerked it away. It felt good, though. "I know what it's like, you know."

"Do you?"

"Yeah. I lost my parents, too. Even though I was too young to really remember."

"But I thought you said…"

"I'm adopted."

"Oh. Sorry."

"It's okay. I'm cool with it."

"So what happened to your birth parents?"

She opened her mouth, then closed it again. "I don't talk about that."

"Sorry. You just said you were cool with it or I wouldn't have asked."

"I *am* cool with it. Just some of it is…private."

"I get that."

"Trust me, you totally don't." She shrugged. "Doesn't matter." She bit into her bagel.

Bryan watched her chew and wondered if she would go out with him if he asked her. Then he said, "So how do you know Beth?"

She washed her food down with a gulp of coffee. "She was my English teacher last year. Part of the year, anyway. Until she moved away."

"You seem closer than that."

She blinked at him. "What do you mean?"

"Well, let's see, you keep in touch with her, you worry about her, you sneak out, cut school and drive all the way out here to make sure she's okay, and you seem to know more about her than anyone I've met so far."

"What makes you think I know anything about her?"

"You knew she was in trouble."

She licked her lips.

"I like her, Dawn. I like you, too. You can trust me."

Dawn drew a deep breath, swallowed, then nodded once. "She's my birth mother," she said.

Bryan felt his eyes widen and just barely prevented his jaw from dropping.

"But you can't tell anyone. Not *anyone*, Bryan."

"I won't, I promise. Jeez."

Footsteps sounded on the porch. "Oh, crap," Dawn muttered. "No way was that a half hour."

"Go out the back door," Bryan told her. "There's a path through the trees and a minipond out there at the end of it. I'll meet you there as soon as I can get away."

She grabbed her bagel, yanked open the back door and ran. Bryan closed it behind her, even as the front door was swinging wide, and his dad and Beth were walking through it. Bry flipped the lock, spun around, looking at the table, at the two coffee cups and the two plates, half a bagel still on one of them. The other bore only crumbs.

Beth and Josh were coming toward the kitchen. Bryan grabbed the extra plate, knife and cup of coffee, spun to the sink to empty the cup, yanked open the dishwasher, tossed the items into it, slammed it closed and lunged for his chair.

He was just sliding into it when they stepped into the kitchen.

"Hey, you two," he said lightly. "So what did Chief Frankie have to say?"

10

— —

Mordecai stood on the bank of the glittering stream that writhed snakelike among the pines and sugar maples. A more picturesque scene, he couldn't have imagined. The last time he'd been here, Beth's little cottage had been a part of the picture. He'd waited, of course, until the ambulances had carried the old woman away and the cottage had been empty. Then he'd slipped inside and found the vial where he expected to—in Beth's refrigerator. The hypodermic had been in the wastebasket.

He'd been fairly certain today would be the day. He'd been careful, that night in the old woman's kitchen, but he couldn't use the first vial in the little row of them in her refrigerator, because it only had a small amount of insulin remaining. She might have noticed the added volume. He'd chosen the next one, the first full vial. Removed a little insulin with a hypodermic of his own, then injected the succinylcholine he'd stolen from a veterinarian's office several weeks ago. He hadn't known, then, why he would need the drug. But the guides had told him to take it, and the guides were always right.

The old woman must have used the remaining insulin in the first vial during the course of the day. Then she took the special vial with her to Beth's, where she injected herself with the poison that had killed her.

And after the ambulances and Beth and the man and

the boy and everyone else had cleared out, Mordecai had returned to the house to retrieve the evidence and, also, to rig the natural gas line. It wasn't difficult. The key was timing. He turned off the main breaker, which was in a box mounted to a pole near the roadside. Then he turned off the gas and drilled a hole in the pipe where it ran to the furnace. Turned the gas back on. Adjusted the thermostat to a low setting, so it wouldn't start instantly when he turned the power back on. After that, all he had to do was wait. The guides had surely protected him last night. No one had found the evidence before he had removed it.

The gas built up in the house, even as the temperature outside dropped during the night. When it got cold enough, the furnace came on. A spark was all it took.

Mordecai dipped into his coat pocket and closed his latex-protected hand around the small glass vial of insulin-and-succinylcholine cocktail, and the spent hypodermic, lifting them out. The label on the vial bore Maude Bickham's name. But Maude wouldn't be needing it anymore. He put the vial into an empty onion bag, added the needle, then laid the bag on the rocky shore and hammered it with a stone, breaking the contents into smaller pieces. He filled the mesh bag with creek stones he plucked from the stream bed and knotted the top. Then he tossed it into the stream. It landed in a deep swirling pool and sank beneath the crystalline water. He didn't think it would ever be found, and if it was, the water would have rinsed away all traces of the succinylcholine he'd added to Maude's insulin. He'd left no fingerprints. Nothing. It couldn't be connected to him. The rock on which he'd smashed the vial bore traces of liquid. He kicked it into the stream. He'd thought of everything.

He turned toward the road, moving past the remains of Beth's house before he made it to his car. He was making progress. Her best friend was dead, and her home and possessions were destroyed.

But there was still so much more to be done. He had to strip her of everything. And he had to make inroads with the boy, his heir. He had to make sure.

Even now, he wasn't sure exactly how he was supposed to proceed with the heir. He assumed he had to teach the child about the scriptures and about the guides, how to listen to them, how to hear them. They had whispered about leaving his gift behind when he moved on from this world. He didn't know exactly how he was supposed to do that, because his gift wasn't something that could really be taught. But he trusted them. They would tell him—when the time came.

Josh knew damn well Beth was waiting to get a word alone with him. He'd been stalling for time all the way home, running several steps ahead of her, keeping the pace so fast she was too breathless to talk.

And then they were in the kitchen, with Bryan sitting nearby. She wouldn't bring her questions up in front of the boy. Bryan, though, seemed edgy, eager to get away from them both. And none of Josh's efforts to keep him around worked. Beth was putting her bowl of rolled oats and water into the microwave and hitting the power button when Bryan left.

She turned around, leaned back against the counter and crossed her arms over her chest. "Alone at last," she said.

Josh lifted his brows. "That sounds interesting. Should I lock the door and clear off the table?" Flirting might help. She was attracted to him. In fact, the only time he felt he was getting anywhere with her was when he was playing up the romance angle. The rest of the time she was as wary and distrustful as a wounded doe during hunting season.

"No," she said. "But you should be prepared to answer a few tough questions."

"That's not going to be nearly as much fun."

"Josh, some things about you just don't add up. I need to know why you—"

She broke off there, interrupted by the ringing of his cell phone. Josh yanked it out of his pocket, glanced at the panel. It was Arthur Stanton. "I have to take this," he said.

"You can't dodge my questions forever, Josh."

"I don't want to dodge any part of you, Beth." He hit the button and brought the phone to his ear, hurrying out of the room as he did. "Art, it's me? What's up?"

"A lot. How are you holding up?"

"Fine. I'm fine. I'm not so sure about Beth, though." He glanced back toward the kitchen to be sure she was still out of earshot. "I assume the local police chief has called you by now?"

"Not yet. Should he have?"

"She. Her name's Parker, and she's on to me. She'll be phoning you to verify who I am. Tell her, Art."

"Will do. We're still working on the cause of that explosion, Joshua, but we have a result from the postmortem."

"And?"

"It's Marcia Black's opinion that Maude Bickham didn't die of natural causes. She believes Maude was poisoned. Death by succinylcholine."

"Jesus." He closed his eyes, racking his brain. "She found proof?"

"Her report says that a relatively new test, a liquid chromatography-tandem mass spectrometry procedure, showed—"

"In English, Art."

Arthur cleared his throat. Papers rattled. "There's evidence of the drug in Maude's urine. Barely. Maude died before more than a trace worked through her system. Black said that a few years ago, this drug was completely undetectable. This test is still controversial. Sometimes the process of decomposition can leave traces of the same chemical. But given the circumstances..."

"What is it, anyway?"

"It's curare based."

"Curare? You're shitting me."

"No, it's for real. Every hospital has the stuff. It's used in surgery, paralyzes the patient's muscles. They have to be on a respirator until it wears off, because the lungs are paralyzed along with everything else. Maude was basically frozen, conscious and aware, but unable to move or breathe. She suffocated, Joshua."

Josh closed his eyes slowly. He couldn't imagine a more horrible way to die, and it burned in his gut to remember Maude, how she'd looked, and to know she'd been conscious, aware, and helpless. God. Beth had been right; she'd seen the life, the awareness, in Maude's eyes during those final minutes. It was like something out of a horror movie.

"Black said it had to be injected?" he asked.

"Yeah. She suspects someone mixed it with Maude's insulin sometime prior."

Which meant, Josh reasoned, that someone must have had access to Maude's insulin. Somehow, someone had been in Maude's house. On his watch.

And then it hit him—that night, when the neighbor's cat had gotten inside! It flashed again in his mind's eye. Maude opening the fridge for the cream, straightening her insulin vials. As if they were out of place. As if something had disturbed them.

He had found a basement window, open just a little. Jesus, he'd screwed up yet again.

"It also means she gave herself the injection while she was at Beth's," Arthur went on. "The reaction is too fast otherwise."

"What about the team that was going over Beth's cottage before it blew up? Did they find the vial? The needle? Anything at all?" Josh asked.

"No. They'd barely gotten inside when you called to warn them she was on her way, and then the place blew up. Your call probably saved their lives, you know."

Josh sighed. Seemed he only managed to save lives by accident. "So the spent hypodermic, and any other evidence, was in the cottage when it was blown to bits," Josh said. His voice dropped. "Or maybe not. God knows he had time to go back for it if he wanted to, while we were all at the hospital with Maude. Perfect."

"What is?" Beth asked.

Josh spun around, wondered how long she'd been listening, then spoke to Arthur. "I've gotta go."

"If someone murdered Beth's best friend, Joshua, it was probably Mordecai Young. We've run Maude Bickham's background. She didn't have an enemy in the world. No one with a motive. Young must be there, in that town, somewhere."

"I know."

"Be careful. He's deadly."

"I know that, too. Thanks." Josh hung up the phone, schooled his expression into something he hoped was casual and turned to face Beth.

She tipped her head to one side. "I take it that was your friend the ghoul, telling you what her inspection of Maude's body turned up."

"I have no idea what you're talking about."

"I heard something about a hypodermic that blew up with my cottage."

He frowned and felt his heartbeat speed up.

"Maude was murdered, wasn't she, Josh?"

"Look, you're nervous. Given what you've told me about your past, I don't blame you. But you're projecting, Beth."

She stared at him, her eyes seeming to pierce his skin, to see inside his mind.

"Okay," he said softly. "Okay, I admit I asked a friend of mine to take a look at Maude's body." That was good, he thought, give her a little of the truth. Just enough. "I wanted it done discreetly, so as not to upset you or all her friends in this town, and yeah, to avoid having to go through formally requesting it. I just wanted to know what killed her. I loved her. Surely that's understandable."

She blinked slowly. "Who are you really, Josh?"

"I'm exactly who I say I am, Beth."

She licked her lips, lowered her eyes. He didn't think he'd sold her on that, not entirely, at least. But she was uncertain. "What did your…friend find out?"

He knew without question she would leave if he told her the truth. She would bolt, and he would have failed in his job. "There was some question about the needle tracks in her arms. I told them she was diabetic." Then it occurred to him. "They wondered if she might have missed a dose of insulin or mistakenly taken two. Asked if I could get the vial or needle she used last so they could try to determine anything from those, but I told them they were probably in the cottage when it blew."

Beth shook her head slowly. "She hardly ever forgot. She'd been living with diabetes for a long time, Josh. It was like remembering to brush her teeth."

He nodded.

"Besides, we'd have noticed symptoms. And the doctor said it was respiratory arrest."

"I know."

She tipped her head slightly to one side as she studied him so closely it made him feel like squirming. "So are you ready to answer the rest of my questions now, Josh?"

He shrugged. "I'll do anything you want, if it'll take that suspicion out of your eyes. It hurts to see it there, Beth."

She averted her gaze, pacing toward the fireplace. "I don't want to hurt your feelings. It's…it's been a long time since I've trusted a man, Joshua. And every time I start to trust you, something comes along to fill me with doubts."

"It's your past causing those doubts. Not me. You're judging me by what someone else did to you. But it's okay. I'm willing to deal with your baggage if that's what it takes."

She thinned her lips. He thought she felt a little guilty, but not guilty enough to let it go. "Why didn't you tell me she wasn't really your grandmother?"

"Are you kidding?" He shook his head as if the idea were ridiculous. "If she found out, she'd have been crushed. I introduced myself as her 'honorary' grandson once, and she actually cried, she was so hurt." He sighed. "Until he was six, Bryan didn't know the difference between his real grandparents and his unofficial one."

"So you've been close for a long time?"

He shrugged, trying to think ahead, to anticipate her questions, not let her trip him up. Beth was sharp, and damned if she wasn't the most suspicious woman he'd ever met. "Yeah. Until the falling out."

"And what was the basis of this falling out you and she had?" She was standing by the fireplace now, but she never took her eyes off him. God, those eyes. Huge and green and searching. They were hungry, her eyes. Longing for something he couldn't have named.

He swallowed hard. "My divorce. Maude thought I should try to work things out with Kathy."

"But you told me you were divorced when Bryan was still a baby."

He nodded. "That's true. But Maude didn't cut me off entirely until my ex-wife remarried. It was only then she realized a reconciliation wasn't going to happen. And she blamed me for Bryan being moved so far away she couldn't see him anymore."

Beth nodded slowly. He thought she was buying his story—so far. "She wouldn't have cut Bryan out of her life just because she was angry with you, though."

"No, of course not. Bryan was cut out of her life by distance. Maude wasn't in any position to travel out there."

She watched him as he spoke—so intently his flesh heated. She watched his eyes, the movement of his mouth as he formed words. She watched him the way a hawk watches a wounded rabbit. One slip, and she would swoop in for the kill, and his cover would be her prey.

"Maude's more stubborn than that," she said. "She wouldn't have just let go."

"Well, they kept in touch. Letters, phone calls."

She nodded. "Then why are there no photos of Bryan?"

"I'm sorry?"

"Where are the school pictures, the holiday photos? Where are Bryan's letters? Shouldn't they be all wrapped up in a ribbon and tucked in a candy box somewhere? I went all through this place this morning, Josh, and I didn't find a thing. Not a hint of Bryan or a hint of you."

He lowered his head, unable to withstand the power of her probing stare. "Maybe she was angrier than I thought."

"'Life's too short to waste time on a nasty thing like anger,'" she said. "That was one of her favorite sayings." She shook her head slowly. "I can't imagine Maude holding a grudge like that."

"Well, I've known her a lot longer than you have."

"Yeah. That's true." She wandered through the dining room and into the kitchen.

Josh followed. "Maybe she just couldn't bear to have the photos around. Maybe they were too painful. Then again, this house is huge. Maybe you just haven't looked in the right places yet."

That was the easiest one for her to swallow. He could tell by the pause in her steps as she crossed the kitchen.

"Were you as close to Sam?" she asked.

Sam, Sam. Who the hell was—right, Maude's husband. He dug into his brain for the conversations he'd had with the old woman. She'd filled him in on so many things, given him all sorts of personal details he could use to convince Beth he really was who he said he was. And then he remembered what she had told him about Sam.

"Sam...wasn't as fond of kids as Maude was. I think that made me less fond of him." He paced to the counter, poured himself a cup of the fresh coffee and sat at the table. "That's why they never had children, you know. Sam didn't want any."

Beth blinked at him. "I didn't think anyone knew that but me," she said softly.

"I knew," Joshua said. And it was the truth. Maude had told him. "And I think I always kind of resented him for it. She would have been a great mom."

That did it. He had her. She believed him; it was all over her face. Thank God.

"Are you going to read that letter she left for you with her lawyer?" he asked.

Beth blinked, maybe surprised by the change of subject. She took the letter from the pocket of her jacket, slid her fingers along its edge. "I'm almost afraid to."

"Go on. Read it."

Licking her lips, she sank into a chair beside his, set

the envelope on the table and slid it across to him. "You do it."

"You sure?"

She nodded.

"All right." Josh tried to hide his relief that the subject of his relationship with Maude had been successfully side-tracked and gently opened the envelope. He tugged the handwritten sheets from it and unfolded them. And then he read aloud. "'Dear Beth, if you're reading this, then I must be gone. On my way to some great adventure. And you probably know that my house, the place that has been my haven for more years than I can count, is yours. It's my fond-est wish that it will shelter and protect you as it has always done for me. A house isn't just a pile of boards and nails, you know. Mine isn't, at least. It has a soul, a life all its own. A life I'm entrusting to you.'" Josh looked up to see Beth wip-ing a tear from her eye. "You okay? Should I keep going?"

She sniffled, nodded.

He kept reading. "'You have to live your life the way you see fit, I'm not such an old fool that I don't know that. But I can tell you what I wish for more than anything else. I wish for you to return the gift I've given you by giving one to me. Fix the place up, Beth. Repaint the sign that hangs on the lawn and reopen the Blackberry Inn. Give life back to the old place and it will return the favor a thou-sand times. I guarantee it. It will breathe new life into you, too, Beth. Stop hiding from your past, and instead, look forward with open arms to your future. Open your heart again. You'll never regret it. And know that I will always be grateful that you came into my life, and that if there's a way, I will watch over you always. All my love, Maude.'"

Josh felt his own throat getting tight on those last words. He refolded the note, replaced it in the envelope and slid it back across the table to her.

Beth's tears were flowing freely now. "She had a way of imposing her will on everyone. She really did it this time, waiting until I couldn't argue with her."

"She sure did." He was uncomfortable with her weeping. He wanted to take away her pain. He got out of his chair, went around the table, put his hands on her shoulders. "Think you can do what she wants?"

She let her breath out in a rush—in response to his hands on her, he thought. "The furnace has to be replaced. It broke down three times last winter. The floorboards on the front porch, too. The whole place needs to be painted, missing shutters replaced, woodwork restained." She shook her head slowly. "I could do it. It would take every bit of my savings and maybe a small loan to boot, but I could do it."

"Will you?"

She closed her eyes. "I can't even think about that until this thing with Mordecai is settled."

"I don't think you should wait. I think you should do what Maude said, stop running from the past, embrace the future instead. If you want this—stay and fight for it."

She nodded slowly.

"What will you live on, if you drain your savings?"

"My tutoring provides a steady income. Not a lot. But I could take on more."

He sighed. "I wish I could make this better."

"You can't."

He swallowed hard, thinking the decent thing to do would be to offer to take his son and leave. It was her house now; they'd been Maude's guests. Only they hadn't *really* been her guests at all. She'd let them in only because he had convinced her Beth was in danger. Their presence here might have gotten the old woman killed. God, it knotted his insides to know that. If he offered to leave now, he was afraid Beth would take him up on it and end up the same way. He couldn't risk that.

He had to save her.

"I have to call the funeral home. Chief Frankie said Maude made her own arrangements, but still—"

"I can do that for you," he offered.

"I should order flowers."

"I can do that, too. Right after I finish with the funeral home. Just tell me what kind she would have wanted, and what you want on the card." He was massaging her shoulders now, feeling like a trainer in a battered boxer's corner.

She lifted her head, looking over her shoulder at him. "Maybe we could do it together."

"Okay."

"She liked daisies," she said. "Those gaudy Shasta daisies in the bright, unnatural colors. I wonder if we can get them."

"We can get whatever you need. If they don't have them here, I'll call someone in Manhattan and have them sent out here."

She sighed, giving in to the pressure of his hands, and let her head fall forward. "I'm not used to accepting help like this. I'm not very good at it. And I'm not comfortable with it."

"Yeah, well, I'm not asking permission to help you through this. I'm just doing it. So don't start thinking you've got a choice in the matter."

"I hope you are what you say you are, Josh."

"That's exactly what I am. Now, why don't you go on upstairs, get showered up and changed? While you're doing that, I'll call the funeral parlor, and when you're ready, I'll drive you into town and we can go to the florist."

"All right." She got up from her chair, but faltered a little, gripping the back of it as if her knees were weak.

Josh closed his hands on her shoulders, and then, before he thought better of it, pulled her close, let her rest against him. She stiffened at first, but just when he was thinking this was a very bad idea, she relaxed and lowered her head to his chest, even, timidly, slid her arms around his waist. He closed his eyes against the feel of it even as he held her a little tighter. So small, so fragile in his arms. Amazing that this woman had survived that raid and a bullet from a high-powered rifle tearing through her. It should have ripped her in half. Should have killed her.

He had believed it had—believed he had snuffed out the very life he now held in his arms. That must be why it felt so good to hold her. It reaffirmed to him that she was alive when he could feel her, warm and breathing, her heart thudding strong and steady against his chest.

"I think I'm more afraid of you than I am of Mordecai," she whispered.

The words hurt more than they ought to.

"Ridiculous, isn't it?"

"Beyond ridiculous, Beth. If you haven't figured it out yet, I, uh…I like you quite a lot."

"So did he."

He lifted his head, stared down into her eyes.

"But at least with Mordecai I always knew exactly what he was. Dangerous. Insane. With you—I get the feeling I don't even have the first clue."

"What can I do to make things easier?"

She lifted her head, stared into his eyes, and he could see her answer there. She was pleading without a word. *Just tell me the truth.* Her eyes were so needy he couldn't help himself. He lowered his head and kissed her, deeply, slowly, and more tenderly than he could remember ever kissing anyone in his life. She tasted of grief and teardrops and fear. And she trembled in his arms.

When he lifted his head away, she said nothing, just stared up at him, her eyes probing for a long moment. Then she turned and hurried away from him, through the doorway into the dining room, beyond it to the living room. He heard her footsteps retreating up the stairs and the closing of her bedroom door, and he knew damn good and well he hadn't given her the answer she wanted. The answer she needed.

He lifted a fist to slam it into the wall and just barely stopped himself before bringing it down. He hated lying to her. Hated it.

He lowered his hand, shook his head and reminded himself that he was only doing what he had to do. He'd destroyed this woman's life once. This time he was here to protect her. It looked as if he might have to break her heart to do that, but that was a small price to pay for keeping her alive.

Hell, why couldn't anything ever be simple?

He was distracted by a knock on the front door. He went to it to find Chief Frankie and one of her officers, each carrying a box. Other boxes were in the open trunk of Frankie's car. The boxes held Beth's belongings, he realized. All she had left from the wreckage of her house. The wreckage of her life.

11

— ◆ —

Beth turned on the shower but didn't get in. Instead, she tiptoed down the hall and, giving a quick glance down the stairs, caught a glimpse of Josh with the telephone in one hand and the Blackberry-Pinedale telephone directory in the other. Swallowing her fear, she kept moving along the hall to the room he was using and quickly slipped inside.

His bed was made. Not neatly, but made. Maude's quilt, patterned with little patchwork houses, was spread over the pine four-poster bed. Knotty pine dresser, matching rocker. Brown carpeting. She went to the dresser and slid open the top drawer, pawed through the socks and underwear there. The next drawer held shirts, and the third one jeans. She went to the closet and searched that. Two suits, some dress shirts, a couple of ties, shiny black shoes standing toe-to-toe with brown leather Timberland work boots. Frowning, she looked closer. Hell, those were not cheap suits. Maybe he'd underplayed the size of his consulting business.

Interesting.

There was a briefcase on the overhead shelf in the closet. She pulled it down and pressed the button, but it didn't open. Locked. Dammit. And not a key in sight. It was as she was putting it back that she bumped against one of the suits and was surprised by the weighty object that bumped back. Frowning, Beth set the briefcase carefully in its spot and ran her hands over the suit, then realized something was inside it. She released the jacket's button, opened it to see the trousers, neatly pressed and suspended from an inner hanger. But that wasn't alarming at all. What *was* alarming, was the gun. Its holster was suspended from the coat's hanger by a long leather strap. The gun it held was large and black.

"What the hell are you doing with a gun, Joshua Kendall?" she whispered. A lot of people had guns, she reasoned. Shotguns, rifles. Few people saw the need to own a handgun. She'd had handguns. But she also had damn good reasons. What reasons did Joshua have?

Josh's footsteps came quickly up the stairs, and her blood rushed to her feet.

"Hell." She closed the closet door fast, then darted into the adjoining bathroom and closed the door loosely. Then she hurried to the other side of the bathroom and opened the other door off it, stepping into Bryan's room. Thank God the boy was out.

She closed his door behind her just as she heard Josh entering his bedroom. Then she slipped through Bryan's room toward the door and the hallway beyond it. But she stopped short when she saw the item on the floor, a white strap just peeking out from beneath the bed. If she didn't know better she would think that was a...

She bent and picked it up.

"Bra strap," she muttered, as she pulled the white bra from under the bed. "Oh, my God."

Licking her lips, she glanced nervously toward Josh's room, could hear him moving around in there. Telling him was out of the question, at least until she could be sure just what was going on with Bryan and how Joshua would react.

A voice in her head told her that just because he had a gun, it didn't necessarily mean he was dangerous.

But until she knew for sure...

Besides, if she told him about the bra, she would have to explain what the hell she was doing in Bryan's room in the first place. No. She wouldn't say anything just yet. There was enough strain between him and Bryan already.

She would have a chat with the boy herself. She shook her head slowly, wondering how Bryan had managed to hook up with a girl already. Had to give the kid credit, she thought. He worked fast.

She wadded the bra up in her hand and carried it with her as she slipped into the hall and back to her own room, where she tucked it into a drawer for safekeeping. Better than leaving it for Josh to find, should he happen to walk into Bryan's bedroom. Then she stepped into her own bathroom and took her time in the shower.

"Now remember the cover story," Bryan said, totally ignoring the little voice in his head that was telling him he sounded just like his father. "You're just passing through town, on vacation with your family, who stopped to enjoy the scenery and are thinking about staying for a couple of days."

"I know, I know, and you and I just happened to meet," she said, rolling her eyes.

He nodded in approval, choosing to ignore her sarcastic tone. "And I'm here because Maude was a relative."

Dawn crossed her arms over her chest, tipped her head to one side. "I thought that *was* why you were here."

"It is."

"Then why are you rehearsing it?"

"I'm not."

"Yes, you are. That's exactly what you're doing. You're drilling yourself as if your cover story is as bogus as mine."

"Look, you're the one who said Beth might be in trouble. That someone might be after her. I'm just trying to help you out here."

"And I'm glad for the help—not that I need it," she added quickly. "But meanwhile, how do I know you're not an informant or something?"

He gaped at her, astonished he was as lousy at this spy game as he was. God, she saw through him already.

"Hey!" someone called. It was a teenage boy, one of the small group who'd been tossing a football around in the town park when Bryan and Dawn had arrived. He was heading toward them, blond and bulky, and while he offered a friendly smile, it was aimed at Dawn, not Bryan.

"Hey," she replied.

"You new in town?"

"Just passing through. Family vacation—you know how that goes." She shook her head and tossed her hair. The wind picked it up, adding to the magic of the action.

"Boy, do I. You here for long?"

"They're undecided on that. I'm Dawn, by the way."

"Tim," he replied. "This your brother?"

"No," Bryan said before she could reply. "I'm *not* her brother." Did that sound a little hostile? What the hell had brought that on? The guy outweighed him by twenty pounds, and his pals were heading this way now.

"Wait," Tim said. "I've seen you around town. You're the one stayin' out at the old Bickham place." He'd looked a little huffy at first, but that look vanished now. "I was sorry to hear about Mrs. Bickham. She was a really nice lady."

"You knew her, huh?"

"Yeah, I shovel her driveway for her in the winter." He smiled. "She always paid me on time and sent me home with a box of cookies or fudge or something. I really liked her."

"Me, too," Bryan said. And that, at least, wasn't a lie.

"You guys wanna get in on a game?"

Bryan glanced at Dawn. "Touch or tackle?" she asked.

"You're gonna say no if I say tackle, aren't you?" Tim replied with a grin.

"Not if you don't mind getting hurt."

He laughed, nodded toward the others who'd gathered around them, two other girls and three guys. "Touch. The local girls don't trust us guys not to tackle them for the wrong reasons."

"Hey, they know you better than I do."

Tim laughed out loud and rattled off a pile of names that Bryan tried to commit to memory—without much luck. They played touch football in the park for the next hour and a half, and he had to admit, it was fun—except for the way the other guys were flirting with Dawn. He didn't care much for that. Not that he had any interest in her—okay, maybe he did, but that wasn't why it bothered him. It was a matter of principle. For all these guys knew, she might be his girlfriend, but they acted as if they didn't care. Then again, the local girls didn't seem too thrilled with the situation, either.

It was after the game, when they were all sitting in the grass sipping Cokes from the cooler someone had brought, that one of the girls, Melissa, asked Bryan, "So how come you're not in school? You graduate or quit?"

"Neither. I just don't want to commit until I know how long we're gonna be here," Bryan said, thinking his words through before speaking. "I'm taking tutoring from Beth Slocum so I won't fall too far behind."

Shelly, the other girl, lowered her head. "She's great, isn't she? She tutored me all last summer. Got me out of summer school. I just wish my stupid mom wasn't making me drop her."

"All because of rumors," Melissa put in. "I mean, God, I *know* a stoner when I see one, and Beth Slocum is no stoner."

Bryan shot a look at Dawn. She looked angry and about to speak, so he cut her off before she could. "I gotta agree with you there. Dawn, you would, too, if you'd ever met her." She met his eyes, got the message. She wasn't supposed to know Beth. She bit her lip. "So who says she's a stoner?" Bryan asked, returning his attention to the other two girls.

"Who the hell knows? Gossip, you know. Someone heard that someone said that someone else heard, blah blah. Grown-ups in this town have too much time on their hands, if you ask me."

"The way I heard it, she was fired from her last teaching job for dealing drugs to students," Tim said. "Weed."

"That's what I heard, too," another of the boys put in. Peter, Paul, something like that. "Only I heard it was coke. They're saying that's why she's not teaching anymore."

"Still, it's nothing but rumors. I mean, I don't know why my mom is being such a total bitch about it," Shelly said.

"She's not the only one. From what I heard, Ms. Slocum will be lucky to have any students left by the time the week is out."

"It's not exactly fair," Dawn said. "I mean, if they don't even have any proof—"

"Yeah, I was saying the same thing at first," Peter-Paul said. "But then her house got blown up, and even I started wondering what the heck was going on. I mean, they're saying it was a gas leak, but that kind of thing doesn't just happen, does it? It's more like something out of a movie. You know, like maybe she screwed her supplier or had a meth lab in there or something?"

"Oh, come on. What do you think, she's in the mob or something?" Melissa asked.

"I was in that house for tutoring," Shelly said. "It was tiny. If there was a meth lab, I'd have seen it."

"Me, too," Bryan said.

The boy shrugged. The third male, Greg, had been silent up to now. He was mostly quiet, blond, skinny, glasses, totally sucked at football. But he spoke now. "I heard someone say she might have had something to do with Mrs. Bickham's death, too. Said maybe the old woman found out something, you know?"

"You have got to be kidding me!" Shelly snapped. Dawn looked ready to hit the kid. "That's the stupidest thing I ever heard. Mrs. Bickham was ninetysomething. Sheesh!"

"Seventy-eight," the skinny one said. "And I didn't say I believed it. I just said I heard it."

Shelly rolled her eyes. "I don't care what anyone says. I like Beth Slocum, and I don't believe a word of it." She pursed her lips.

"She owns the old Bickham place now," Tim said. "That's what my dad heard, anyway. Damn lucky timing, with her own house gone."

"Yeah, damn lucky," Greg the Geek said.

"You and your father are still staying there, aren't you?" Tim asked Bryan.

"Yeah."

"So what do you think?"

"I think if she found a joint in the house she'd kick ass and take names. She's straight up."

Tim nodded, his face serious. "I don't know her, but from what I've seen, I think you're right."

"I know I'm right."

"She's hot," Peter-Paul said, and when every female

there turned to glare at him, he added. "For her age, I mean."

Tim and Greg nodded in agreement. "Anything up…you know, between her and your old man?"

"Like I'd tell you guys if there was?" Bryan asked. "Sounds like she's got enough trouble with gossip already." He got to his feet, knowing it was time to leave. He had to relay all this information to his father as soon as possible.

"Shit, you guys can be so tacky!" Melissa put a hand on Bryan's arm. "Don't leave, Bry. They're not complete jerks. Not all the time, anyway."

Dawn cleared her throat, and Bryan looked her way, only to see her frowning at the pretty redhead with her hand on Bryan's arm. Dawn said, "We have to go anyway. I promised my mom I'd be back in an hour, and I've been gone for three. And, uh, Bryan, you did promise to walk me back."

He blinked. Was she delivering a not so subtle message to Melissa? Hell, that made his day. "Yeah, we should go. Maybe I'll see you guys around," he said to the others.

"You should come to school, Bryan," Tim said. "You're no slouch on the field. We could use you on the football team."

"I'll think about it."

"Cool." Bryan reached a hand down to Dawn, who was still sitting on the ground. She reached up and took it, and he went warm all over as he tugged her to her feet.

When Beth finished in the shower, she returned to her room to find boxes of her belongings stacked near the bed. More of her clothes had survived than she had expected— all of them freshly laundered and smelling of fabric softener. She went through the boxes, but there was no sign of her gun. Sighing, she picked out something to wear, relieved to have so many of her possessions returned.

When she came back downstairs, Josh was clean, fresh, his hair still damp. He sent her a look, one that conveyed the notion he cared about her, or was perhaps designed to convey it, and asked, "Feeling any better?"

"Not yet. I will be when this is over. How did you manage to shower so fast?"

"I'm male. I've never been able to figure out what it takes you women so long to do in there."

"I can't figure out how you managed to do more than pass briefly through the spray."

"I promise, I did more that pass through the spray."

She forced a smile she didn't really feel. "I believe you." At least that part was sincere. He smelled damn good.

"You look nice."

She pursed her lips. Making funeral plans for a friend seemed to her to call for something more than her usual jeans and sweaters. She'd put on dressy black pants with a slender belt, an ivory shell and a tailored black blazer. She'd even donned her most comfortable pumps, which someone had polished for her, and she thought Maude would forgive the trouser socks instead of nylons. No nylons seemed to have survived the blast. The way he was looking at her, Beth thought she might as well be wearing a slinky evening gown. Then again, he had never seen her in anything other than blue jeans or her running clothes. Or a T-shirt nightie. He seemed to like what he saw. Or was that just a part of whatever game he was playing?

"Thank you," she said, and before he could say another thing, she asked, "What did you find out from the funeral home?"

He looked absent for a second, then stared around the room as if he'd lost something. Finally he headed for the coffee table and grabbed up the yellow legal pad that lay there. He sat down on the sofa and patted the spot beside him.

Warily, she crossed the room and sat down. Josh nodded to one of Maude's antique china cups on the table. "I made that for you. It's still good and hot."

She blinked in surprise, felt her throat tighten just a little and wondered why. "You found Maude's teacups."

"Yeah. And I remembered to add the honey." He took the cup from its saucer and held it to her lips. "Taste," he said. And she found herself complying, sipping just a bit of the tea. He withdrew the cup, watching her face. "How did I do?"

"It's perfect. Thank you, Josh." She took the cup from his hand, so he wouldn't feed her from it anymore. It was too intimate a gesture, too tender. She didn't need him building her ill-advised, and perhaps self-destructive, attraction to him any further. Not when she wasn't even certain she could trust him.

He leaned back on the sofa, picking up the notepad. "Maude wanted only one set of calling hours, held at the funeral home, and a very brief graveside service the following day. She has her headstone and plot ready and waiting, her casket's already been chosen, and Reverend Baker knows what she has in mind. The funeral director says he plans to hold the calling hours tonight, if that's okay with us. Though I didn't get the feeling we had much choice in the matter."

She shook her head slowly. "It's so soon. But…I guess if that's what Maude wanted…"

"It wasn't all she wanted."

Beth looked up quickly. "No, Maude never did let people off easily. What else?"

"She left word with the funeral director that she wants

a memorial service held in her memory. And she wanted it held here, at the house, exactly a week after her death."

Beth frowned, drawing her brows together and trying to remember what day it was. "Next Sunday?"

"Yeah." He handed her the pad. "He gave me the details."

Beth took the pad and skimmed Josh's handwritten notes. He had nice handwriting, neat and compact. "She wants the house thrown open to the entire town? In one week?" Josh nodded, and Beth read from the notes he'd taken. "To be catered by Sally Peterson. Beverages from the Brown Beaver Inn. Extra folding chairs can be borrowed from the Legion Hall. Cake has been preordered from Susie Q's Bakery." She lifted her head and her eyebrows. "Cake?"

He nodded. "Not only that, but the announcement was sent to the paper months ago, with instructions to run it the same day news of her death was published. And they did. It ran this morning, along with the time for the calling hours. The dates can't be changed. She arranged all of it, paid in advance for everything."

Beth shook her head slowly. "Maude liked things done the way she liked things done. Guess she didn't want to leave anything to chance."

"We should get over to the funeral home. Mr. Miller said there was more to discuss, but he kept getting interrupted. Said it would be easier in person."

"All right." She finished her tea and got to her feet. By the time she did, Josh had fetched her coat and was holding it for her. She let him help her slide into it, and then he opened the door for her.

"Enough already," she said. She didn't say it harshly, but she did make it firm. "I'm not falling apart. I don't need quite so much of you fussing over me, all right, Josh?"

He licked his lips. "Sorry. I…kind of enjoy fussing over you."

"I've taken care of myself for a long time. I like knowing I can."

"Just because you can, it doesn't mean you have to. Not constantly." He shrugged and took a garment bag she hadn't noticed before from the coat tree just inside the door.

"What's this?"

"Maude's clothes, I guess. Apparently she had them picked out, packed and ready. The funeral director told me to bring the cranberry garment bag from her closet."

Beth swallowed hard, silently grateful she didn't have to go through Maude's things and try to decide what she would want to wear for her own funeral. It would have been painful. "She thought of everything."

"She did. Like you said, she liked things done her way."

"Yeah, but she also hated being a bother to anyone. I think a lot of this was her way of not putting anyone to any trouble." She shook her head slowly.

Josh nodded his agreement; then he glanced outside. "I wonder where the hell Bryan has gotten to?"

"Don't tell him I said so, but I think he's met a girl."

Josh looked at her sharply. "What makes you think that?"

"Just a hunch." She frowned, too, though. "It's not like him not to check in, though, is it?"

"No. Not…up to now, at least."

She stepped out onto the porch and looked around, but she didn't see Bryan. She did see her VW Bug sitting in the driveway, though, parked beside Josh's pickup.

"How did that get here?"

"Frankie said they'd found the keys in the rubble. She had an officer bring it by." Josh dipped into his pocket for her keys, then handed them to her.

She wondered why people in this town were taking care of her the way they were, and then she knew. It was because of Maude.

Josh was back to scanning the surroundings, a frown etched between his brows. He was worried. Did he have cause to be? "Bryan will come along," she said. "It's not like you have any reason to be worried. My house exploding was an accident. And Maude died of natural causes." She licked her lips, focusing on his face once more. "Right, Josh?"

"Right."

"Because if there's some chance Bryan could be in trouble, then you would say so, wouldn't you? Even if you were trying to keep me in the dark about things for some reason, you wouldn't do it at the risk of your son."

Josh looked honestly perplexed as he searched her face. "You really don't trust me at all, do you?"

"Maybe we should go looking for Bryan, Josh."

He looked as if he were going to agree with her, except just then Bryan called from the driveway. "Did I hear my name?"

Josh swung his head in the direction of his son's voice, but Beth didn't take her own eyes from Josh's face, and she saw the relief that surged there. He *had* been worried about Bryan. And that meant he had reason to be—or at least thought he might. She supposed the things she had told him about her past, about Mordecai, might have been enough to shake him, make him nervous about his son. But she had a feeling there was more to it than just that.

Damn him for keeping so much from her.

"Where have you been?"

He shrugged. "Checking out the neighborhood. Did you know there's a trail in those woods out back that leads into town?"

Josh was shaking his head from side to side while Beth said, "Sure. It runs along the bank of the stream. Cuts half the distance off the walk to Blackberry."

"I thought it seemed like a shortcut," he said, nodding.

"Be careful about those woods, Bry," she went on. "There's twenty thousand acres of state forest back there. It would be easy to get lost."

"Got it."

She nodded. "So, um, what did you do in town, Bryan? You meet any of the local kids yet?"

"Yeah, a few were hanging out in the park, playing football. I got in on it for a while. They seem cool."

"Yeah, there are some nice kids around here. Which ones did you meet? Any of my other students?"

He shrugged, averted his eyes. "I didn't write them down. Let's see, there was a Tim, and, uh…Greg, and a Peter or Paul, I keep forgetting which."

"All guys, huh?"

"There were some girls there, too." He avoided her eyes when he said that and didn't mention any of the girls' names. She was sure he was keeping something to himself. It must run in the family, she thought. "Why do you ask?"

She shook her head, not about to push it in front of Bryan's father. "No reason."

"We have to go into town, Bry," Josh said, and she thought he was interrupting on purpose—whether to tell her his son's love life was none of her business or for some other reason, she couldn't tell. "Gotta take care of the arrangements for Maude."

"Oh." Bryan looked again at Beth, his eyes sharp and thorough now. "How are you doing? You okay?"

She couldn't help but warm to the boy's genuine interest—even concern. "I'm hanging in there. You?"

"I'm okay."

"Are you sure, Bryan? You've lost a lot these past few months. And I know you cared about Maude, even if she wasn't your real grandmother."

Bryan's eyes went huge and shot to his father's, the look in them unmistakable. It was clear this was information they had both decided Beth was not supposed to have. And even though Bryan tried to hide the look quickly, and Josh jumped in to ask Bryan if he wanted to come into town with them, they both had to know that the damage was done.

Bryan declined and hurried into the house, eager to be away from her, she thought. She eyed Josh. "It's pretty clear I was never supposed to know that."

"You're being paranoid," he said. "Not that I blame you, Beth, given what you've been through. What you're still going through."

"Am I?"

"We never told anyone she wasn't a blood relative, because it would have gotten back to her and hurt her feelings. Bryan is so used to that, he was surprised I had told you the truth. That's all."

She pursed her lips. "You didn't tell me the truth. Bert Hammond did."

"I would have told you myself. Especially if I'd known it was going to make you this suspicious of me." He shook his head. "I don't know what it is you think I might be up to, Beth, but surely you don't think Bryan's in on it with me. Much less that Maude was."

It did sound ridiculous and paranoid when he put it that way. Besides, did she really think this man could be in league with Mordecai Young? She'd known many of Mordecai's lapdogs. They were not identical, but they were alike in many ways. They were soft men, needy men, men with holes in their characters big enough to drive a truck through. They were never charismatic, strong men. Mordecai didn't like those under him to be able to offer him any competition. There was only room for one charismatic, charming, handsome leader in Mordecai's life, and he was it.

He would have hated Joshua Kendall on sight.

No. She seriously doubted Josh was working for Mordecai. And yet it would be just like Mordecai to hire someone who could fool her so thoroughly. He was brilliant that way.

Maybe Josh worked for the government, after all. She tipped her head to one side as she considered the possibility. God knew he was nothing like the bodyguards Arthur Stanton had sent to nip at her heels, which would have made him a smart choice.

But that couldn't be right, either. This man might lie to her, but not Maude. Maude wouldn't have deceived her.

Josh's hand on her arm startled her out of her thoughts. And she was angry with her body for feeling a trail of heat in the wake of his fingers.

"Come on, let's get this over with, hmm?"

"All right."

He had to work harder, he thought, because Beth was just too damn smart for him. She was seeing holes in his story, watching Bryan's reactions to every word and doubting the sincerity of his doting suitor routine. Not only that, he was pretty sure she'd been snooping in his bedroom this morning, and if she had been, he had a feeling she'd found his 9 mm. It had been hanging in the closet, with a suit jacket buttoned over it to prevent it accidentally being seen, while ensuring it was within quick and easy reach.

Since Maude's death, he'd been carrying his other weapon on him at all times, but the little snub-nosed .38 only fired six rounds. The 9 mm Ruger was his weapon of choice. Semiautomatic, multiround clip, with a glow-in-the-dark sight. Normally he would have carried it and left the .38 at home with the trigger lock on it, but the Ruger was considerably tougher to carry around without it being seen.

This morning, after Beth had gone up to shower, he'd gone to his room and seen that the closet door wasn't closed as tightly as it had been and the suit jacket was un-buttoned. He had no doubt he had left it buttoned.

So Beth probably knew about the gun, and that was probably feeding her suspicions about him and his reasons for being here. The only way to alleviate them was with a grand show of honesty—if he hadn't learned another thing about her in the past few days, he'd learned that she valued honesty above all things.

Besides, he reminded himself for the second time since he'd known her, the best defense was a good offense. Hell, when had he ever needed such a strong defense?

He took her to the funeral home. Beth added her own touches to Maude's preplanned event—which would be held this very evening. Despite all her planning, Maude had left a few things undone, making it painfully clear she had imagined she would have a lot more time. She hadn't yet chosen the music to be played. Beth did that, choosing the hymns she knew to be Maude's favorites, "In the Garden," and "Amazing Grace." She promised to go through Maude's photo albums for some pictures of her that could be displayed, and picked out the memorial cards to be rush printed that afternoon.

It wasn't easy on her. Josh could see that. And he couldn't be sure if his presence was making things easier or all the harder.

They were leaving the florist's, where they had ordered piles of Shasta daisies, when a hardy-looking man in overalls approached them on the sidewalk. "Beth Slocum?"

She went stiff instantly. "Yes?"

The man extended a hand. "Will Ahearn," he said. "Ahearn's Contracting?"

She relaxed a little—obviously the name was familiar to her—and took the man's hand.

"I'm so sorry about Maude," he said. "How are you holding up?"

"It's not easy. I miss her so much."

"The whole town does," he said.

She nodded, glancing at Josh. "Forgive me. Will, this is Joshua Kendall."

"Ahh, the long-lost relative. Good to meet you," Will said, shaking Josh's hand. Then he returned his attention to Beth. "Word around town is that Maude's house belongs to you now. I sure hope you don't mind my bringing up business at a time like this, but Maude had hired my crew to repaint the old place. I'm wondering what you want to do about that now."

Beth blinked, clearly surprised. "She didn't tell me."

"Well, we hadn't gotten very far. She was supposed to sign the contract and give me the down payment this week." He nodded toward the diner across the street. "Do you have time for a cup of coffee? I can tell you where we left things."

She looked at Josh. "Fine with me, if you're up to it," he said.

She looked at the town around her, then back at him. She drew a breath, then nodded. "I'll meet you over there in just a minute, Will. All right?"

"Sure. I'll go grab a table."

Will nodded goodbye and crossed the street. Beth

turned to Josh, her eyes big and slightly damp. "Looks like it's decision time."

He shook his head. "You don't have to decide now. You've got time, Beth."

She sighed. "I've had a lot of trouble admitting it, but I think I love this town."

He smiled a little, looking around. "What's not to love? Fresh air. Fall foliage." He searched her face then. "You've already made up your mind, haven't you?"

"No, not by a long shot. I think I'd like to stay, but I don't know if I can."

"You can do whatever you want to do, Beth."

She shook her head slowly. "I'm going to honor Maude's agreement with Will. God knows Maude would have done all the research in advance. If she trusts him, he must be on the level."

"Wish the same applied to me."

She ignored that remark. "I'll pay him from my savings. I can live on my tutoring income. I'll sign that contract and get the house painted, the repairs made. If I end up having to leave, it will only mean the house will bring that much more on the market."

"What about reopening the Blackberry Inn?"

She looked up at him, and for just a moment he saw in her eyes, shining from their depths, the excitement and joy that idea brought her. But she tamped it down, covered it up with bleak realism. "We'll see."

12

◄ ►

Josh, Beth and Bryan sat in the front as what looked like every resident of Blackberry and the surrounding communities filed through to pay their respects to Maude Bickham. Frankie said even some of the tourists, the regulars who had returned year after year and had gotten to know Maude over time, had shown up to say goodbye. The casket was closed, at Maude's request, and there were so many flowers in the room that Josh couldn't inhale without filling his lungs with their scent.

"How are you holding up?" he asked Beth when there was a brief lull in the procession.

She glanced his way, gave him a wet, shaky smile. She looked exhausted, pale and unsteady. "I'm okay. It's great that so many people turned out for Maude, isn't it? And on such short notice."

"She deserved it."

Beth nodded. "In case I didn't say so, Josh, thank you for today."

He started to shake his head, but she went on. "After this morning, the last thing I felt like doing was shopping for clothes, but I'm glad you convinced me. I would have ended up panicking at the last minute with nothing to wear tonight."

He nodded. The things salvaged from the wreckage of

her house hadn't included anything suitable for saying goodbye to Maude.

"I hated to push you. You would have been better off if you could have spent the afternoon relaxing at home. I just thought—"

"No, you were right. I needed clothes. It was nice of you to come with me. It couldn't have been much fun for you. And poor Bryan, spending the entire day home alone." She turned to Bryan. "I hope you weren't too bored."

"I was fine." He glanced past her, catching his father's eye.

He'd done that three times since they'd arrived tonight, Josh thought, and he knew his son wanted to talk to him alone, but for the life of him, he couldn't leave Beth by herself right now. Sitting beside the casket of her only friend, receiving the condolences of the locals. It was odd, the way people were behaving toward her. While it was clear Maude was a beloved member of the community, it wasn't so obvious how they felt about Beth. Their condolences ranged from flat to downright chilly. The looks being sent her way were wary, even suspicious, and more than once Josh had noticed small groups speaking in low voices while looking in Beth's direction.

Something was definitely off about the town's attitude toward Beth. And it wasn't going unnoticed by her. This morning he'd been touched by Blackberry's kindness to her, the way the police department had gathered her belongings, one of the wives cleaning them. The way they'd brought her car to her. But maybe that didn't extend farther than the police department—Frankie Parker being Maude's best friend might be more responsible for that than he had guessed. Oh, Will Ahearn had been kind to her, as had Stu Miller, the funeral director, and the woman at the flower shop. But to them, she was a customer, a paying customer. The others in the town seemed chilly toward her tonight. Sympathetic, but wary. He'd seen her noticing and pretending not to.

"Could I have your attention?" Reverend Baker said in a voice that carried over the hushed discussions of the mourners, "We'll begin the service in five minutes, so you all might want to wrap up your discussions and find your seats."

He stepped away from the podium, rejoining the funeral director, who stood near the door, greeting people as they arrived.

Beth drew a breath. "I'm going to freshen up before things get underway. Be right back."

Josh got up when she did and watched her go.

"Thank God," Bryan said when she was out of earshot. "Dad, I've got to talk to you. Something's going on."

"I picked up on that. Look, I screwed up our cover. Maude assured me that there were very few people who knew her well enough to have known she never had kids. I didn't realize one of them would be the police chief. But it's okay. I gave Frankie a little of the truth and Art's number to verify it, and I convinced her to keep quiet. I think I covered it with Beth, too—told her Maude was more like an honorary grandmother, and we—"

"It's not about that. It's about Beth."

Josh stopped speaking, frowning down at his son. "What about her?" he asked, keeping his voice low.

"There are some nasty rumors going around about her. They're saying she was busted for dealing drugs to students in her old school district. Some of the bigger imaginations in town even think her house blowing up was part of some kind of organized crime retaliation thing."

Josh felt his jaw go slack. "That's...you're kidding me. God, where the hell did you hear this garbage?"

"The kids in the park today. They were just repeating

what they'd heard their parents saying. One kid even mentioned that maybe Maude found out and Beth or one of her criminal cohorts had her murdered."

"Jesus."

"One of the girls there, Shelly, is one of the kids Beth tutors. But she says her mother is going to make her stop going, and that she'll be surprised if Beth has any students left by the end of the week."

"Hell. That's all she needs."

"I just don't get it. It's got to be that cult leader, who's been after her all this time, doing this, right?"

"I can only assume," Josh said. "I can't imagine anyone else wanting to ruin Beth's reputation."

"But why would he? Why would Mordecai Young want to start stories like that about Beth? What could he gain from it?"

"I don't know." Josh lowered his head, then raised it again. "I'll tell you one thing, son, you're damn good at this game."

Bryan looked away.

"I'm serious. You're doing better than I am. She's getting more suspicious of me by the day."

"Maybe that's because all you do is lie to her."

Josh felt his jaw firm. "It's my *job* to lie to her."

"That doesn't make it the right thing to do, Dad."

Josh looked up, saw Beth coming back across the crowded room. "Here she comes. Good work, Bry. Keep it up."

Bryan sighed, but he didn't touch on the subject again. The minister returned to the podium, then spoke long and eloquently about Maude, all her contributions to the community, how loved and respected she was. Then he made room for the locals to come up and talk about her themselves. Many did. Beth declined, and it was understandable. The words of the others had reduced her to tears, and speaking was probably beyond her by then. Josh felt too phony to get up there and wax on about a woman he had barely known, so he shook his head when the minister looked his way, and the man nodded as if he understood perfectly, then returned his attention to the crowd.

"There will be a graveside service tomorrow at two at Brookside Cemetery. And next Sunday at 8:00 p.m., as per Maude's wishes, there will be a gathering at her home, to which all are invited. In the old days, Maudie told me, when Sam was alive, they always threw the place open at holiday time. Most of the town would gather, and there would be food, music, laughter. She wanted that one last time. For the town, she said, and for the house." He smiled, shook his head. "She wants it to be a celebration and a send-off, not a time of mourning. And I hope to see you all there."

Things wrapped up and people filed out. When the last of them had left, Josh got up, but Beth remained seated, staring at nothing, lost in her thoughts. He touched her arm. "Time to go, hon." The endearment slid out before he could stop it, drawing a look from Bryan that conveyed something between surprise and disapproval.

But by then Beth was gripping Josh's forearm, letting him help her to her feet. He put an arm around her, resting his hand at her waist as he led her to the exit, pausing only long enough to thank the minister and funeral director on the way out.

Dawn was at the house alone, and she didn't much like it. At first it had been nice, not having to hide, being free to get snacks, watch TV, wander around the place. But once darkness fell, it became creepy. She had to keep all the lights turned off, because Beth and Joshua would be back soon, and if they saw a light on they would know someone was there.

So she left them off. And she sat in the living room, because it seemed less scary than being upstairs alone. She would hear them pull in. There would be time to slip up the stairs and into Bryan's bedroom.

She sighed, flipping channels on the TV and hoping the light from the screen wasn't visible from outside. Every nerve in her body was prickling and jumping. She got to thinking maybe it wasn't entirely because she was sitting alone in the dark, or because she was in the house of a dead woman, or because she knew her lunatic father was probably in this same town or on his way there.

It was something more.

Dawn got feelings sometimes. Hints of things that were going to happen just before they did. And she hated it. It terrified her. She didn't want to be like her birth father. She didn't want any part of him inside her, and she secretly hoped it would just go away.

But right now, it—whatever *it* was—was quivering, and she knew that he was close.

She closed her eyes, tried to calm her fears, told herself it was her imagination—just before she heard the soft footsteps crossing the front porch. Reflexively, she snatched the remote and hit the power button, shutting the TV off and plunging the room into blackness. She swallowed hard, rose slowly to her feet, her eyes glued to the front door. The knob wiggled, twisted.

Her heart leaped into her throat. She fought the instinct to run and instead squinted through the darkness at the lock, managing to verify that it was engaged. Then she backed slowly toward the kitchen, her throat bone dry, determined to make double sure that door was locked, as well. She moved silently, unable to see, chills racing up her

spine as the fine hairs on her nape stood erect. Feeling her
way, scuffing her feet, terrified she would make some
noise and give herself away, she managed to get through
the pitch-black dining room and, finally, into the kitchen.

Trembling, she scuffed across the linoleum floor, her
heart pounding faster and harder with every step. She
reached out both hands, feeling for the knob, searching for
the lock, eyes staring so hard at the curtained glass window in the top half of the door that they watered. She felt
the lock. It was engaged.

Her pent-up breath escaped in a sigh—just as a silhouette, a head and shoulders, appeared beyond the curtain.

The sigh became a scream. Dawn clapped a hand over
her mouth, then turned and raced through the house,
banging into things, tripping, careening. She found the
stairway and rushed up it, then dived into Bryan's bedroom, closed and locked the door, and crouched in a corner, trembling....

And waiting.

Joshua drove the three of them back to the old Bickham
place. It looked like a typical haunted house tonight, its
paint dull and peeling, the porch slightly sagging in the
middle, the lawn unkept. The only hint of color came from
the vivid foliage of the trees beyond the back lawn, and already those leaves were starting to fall. Patches of brown
were tiny scars on a rapidly fading masterpiece.

The porch light was on. The rest of the house was dark.

Beth sighed. "It's good to be home." Then she shook her
head slowly from side to side. "Hell, I lived in the cottage
for a year and never thought of it as home. That's odd, isn't
it?"

Josh nodded. "Maude's house is like that."

"Yeah. She said it had a soul."

He nodded, and she opened her door to get out of the car. He got out, as well, and the three of them walked to the porch, up the steps to the door.

"I'm going straight to bed," Beth told him as he unlocked the place, and turned on the lights.

Josh said, "I know you've been through hell today, Beth, but I need to talk to you about something. Can you stay awake a few more minutes?"

"Sure."

"I'm heading up to my room," Bryan said. "Good night."

"Night, Bry. Call if you need us," Beth told him.

He nodded at her and hurried up the stairs.

As soon as Bryan opened his bedroom door and flipped on the light, Dawn lunged at him, snapped her arms around his neck and hugged him so hard he almost fell back out into the hallway again. "Thank God you're back!"

"Whoa, hey, what's this about?" He hugged her in return. Hell, this was like the opening scene from the fantasy he'd been having about her all afternoon. Of course he hugged her.

She stepped back a little, staring up at him. "While you were gone, someone tried to get into the house."

"What?" He took his arms from around her waist and crossed the room to the window, tugged the curtain open and looked out onto the back lawn. There was nothing there. "Who? When?"

"It—it was too dark to see his face." She moved behind him to peer over his shoulder out the window. "I got bored, went downstairs to watch some TV. I heard someone at the front door, not knocking, just rattling the knob, you know? I shut off the TV and felt my way to the kitchen to be sure that door was locked, and then there was this dark shape right on the other side of the window." She pressed her hands to her chest. "God, I almost died. I didn't mean to scream, it just sort of jumped out of me."

"What did he do?"

"I don't know. I ran up here and hid. Kept the door locked until I heard you guys pull in. I guess I scared him off."

Bryan was riveted, watching her, and he put his hands on her shoulders, thinking how scared she must have been. "Are you okay?"

She nodded rapidly. "I didn't see him, but I think…no, I know. I know it was him, Bryan."

"Who?"

"Mordecai Young," she told him. Then she looked him in the eye. "My father."

Josh took Beth into the kitchen and put on a kettle of water as she sank tiredly into a chair. "Maude's tea is great," he said, "but I'm in the mood for cocoa."

"Sounds good," she said. "What is it you wanted to talk to me about?"

He licked his lips. "Well, this is your house. You've been gracious enough not to ask Bryan and me to leave, so far, and—"

"I don't want you to leave." She blurted the words as if on impulse, and the silence that followed them confirmed his guess that they hadn't been preplanned. She seemed to gather her thoughts; then she started over. "You're welcome to stay as long as you want. Maude would have wanted it that way."

"She would also have wanted me to return your hospitality with good manners. At the very least."

"Your manners are fine, Josh." She tipped her head to one side, studying him as he emptied packets of hot cocoa mix into a pair of coffee mugs with roosters on them. "But you're getting at something, aren't you?"

"Yeah. How do you feel about guns, Beth?"

She lifted her eyebrows. "Guns?" Clearly, it was not the topic she had thought he was working up to. "I don't like them. I don't think anyone should be allowed to have them. And I own one."

He almost gaped at her. Man, she could turn the tables on him faster than anyone he'd ever met. He'd known, of course. He just hadn't expected her to admit it. "You do?"

She nodded. "A nearly useless little derringer. I had a bigger one, but it was in the house and I guess it's gone. Don't worry about it being where Bryan can get at it. I'm very careful about that."

He nodded. "I suppose it's logical you'd have one, given your situation. Do you think you could use it?"

"I've already proven I could."

He blinked, recalling what he knew about her past, realizing she was right. "So why did you bring up the subject of guns, Josh? You thinking of getting one?"

"I already have one. Two, actually. I thought you should know that."

She lifted her brows. "Now why would a guy like you feel the need to keep a gun?"

He sighed. "A lot of reasons. Living in the city, I saw a lot. Makes a guy want a little added security."

She pursed her lips.

"Like you I'm careful. There are trigger locks on them when they're not on me, and I have the only keys. I just thought you ought to know they were in the house."

She nodded slowly. "Think you could shoot someone, if it ever came down to it?" She watched his face as he thought about how to answer.

"Yeah, I think I could."

Her eyes narrowed, head tilted just slightly to one side. "Have you?" He frowned at her, and she said, "Have you ever shot anyone, Joshua?"

The question hit hard, virtually knocking the wind out of him. He *had* shot someone. He'd shot *her*.

"You have, haven't you?"

"Of course not."

"Then why did you take so long to answer?"

"I was surprised by the question." He was saved by the teakettle's whistling, so he got up to get it, then brought it to the table and poured the bubbling water into both mugs. "Do you mind my having guns in the house?" He sat down in his chair, stirring his cocoa with a spoon.

"Depends on whose side you're on, I guess."

Josh stopped stirring, smelling an opportunity. He reached across the table, covered her hand with his. "Yours, Beth. No matter who the enemy is, I'm on your side. Understand?"

Her gaze glued to their joined hands, she shook her head slowly from side to side. "No. I don't think I understand you at all."

Josh got to his feet, and went around the table. He saw her tremble, saw her tongue dart out to moisten her lips in anticipation. He still had her hand in his, and he used it now to tug her to her feet. When she was standing, he slid his arms around her waist, tugged her gently to him, found she didn't resist. Sliding one hand up her back, over her nape, until it cupped the back of her head, he lowered his own head slowly and kissed her. And when he lifted his head again, he said, "Now do you understand?"

"Even less," she whispered. "What do you want with me, Joshua?"

He let his lips pull into a gentle smile. "I like you.

Maybe…more than like you. I think I'm starting to fall for you, Beth."

Her brows came together. "You don't even know me."

He did, he thought. He knew her. She'd been living inside his mind for almost twenty years, a ghost he could never touch. Being here with her, being able to touch her, to feel her living warm skin and taste her breath, just added to that knowing. He thought he knew her on a level far deeper than he'd ever known anyone. He thought he knew her soul.

Joshua blinked suddenly, reminding himself that this, what he was doing with her right now, tonight, was an act. A confidence scheme, designed to win her trust. He needed her to stop mistrusting everything he did or said, so that he could protect her and keep her alive.

She was staring up at him now, waiting for him to explain. He stared into her eyes, and something twisted in the pit of his stomach. Genuine attraction—because he wasn't a monk or a dead man, after all—and guilt so big it nearly choked him. He managed to force the words out all the same. Maybe he would burn in hell for this, but if he could save her life, it would be worth it.

"Is it really so confusing, Beth? I'm falling in love with you."

She stared up at him for a moment, her eyes stunned, then suddenly brimming with moisture. She opened her mouth to speak, but no sound emerged, and then finally she pulled free of his embrace, turned and hurried from the room.

Josh was still standing there when Bryan said, "You're colder than ice, you know that?"

Josh looked up fast, saw that Bryan had come into the kitchen. "Don't start on me, Bry, not now."

"How the hell could you do that to her? Especially after what she's been through today?"

He shook his head. "I'm not discussing this with you. It's my job. If I don't win her trust, she could end up dead."

"And if you do, she's going to end up finding out the truth, and having her heart broken and her entire world torn apart all over again. Jesus, Dad, there has to be a better way."

"You think I want to mess with her head this way? You think I'm enjoying this or something?"

"Hell, I don't know. You looked to be enjoying it plenty a few seconds ago when I started to walk in here and saw you kissing her."

"Watch yourself, Bryan. You're walking on thin ice."

Bryan lowered his head, sighed.

"Did she see you when she went tearing out of here?" Josh asked, tempering his tone a little.

"I doubt it. She looked pretty upset." He searched his father's face. "You sure this whole thing isn't going to backfire? You're not going to wake up tomorrow to find all our stuff sitting on the porch?"

"It won't backfire."

Bryan pursed his lips and was quiet for a moment. Then he said, "I have to tell you something. And I can't tell you how I know, so don't ask."

Josh frowned, finally tugging his attention away from the kiss and Beth's reaction to it, not to mention his own unexpected reactions, to focus on his son. "What is it?"

"Someone tried to break in here tonight."

"*What?*"

"While we were at the funeral home. A friend of mine saw it, made some noise or something, and apparently scared him off."

"A friend of yours, huh?"

Bryan didn't elaborate. "My friend wasn't able to see his face, but…he was pretty sure it was a man, from the build.

He tried the front door, then went around to the back, but ran off before he could get inside."

"Hell. That's it, then. It's got to be him. It's got to be Young."

"I was afraid you were going to say that. Hell, it's what I thought, too. Just how dangerous is this guy, Dad?"

He looked at his son, knew damn well he was going to have to get the boy out of town. When he thought about Bryan being here in this house alone all day—God, he got chills.

"I was never really sure he'd track her down or I wouldn't have brought you here." He shook his head. "Young is a killer, but more than that, he's insane. If he *is* around here, he's well hidden—not too tough, with all the tourists in town right now, but still…"

"Not answering the question, Dad."

Josh licked his lips. "I can't think of anyone more dangerous."

"That's what I figured."

"This friend of yours…if Mordecai saw him…"

"He didn't. But thanks. I'll keep an eye out."

Josh nodded. He didn't tell Bryan he was going to be shipping him out of there first thing tomorrow, because there was no point in starting the argument that might very well erupt if he did. He was going; it was that simple. Maybe if Josh offered him a visit to some of his old friends in California, he wouldn't fight it too hard. Hell, he would probably welcome it.

"Thanks for telling me about this, Bryan. You've been a lot of help on this."

"I could be more, if you'd just listen. Don't you think Beth ought to know if this guy has tracked her down? Don't you think she ought to be aware of the danger she's in, and that you're here to protect her? How's she going to know to watch her back if she doesn't even know all the facts?"

Josh licked his lips. "I'll think about that. You go on up to bed and try not to worry. I'll stay up tonight, keep an eye on things."

Bryan nodded. "I can set my alarm, stand watch for a couple of hours later if you want to get some sleep."

Josh stared at him, still irritated with the boy, but amazed by his offer. "Thanks. I'll give you a holler if I need you."

Bryan paused a second, then said, "You'll have to knock. I'm gonna keep my door locked tonight, just in case."

"Okay."

"Think about telling her, Dad."

Josh nodded and watched his son go back upstairs to bed. Then he slipped up to his own room, and took the 9 mm from its spot, unlocked and removed the trigger lock and loaded a full clip. He buckled the holster around his shoulder, put the .38 away and went back downstairs to brew a pot of very strong coffee.

Beth went to her room, closed the door, sat on her bed and held her head in her hands. What the hell was happening to her cautious, calm life here in this town? Everything had gone crazy—and it seemed to have started with Joshua Kendall's arrival. The next thing she knew, her house had blown up, her belongings had been annihilated, her only friend was dead, and some strange man she didn't even know was falling in love with her.

Or trying to fool her.

And God, she was an idiot, because her heart had raced and her stomach had churned at his words, at his touch. She'd wanted to believe him. It had been so long since any man had felt anything for her, cared about her, even pretended to.

It had been since...

Since Mordecai.

She closed her eyes.

She'd fallen for everything Mordecai had said, lost all sense of judgment, fallen for him so hard she had nearly died because of it. Her baby daughter had nearly died, as well. God, and here she was again, falling for a man when she knew damn well it made no sense. He wasn't being honest with her, she knew that. And it didn't matter that she was attracted to him, that when he kissed her she went molten inside, or that she couldn't stop thinking about him, even now.

He was dangerous. Not just because she didn't know him, not just because he was hiding something, but because she wanted him. God, she wanted him with every breath she drew.

Beth knew her strengths, and, as painful as it was to face them, she knew her weaknesses, too. She wasn't going to let emotion overrule common sense again.

No. Not ever again.

"Not even for you, Joshua Kendall. Whoever the hell you are."

13

Mordecai lowered the night vision binoculars and wiped the tears from his face. The boy had come into the kitchen after that tender kiss. But Mordecai had been too upset to continue the surveillance, even though he still didn't know who had been left behind in the house while the others had gone to Maude Bickham's calling hours.

At the moment, he didn't care. The vision of the stranger kissing his Lizzie had burned all else from his mind. "I'll kill him," he whispered. "I'll kill him for this."

You killed the old woman. It didn't break Beth. You destroyed her home, and that only drove her to him.

"I'm far from finished with her. Wait. She'll be working at the school soon. And the boy will be there, as well. I've made it essential. Now that her reputation is ruined, no one will hire her to tutor their children. She'll have to apply for a job, and teaching is what she does. I'll see to it that the rumors are explained away as soon as she submits an application. She'll be there soon. They'll be mine, then, close to me, day in, day out, and they won't even know."

The man is not what he seems.

He's up to something. He knows more than he pretends.

You saw him at the funeral parlor that night! Someone was examining the old woman's body. He was involved with that.

He must suspect.

"They'll never find a trace."

Don't kill him, Mordecai. Not yet. Better to let this thing de-
velop. Let her feelings for him grow until they reach their full
power. Only then will taking him from her have the ultimate im-
pact on her.

"I can't," he whispered.

You must.

"No. God, no, how can I do this? How can I stand by
and watch her fall in love with another man? How?"

Let this be a lesson to you, Mordecai. You dared to question
your guides. You dared defy our will.

You will destroy her spirit, and then you will kill her, just as
you have been instructed to do. That is what has to happen. That
is the only part of your mission that involves her. The rest is
about the heir. About passing on your powers to the one worthy
of receiving them.

"Powers. They're not powers, they're—"

When Abraham was instructed to sacrifice his precious son,
Isaac, even he obeyed, Mordecai. Even he. Surely your faith is
as strong as his. You will obey Spirit. You will.

"Please, take this cup from me," Mordecai moaned,
lowering his head. His tears were hot, acidic on his skin.
His chest spasmed in his anguish. "Please, I can't bear it.
Anything else, yes. Ask me to sacrifice my child, I'll do so.
But don't force me to witness Lizzie's betrayal of our love.
I can't bear it. I can't!"

You can.

You must.

You will.

And then you will kill her.

He had sunk to his knees in the grass of the old house's
back lawn, pleading with Spirit. But it was no use. He'd
been stubborn, arrogant, assuming he knew what was
best, determined to prove Spirit wrong. This was his
punishment. He was living his own private hell.

He would never question Spirit again. And in the meantime, he would do what must be done. For now, he had seen enough. He needed to obey, and obey without question.

The guides had withdrawn for tonight. He felt the emptiness in his mind that only came when they were angry or displeased with him. They wouldn't return before tomorrow. He had been given his orders, anyway. He was to find out who this strange man really was.

Monday

"No way in hell, Dad. No, absolutely not."

Josh took a deep breath, and Bryan would have bet he was counting silently to ten. Beth was upstairs taking a shower, and Josh was in the kitchen adding to a stack of pancakes and trying not to burn the sausage links. Bryan had just come in, lured by the smell and hoping to fill up a plate big enough to share with Dawn. He'd slept on the floor last night and let her have the bed.

God, it had been good, having her that close to him all night long. He really liked Dawn. There was something special about her, something he couldn't put a name to, but it was real. And powerful.

So he came down, slipped a spare fork into his back pocket, started filling a plate, and got a bombshell dropped onto his head.

"Look, Bryan," his father said, "a few days ago, you were wishing me into hell for taking you out of California. Now I'm offering you the chance to go back and you're turning it down?"

"That's about the size of it. So can we move on to a new topic now?"

Josh shook his head as if confused, and flipped pancakes. "I made the arrangements last night. Ticket's waiting at the airport, and the Malones will be expecting you to land at 5:00 p.m. You've got a bit of a layover in Chicago, but—"

"I'm not going." Bryan couldn't even believe the way his father was trying to run his life.

"It'll only be for a week or two," Josh said. "I thought you'd be glad."

"Was I glad the first time you decided to move me across the country without consulting me first?"

Josh set the spatula down and turned around to face him. Bryan was angry as hell. "Bry, if Mordecai Young is in town, your life is in danger."

No crap, Bryan thought. "So is Beth's. So is yours."

"It's *her* problem and *my* job. You don't need to be here."

"Maybe I do."

"I'm not willing to put you at risk, Bryan. I'm your father. I can't let my job put your life in jeopardy."

Now he was trying to be father of the year. Great. "I can help, Dad. You already said yourself how much help I've been—you said I was doing better than you were on this thing."

"And that was the truth. But, Bryan—"

"I'm almost eighteen. I'm not a kid, I'm an adult."

"Doesn't matter. You're going, and that's final. And you may as well get packed, because we leave for the airport in two hours. That'll just give me time to run to the hardware store for some dead bolts and get them installed on these doors."

Bryan glared at him, but it seemed to have no impact. He knew his father well enough to know that once his mind was made up, there was little hope of changing it. God, how had his mother ever lived with the man?

Bryan turned away with a sigh, poured maple syrup all over his plate, and carried it with him out of the kitchen and up the stairs. When he passed Beth's room he could hear the shower running. He kept on going to his own room, tapped twice to let Dawn know it was him, and then went in.

"God, that smells good," she said. She was wearing an oversize hockey shirt and a pair of white ankle socks. They were what she had slept in, and her hair was long and loose and hanging over her shoulders, and he thought he'd never seen anything better looking in his life.

He handed her the plate with the fork on it and tugged the extra one from his pocket. She sat on the bed and dug in. He sat down beside her and took a bite or two himself.

"Something's wrong," Dawn said after cleaning half the stack. "You aren't eating."

"My father has a ticket to San Francisco waiting with my name on it. I'm supposed to be packing. He's driving me to the airport in two hours."

She nodded. "It's just as well. Mordecai's a maniac."

"No way am I going and leaving you here alone."

She smiled. "I was hoping you'd say that."

"Yeah, but what can I do about it?"

She shrugged. "You mind getting into heaps of trouble?"

"Not particularly. Why, you have a plan?"

She nodded. "Those two are going to be in a hurry when they drop you at the airport. Maude's graveside service is this afternoon, and the airport is a good hour away. So let them walk you as far as security, where they probably can't go through anyway, and then say goodbye. You go on to the gate alone."

"And?"

"I'll walk into town and grab my Jeep from the parking lot where I left it. Then I'll follow you guys to the airport. When I see them leave, I'll let you know the coast is clear, you come out, and we drive back here."

"And then what?"

She shrugged. "And then we catch a killer who should have been in prison a long time ago."

He blinked slowly, wondering why he was feeling a rush of adrenaline instead of any hint of nervousness. "How are we going to do that?"

"We'll figure that out on the drive back from the airport. You got a cell phone?"

"Yep."

"Me, too. So we're set, then."

He smiled at her. "You're brilliant, you know that?"

"Mmm-hmm. Now you'd better eat the rest of this, then pack a bag just to make it look convincing."

He took the plate from her, his appetite suddenly restored.

Beth couldn't help the emotional storm that surged up in her when she watched Joshua say goodbye to his son at the airport. He hugged Bryan—a massive, manly hug that nonetheless conveyed a wealth of feeling. Even Bryan seemed moved.

When the two men pulled apart, he said, "It'll be all right, Dad. Try not to worry."

"I'm not worried. I *am* gonna miss you, though."

"Yeah, me, too." He turned to Beth. "Take care, Beth."

"You too, Bry."

Nodding, Bryan spun around and took his turn in line, going through the metal detector. On the other side, he grabbed up his backpack, the only luggage he'd taken, and headed around a corner toward the gates and out of sight.

Josh didn't turn to face her. He remained where he was, with his back to her, and she thought his shoulders slumped forward a little.

She touched his shoulder, then moved around in front of him, but he lowered his head fast.

"He'll be all right, you know."

"I know."

She was trying to hold on to her anger with Josh, because she just *knew* he was lying to her yet again. According to him, this trip was a gift for Bryan, an effort to show him that his father understood his feelings and homesickness. And though Bryan was doing a great job of acting, Beth didn't believe for a minute he really wanted to go.

She was sure Josh was sending Bryan away to protect him. And that could only be because Josh knew something she didn't. She would be damned if she didn't get the truth out of him before this day ended.

But not right now. Because right now, when he lifted his head to look at her, she saw traces of moisture in his eyes.

It did her in. "You okay?"

He nodded, then turned with her to walk out of the airport. "Fine."

"No, you're not. I know how it is, you know. I've had to say goodbye to my Dawn twice now. Once in the middle of chaos, with gunshots and fire all around me. And a second time when I left her because the government said I had to. It's heart wrenching."

"It's torture."

She slid an arm around his waist, and he put his around her shoulders and held her beside him as they walked out to her waiting car. They'd left the pickup at home. "And now we've got the funeral to get through," she said.

"We'll have time to get home, change clothes, grab a bite of lunch."

"I don't think I could eat."

"I think you have to, Beth. You skipped breakfast."

She lowered her head. "Fear makes me queasy, Josh."

"You don't have anything to be afraid of. Not as long as you stick by me."

She fastened her seat belt, started her engine and bit her lip, vowing not to bring her questions up now, while he was still bleeding over the painful separation from his son.

An hour later, though, she had lost the ability to censor herself.

"You say I have nothing to be afraid of. But it's a lie, isn't it? I have everything to be afraid of, Josh. And I think you know that better than anyone."

He frowned at her.

"You sent your son away because you believe Mordecai has finally tracked me down."

"I don't—"

"Yes, you do. It's not a conclusion I haven't already reached on my own, Joshua."

He lowered his head.

"I've been through all Maude's things, all her photo albums by now. Even the ones she had packed away." She drove as she spoke, taking the exit that would lead them into Blackberry. "Every last one of them. There's not a shot of you or of Bryan anywhere. And the woman had pictures of everyone she ever knew. Every pet she ever had and every town she ever visited."

He licked his lips, looking nervous.

"I went through the family bible, too. The pages in the back had records of more than two hundred births, deaths, marriages. Not a word about you or Bryan."

"Look, Beth, it's not what you think. I told you we were estranged. I explained all that."

She glanced at him quickly. "No, that's not good enough." She was quiet for a while, following the directions she knew by heart, over roads that got progressively smaller, narrower and bumpier. "I know you're having a bad day, Josh. I wanted to put this off, but I have a feeling it would be a mistake to wait any longer for the truth. You're lying to me. I won't live with a man who lies to me."

He blinked. "Are you throwing me out?"

She pursed her lips. "You can pack your things while I'm at the funeral."

"Bullshit. I'm going to the funeral with you."

The town was coming into view now. She slowed down to within five miles an hour of the speed limit and called it good enough as she drove through the place. "Come on, Josh, there's no need to keep up the pretense."

"What pretense?" he asked, his voice impatient.

"That you even knew Maude Bickham, at least prior to your arrival here. Somehow you convinced her to play along with this scam of yours. And it must have been a damn good story, because it would take a lot to get Maude to lie to me. I didn't believe it was even possible, but now I know it has to be. Nothing else makes sense."

She cussed herself for the way her throat was tightening up, the feeling of pressure in the middle of her chest, when he said, "Okay. All right, you win."

She glanced at him, almost missed the driveway and had to brake too hard. "I win?"

He nodded. "I've been lying to you. I want to tell you the truth. I want to make things right with you again, Beth, but you have to give me a chance."

She shook her head, refocused her attention, and got the car moving again, pulling it into the driveway and shutting it off. "Did Mordecai send you here?" She had to ask the question, even though her heart knew it couldn't be true.

"Of course not."

She pursed her lips, tears brimming now, so it was no use trying to hide them. "Would you tell me if he had?"

He didn't answer that, so she wrenched open her car door and started toward the house. She heard Joshua get out, and then he was behind her, gripping her arm and tugging her around to face him.

"I came here to protect you from him, Beth."

She stared at him, pinning him with her eyes. "You work for the government." It wasn't a question.

"No, not really, I—"

"You do, you work for the government. You came here spouting lies as some kind of…of cover."

"No."

"No?" He averted his eyes, so she knew she had hit the truth. "Is anything you ever told me true? The things you told me about your past, your ex-wife's death, your son?"

"Everything. All of it. I've never lied to you, Beth."

"You've done nothing *but* lie to me. God, how can you expect me ever to believe a word you say to me again? How do I separate the truth from the lies?"

"Beth—"

"Were you lying last night, Josh?"

He shook his head. "No."

She sighed. "See? Now how am I supposed to believe that? I don't trust the government. I don't trust the men who work for it. And I don't trust you." She unlocked the front door and went to open it, surprised when it wouldn't budge. Then she remembered Josh's early morning project. She held out a hand. "Give me the keys for the dead bolts."

He fished both of them from his pocket, handed them to her. She tried one, got it right the first time, opened the door, and marched through the house and straight up to her room.

Josh told himself to calm down. He hadn't blown it. Not by a long shot, not yet. He could still salvage this. He knew he could.

One thing he knew, she cared about him. Maybe she was even falling for his seduction routine, because otherwise, she wouldn't have had such an emotional reaction to finding out he had lied to her. And what had she homed in on? What was the one lie she seemed to hate the most? The one he'd told her last night: that he thought he might be falling in love with her.

That spoke volumes, didn't it? He was all right; he was still all right.

He just had to alter the plan, that was all.

God, it did stuff to his insides to see her as wrought up as she was. It twisted him up, tugged knots in his spleen. It shouldn't. This was a case, she was a client—willing or otherwise—and his job was to do whatever it took to keep her alive. If her feelings got hurt in the process, too bad. At least she would be alive when this was over.

But while his head knew all of that, the rest of him was having some trouble with it. Maybe he was becoming more sensitive in his old age, or maybe being a real, full-time father to his son for the first time was making him soft somehow. At any rate, just because it made him feel like hell, that didn't mean he could change his tactics.

So he would tell her the truth. Not the whole truth. Just his real reason for being there—who he worked for, how he'd gotten the job and how he planned to protect her. But he would keep on lying to her about everything else, laying it on thick with the attraction, because that had been working up to now. And because it was so easy.

Maybe a little too easy. But he wasn't going to start analyzing himself about that, not now. There was too much at stake. Her life.

And he damn well wasn't going to cost Beth her life for a second time.

14

Joshua filled out the dark suit as if it had been designed just for him. He stood very close beside her at the cemetery, holding her hand in his and using his body to shield her from the brisk autumn wind. It was whipping hard today, colder than it had been so far this year, stripping leaves from the trees with every gust, so that it seemed as if it were raining in Technicolor.

Beth couldn't shake Joshua off without causing a scene, and she found she didn't really want to. Let him pretend to care—she could pretend it, too, for an hour or so. She would take a little comfort wherever she could find it.

It didn't matter, in the end. It almost had, though. She had almost let it matter, almost started to believe she might be able to have a man in her life besides Mordecai. She'd been an idiot. She would never have anyone else in her life. Never. Mordecai would not allow it.

When the service was over, Beth tossed a handful of soil onto Maude's casket, then turned and walked to the car, not even waiting for the well-wishers to come up to her. It was too much. All of it was just too much.

Josh kept pace with her all the way to the car, and then he drove her home.

"Doesn't look like they're getting along too well, does it?" Bryan whispered.

"Looks like she's been hurt again. What do you suppose he did to her?"

"How do you know he's the guilty one?"

Dawn rolled her big expressive eyes.

Bryan sighed. "As long as we're in this deep, I should probably be as open with you as you've been with me," Bryan said. "It's pretty clear you're not working for the other guy."

"Gee, thanks. Why, what haven't you told me?"

"My father is a private security specialist. A…bodyguard."

Dawn blinked.

"He was hired by the government to come out here and protect Beth. It was supposed to be routine, but—"

"So he's been playing up to her romantically in order to do his job?"

"Look, he's trying to keep her alive. Hell, it's not like I haven't told him I think it's a huge mistake to go about it the way he has been, but—"

"That's what it is, then. She knows," Dawn said softly. She nodded toward the couple as Beth marched to the car and Josh went after her. "She must know. Look how angry she is."

Bryan shook his head. "He looks pretty upset, too."

"Well, duh. That's because he really does like her. If he thinks otherwise, then he's just too dense to have figured it out yet."

Bryan stared at Dawn in surprise. "You think?"

"Look how miserable he is," she said. "We oughtta follow them home, see what he intends to do to fix this mess."

"That might be too much information for me to handle," Bryan said. Then he frowned, tapped Dawn on the shoulder and pointed. "Besides, I think we have more important things to do."

She looked and saw what he did, the dark form standing alone in the distance, amid trees and tombstones, watching the proceedings. "I knew he'd show up here," Dawn whispered harshly. "I knew it."

"So now what?"

"We follow him." She trembled when she said it.

Bryan swallowed hard. "You sure that's a good idea?"

"How else are we going to know where to find him, much less who he is?"

"I thought you already knew who he is."

"I know who he *really* is. We need to know who he's pretending to be. What kind of getup he's wearing, what cover he's using."

"Suppose he sees us?"

"He won't need to see us to know we're there." She turned to Bryan, clasped his forearm. "Bry, we have to be very careful. He's…powerful."

"Powerful like The Rock?"

"Powerful like Gandalf."

"Gray or white?"

She frowned, considering. "Gray," she said with a firm nod.

"Okay. Gray we can handle." He smiled at her.

She didn't smile back, and that worried him.

"We'll keep a safe distance," she said. "Just get a look at where he goes and then back off. Okay?"

He nodded. "Okay."

They got into Dawn's Jeep, which was parked several rows away in one of the dirt lanes that crisscrossed the cemetery. Then they moved it until they could see the man, and watched until he walked back to his own car, which was hidden among the greenery. "Did you call your friends in California?"

"From the airport," Bryan said. "Told them I'd be a couple of days later than planned and would call with the new details when I knew them."

"They won't call your father to verify?"

He shook his head. "I don't think so." Then he nodded toward the strange man's car. "He's moving. Let's go."

Beth had gone straight to her room upon returning to the house. She didn't think she would come out again until Joshua and his phony longing looks and potent kisses were gone. She was exhausted, having barely slept the night before—largely because of what he'd told her. That he was falling in love with her. What garbage! And to think she'd spent half the night lying awake torturing herself over it, believing it was true. She was so gullible. Worrying about how to let him down easily, waffling over whether to let him down at all.

God.

At least now that she knew it was all make-believe, she could sleep. And she did.

She slept, and floated into a deeper and darker place. A place of stillness, silence. A place where she had been before.

The word *coma* whispered through her mind. But it didn't frighten her. Instead it was almost comforting. A familiar warm, safe place where no one lied, no one hunted her. No one even knew her there.

And then there was a gentle warmth on her hand, a soft, but familiar voice speaking close to her ear. "I'm sorry. God, I'm so, so sorry."

Frowning, she whispered, "Joshua?"

"Right here," he said.

She opened her eyes, and a tantalizing aroma tickled her senses. Josh was standing in her doorway, as if just entering the room. In the dream he'd been right at her side. But he hadn't been. Not really.

"I was just coming to see if you were awake. I'm making dinner."

She tightened her lips, about to say she wasn't hungry, but her stomach growled so loudly it gave away the lie before she even told it.

He took her hand and tugged her gently until she sat up and the blanket fell away. She was wearing the same clothes she'd worn to the funeral. "Come on. I ran you a bath."

"You ran me a bath?"

He nodded, tugging until she was out of the bed, on her feet. "Yeah. Dinner won't be ready for a half hour, and I'll keep it warm if you want to soak longer. Come on now."

Frowning, she let him tug her into the hallway. "But my bathroom is—"

"I didn't want to wake you, so I ran your bath in mine. Here we go." He opened the bathroom door.

There were no lights on, only candles, dozens of them, lining the room, and the scent of roses rising into the steamy air. Music, soft and low—Celtic harp music, she thought—wove a mystical spell. And a white muslin nightgown and warm terry robe were hanging on the hook, with a pair of new slippers on the floor underneath.

"Enjoy," he told her. "And call if you need me…if you want me."

She blinked in shock as he backed toward the door.

"Joshua, what is this?"

"It's…an apology. An overdue one. Just relax and enjoy it, okay?" He closed the door.

She looked at the tub, at the steam rising and the candles reflecting on the water. Hell, he did owe her an apology, she thought, and she began to undress. Then, almost as an afterthought, she turned and locked the bathroom door. If he thought he was going to seduce her, make her stupid enough to believe his lies by getting her into bed, he'd better think again.

She stepped into the water.

Besides, women didn't lose brain cells at the thought of sex. Only men did.

She sank slowly down into the hot, scented luxury and closed her eyes. He'd added bath salts, something soothing. She identified the smell of roses, but there were others mingling with it that were harder to identify. Combined, it was heady and more. It wasn't just aroma-therapy she was experiencing here, she thought. The salts in the water were soothing, working knots out of her muscles and relaxing her.

She decided to take his advice and just enjoy it without worrying about his motivations. She could handle Joshua Kendall.

Mordecai had watched three of them walk into the airport and only two walk back out again. The boy was leaving. Either Beth or her new lover must have sensed the impending danger and sent young Bryan away. It angered Mordecai, nearly sent him into a panic. If his heir was sent away, then his mission would be a failure! But his guides assured him that he would have ample opportunity and easy access to the boy soon. Very soon. He wasn't to worry, only to trust in them. And for right now, he must focus on Beth, on getting to her, on destroying her.

He drove back to Blackberry, substituted for Nancy Stillwater's social studies classes, and checked her notes to learn which students had been taking tutoring lessons from Beth Slocum before the rumors he'd started had destroyed her reputation. He paid special attention to those students. Because even if they were no longer working with Beth, she would still care about them. He might need to use them to cause her further pain soon.

After classes ended, he drove to the Brookside Cemetery, where he stood among the shadowed tombstones, beneath the cavelike canopy of a weeping beech tree and watched Maude Bickham's funeral service. The preacher was terrible, in Mordecai's opinion. Typical, but terrible. Talking about what a great woman she was, never mentioning the shortcomings of others or wrongs they might have done her. Funerals were the perfect time to drive home the need for redemption. People faced with death became powerfully aware of their own mortality. It was easy, then, to lay them down low, humble them until they prostrated themselves before almighty God in remorse and vowed to sin no more.

This fellow did nothing but try to take away the sting of death. The fear of it. He did nothing more than try to comfort the mourners and make it easier on them, rather than using death as a scourge with which to whip them into submission to the All Holy. He was useless—unworthy of the collar he wore and the Bible he held.

"I should remove him from the planet. It would be a service to the Father."

If and when you have the time, Mordecai. But you can't let anything sidetrack you from your goal. Look, look at the two of them. Something's wrong.

Mordecai heeded the voice of his guide, and focused on Beth and Joshua. They were holding hands, but Beth's face revealed a great deal. She wasn't happy to be holding Joshua's hand. She stood as far from him as his grip would allow, and there was more on her face than grief. There was anger. A wariness. A mistrust of her companion.

Mordecai smiled broadly, relief flooding him. There was something wrong between the two of them.

Don't be so selfish, Mordecai.

If she loves him, you can bring her down harder. Her love is your most powerful weapon.

Don't rejoice in its loss.

He pursed his lips. "I'm sorry," he whispered. "But maybe she doesn't love him. Maybe she's not meant to."

This is a temporary setback. She'll be in his arms by sunrise.

Mordecai lowered his head and closed his eyes against the rush of acidic moisture. His stomach clenched, and his throat tightened.

It's for the best, Mordecai. Let them be now. You have homework to do.

Indeed he did. He had begun digging into Joshua Kendall's past. Mordecai was well networked and powerfully connected, and his sources should be reporting back by now. Before this night was out, he ought to know as much about Kendall as the man himself did.

Bryan and Dawn kept a safe distance from the madman. It wasn't hard to keep his car in sight, even so. It was a small town. There were few roads and scant traffic. They followed him from the cemetery to the nearby hamlet of Bonnie Brook, where he pulled into the driveway of a beautifully restored Victorian house, right off the main road. There were several houses like it nearby, though each one was unique. The one he was apparently using was white, but the fancy trim and scrollwork were painted pink and green, as were the shutters, porch posts and window casings.

"He always did have great taste in houses," Dawn muttered.

"Did he?"

"Yeah. You should have seen the place he had in Virginia. It was like a dream-house."

She had pulled the Jeep into the driveway of one of the

neighboring houses. Bryan glanced at the place; it looked occupied but currently empty. No one was home. Dark windows, not a car in sight. "I can't quite make sense of the fact that this maniac we're all so terrified of is your father."

"Birth father." She shrugged. "Hell, I've got three fabulous parents and one psychopath. It balances out."

"Guess that's one way to look at it."

"He came after me a year ago. Thought I was going to inherit his so-called gifts and decided it was time to start my training."

"What kind of gifts?"

She shrugged. "He's so crazy it's hard to tell, but there's definitely some genuine talent there, too. I think he's psychic, and he might actually be able to channel things from…you know, from the other side or whatever. But his mind is so twisted, it's hard to tell what's real and what's delusion." She sighed, shook her head. "After Beth got me away from him, he sent papers surrendering all parental rights to me. I guess he decided I wasn't worthy of his gifts after all."

"You should be thanking your lucky stars." Bryan searched her face. "But you're not, are you? You almost sound a little sad."

Dawn met his eyes, and hers were unguarded and potent. "There are such beautiful parts of him. It's like… when he first kidnapped me. He ran Julie's car off the road, but he only meant to force her onto the shoulder."

"Julie your adoptive mom?"

She nodded. "She's such a lousy driver, we wound up over an embankment. Julie was hurt bad, unconscious. I climbed up to get help, and he was there."

Bryan narrowed his eyes on her. "Not seeing the beautiful part yet, Dawn."

"I think her injuries were serious. I don't know how I

know it, I just do. I begged him to do something, to help her. And he did. I mean, he didn't want to, I could see that. But then he said it wasn't her time, and he looked down there at the wreck and was just quiet for a moment. And then he told me she would be okay. And she was."

"You think he…healed her?"

She shrugged. "Maybe. I think he tried. I think he knew she would come after me, and that it would be better for him if she died in that wreck, but he tried to save her. I think there's a goodness down deep inside him."

Bryan tipped his head to one side. "He's killed a lot of people. I think my dad suspects he killed Maude. No good in that, Dawn."

"No. But he thinks he's following instructions straight from God. He won't hurt anyone unless he believes God tells him to, even if it would be better for him. You see what I mean?"

"That deep down he's a *nice* homicidal maniac?"

She sighed. "I don't expect you to understand."

He studied her for a moment. "You have to see something good in him, because you know his genes are in you. You're part of him. And you want to believe the part you came from was the good part. I totally get it." Reaching out, he smoothed a hand over her hair. "And looking at you, I can't believe you came from anything else. There must be good in him. And you got all of it, Dawn."

She sniffled, lifting her head, and he was surprised to see that her eyes were wet. "It scares me sometimes. I wonder if I might have gotten some of the bad, too."

He shook his head slowly. "There's nothing bad in you."

Her lips thinned. "Sometimes…I know things."

Bryan was silent as a little jolt of surprise zapped through him. His hand stilled in her hair.

"I knew Beth was in trouble. I knew Mordecai had found her. I knew Maude was going to die before it ever happened." Her tears spilled over. "I think I have whatever it is that he has. And what if that's what made him insane?"

"Oh, hell, no, Dawn. That's not it." Bryan slid his arms around her, and she collapsed against his chest and let him hold her. Her shoulders spasmed as she cried, giving way to the fear that must have been eating at her for a long time. "Dawn, I swear that's not it. There are plenty of people who have…you know…a little something extra. You see them on TV all the time. They write books, lead seminars, have great careers, and they help people. You know that. You've seen them, read them."

"But—"

"But nothing. He had a gift, but his mind wasn't right. His insanity twisted and corrupted his gift, not the other way around. You're not crazy, Dawn, and you're not evil. God, when I first saw you, I thought you were an angel."

Sniffling again, she lifted her head from his chest. Her cheeks were tear-streaked, her eyes wet and red. "You did?"

"Yeah."

She swallowed hard. "I've never told anyone about this. Not anyone."

He could hardly believe she'd told him something so private, something she hadn't shared with anyone else. It made him feel special, and strong. "I'm not going to tell anyone," he said. "You can tell me anything you want. Any time you want."

"I'm glad you're here, Bryan. I'm not sure I could get through another encounter with my father alone."

He nodded. "I'll make sure you won't have to."

She smiled just a little, wiping her tears from her eyes. Bryan drew a breath for courage, leaned closer, and very gently, very slowly, pressed his lips to hers. She didn't push him away. In fact, she leaned in a little, kissed him back a little. But when they parted, she was searching his eyes again.

He looked past her. "It's dark outside."

She nodded. "We should try to get a closer look at Daddy Dearest before we leave here. I didn't see what he looked like, did you?"

"I figured you'd be able to recognize him."

"No way. He's way too good for that. Come on." She opened her car door and got out.

Bryan didn't like admitting, even to himself, that he was scared shitless as he got out, too. But at that point, he thought he would have followed Dawn Jones McKenzie straight into hell if she asked him to. He just hoped that wasn't exactly what he was about to do.

Beth followed her nose and grumbling stomach down the stairs. She'd combed out her hair, partially dried it, and put on the muslin nightgown, terry robe and fluffy slippers Joshua had laid out for her. She felt cozy. Refreshed, clean and warm. And though still wary of him, and his motives, lies and intentions, she was grateful for the royal treatment.

When she stepped into the dining room, she stopped walking and stood still, surprised yet again. Maude's old table had been polished to a high gloss shine and set as if for a queen. Silver and china glittered in the light of two tall, white tapers set in silver holders. A candelabra sat on the sideboard, glowing and casting dancing light into the room. And the smells from the kitchen were tantalizing.

"I hope you're hungry," Josh's voice whispered from very close behind her. Then he moved past her and pulled out a chair. "Sit, relax."

"I don't know what you're trying to pull, Joshua, but—"

"I'm not trying to pull anything. I lied to you. I feel bad. I want to make up for it and come clean."

She lifted her brows, staring at him as he stood there, his hands on the chair. "You're going to tell me the truth?"

"About everything. Over dinner. I promise." He nodded at the chair.

She wasn't sure she believed him, but she moved forward anyway, taking the seat as he pushed it in for her. His breath warmed her neck when he leaned over her to take an immaculate white napkin from the table and lay it in her lap. She tried not to let her shivery reaction show too much.

"Be right back with the food."

He hurried away into Maude's kitchen, returning moments later with silver serving bowls, covered and steaming.

She started to get up. "Let me help—"

"No, don't you dare. You'll ruin my plans." He set the bowls on the table and started back.

"And just what are your plans, Joshua?"

"To give you a little pampering, a little TLC. Something Maude told me you'd been too long without."

She opened her mouth to speak, but he was gone again. When he returned, he brought a huge covered basket and another silver bowl, this one uncovered and brimming with a tossed salad. He took the cover from the basket, revealing hot, freshly sliced garlic bread. The other two dishes held spaghetti, and a sauce so full of meatballs and veggies that it held the serving spoon upright.

"I hope you like spaghetti."

"Everyone likes spaghetti," she said, and she let him wait on her, deciding she wasn't being given a choice in the matter. He filled her bowl with tossed salad and set the selection of dressings and toppings in front of her, waiting for her to finish before fixing his own. She took a handful of croutons and some Italian dressing. He used the croutons, as well as the bacon bits and shredded cheeses, before soaking the bowl in creamy ranch dressing. But before he sat down to eat, he ran back to the kitchen, returning this time with a bottle of chilled wine and two glasses. He filled them both, then raised his own. "To honesty and maybe, if I'm very lucky, a fresh start?"

She lowered her eyes. "To honesty," she said, and she clinked her glass to his.

15

————

Bryan could see Dawn shivering as they crept from the back lawn of the empty house to the back lawn of the one next door. The thing that got to him was that it wasn't all that cold outside. He tried to edge a little closer to her as they moved, bending low, almost tiptoeing through the grass and dry leaves that crunched with every step they took.

Damn noisy leaves.

The darkness seemed to grow thicker, denser, by the second. Or maybe that was just the thick black clouds gathering and shifting, breaking apart and regrouping over the thin cradle moon.

Just as well. When the moon did shine through, it only reminded Bryan of a scythe, and that made him think of the Grim Reaper, and that was too damn close to his image of Dawn's demented father for comfort.

They walked like cartoon characters trying to be sneaky, backs bowed, knees bent, with their arms bent at the elbow and hands hovering in front of them in an almost defensive position. The only difference between them and a classic episode of Bugs Bunny was that they were tiptoeing more slowly and lacked the accompaniment of a tinkling piano.

When they were close enough to touch the white clapboard siding on the back of the house, Dawn stopped moving. She stood still, one hand braced on the house, and Bryan thought she was listening, so he listened, too.

The wind rattled through dead leaves that still clung to the trees and littered the ground. An owl hooted. A car passed by on the highway.

"He's in there," Dawn whispered.

"Well, yeah. We know that. We saw him go in there."

She nodded. "We have to get a look at him."

"I was afraid you would say something like that."

"Maybe…maybe you should go back. Wait in the car."

Bryan made a face. "Yeah, right. I'm gonna go cower in the car like a little girl while you risk your neck spying on a lunatic. *Not.*"

"He's my father. My problem, not yours."

"Actually, right now he's my dad's problem, which sort of makes him mine, too." He shrugged. "Hell, maybe *you* oughtta go wait in the car."

"He's Beth's problem. That's what he really is," Dawn whispered.

"Is that why you're doing this?"

"Partly. I guess. I owe her. But it's more than that. It's like—you gotta clean up your own garbage, you know what I mean?"

He shook his head side to side.

Dawn pursed her lips. "Well, as far as I know, I'm the only blood relative he has. I feel like…I ought to be the one to rein him in. You know?"

"Yeah. I guess I get that." He turned to look at the back of the house. Uncomplicated, a flat broad wall, with several windows and a back door with no porch, just a simple concrete stoop, three steps up, wrought-iron railings. "How do you want to do this?"

"Fast and silent," she said. "And…with you holding my hand."

He would have smiled if she hadn't looked so damned petrified. Even in the dark, he could see it. It was in her eyes. He quickly closed his hand around hers and let her lead. They crept along the rear of the house, but each window they came to was blocked by carefully drawn curtains. It was looking more and more like the glass panes in the back door were the only ones through which they might be able to steal a glimpse of the man. Light spilled from that doorway.

It was only as they drew still closer that they realized the reason why.

The door stood wide-open.

A sound, metal clanging against metal, shot through Bryan's chest like a lightning bolt, and he jerked in reaction. It came from the side of the house, the opposite direction from which they had approached. Dawn's hand clutched his hard enough to crush his bones as he peered through the darkness to see a dim silhouette that included one man and two trash cans. The man was at the corner of the house, facing away from them, cramming a bag into one of the cans.

Three things zipped through Bryan's brain at the speed of light. That man was going to turn in their direction any second now. When he did, he would see them, because they were standing in the pool of light from the back door. And there was no time to run back to the opposite corner of the house, and no cover between here and there.

There was only one option to keep from being seen. He knew it, though it made him want to throw up. Dawn knew it, too. He knew she did when she lunged forward, jerking him right along with her, up the three concrete steps and *inside* Mordecai's house.

His heart hammered rapid-fire, and he could hardly stop panting, though they'd only moved a few yards.

They stood in a kitchen, yellow and white and spotless. There was something that smelled fantastic bubbling in a Crock-Pot, and a waft of heat that was coming from the oven.

"He's coming back," Dawn whispered. She was peering out the door, backing away from it now. "God, we're trapped!"

"Come on." Bryan pulled her with him, out of the kitchen, into the next room, a large formal dining room. The table was set for dinner. Dinner for a group, not one man alone. He didn't have time to count the place settings—barely noticed them, in fact—as he ran through the room. Then he slowed his steps, quieted them, because he heard other footsteps. Mordecai Young's footsteps as he came into the house. The back door creaked softly as it closed. The man was humming a little tune.

Bryan's throat went dry, and he kept moving, straining not to make a sound. Through the dining room and into another room—sitting room or living room. Soft furniture, fireplace, coffee tables. No TV. God, the man *was* insane. Where the hell was the front door?

The humming stopped abruptly. The man said, "Oh, really? Well, I wasn't expecting more company, my dear guides, but if you're sure...."

Bryan swung his gaze to Dawn's. Her eyes were huge. "Who the hell is he talking to?" he mouthed.

She shrugged, and they kept moving.

"Hel-looo," Mordecai called. His footsteps were coming softly. Crossing the dining room now, Bryan thought.

The sitting room was dim; a hallway led off it in one direction, a stairway in another. An archway at the end. He chose the arch and hurried toward it.

"A little birdie tells me someone is in my house," Mordecai called, his voice lilting and light, as if he were speaking to a small child. "Don't be afraid now. Come out and say hello."

They ducked through the archway and into what appeared to be a foyer just as Mordecai's footsteps entered the sitting room. There, Bryan thought, spotting the front door. A way out at last! They ran toward it, and Bryan grabbed the knob, twisted and pulled.

Locked!

Dawn shoved his hands aside, gripping it herself, even as Bryan turned to look behind them. The man stepped into the archway. Backlit, and that just barely. He was a dark shape, a ghost.

A demon.

"There you are. Let me just get the light so I can greet you properly."

"*Hurry,*" Bryan whispered.

Dawn was shaking, rattling the door. She twisted the dead bolt, yanked the door open, only to have the chain stop it. She was shaking so hard he didn't know how she could function as Mordecai started across the room toward them—and the light switch.

She slammed the door closed, fumbled with the chain.

"Who are you? Don't run off. I've made a lovely soup, and there are rolls in the oven."

Dawn yanked the door again, and the two of them stumbled through, then launched themselves into a sprint, running for all they were worth even as the light flashed on behind them, first the foyer light, then the outdoor lights. The pools of brilliance pursued them and stopped just short of Bryan's heels.

The man stepped out onto his porch, calling after them. "Was that you, Bryan? I thought you'd gone out of town? Who is that with you?"

Bryan's blood seemed to turn into ice water when the

man said his name. They dived into Dawn's Jeep, Bryan ending up behind the wheel without either of them consulting on it. He twisted the key, ground the gears, almost stalled it, but managed to back them rapidly out of the driveway. Then he slammed the car into second, skipping first altogether, and the vehicle jerked itself into forward motion.

"Jesus, that was close," he muttered, belatedly fastening his seat belt and glancing sideways at Dawn to see if she was okay.

She wasn't. She'd buckled up, but now she sat there, staring at nothing, her eyes kind of dazed, her skin pale in the greenish glow of the dashboard lights. She looked bad. Close to tears, or maybe even something worse. Shock or something. He didn't know.

"Hey." He reached over, closed his hand around hers. "It's okay, we're clear."

She closed her eyes, shook her head. "He knew who you were. Dammit, Bryan, I'm sorry. I never should have brought you here."

"So he knows it was me. So what?" He shrugged, tried to seem unconcerned. The truth was that when that maniac had called his name, he'd been so creeped out he'd almost keeled over. "He'll think I'm a punk playing Halloween tricks or something. Hey, we can sneak back later and toss some toilet paper on his hedges. He'll think that's all we were up to."

Dawn opened her eyes, looked dead into his. "You don't understand, Bryan. We can't fool him. He knows things."

"Yeah, I'll bet he knows lots of things. Like two and two equals eighty-seven. The guy's freakin' fried, Dawn. I mean, no offense, but he's buggy. Sets the table for a crowd when it's just him there all alone? And talking to someone who isn't really there?"

"His guides. He calls them his guides. Spirit guides. They tell him things."

"Right. Dawn, the man's insane. Don't let him draw you into his delusions. There was no one there."

"If there was no one there, Bryan, then who the hell do you think told him *we* were there? How did he know you were supposed to have been out of town today? How does he know any of the things he knows?"

A little shiver crept up Bryan's nape. He shrugged his shoulders a little to try to chase it away. "We, um…we need to find a place to spend the night." Better to let the other subject go, he decided. Better not to argue against the existence of a homicidal maniac's supernatural helpers. If he lost the debate, he would be too scared to continue. He would probably hop on the next plane to the West Coast, where the crazy people were normal.

"There's a motel outside of Pinedale. I passed it on the way in. It didn't look very busy—I guess it's far enough beyond the tourist area that it doesn't get overwhelmed like everything in either town does. And there's a parking lot in the back, too, so we can park the Jeep out of sight, in case he got a good look at it."

"Good plan." Bryan was pretty sure the nutcase *had* managed to cop a look at it, and he didn't want to think about that guy creeping up on them while they were asleep. "We should get something to eat." He nodded at the control panel. "This thing needs gas, too."

"How much money do you have on you?" she asked.

"Around fifty," he said. "You?"

"I've got eighty in cash, and the credit card my mom gave me for emergencies."

"We won't use the plastic," Bryan said. "She'd know where you were if you did, wouldn't she?"

She shook her head. "You watch too many cop shows.

She won't know until the statement comes, and by then I'll be back home. I'll probably tell her anyway, once this is over. Speaking of which…" She pulled her cell phone from her pocket, reached for the charger that was plugged into the car's cigarette lighter and plugged the phone in. "Better keep this baby charged. Mom will be calling to check in."

"She hasn't already?" Bryan asked.

"I circumvented that by calling her first. And I told her to use the cell if she wanted to reach me tonight, 'cause I might go over to my friend Kayla's house."

"Smart. So she's not suspicious?"

"It's been a year since I pulled anything this hare-brained on her."

"Yeah? What happened the last time?"

She lifted her gaze to his, her smile vanishing. "Mordecai got me."

"So you're going to be honest with me," Beth said.

She sat in the antique settee—though Maude had always called it a love seat—in front of the fireplace. Josh had built a small fire in the hearth, poured them each a third glass of wine and settled himself there beside her.

She wasn't entirely comfortable with his proximity. No, scratch that, she thought. If honesty were the theme of the evening, she might as well be honest with herself. She was entirely *too* comfortable with him this close. She was tempted to curl into his strong arms and just forget about everything else.

He nodded. "When we finish the wine."

She set her glass down on the end table beside her. It made a loud tap when it landed, punctuating, she hoped, the look she sent him. "Until I'm too drunk to care?"

"You've only had two—"

"You put me off through salad and dinner and dessert, Josh. I'm done waiting."

"Did you like it?" He took a slow sip and met her eyes. "The fudge brownie?"

"You make a mean brownie. But if you change the subject one more time, you're going to be wearing the rest of the pan. Or maybe just my wine, since it's closer."

He sighed, lowering his head.

"Who are you really, Josh?"

Lifting his head slowly, he nodded. "I'm a security expert—a glorified bodyguard, if that makes it simpler. My partner and I own a company that specializes in protecting high-profile clients."

"You work for the government."

He shook his head. "No. I own my own business. Hell, most of the time we don't even do the legwork ourselves anymore. We have a lot of good men on the payroll to do the actual hands-on work."

"Then why are you here?"

He lowered his head. "Arthur Stanton—the man in charge of protecting you—contacted me and asked me to take some time off to handle a special project for him."

Arthur Stanton—the man in charge of her relocation and, supposedly, protection. "And I'm the special project," she surmised. God, why was it so disappointing to hear the truth at last? This was what she had wanted. The truth. That didn't mean she had to like it, though.

"He said the guys on Uncle Sam's payroll were too obvious, and you would send them packing every time he sent one into town. He wanted me to be…more discreet."

"To lie to me. Pretend to be someone else."

"Yeah," he admitted.

"Sneaky son of a bitch."

"He's only trying to do his job, Beth. And obviously,

given what's been happening here, it's a damn good thing he did."

She frowned then. "And just in the nick of time, too." Her eyes narrowed. "How did he know Mordecai was about to track me down?"

"He didn't."

She narrowed her eyes. "Then it's coincidence, him sending you out here just in time? No way. It's been months since he tried saddling me with any of his henchmen." Beth reached for her wine, took a long sip, then stared into the glass. "You're either lying to me again, or you really believe that. I don't."

"I'm not lying to you, Beth."

"Then you're way too trusting of Arthur Stanton."

She looked at him, saw him frowning as if considering her words. Maybe he'd already been wondering the same things. "So you never really knew Maude at all."

"No. Arthur's reports on you named her as your closest contact in town, so she seemed the natural way in. We took a shot. I approached her, told her you might be in danger, and that I had to get close to you in order to protect you." He shook his head. "She was more than willing to cooperate. Hell, the whole long-lost grandson bit was her idea. If I'd known the only person in town who would know better was also the police chief, I'd have thought of something else."

"Frankie knows?"

"She knows a little. That I'm here to protect you, not why."

She pursed her lips. "I can't believe she lied to me. Much less that Maude did."

He lowered his head, swirled the wine in his glass. "She really loved you, Beth."

"And you used it against me."

"Not against you. Never against you. I came here to protect you."

Beth drained her wine in one gulp. "And Bryan?"

"Everything I told you about Bryan is the truth. And yes, he did know the real reason we were here, and he hated it. He's been bitching at me nonstop to just tell you the truth, threatening to do it for me if I waited too long."

She nodded. She would have guessed as much about Bryan. The boy had a good heart. As for his father…

She focused on the fire burning in the hearth, rather than on him. "So that's it, then? That's all of it?"

"That's not even close to all of it." Joshua took the glass from her hand and set it down. "As soon as I met you, things started to change. Beth, I think we both know there's something between us. Something…good. It's been killing me to keep the truth from you. But I was scared to death that when I told you, you'd throw me out of your house and out of your life. And maybe you'd end up dead because of it." He lowered his head, shaking it slowly. "I painted myself into a corner, Beth, and I didn't know how to get out. So I told myself my feelings didn't matter. Your finding out the truth in the end and hating me for it didn't matter. The only thing that did matter was keeping you safe, no matter what it might cost me."

"And what about what it might cost me?" Damn the tears for springing into her eyes.

"I'm sorry. God, you don't know how sorry I am. I didn't mean to hurt you."

Her brows pulled together—the words, the sound of them, were so familiar. As if she'd heard him say them before. Long, long before.

"I never meant to have feelings for you. It's completely unprofessional, totally against everything I've taught the men who work for me, and something I never thought would happen to me, not in a million years. But I do feel something for you, Beth. I do, and I can't help it."

She forced herself to meet his eyes, even though it meant revealing the moisture in her own. "Please don't lie to me...not about this.... I can't—"

He stopped her whispered plea with a kiss. His lips touched hers, lightly, softly, at first. And then his arms slid around her, one encircling her waist to draw her closer, the other slipping to her nape so his fingers could thread upward into her hair.

A shudder worked through her body, from the soles of her feet all the way to the top of her head. She told herself to pull away, but she didn't listen. The kiss grew. It deepened, ripened and heated. She found herself clinging to him, kissing him back, opening to his tongue and then tangling hers with it. He kissed her, and kissed her and kissed her some more, until her heart was racing and she couldn't catch her breath and didn't care. Her entire body was alive with wanting him.

But finally he lifted his head away.

Somehow she'd ended up reclining on the love seat, with him leaning over her. He was staring down at her when she opened her eyes, and the look in his was one she tried hard to read. Surprise, confusion and desire all mingled there, and she only understood the latter.

He was everything she had vowed never to trust again. Male, less than honest with her, keeping secrets still, she sensed, and working for the government on top of all that. And yet she wanted him. God, was she doomed to keep repeating the same mistakes over and over? And then again, she reasoned, what did it matter? She had nothing to lose now. No daughter. No lover. No life, really.

What did it matter?

He started to sit up, avoiding her eyes.

She gripped his shoulders, stopping the retreat. "All right, Joshua. All right."

Facing her again, he frowned.

"You win," she said.

His frown deepened. "I win? This isn't a battle, Beth. All I want is for you to believe me. To trust me."

She let the bitter smile cross her lips. "I almost believe you. I'll probably never trust you, not fully. But, as stupid as it may be, I do have feelings for you. And I do want you. Now. Tonight."

He stared at her—stunned, maybe. "I wasn't trying to get you into bed. I didn't mean for that kiss to... I got carried away."

She unbuttoned his shirt, one button. Then the next. "You know what? I don't really care."

"Beth, you've been through too much in the past couple of days—this isn't the right time—"

She kept unbuttoning, noting that he didn't put his hands over hers to stop her. She got the last button free, slid her hands over his chest, upward to his shoulders, and watched him close his eyes. "Do you have any idea, Joshua, how long it's been since I've been with a man?" Sliding her hands lower again, she raked her nails lightly over his nipples, and he sucked in a sharp breath. "Make it good, Josh."

He opened his eyes slowly, staring down at her. His hands—were they shaking a little?—moved to the sash of her robe and tugged it free. Then he was lifting her gently, so he could slide the robe off her shoulders, down her arms. The white linen nightgown was thin. But the firelight warmed her. She watched his gaze focus on her breasts, and knew her nipples were hard and visible beneath the fabric. He wasn't moving, so she reached to the neckline and began undoing the tiny buttons herself. One by one, all the way. The linen fell open, just slightly, with every button she unfastened, revealing a ribbon of flesh down the center of her body.

She lay back again, waiting.

Almost hesitantly, his hands pushed the nightgown open, and the breath stuttered out of him when he did. "Beth," he whispered. And his hands smoothed a path over her shoulders, breasts, belly...and then back again to her breasts, where they lingered.

She let her head fall backward. His palms on her were not enough, even when he squeezed. "Please, Josh."

He drew his fingertips over her nipples then. Finally. Pressure, tugging, tender pinches. She opened her mouth and trembled with every touch.

He drew back, sliding off the love seat so he knelt on the floor beside it, and then he finished unbuttoning the gown, pushing it open, exposing her hips and her thighs. Then he slid his hands over her abdomen, down her legs, as if compelled to touch every part of her. "You're more beautiful than I ever dreamed," he whispered. He stroked a hand over her center, hesitated there. Beth moved her thighs apart, letting one leg drop to the floor. Joshua swore softly and let his fingers burrow between them, softly exploring, probing, just a little at a time, his movements slow. When one finger slid inside her, she whimpered, moaned, and that seemed to be what finally broke the dam of his restraint.

Bending over her, he captured a breast in his mouth, sucking the hard nipple between his teeth even while his fingers deepened their invasion, sliding in and out, the pace faster than before. The fire inside her was alive, and he was building it higher. God, how she wanted. She had never wanted like this. She was moving her hips against his hand, silently begging for more. At last his mouth released her breast and moved down her body. Lips and tongue and teeth making a fiery wet path over her belly and lower, then still lower. And then his fingers withdrew, and his hands spread her open, and he bent lower, pushing his face between her legs. His tongue snaked out, a hot, slow lick. He spread her open even wider with his fingers, so his tongue could delve inside. One hand slid beneath her buttocks, to tip her up, and he plunged even deeper, devouring her from the inside out.

Beth cried out, her hands pressing to his head. Every sound she made seemed to drive his hunger, until his feeding became so frenzied that his teeth scraped over her clitoris with every lap of his tongue, and still he strove to lick more deeply, to taste more of her. It was as if he couldn't get enough.

She screamed aloud when she came, her entire body spasming, twitching, and that only served to make him keep lapping, sucking, biting her gently, until she was shaking so hard she thought she would break apart.

But it wasn't over.

He'd shed his jeans at some point, and now he gripped her shoulders, pulled her upright and around on the love seat until her legs were on either side of him, where he knelt on the floor. His hands gripped her buttocks, and he pulled her forward, off the settee, and onto his rock-hard erection. So big, she felt him stretching her as he sank himself into her, and yet she was so wet he entered her easily, deeply. She was still spasming from the orgasm, on the verge of begging for mercy.

But then he moved his hips, and she had no desire to be free. Only to take him, more of him, all of him. She clung to his shoulders, moving over him, and he caught a breast in his mouth again, using his teeth far more aggressively this time than he had before. His hands on her backside squeezed, fingers pinching now and then as he pulled her down onto him, harder with every thrust.

She sucked in a sharp breath, going still with shock and sensation. He jerked her hips forward, driving his cock deeper; then he pulled back and drove in again and yet again. Harder, deeper, and it felt good. Then she was helping him invade her, possess her utterly, by rising up and driving herself down over him. "Oh, God!"

She was coming again, and she thought he was, too, but the sensations were overwhelming, blinding, deafening. As he drove to the very depths of her, she crushed her body against him, taking everything he gave her.

He held her there, her body wrapped around his, and slowly, he lay back on the floor, snuggling her with him, holding her so tenderly she felt almost cherished. As the echoes of passion slowly ebbed, she rested her head against his chest and whispered, "I love you, Joshua."

16

◄—►

Mordecai sat alone in the darkened dining room long after he'd finished his dinner and cleaned up the dishes. There was no doubt in his mind that the shadowy figure he'd seen running from his front door tonight had been young Bryan Kendall. His guides didn't correct his assumption, and that, more than anything, confirmed it. Even though he'd seen the boy taken to the airport this very morning.

Obviously Bryan hadn't left town after all. Why the trip to the airport, then? he mused, twisting a long-stemmed wineglass in his hand, watching the bloodred contents swirl. Had he been meeting a new arrival in town? But then, why would Lizzie and the boy's father have left him there?

No, they had dropped him off. He'd been carrying a bag. He must have been planning to leave. Something had happened to change those plans. And who was the girl who'd been with him? Why was the boy's identity made known to him, even in the darkness, but not the girl's?

Because she's unimportant, Mordecai.

It worried Mordecai that the boy had been sneaking around his temporary home tonight.

He knows something, a voice whispered inside his mind. *Something about you.*

"What could he know? He's only a boy." For a moment he feared the guides would tell him the boy was a threat and had to be dealt with, and a knot of dread formed in his belly. Sometimes he hated them.

God, that was sacrilege!

It's not the boy. He's not the problem. It's that father of his. Joshua Kendall.

Mordecai nodded in silent agreement. Kendall *was* a problem. The knot in his belly loosened. He almost hoped they would tell him to rid the world of that man. Petty jealousy, yes, but he was still human, after all.

Knowledge is power, Mordecai.

"Yes," he whispered. "And soon we'll have all the knowledge we need." The name *Joshua Kendall* had been haunting him since the first time he'd heard it. Internet searches had turned up nothing other than references to other men of the same name. It had taken hours to go through all the hits, eliminating them one by one.

But he had other connections—friends in high places, as the saying went—though in his case, they were not friends at all. Just people with things in their past that they wished to keep there. Many skeletons in many closets. And Mordecai had been rattling the bones.

Time to see what had resulted.

He sipped his wine and got to his feet, refilled the glass and carried it with him into the den, where he'd set up his computer. There were no high speed, always-on connections here in this small town. Just an old-fashioned dial-up server. He clicked on the Connect icon, then waited for the modem to finish its squealing and log on.

The mailbox logo lit up, and he clicked on it. Three e-mails, the third one with a file attached. He clicked on the first, from a judge in San Diego.

"Joshua Kendall and Kevin Russell own a private security firm with offices in Manhattan and Washington, D.C. While neither man publicizes his name, for obvious reasons, the firm has a Web site, RK-Security.com. It's owned, hosted and maintained by a third party, however, so no personal information on either of the proprietors shows up in WHO IS records. I was unable to get a home address on either man. That's all I know."

Security firm—well, that made sense. Perhaps Beth had sensed Mordecai closing in on her and hired him for protection.

"I knew he wasn't who he was pretending to be."

He clicked on the second message, from a Congresswoman in South Carolina. "I won't help you. Don't contact me again."

He pursed his lips, sighed softly. "What a shame," he said. Then he took an extra moment to skim through his files and find the ten-year-old photographs he'd scanned in. So much easier to keep track of one's records since computers came along. He had files on hundreds of people. Ammunition.

He opened the file folder for a quick look. The Honorable Sheila McGruger's long limbs were wrapped around a naked man. She'd been very good back then. Only a lawyer, but just as married as she was today. He wondered sometimes if she remembered their dalliance fondly. There were several shots, and he flicked through them, pausing longest on his favorite—the one of her on her knees in front of him, taking him halfway down her throat. He'd made sure they were very close and presenting a side view to his hidden camera for that particular carnal act. His face didn't show, but the tattoo on his thigh did. She was clearly not with her husband.

He flipped through his address book for North Carolina newspapers and sent the entire file folder to the largest one, all with a click of his mouse.

"She really should know better than to defy me," he muttered.

Sighing, he moved on to read the third e-mail.

It was from Martin Phillips, the assistant warden of the prison where David Quentin Gray had been held, before Mordecai had helped to arrange his escape and subsequent demise.

"Yes, I know who Kendall is," he had written. "The Feds have gone to a lot of trouble to help him keep his past quiet, and the press on him is too old to be found on the Net. Plus, he's shortened his name since then. It was Kendalson. He was in the papers, years ago. He was on the team that stormed your compound. He accidentally shot a girl, killed her, and was fired over it. I've attached a news clipping for you.

"By the way, I found Gray right where you said I would and got all the credit for locating him. Even though he was dead, as I'm sure you know. I figure we're even now."

Mordecai smiled. "Not even, my friend," he said to himself. "But I'm glad you've provided more leverage for my use, should I need to solicit your aid in the future." He saved the e-mail containing the assistant warden's confession to his file on Martin Phillips, then opened the clipping.

It was a front page story, and the scan was excellent. The photo of Kendall—probably taken from his badge when they made him turn it in—was a good likeness, though obviously taken when he was much younger.

The headline was the best part. ATF Agent's Bullet Killed Unarmed Seventeen-Year-Old Girl in Raid on Young Believers.

Mordecai smiled slowly. "This is too good. *He's* the one who shot Lizzie?"

Now do you understand? the voices whispered. *Now do you see why you had to let her fall in love with him?*

He nodded. "If she has…then this will destroy her."

Timing is crucial, Mordecai. You have to show her at just the right time.

Again he nodded. Then he hit the print button on the PC screen and waited while the printer spat out a hard copy of the truth about Lizzie's new savior.

"I love you, Joshua."

Her voice, soft and breathless, whispered those words again and again in Joshua's mind as he lay in her bed, holding her in his arms while she slept.

She loved him.

Hell.

He'd never intended to take things this far. Something had just…happened. When he'd kissed her tonight, he'd let himself fall for his own act. It was as if he really had fallen head over heels for the woman. As if he really did…

It was utterly unethical of him to have allowed things get to this point. Convincing her that he loved her was bad enough. Letting her fall in love with him was considerably worse, though still within the realm of necessary evil. But making love with her—that was beyond the rest. It was cruel. He wasn't a cruel guy. And he wasn't a caveman.

She muttered something in her sleep and rolled over, spooning up against him. His arm slid around her waist automatically, and he could smell her hair. With their bodies nestled this close, he knew at least part of the answer. The attraction he felt for her was real. Had been all along. And he liked her, making the attraction more potent. Above and beyond all of that was the past—his bullet cutting her down, costing her damn near everything. So, sure, part of it was probably guilt, mingled with the overwhelming relief of knowing she was alive.

Hell, it would take a shrink a year to figure out why he'd wound up in this woman's bed. He certainly wasn't going to work it out in one night. And he wasn't sure it would matter if he did, at this point. The deed was done; there was no turning back. If he backed off now, she would want to know why. So he would just have to play it out, live the act, pretend that he was in love with her.

He snuggled closer, kissing her hair and relaxing onto the pillows. If nothing else, he thought, he had at least won her trust. To bad he was going to end up dashing it on the rocks of truth once she was safe and her nemesis behind bars.

Tuesday

She didn't trust the man as far as she could throw him, Beth thought while she poured them each a cup of morning coffee. He was too good-looking to be trusted, to begin with. He'd been lying to her since he'd met her, and he was convincing and charming enough to fool anyone. Even Maude. Which meant he could fool her just as easily.

Mordecai had been like that. Charismatic. Charming. Beautiful, with his dark-brown soulful eyes and those thick lashes. He had little-boy eyes. Angel eyes. As windows to the soul, they were miserable failures. Or maybe his soul really was a thing of beauty beneath the madness that had corrupted it.

There's nothing as precious as an honest man, Maude used to say. *Unfortunately, there's nothing as rare, either.*

She set Joshua's cup on the table, studying him closely and wondering if he was precious and rare, dropped on her doorstop by some higher power that thought she'd finally earned a break, or if he was just another beautiful liar. One who smelled sinfully good, freshly showered, and looked good, freshly shaved.

"What are you thinking about?" he asked.

Ah, right. She'd been staring. Caught. "That Maude probably agreed to go along with your little charade in the hopes that something would happen between us."

He smiled just a little, and a dimple came into his cheek. "Yeah, she was trying all along. Nothing subtle about it, either."

"No, there never was." She frowned then, tilting her head to one side. "Those people who were examining her body...?"

"Worked for Uncle Sam." He tightened his lips, as if debating whether to tell her something; then finally he sighed. "She was murdered, Beth."

She almost dropped the coffee cup. "How?"

"We suspect a drug was mixed with one of her vials of insulin."

Beth blinked as Maude's panicked face and straining, terrified eyes replayed through her mind. "She couldn't breathe."

"That's how this particular drug works. Paralyzes the muscles, including the lungs. Bastard could have used a tranquilizer—knocked her out so she wouldn't have suffered like that."

She drew a breath. "It was Mordecai, wasn't it?"

"I think so."

"And my house?"

He shook his head. "Nothing definitive. Everything points to a gas leak. But that's not a tough thing to set up. Tough to prove, though. We may never know for sure. But according to the Feds, he's a genius with explosives."

She frowned. "I never knew that."

"It was classified information. It's long been suspected he may very well have rigged the compound to burn himself, and that something went wrong, set it off early."

Lowering her head, she let her eyes fall closed. "No wonder you sent Bryan away."

He frowned at her.

"I'm dangerous, Josh. Anyone who gets close to me is putting themselves at risk."

"I sent Bryan away because of Mordecai, Beth. Not because of you."

"Mordecai wouldn't be here if it weren't for me. I know him. I know the way his mind works. What Mordecai loves, he has to own, and once he owns you, he never lets go."

"He let your daughter go."

She lifted her head, nodding slowly. "I still haven't figured that out. It's completely out of character. I wouldn't be surprised if it was part of some convoluted plan to get her back in the end."

He sighed softly. "He doesn't own you, Beth. You got away. You survived, made a new life. He can never own you."

"What he can't own, he destroys." She studied his face for a long moment. "I know what he's doing," she said softly. "He's trying to take away everyone I care about. Maude was first—you'll be next."

"Don't even—"

"You should leave here."

"—say it," he said, finishing the sentence her own had cut in half. Shaking his head, he faced her, his eyes solemn but stubborn. "I'm not going anywhere."

"You're putting your life in danger."

"It's my job to put my life in danger."

"You have a son to raise."

"And you have a daughter."

"I'm not raising my daughter. I'm not even in her life except for phone calls and e-mail."

"You can be, once Young is behind bars where he belongs."

"That's not your—"

"Enough, Beth." She flinched at the words, and Josh got to his feet as he said them. "I'm here, and I'm staying until this thing is finished. Period."

She pursed her lips, lowered her head. He was making a whole lot of progress in winning her trust, she thought, and a little shiver raced up her spine. She didn't want to trust him. Didn't want to put herself in that precarious a position with any man ever again, loving and trusting to the point where common sense and her own mind failed her, and the love and trust became the controlling force. Where the voice of the man overwhelmed her own innerspeak, until she couldn't hear herself anymore.

That's how it had been with Mordecai.

But Joshua was nothing like Mordecai. He said he wouldn't leave her until this was over. And even though she didn't want to, she believed it. She believed *him*.

She swallowed her fears and let herself accept that, like it or not, she trusted this man.

"I should shower. Shelly Bryce is supposed to come by this morning to cram for a second period English test. Though given the situation, I should probably cancel."

She saw the way his face changed, the way he averted his eyes all of a sudden. "Maybe you won't need to," he said.

She frowned, studying him. But before she could ask what he meant by that, the telephone rang. Beth got to her feet and crossed the kitchen, picked up the telephone and brought it to her ear. "Hello?"

"Hi, Ms. Slocum. This is Mrs. Bryce, Shelly's mom."

Slanting a look at Josh, Beth wondered how he could have known. "Hi, Mrs. Bryce."

"I'm afraid Shelly won't be coming by this morning."

"I hope she's not ill."

"No, I just, uh…well, I decided against letting her skip first period to study for that test."

Beth blinked. "But she said she only had study hall first period."

"Yes, well…the thing is, we've decided to drop the tutoring altogether."

"Oh." She was being fired. She had no idea what to say. "I hope you haven't been unhappy with my work, Mrs. Bryce. Kelly's grades have come up significantly since—"

"Yes, I know they have. Frankly, Ms. Slocum, we're concerned about more than just our daughter's grades. And…well, it really doesn't matter now, does it? We've made our decision. Have a nice day."

She hung up the phone before Beth could get another word in. Beth just stood there for a moment, staring at the receiver in her hand, and looking again at Josh. "You knew about this?"

He nodded.

"How? What's going on, Josh?"

"Bryan heard some of the other kids talking. Seems there are some wild rumors being spread around town."

"Rumors. About me?"

He nodded.

"What kinds of rumors?"

"Drug abuse, mostly. There's some suggestion that you may have gotten on the wrong side of some dealer, who decided to blow up your house in retaliation."

She closed her eyes. "So I should expect more calls like that one."

"People are idiots," he said, rising from the table, coming across the room to her and sliding a hand over her shoulders.

"I can't blame them. After all, I'm the mysterious stranger with no past. The teacher who won't take a job at the local school. Secretive, hermitlike. This is the first plausible explanation anyone has come up with."

"And the most ludicrous one anyone could think of."

"You can't blame them for wanting to protect their kids. God, if they think some criminal is after me—" She stopped there, looked up at him slowly. "Actually, there *is* some criminal after me. They're right to keep their kids out of the cross fire." She sighed. "It's not just this one student, is it, Josh?"

He shook his head slowly. "Bryan didn't think so."

"It's for the best. But what am I going to do? The workers are supposed to start on this place tomorrow. Everything I have in savings is earmarked for the renovations. Hell, I put a good chunk of it down already. What am I going to live on?"

"What I don't understand is how a rumor this insane got started."

"Mordecai," she whispered. "Who else?"

"I thought the same thing at first, but that doesn't make any sense. Why would he want to ruin your reputation like that?"

She lowered her head, staring at the floor. "He has a reason. Everything Mordecai does has a reason. It's all part of whatever he's up to." Swallowing the lump that rose in her throat, she lifted her eyes again. "Maybe he's trying to take away everything I have, as well as everyone I love, before he finally kills me."

"He's not going to kill you. And this gossip fiasco isn't going to work, either."

The telephone rang again. She recognized the number on the caller ID screen. Another of her students. She looked at the phone, then at him. "I think it already has, Josh."

* * *

Josh put in a call to Arthur as soon as Beth was busy elsewhere in the house. And Arthur's first words were, "Has Mordecai made contact?"

Josh pursed his lips, frowning as he recalled Beth's earlier warning—that he trusted this man too much. "Not directly. What I'd like to know is how you knew he would find her."

"What do you mean, Josh? It's always been a risk."

"Yeah, but this is a little too coincidental to be for real. Beth's been living out here for a year without so much as a ripple. Now, a few days after you send me to protect her, he tracks her down? Come on. Don't mess with me, Art. You knew this was coming."

Arthur hesitated before replying. "I got a tip that a convict, Young's former lawyer, might have had some idea where Beth was hiding out," he admitted.

"How?"

"Newsclipping. Photo that caught her by accident. She was watching some town event last fall. Harvest parade, something like that. Goddamn bad luck."

"But the guy's in prison, isn't he? You could've had him watched, had all his outside contact monitored—"

"Did that, son. But he didn't try to get word out that way."

"Then how—"

"He escaped."

Josh closed his eyes slowly. "Jesus Christ, Arthur, why the hell didn't you move Beth the second you learned about this?"

"Because she wouldn't have gone. And because…I thought we could get him, all right? I thought we could get this son of a bitch Mordecai Young at last."

"Using Beth as bait?"

"I sent you to protect her."

"I brought my *kid* with me, Arthur! You put my son at risk, and you didn't even bother to tell me. If I'd known Mordecai knew where she was…"

"I didn't know you had your son with you, Josh. Not until after you took the job. It had been years since we'd been in touch. Last I knew, Bryan was living with your ex in California somewhere."

That much, at least, was true. "You should have told me the truth," Joshua said. "You should have given me all the information. Instead of using me—and *her*—to try to blot out the only stain on your career."

"Not on my career. On my soul." Arthur Stanton drew a raspy breath. "And I thought you'd appreciate having the chance to right some old wrongs of your own."

"I don't appreciate you putting my son's life in danger. Or mine. Or Beth's all over again. She doesn't deserve this. Hell, an innocent woman has been killed because of what you did."

"One more on an already crowded list," Arthur said softly. "Is Bryan safe?"

"I shipped him back to the West Coast yesterday."

Arthur sighed. "Do you want to move Beth Slocum?"

"Damn straight I want to move her." He could hear Beth now, upstairs in her bedroom. Hard rock pounded from the clock radio as she moved, no doubt working out yet again. "But I'm not sure I can convince her to go."

"I'm coming out there."

"You don't have to—"

"Yeah, I do, Josh. I've screwed up too many times. I'm the one who needs to fix this, and I think you know that. You just keep the woman alive until I get there, huh? I'll be there tonight, Josh."

He disconnected, leaving Josh with a dead telephone in

his hand and a feeling of betrayal gnawing at his chest. But the anger overwhelmed everything else. He was furious at his old friend for using Beth this way. Furious. Maybe a little more so than made sense; maybe he was buying into his role as her lover a bit too deeply. But knowing it didn't make the anger go away.

If he'd been face-to-face with Arthur just now, he thought, he would have decked him. The man he admired most in the world. He would have hit him, laid him out.

He was too close to this job. Things were getting confused in his mind; he was letting the act, the role, the job, get all mixed up with his real feelings of guilt and admiration and attraction. It was a dangerous thing to let happen, and he told himself he'd damned well better get a handle on it—and soon.

17

Beth slipped out of the house while Josh was on the phone. It probably wasn't a very nice thing to do, because it would worry him to death should he discover her gone. And with Mordecai in town, it wasn't a very safe thing to do, either, so she took the derringer with her, tucking it into the back pocket of her jeans.

She slipped out the back door without making a sound, and walked over the back lawn and into the woods. Brilliant sunlight gave way to cooler shadows once inside the trees. The vivid leaves were thinning now, turning to brown and carpeting the trail so that her footsteps crackled.

Beth told herself, as she always had, that she would have to face Mordecai sooner or later. She would far rather that showdown come when she was alone—when Josh wasn't standing in the cross fire. She told herself that. But she knew it was a lie. She would feel far, far safer if Josh was by her side. But that was selfish, not to mention foolish. She was in no position to let herself become needy or dependent. No one could end this but her. When the time came, she would face Mordecai alone.

But she really hoped this wouldn't be the time. She had another mission in mind, one far more important.

She'd changed into a pair of well-worn jeans, a T-shirt and a hooded sweater, and traded her shoes for suede hiking boots. It wasn't a cold day, though the breeze that found its way among the trees to ruffle her hair carried the bite of autumn. By the time she made her way to the narrow winding stream and the path that ran alongside it, she was wishing she had come out here more often. The spot between the path and the stream had been one of Maude's favorite places. There was a park bench there, a bird bath, a feeder hanging from a tree and a miniature pond, fed by the stream itself. In the summer, she and Maude had their tea out there more often than not. One time a deer had been sniffing along the banks of the stream and come within ten feet of them.

Her heart ached with missing Maude. She hoped with everything in her that the wonderful woman was at peace, maybe with her beloved Sam in some heavenly paradise.

It wasn't a long walk into town. Long enough, though, that Josh would have plenty of time to realize she was missing and to come looking for her before she reached her destination. It worried her. But she would be quick. What she had to do wouldn't take long.

She emerged from the woods and onto the road, where a narrow, ancient, one-lane bridge spanned the tiny stream, and picked up her pace as she headed into town, gripping the small envelope she carried in one hand. Finally the town's storefronts, rows of green-and-white awnings and perfect sidewalks spread out before her. She glanced up and down the road, eyeing every one of the three vehicles that drove past as she walked. She watched the face of every passerby on the sidewalk, jumped every time a shop door opened with a jingling of bells. The town wasn't too full today. It was a weekday, and the leaves were past their peak. The tourists were beginning to thin out a bit.

Finally she went through the door that read *Blackberry Gazette*.

The office of the small-town newspaper was tiny. Three reporters and a receptionist occupied the space, and one of the reporters was also the managing editor, a sixty-something widow who had taken over the paper when her husband had passed away years ago. Another was Eric Lewiston, a reporter with a career behind him at far more prestigious papers, who had retired to Blackberry a few years back. The writing bug wouldn't leave him alone, so he'd taken it up again for the small paper. No rat race. No pressure.

"I'm here to see Mr. Lewiston."

The receptionist looked up with a smile—one that froze in place as soon as she saw who was standing there. "Aren't you Beth Slocum?"

"No. I'm not, not really. My real name is Marcum. Elizabeth Marcum. I'd like to talk to Mr. Lewiston about that and a few other things, actually. I have an exclusive for him that's going to rock the whole town."

Bryan came awake with a start, only to see Dawn leaning over him, looking sympathetic. "You slept in that chair all night?"

He sat up slowly, looking around the motel room. TV, twin beds, window that was way too big, and only one exit. The back of his neck hurt when he moved it, and his back ached a little. He ran a hand over his nape. "The idea was to stay awake in this chair all night. If I'd planned to sleep, I'd have done it in the bed. I guess I blew it around 4:00 a.m."

She heaved an expressive sigh. "You didn't have to do that. He didn't follow us."

"How can you be sure of that? And hell, with his...abilities, how do you know he'd even *have* to follow us to know where we are?"

He watched her face. She averted her eyes, unable to even drum up an argument. Instead she said, "Hell, Bry, if he knew where we were, staying awake all night watching for him wouldn't do us any good anyway."

"Oh, that's reassuring." He rolled his eyes, got to his feet and stretched, arching his back and pressing his hands to the small of it to work out the kinks. "What the hell are we going to do about this, Dawn?"

"I've been thinking about that all night. I think we have to tell someone. I mean, he's a wanted felon. If the authorities know where he is, they'll go arrest him, and that will be the end of it."

He nodded. "So we call the police, just like I wanted to do last night."

She shook her head firmly. "No. That would be a huge mistake. This is a small town, Bry. They couldn't handle him by themselves. They'd only tip him off, and he'd end up getting away. That's why I was against calling them last night."

Bry paced across the small room, his stomach growling. "He's one guy."

"Yeah, and he's managed to get away from the FBI, the ATF and every other government agency that's tried to take him in. God, I wish I had Jax's number."

"Jax?"

"Lieutenant Jackson. She was one of the cops who helped track him down last time, when he'd kidnapped me. She was really good. I'd rather have her here than the FBI *and* the ATF."

"TTB now," Bryan said.

"Huh?"

"The ATF is the TTB now. Alcohol and Tobacco Tax and Trade Bureau."

She frowned at him. "How do you know that, Bryan?"

He shrugged. "It's a guy thing. We're into that stuff.

I'm starved. You think it's safe to venture out for some breakfast?"

"No. But I don't think it's any safer not to, so we may as well."

He nodded. "You want to shower up first?"

"You can take the first one if you want."

He shook his head. "I took one last night while you were sleeping. Figured that way I could leave the door open so I'd hear if anyone tried to get in."

She smiled slightly. He didn't know why. Then she hugged his neck without warning, grabbed her overnight bag and headed into the bathroom.

He spoke to her again through the closed door, trying to keep his voice nonchalant. As if her tender hug hadn't sent his pulse through the roof. "So if we can't call the cops and you don't have your friend Jax's number, who are we going to call?"

"Beth has a government contact. The guy in charge of keeping her safe. He's the only one I can think of."

He nodded slowly. "You mean Arthur Stanton?"

"You know about him?" She sounded shocked.

"He's the man who hired my father. Actually, contacting him with all this isn't a bad idea. Do you have *his* number?"

"No. But Beth does. Hell, she might have Jax's, too. We're gonna have to get back inside the house, go through her stuff and find it."

He heard the water crank on, raised his voice higher. "What stuff? Everything she had went up with her house."

The door opened, and Dawn peered out. He could only see her from the neck up, and he got a little breathless wondering what she was wearing and guessing it was probably just a towel. "Not her purse. Or cell phone. They'd have been with her wherever she was. Right?"

"I guess so."

"So if she had the numbers, that's where they'd probably be. In a little address book in her purse or programmed into her cell."

"So we're going back to Maude's house?"

"We'll slip in while they're out running. You have a key, right?"

"Uh, no. Dad replaced the locks just before I left. Probably didn't see any need to give me one, since I'm not supposed to be here."

She bit her lower lip. "I'll figure something out." She closed the door.

"Yeah, that's what I'm afraid of," he muttered.

Two minutes later the bathroom door opened again, and this time, when her head popped out, her hair was dripping. "After we eat, we'll go stake out the house."

"Stake out the house?"

She nodded. "We'll just watch the place until they leave, and then find a way to get in." Her head vanished, and the door closed again.

Great, he thought. "So while trying to avoid my dad seeing me still in town, I'm going to keep him within sight all day."

"Speaking of your dad," she yelled above the shower spray, "you'd better call him, don't you think?"

He looked at his watch, wondering if his father would believe he'd gotten up before 7:00 a.m. West Coast time. "Okay."

"Hello?"

"Hey, Dad. It's Bry. Just wanted to check in."

Josh smiled at the sound of his son's voice on the telephone. "I'm glad to hear from you, son. How was the flight?"

"Completely uneventful."

"Well, boring is a good thing in this case."

"Yeah."

"Bet Mickey was glad to see you, huh?"

"That's an understatement."

He nodded, missing his son with an ache that gnawed at his chest. It was beyond the way he'd missed Bryan before. Hell, he'd spent most of his life missing the boy. But now it was different. Bigger. Deeper, somehow. He felt as if one of his vital organs were three thousand miles away.

"So how's the weather there, Bry?"

"Oh, you know California weather. It's always the same."

"Yeah. So you have everything you need?"

"Yep. I'm all set."

"Great. Then I'll say so long for now. I miss you, Bryan."

"I miss you, too, Dad."

"It won't be for long, I promise."

"I know."

Josh sighed. Then, "So can I speak to Mr. Malone?"

"Mr. Malone?"

"Mickey's dad?"

There was a hesitation. Then Bryan said, "Uh, he's not here. But you can talk to Mrs. Malone, if you want."

"Fine. That'll be fine."

Josh looked around the house, frowning at how quiet it was. He wondered if Beth had decided to take a nap. Then, finally, a woman's voice came on the line, though it was raspy and hoarse.

"Hello?"

"Janet? Gosh, you sound terrible."

"Oh, I've picked up a cold. It's not as bad as it sounds."

"I should hope not. I, uh—I just wanted to thank you and Mark for taking Bryan for me on such short notice."

"Don't be silly. We love having him."

"I do, too. I hated having to send him to you, Janet, believe me. It's killing me."

"You miss him that much, huh?"

He sighed. "It's like someone pulled out my heart. If this wasn't absolutely necessary, I swear—"

"We understand."

"It won't be for long. A few days, a week at most."

"That's fine. Don't worry about a thing."

"Can't help but worry. I'm the farthest thing from father of the year. I've probably messed the poor kid up as much as losing his mom did, but I'm trying my best."

"From where I'm sitting, I'd say you're doing fine."

"Thanks, Janet. You know where to reach me?"

"Sure. Take care…Josh."

"You, too."

Josh hung up the phone, frowning, focused more on the silence in the house around him than on the oddness of that phone call. He walked slowly up the stairs, expecting to find Beth in her room, but when he peered into her bedroom, she wasn't there. The bed was made, hadn't been disturbed. She hadn't been napping, then.

"Beth?"

He moved from room to room looking for her, growing more afraid with every echoing nonanswer. Nothing. She was not in the house.

Jesus. His heart jumped into his throat, choking him. He ran to the front door and out onto the porch, calling her name. Her car was still in the driveway, right beside his pickup. Hurrying around to the side of the house, he checked the back lawn but again, saw no sign of her.

"Beth!"

He was close to panic. He didn't get this way, not ever. He was trained to stay calm in any situation. What the hell was the matter with him?

He hurried inside, snatched up the phone and called the Blackberry Police Department. He told the receptionist to put him on with Chief Parker, and she did so without any questions, which he appreciated to no end.

"Frankie Parker here," she said. "That you, Kendall?"

"Yes. I've lost track of Beth. And I'm worried."

"How long since you've seen her?"

He thinned his lips, looked at his watch. "Forty-five minutes."

"Forty-five—Kendall, you have some reason to think something's happened to her?"

"I just can't believe I let that much time go by without—" He broke off at the creak of the screen door, and spun around to see Beth coming inside.

"Never mind, Frankie. She just came in."

"I still think you need to tell me a little more than you have, Joshua. If the threat to her is so severe that you panic when she's out of your sight for more than a few minutes—"

"I have to go."

He hung up the phone while Frankie was still talking, reached Beth in three strides and snapped his arms around her waist, pulling her close, burying his head in the crook of her neck.

"Josh, what in the world?"

He lifted his head, leaned back just enough so he could look down at her face, and then he was kissing her in a way that probably gave away everything he'd been feeling. He kissed her fiercely, almost desperately, his hands tangling in her hair, his mouth invading and then possessing hers.

When he finally came up for air and stared down into her sparkling, confused eyes, he took a moment to ask himself just what the hell he was doing. This hadn't been planned, hadn't been part of any effort to fool her, hadn't been part of the role he was playing. What was it, then?

He avoided her probing, questioning eyes. "Where were you?"

She shook her head. "Needed some air, had some thinking to do. So I took a short walk out back."

He spun to face her. "Do you have any idea what kind of risk you were taking? Going out there alone like that?"

She blinked twice. "No more risk than I've been taking every time I've left my house for the past year, Josh."

"A lot more than that, and you know it. Jesus, Beth, do you *want* him to find you? Alone, defenseless—"

"I'm far from defenseless."

He had to forcibly restrain himself from barking at her, calling her a fool. He drew a breath first, all too aware that he was in an emotional state he'd rarely experienced. "I know that," he said, keeping his voice level. Careful. "But I'm here to protect you. I'm one more tool you can use to protect yourself. Slipping away without me is like—like driving without your seat belt. It's an unnecessary risk."

She lowered her head. "I don't think as clearly when I'm with you," she said softly. "Frankly, I think you could probably get me to believe just about anything you wanted to. You touch me, and my common sense goes to hell."

"Beth, don't. I've told you the truth, I've told you why I'm really here. I'm sorry I lied to you in the beginning, I just—"

"I know. I know, Josh." She paced away from him. "I needed some space, that's all. There were things I needed to do."

He frowned, noticing for the first time the shadows in her eyes. She was keeping something from him. "What kinds of things?"

She thinned her lips. "Nothing you're going to like."

"What?" He blinked, searching her face.

She shook her head. "Have you heard from Bryan?"

"Yes, and stop changing the subject."

"It's none of your business, Josh. I'm not telling you until it's too late for you to do anything to stop it."

"Stop what? Jesus, Beth, what the hell are you talking about?"

She shook her head. "Ask me again, about six-thirty, and I'll tell you."

"Beth—"

"I'm tired, Josh. Can we skip this for now? God, we've got so much to do. The place is in no shape for Maude's memorial service."

Josh could only frown at her as she headed up the stairs. He followed her, but she walked into one of the unused bedrooms instead of her own. It wasn't one of the usable ones; it was stacked full of boxes and smelled slightly musty. She was peeling off her sweater on the way. Then she pulled on an oversize T-shirt she'd left hanging from the vacant room's doorknob at some point.

"Beth, what on earth are you doing?"

"Cleaning the place," she said.

"Why?"

She shrugged. "I spoke to Will Ahearn. He's not amenable to returning my deposit—I signed a binding contract and that down payment is nonrefundable. He says it covers his coming out here, inspecting the place, generating an estimate and so on."

"He did all that before it was yours."

"Technically, he didn't. It was already mine on paper. Remember what the lawyer said?"

"Still—"

"I told him to start today. And since he and his crew are taking care of the outside, I'm suddenly in the mood to take care of the inside. So I'm cleaning. You care to join me?"

Sighing, Josh walked into the room, picked up a box and carried it out. She'd made it clear he wasn't going to get another thing out of her until she was damn good and ready.

The *Blackberry Gazette* was delivered at the usual time. 6:00 p.m. Beth had thrown herself into her work on the old house all day, and the time had flown past. It was good, working this hard. Kept her mind off her impending and inevitable confrontation with Mordecai, and her growing feelings for a man she knew was lying to her. But she was finished with lies.

As the afternoon wore on, the two bedrooms Maude had used for storage were cleaned out, things sorted, stored in the attic or basement or the garden shed beside the house, or stacked on the porch to be given away. Beth polished hardwood floors and washed woodwork, dusted corners and buffed light fixtures. She took her time, partly in order to do an extra good job—but mostly to avoid having to have a real conversation with Josh before the newspaper arrived.

As she worked, Josh brought down furniture from where it was stored in the attic: beds, dressers, trunks. It was like a treasure hunt up there, and they scrubbed and polished and set things up. A few new mattresses, a little paint here and there, and the two rooms would be as ready to use as the rest.

As much as Beth had told herself not to, she was starting to get excited about the idea of reopening the Blackberry Inn.

She was wiping the streaks from a bedroom window when she saw the newspaper boy whiz past on his bicycle at top speed, canvas sack over his shoulder. He reached back, tugged out a rolled-up newspaper, whipped it toward the porch and never even missed a beat.

She drew a breath, set down her paper towel and wiped her hands. "Ready for a break?"

Josh had removed a couple of doors from their hinges, put them on sawhorses, and was sanding them down, getting rid of old paint. "Just about."

She saw that he was nearly finished with the second one. "Meet me downstairs when you're ready. I'm gonna make fresh coffee."

"Okay."

She went past him, out of the room and down the stairs, and felt his eyes on her as he finally got the message that something was up. He was washed up and in the kitchen before she finished measuring ground roast into the basket.

She looked up at him, at the question in his eyes, gave him a single nod and said, "Would you go grab the evening paper off the front porch for me?"

"Sure."

He left. She ran water, poured it and braced herself, knowing he wasn't going to be happy. When he came back with the newspaper in his hand, she could see that was an understatement. He blinked down at the front page, then looked slowly up at her, his eyes wide with disbelief.

"Jesus, Beth. What the hell did you do?"

She sighed. "What I had to do."

"This is insane. My God, the government has bent over backward to keep your whereabouts and identity secret."

"From Mordecai," she said. "But he's already found me. There's nothing to gain by keeping my past a secret any longer. Besides, this will flush him out. Even though the tourists are starting to go home, the town is too crowded for us to find him otherwise. The place is still full of strangers."

Josh lowered his head, pinching the bridge of his nose. "Yeah, it'll flush him out. Him and every reporter in the freaking country."

"It's a small-town newspaper."

"It's a huge story." He shook his head and set the paper on the table.

She sat down, pulling it closer to her and reading the headline. "'Sole Survivor of Long Ago Raid Alive and Well in Blackberry.'"

"It's going to be a circus here by this time tomorrow, Beth."

She hadn't thought that far ahead. The article told the story of her time at the Young Believers' Compound, her injury in the raid, the long, slow recovery that followed, and the fact that fugitive cult leader Mordecai Young's obsession with her had been renewed a year ago, when she "single-handedly rescued one of her students from the madman, risking her own life in the process."

"It makes me sound like some kind of hero."

"You are, Beth. You went after a man you should have been avoiding at all costs."

"But not for just any student. For my daughter."

He shrugged. "I take it you didn't tell the reporter that part."

"Of course not. That's no one's business." She gave the paper a shake. "He makes me sound like some kind of superhero teacher, rushing after kidnappers in defense of her students."

He smiled just a little. "I'm not so sure he was all that inaccurate."

"Please."

Josh shrugged and went to read over her shoulder as Beth bent over the paper again. The story went on to describe how the government had given her the new name

Beth Slocum and relocated her in Blackberry, Vermont. It talked about how, though voted outstanding teacher of the year in her former district, she'd never sought employment in the local school system of her new town, knowing the still-at-large murderer would be more likely to look for her at schools, and that if he found her, her presence would put the student body at risk.

"Looks like Eric Lewiston did a little research on his own today. Phoned my old district. I never told him any of this, and a lot of it's pure speculation." She read aloud. "'Her past, and the threat that this woman has lived with every day, ought to raise some serious questions in the minds of all of us—especially given the recent explosion of her home, allegedly due to a gas leak. Elizabeth Marcum claims she has reason to believe her nemesis has tracked her down and may be in our area even now, using an alias, likely disguised, just biding his time. While Marcum would neither confirm nor deny it, I believe she plans to relocate as soon as arrangements can be made, rather than giving the madman reason to linger in our town. In the meantime, residents should be vigilant and watchful. Granted, we've grown used to the presence of strangers. And I'm not advocating panic or mistrust of the tourists that are this town's lifeblood. Just vigilance. Watch out for each other. That's what we do in Blackberry.'"

She set the paper down, sighing.

"You're planning to leave after all?" Josh asked, leaning closer and searching her eyes.

"I didn't say that."

"According to him, you didn't deny it, either." He narrowed his eyes. "What is this, Beth?"

She drew a breath, pushed her chair away from the table and paced to the sink to stare out the window into the backyard. "I might have hinted that I was going to leave town."

"Why?"

Straightening her spine, she turned, hands braced on the sink counter. "Because Mordecai won't wait if he thinks I'm about to run again. It's taken him a year to find me. He won't risk me slipping away, going into hiding again."

"You're forcing his hand."

She nodded.

Josh got up and strode across the room to where she stood. He put his hands firmly on her shoulders. "You've ensured he'll come after you as soon as he can."

"Maybe even as soon as he reads this," she said, lowering her eyes.

"God, Beth."

"I know you're angry. But I'm tired, Josh. I need this to be over with. I'm either going to get my life back or lose it for good. Either way, it's long overdue."

He closed his eyes, sighed and slid his arms around her. God, it felt good, his solid form pressing against her, supporting her.

"I'm not angry. I'm…I don't know what the hell I am." He sighed. It was a deep sigh that seemed to come from his core. And then he squeezed her and stood back to look into her eyes. "It's done. We'll deal with it. And no matter how fast the bastard moves, he's not going to lay so much as a finger on you, Beth. I promise."

She smiled through her fear. "Now who's the hero?"

His expression changed then. Something clouded his eyes. Something she couldn't name. "I'm no hero."

"No? You mean you *didn't* come charging into Blackberry with everything but the white steed for the sole purpose of keeping one lonely woman alive?"

He lowered his head. "Beth, there are things…you still don't know about me."

"I know there are."

His eyes snapped back to hers.

"You don't think a woman who's been through what I have is easily fooled, do you, Josh? I know there are things you've been keeping from me. I've known it all along. But I also know that you mean it when you say you want to protect me. That you're on my side in this. I believe that. And I…I think I'm starting to believe that you aren't lying about…about having feelings for me."

"I'm glad to hear that."

She nodded. "So what else is there?"

He licked his lips. "We've hit a crisis point here, Beth. Let's get through this, and then…then we'll deal with the rest."

She stared at him, searching his eyes, wondering what he was still keeping from her and aching inside because she was so afraid it would change everything between them. God, she was more afraid of his secret than she was of Mordecai. Her priorities were skewed to hell and gone.

"Do you trust me enough to do that, Beth? To wait a little bit longer for the answers to your questions?"

She sighed. "You're not giving me much of a choice.".

His lips thinned. "I can't. I'm sorry."

She sighed, slipping free of his embrace to walk to the table, where she picked up her now cold coffee, took a sip and grimaced. "It's a major thing, Josh. As badly as I've been burned by men who keep secrets—this is a lot you're asking of me."

"I know that." He walked up behind her, slid his hands along her outer arms. "Believe me, I know."

She lowered her head, his touch warming her, coaxing

her. The telephone rang, and she let out a sigh and moved away from him to pick it up. "Hello?"

"Beth, it's Chief Frankie. Why the *hell* didn't you two tell me any of this?"

She licked her lips, lowered her head, taken off guard by the lack of preamble or small talk. "I don't imagine you're too happy with me right now, are you, Chief?"

Her eyes met Josh's. He nodded, as if he'd expected Frankie to be calling.

"Not thrilled, no," Frankie said. "Don't you think this is something you might have considered telling me? By God, woman, Josh told me he was here to protect you, but not the rest. Don't you think the fact that one of the FBI's Ten Most Wanted felons is in my little town is something I ought to know?"

Beth lowered her head. "There were reasons."

"I've got no doubt about that. As far as your protection—"

"It's covered, Frankie."

"It's my job, Beth. Or should I call you Elizabeth now?"

She closed her eyes, not answering.

"Did Maude know about this, child?"

"No," Beth said softly. "She didn't know any more than what Josh told you."

Frankie sighed. "We don't have the resources to deal with this sort of thing on our own. I have a call in to the state police requesting help, though I have no doubt there are federal agencies we should be working with on this, too. I thought you might have a name for me. Tell me who's in charge. The same fellow whose number Joshua already gave me?"

She wasn't too overwhelmed to be surprised by Frankie's brisk efficiency—or to be disappointed in herself for that surprise. Had she just blithely assumed Frankie was incompetent because she was female and over fifty? Shame on her.

"You probably ought to talk to Joshua," she said. "I'm putting him on now." Beth handed Joshua the telephone, sighing and walking away, leaving him to handle things, even though she hated how dependent she had become on him in such a short time.

"Hold on, Chief." Josh put his hand over the phone. "Where are you going?" he asked Beth.

"Upstairs," she said. "I have to get ready. I don't imagine it will be long now."

18

Josh confirmed for Frankie that Arthur Stanton was indeed the man in charge of Beth's case and informed her that he was on his way to town as they spoke. Then he called Arthur and filled him in on the latest developments. He put the phone down and glanced toward the staircase.

Beth was starting to believe his feelings were genuine.

And she wasn't the only one.

Josh sighed as his stomach knotted up and his throat went dry. He could barely tell what was true and what was a lie anymore. What did he really feel, and what was he pretending to feel, and what was leftover guilt from what he had done to her in the past? He didn't think this was any time to be trying to work all that out, anyway, not when her life was hanging in the balance.

He drew a breath and headed up the stairs. Her bedroom door was open, and beyond it, she sat on the edge of her bed, with her pathetically tiny derringer in her hands. She held the nickel-plated barrel of her little gun as she ran a tiny wire brush through it. Then she set the brush aside and held the barrel up, peering into it.

He stepped inside, and she looked up at him. "Thought I'd better get this in shape. Hasn't had a thorough cleaning in a while."

He nodded at the cleaning kit, open on the bed beside her. "You went shopping, huh?"

"Picked it up while I was in town this morning. The old one got blown away."

He sat down on the bed beside her, replaced the wire brush in its slotted spot in the case, took out a yellow felt square and a bottle of gun oil, and handed them to her. "I have a kit in my room."

"I didn't think of that before I left or I'd have asked."

"Never hurts to have a spare."

She nodded. He watched her drip oil onto the gun barrel and then buff it with the felt. She knew what she was doing. She used another tool, sliding the felt through a slot on the end, to oil the inside of the barrel. The familiar, powerful scent of gun oil would cling to her hands for hours, he thought. Finally she snapped the barrel back onto the rest of the weapon, which had clearly already been cleaned.

"You need a bigger weapon," he said.

"Had one. Lost it."

"Did you have a holster for it?"

She shook her head. "Never got around to buying one. Guess I didn't want to think about the time when I'd need to have it with me 24/7."

"I don't blame you. But that time is here. I want you to carry one of mine. And I don't want it farther than arm's length from you from here on. Okay?" She nodded, repacking items into the gun cleaning kit, wiping her hands on a rag.

"Okay." She slipped the two tiny bullets into the derringer, then held it up and sighted down the barrel at a spot on the wall. "You ought to be wearing your own from here on, too, Josh." He glanced at her. She didn't lower her weapon. Her finger caressed the trigger, and she closed one eye. If Mordecai Young were on the other end of the room, Josh had no doubt he would be hurting. The tiny gun wouldn't stop him, but it would sure slow him down.

"Headshots only," she told him, still sighting.

"Headshots?"

She nodded. "Smaller target, but the only sure thing. Last time I killed him he was wearing a vest. If I'd put one between his eyes then, he wouldn't be a threat now."

No, he wouldn't be, Josh thought. Even the derringer might do the trick if she hit him there. But if she had killed him, other things wouldn't be happening now, either. He would never have found out that the woman he thought he had killed was alive after all. He would never have found her again. He would never have kissed her, touched her, made love with her.

"I'll get that gun and extra holster for you," he said, and it came out gruff and hoarse. He got his own guns, both of them, and his holsters, and a heavy knit sweater, then headed back to Beth's bedroom. He handed her his 9 mm. "How about you carry this one for a while?"

She took it with a frown, hefted it in her hands. "I had one something like it. Mine was a .45. Never carried it around with me. Too bulky, too heavy, too slow." She met his eyes as she handed it back, then nodded at the gun in his other hand. "What's that one?"

He tossed the sweater and holsters onto the bed and handed her the gun. "A .38. It's a revolver, though. Only holds six shots."

"I don't plan to need six shots." She looked the gun over, nodding in approval. "I like this one better."

"Keep it, then. And if you should happen to need more than six, you'll have the derringer as backup."

Josh set both guns on the bed and reached for one of the holsters, held it up. "You ever use a shoulder holster?"

"Nope."

"Handy as hell. We'll have to adjust it to fit you, though. Put it on under a bulky sweater and no one will be the wiser. Just make sure you can grab it in a hurry." He glanced at her, rapidly adjusting the straps to an approximation of the right size. "We'll adjust it once you get it on. Here."

He held out the holster. She took it. Then he peeled off his shirt and grabbed his own holster. "Put it on like this." He held the holster up to show her. She wasn't moving, though, and when he looked at her, her eyes were on his chest, not on the holster he held in his hands.

The way she was looking at him made his blood heat. But then she looked away, licked her lips. Set the holster down and peeled her sweater off over her head. She picked the holster up again, held it awkwardly. "Like this?"

Josh cleared his throat, told himself he'd seen her naked, so there was really no earthly reason why the sight of her standing there in her lacy purple camisole should turn him into a drooling idiot. "Here, let me show you." He put his own holster down, took hers from her hands, moved closer to her. But before he could slide the holster onto her, her palms were touching his chest, sliding slowly over his skin. Josh closed his eyes and let the holster go. It landed on the floor, and he kicked it aside, his hands going to her waist to pull her closer. Silk against his skin, under his hands. She was soft, warm, beneath it. He needed to taste that smooth skin again, and he did, bending his head to kiss her shoulder, the crook of her neck, the hollow underneath her ear. Her hands slid around to his back, and she returned every kiss. His shoulder, his neck, his chin.

With a low growl, he pushed her backward onto the bed, shoving the weapons aside with a sweep of his arm. His body covered hers, and he ground his hips against her as he finally took her mouth. She opened to him. Her lips, her legs. All of her. God, she had a way of turning him on like no woman ever had. He'd decided this was a bad idea. That he shouldn't do it again. But he'd be damned if he could stop himself. It wasn't just wanting her—it was a compulsion, a need that couldn't be denied. He needed her like he needed air.

He worked one hand in between their straining bodies, fumbled with her jeans to get them undone, then managed to shove a hand down the front of them, inside her panties and into the warmth, the wetness, beyond. She shivered at his touch, so he made it deeper, probing inside, one finger, then two. She moaned his name around his tongue, encouraging him. So he used his free hand to slide the straps of the camisole from her shoulders, pushing it lower, baring her. And then he slid his mouth from hers and went to work on her breasts, first laving, then sucking hard on one stiff nipple. Her hands gripped the back of his head, and she arched her back. He nipped with his teeth and she whimpered, so he did it again. He moved his fingers inside her still deeper, then attacked her other breast with his free hand, pinching its little nipple as he bit down.

"Good, baby?" he asked, mouthing her with the words.

"Good, more. Harder, Josh."

Even as she spoke, she shoved her jeans and panties down, lifting her hips against him and then freeing him of his jeans. She wrapped her hand around him, guided him. And then he was inside her, plunging into her, suckling and biting and pinching and driving deep inside her.

The way she clung to him, pressed against him, matched his every move with one of her own—it was as if she could read his mind. As if they were one being. And she was the most enthusiastic lover he'd ever had, whispering to him, telling him what she wanted, needed, snapping her hips to meet his, wrapping her legs around his waist to take him deeper.

He would have hated himself for not lasting longer except that she climaxed just before he did, her heels digging into his back as her spasms and cries sent him spiraling over the brink.

He collapsed on top of her, panting, breathless. "Damn, Beth, you're incredible."

"Mmm." She nuzzled his neck with her nose, kissed it and sighed. Then she went stiff, hearing what he heard. A car pulling up out front.

"Shit." He got off her, yanked his jeans up, pulled on his holster and jammed the gun into it. Then he reached for her. "Here, babe." He put her holster on her, over the camisole. "We'll tighten it up later." He thrust the .38 inside. "Put on a sweater."

She spun to snatch a sweater from the nearest pile of clothes—she'd been sorting, and most of them hadn't yet been put away. He saw her tuck the derringer into her jeans even as he pulled his own sweater over his head and started out of the room. She was behind him within a second, had to hear the footsteps on the front porch.

Beth came out of the bedroom into the hall, met his eyes, and there was no mistaking the fear in hers. But there was determination there, too. God, she was something.

"I expected him to come in quietly," she said, pulling her sweater down over her waist, adjusting it to hide the bulge of the weapons.

He took the lead, heading down the stairs and toward the front door, never standing directly in line with it. He was just about to peek through the curtain when someone knocked, startling him.

Beth was standing about four feet back. Not far enough, in his opinion. "Who's there?" she called.

"Chief Frankie," a voice replied. "And, uh—and company."

Beth frowned at Josh. He shrugged and moved to the nearest window to take a look outside. A half dozen people were standing on the front porch. A few he recognized. Most he didn't, and he didn't like that. But then Beth was beside him, her breath warm on his neck as she leaned in close to look outside. "What in the world...?"

"More cars are pulling up," he said, nodding toward the headlights. "What do you want to do?"

She lifted her brows. "Open the door?"

He sighed, but went to the door and opened it. Chief Frankie stood front and center, a small crowd gathered behind her.

"What's going on, Chief?" Joshua asked, even as Beth crowded up beside him.

Frankie shrugged. "I came by to check on things. These others—well, I'm not real sure. But my best guess would be that they read their newspapers."

"Darn straight we did," a woman said from behind her. "Beth Slocum—or Marcum or—well, hell, you've lived here a year, girl. Maude loved you enough to leave her home to you, and in my book, that makes you one of us."

"That's right," someone else said. "And in Blackberry, we take care of our own."

Frankie lifted her copper-red eyebrows, glancing from Josh to Beth.

Beth tapped Josh on the shoulder, then stepped aside and said, "Come on inside. It's cold out there."

The chief backed away and stood beside the door, her eyes telling Josh without a word that she would make sure no strangers were among those filing into Beth's living room.

One woman was carrying a pie, another a cake, another a bouquet of flowers. Before Josh knew it, the living room was full, and one of the women was hustling Beth into the kitchen, talking about putting on a fresh pot of coffee.

"Hold on a moment, sir. Just wait right there," the chief said, drawing Josh's attention back to the doorway.

A large man stood there, turned partly to the side as the far smaller woman in the police uniform waylaid him, apparently because she didn't recognize him. Josh did, though.

"It's okay, Chief. This is Arthur Stanton, the man I told you would be coming. Art, this is Blackberry's Chief of Police, Frankie Parker."

Art looked surprised, but hid it quickly and offered a hand to shake Frankie's. "Nice to meet you. Good to see you're on the job here." He glanced inside. "What is this, some kind of party?"

Josh followed his gaze to see that several women had cleared off the buffet in the dining room, draped it in one of Maude's crisp white tablecloths and were setting food they had brought there. A whole group had gathered around Beth. Snippets of their conversation reached him from the noise in the room.

"…so sorry…"

"….you don't need to go…"

"…for having misjudged you…"

"…didn't know, didn't understand."

"…proud to have you tutor our daughter…"

"…anything we can do to help you through this…"

"…Maude would have wanted you to stay…"

"Blackberry is lucky to have a woman like you living here."

Beth seemed to sense his eyes on her, met them through the ever growing throng, found them, clung to them. He saw something he had never seen before shining there amid the tears that seemed to be gathering.

He saw peace.

* * *

Mordecai drove past the old house slowly, because driving quickly would have been impossible, with the cars, pickups and SUVs lining both sides of the road. People were exiting vehicles, some of them carrying covered dishes, others empty-handed. They were bundled in coats, their breath making steam clouds in the chilly air. The house blazed with light and movement. It looked as if there were a party going on inside.

He glanced down at the newspaper on the seat beside him. "No doubt they're rallying around her. This pile of garbage makes her sound like a saint. No mention of her lies, her betrayal."

He kept driving, knowing he couldn't get close to her tonight. "What if she leaves before I get to her?" he asked.

Don't you think we would have told you if she were about to flee? Where is your faith, Mordecai?

He sighed. "The newspaper says—"

Stop speculating and trust Spirit.

He closed his eyes and prayed for patience, pulling his car, a gas efficient blue hatchback this time, onto the shoulder near the end of the line of vehicles. No one would notice one more in the pack. Then he got out, hopped over the ditch and moved carefully through the scrub lot beside the Bickham property. He kept to the cover of scraggly trees and brush, tall dry weeds and grasses brushing his legs as he walked. It was dark. He wouldn't be seen. He needed to get a closer look at what was going on at the house, and he thought the woods in the rear would be the safest vantage point.

He half expected the guides to forbid him from this little expedition, but no voices rose in objection. It was cold tonight, a visitation perhaps from the icy breath of the winter ahead or the death to come. To her, maybe to both of them. Maybe if they couldn't be together in life, they could be in death. Assuming he could cleanse the stains from her soul in time to save her from hell. And assuming, of course, he could get to the boy in time. The guides wouldn't let him leave until he had connected to his heir—done whatever they wanted him to do to leave his powers behind.

He trudged through the waist-high weeds until he reached the denser cover of the woods; then he moved behind the house, keeping just inside the tree line.

But before he'd decided on the perfect spot from which to approach the house for a closer look, he heard a harsh whisper.

"What in the heck is going on in there?"

A boy's voice. Mordecai went motionless, straining his eyes in the darkness.

"I don't know, Bry. But we're never going to get in there now," a female whispered back.

It was the boy and his little girlfriend, Mordecai realized. All day he'd been wondering where the young man and his female companion were hiding, whether they had told anyone where Mordecai was staying or what sort of car he was driving when they'd seen him. He'd spent the entire day preparing, in case he should have to flee the house. Everything was ready. He'd taken the computers down and stored them in the back seat of the newest car. Oh, he had no doubt a good forensics team could prove he had been in the house with little effort—a stray hair, a used water glass, a thousand other minuscule traces of his presence would remain long after he left the house behind. He didn't plan to leave a house for them to search. The name on the rental agreement was that of the unfortunate Oliver Abercrombie, a man whose body might never be found. The house would not be readily connected to *him*. He'd covered everything.

"I'm going for a closer look," the girl whispered. And then she was out of the trees, her body silhouetted in the lights that spilled from the house as she crept closer. She wore a down-filled coat, and her hair was bundled up beneath a knit cap.

Who was she?

The girl is unimportant. She'll only distract you from your purpose here. It's the boy you need to get to. Don't forget, Mordecai, that boy is his son.

"But she knows where I'm staying as well as he does," he whispered.

Where you're staying doesn't matter. It's your mission that matters, Mordecai.

His mission. God, it all got so twisted around in his mind. He had come here to destroy Lizzie. To tear everything away from her and make her realize the error of her ways. To humble her before the living God, to bring her to her knees before Him.

And then to kill her. Unless the guides changed that order.

But that wasn't the entirety of it, and he knew that too well. His priorities were skewed due to the power of his emotions. He was too human to be entirely detached. He needed clarity of mind, and God, it was getting harder and harder to cling to that. His mission was to locate and train his heir, the child who would carry on when Mordecai left this world. That child was Bryan.

The guides were right. The girl didn't matter.

He approached the boy, moving silently, slowly. But before he reached the lad, the girl came creeping back to his side. "I can't get close enough without being seen, Bry. Maybe we should get out of here, try again tomorrow."

"No way. We need to tell someone where Mordecai is hiding out. Tonight. Even if it means blowing our cover and admitting I never left town."

The girl's head bent lower, and she sighed.

Mordecai moved closer, closer, and then stepped on a twig that snapped like a gunshot in the night. Bryan's head swung toward him, his eyes widening as they picked out Mordecai's face, locked with his steady gaze. The girl stared, too, but the lights from the house stood at her back, so she was little more than a dark silhouette.

Bryan choked out one word, his wide eyes fixed to Mordecai's in the darkness. "Run!" Then he turned into the forest, clasping the girl's hand, and followed his own advice.

19

Bryan ran, Dawn's hand in his own. He had no idea where they were going, except away from Mordecai Young. God, he wished Dawn had taken off in the opposite direction. He wished he'd thought to hide her in some brush and keep on running. He didn't think Young had realized who she was yet, and he was afraid to think of what would happen if he ever found out. So they ran, and the man ran after them.

Chills raced up Bryan's spine as his brain tried to wrap itself around this situation. It didn't seem real that he was being chased through the forest by a crazed killer.

"Bryan! Wait, I must talk with you!"

Bryan didn't reply, because doing so would take much-needed air, and he was already starting to run out of breath. Beside him, Dawn panted roughly, and her hand jerked tighter on his at the sound of the man's voice. That he had called out to Bryan, not to Dawn, confirmed Bryan's suspicion: Mordecai didn't know that it was his own daughter he was chasing through the night.

Running wasn't easy. The woods grew thicker, darker, with every yard they gained. Roots and stumps tripped him every third step, and when he wasn't stumbling over them, Dawn was. He tried to help her, tried to use his arms to push limbs and low branches aside, but they were both being smacked repeatedly anyway. The ground sloped upward, and the farther they ran, the steeper the slope.

After twenty minutes of nonstop, panic-powered flight, Bryan paused, bending over, hands on his thighs, breaths rushing in and out of his lungs as his heart pounded. Dawn sank to her knees, gasping for breath.

Bryan tried his cell phone, then hers. No signal. He looked behind them, knowing he couldn't listen for their pursuer the way he was panting, with his own heartbeat thrumming in his ears. His face was hot. He couldn't see anyone coming, but then again, the forest was thick with darkness. He could only see clearly for a distance of about a yard. "I think we lost him," he whispered. Then, sighing, breathing a little easier, Bryan rolled his eyes at his own stupidity. "Of course we lost him. The guy has to be in his forties. No way could he keep up with a pair of teens in the peak of health, running uphill, in the dark."

Dawn lifted her head, stared at him. "He's forty-eight," she whispered. "And don't underestimate him."

Something moved behind and below them, and then a voice came, clear and kind. "Why are you running from me, Bryan?"

Bryan straightened up so fast he almost lost his balance, and Dawn shot to her feet and gripped his arm.

"I'm not going to hurt you, son. I only want to talk to you."

"How the hell did he keep up with us?" Bryan whispered. "He doesn't even sound winded."

Tugging his hand, Dawn started moving again, angling toward the left this time. In seconds they were moving fast again, pouring it on, lunging up the hill with every ounce of energy they possessed. Bryan tripped once, fell on his face on the damp, spongy ground, and because she was holding on so tightly, Dawn fell, too, landing right beside him. They pushed themselves up, helping each other, and kept right on going. They pushed, pushed, pushed, and Bryan kept thinking they would have to come to a road or a town or *something* sooner or later, and then he could flag someone down and get some help. Or find a phone and call his father.

God, he would love to be able to hear his father's voice right now.

But they didn't come to a road or a town. The woods only got thicker and darker, the hillside steeper. And, grimly, Bryan remembered Beth's warning. She'd told him the forest spanned some twenty thousand acres.

God, would they ever find help? And what if they didn't?

When he didn't think either of them could go another step, Bryan stopped, leaned back against a tree, fought the urge to suck loud gasps of air into his starving lungs. He'd pushed so hard his thigh muscles were quivering. And Dawn...God, Dawn was rasping and hot to the touch. But she wouldn't say a word about stopping to rest—hell, he thought, if left up to her, they would still be moving. But when he stopped, she stopped, too, leaned on a tree of her own, fought to catch her breath.

"Maybe we finally outran him," Bryan whispered between gasps.

"Maybe," she whispered back.

Please, God, he thought. And he tried to listen over the pulse beating in his temples. It was quiet for so many minutes he began to think they were safe. But then...

"Bryyy-annn."

The call chilled his blood. And the look in Dawn's eyes when they shot to his was enough to freeze it entirely.

"Come, on Bryan. I'm not going to give up. Just talk to me."

"Jesus," Bryan whispered. "You told me he had powers. But you didn't mention that he was superhuman."

* * *

Josh managed to make his way closer to Beth through the dozen or so neighbors gathered around her. They were coming and going, mostly. Walking in with a gift, a bottle of wine, a casserole, a pie. Telling her how proud they were to have her living in their town, asking if she needed anything, if they could do anything to help. Some stayed long enough to share in the snacks and casseroles that had appeared on the buffet. Amazing, the change in attitude a simple newspaper article could make.

Arthur Stanton and Chief Frankie were handling crowd control, watching everyone carefully. Frankie seemed to know everyone, which eased Josh's mind considerably. If a stranger showed up, Frankie would spot him. Though Josh doubted Mordecai Young would make his move among a crowd. Still, the man was unpredictable.

"How are you doing?" he asked when he got close enough to Beth.

She looked up at him, smiled a little. "I'm a little overwhelmed. People keep telling me they want me to stay."

He nodded. "You've become their new hometown hero."

She lowered her eyes then. "That won't last long. Only until one of them gets caught in the cross fire."

"We're not gonna let that happen."

"It could happen right now. Tonight. Look at them all. Don't they realize they're standing around a live target?"

He followed her gaze, scanned the people milling around.

"Will Ahearn was here," Beth said. "He told me that if I still wanted my deposit back, he'd return it and tear up the contract."

"Really? What did you say?"

"I told him I couldn't think about it right now."

"That's probably for the best." Then he said, "I think they're starting to thin out."

"I wish they'd hurry it up."

He frowned, then, as a sound made its way to him. "Is that the phone?"

Beth tipped her head, listening, then nodded. "I'll get it." She turned to head toward the telephone, but Josh kept pace. He didn't want to be far from her tonight. Something was off; he felt it in his gut, a nervous, hyperalert state. Maybe it was because he expected her write-up in the paper to spur Mordecai into action. Or maybe it was instinct. He didn't know which, and he wasn't willing to take any chances.

Beth reached the phone first, picked it up, then handed it to Joshua. "It's for you."

He took it, covered the mouthpiece. "Stay close, okay, Beth?"

Her lips pulled into a slight smile, and she nodded.

Josh brought the phone to his ear. "This is Joshua Kendall."

"Josh, hi. Mark Malone. We just wanted to call and see whether you had any idea exactly when Bryan will be coming out."

For a second Josh went blank. "You mean—when he'll be coming back here?"

"No, when he'll be flying out here."

His throat went dry, and his eyes sought Beth's. She frowned at him and rose to her feet. "Mark, Bryan was supposed to have arrived yesterday. Are you telling me he never got there?"

He heard the swift intake of breath before the other man said, "We had a call from Bry. He told us there'd been a change of plans, that he'd be coming out in a couple of days."

"Bryan's not there." The words fell flatly from Joshua's lips.

"No, Joshua, he's not here. Are you telling me he's not with you?"

"No. Listen, I have to go. If you hear from him again, call me immediately. All right?"

"Sure. Damn, Joshua, I'm so sorry about this. If there's anything—"

"I know. Just...just call if you hear from him." Josh put down the phone. He felt dizzy, shocky and slightly panicked—not like a trained law enforcement professional at all. More like a frightened parent.

Beth was gripping his shoulders. "Bryan didn't go to California?"

He shook his head.

"God, where is he?"

"I don't know. I don't..."

Beth turned, saw that some of the others in the room had noticed something was up, were watching her and Josh, speaking softly, looking worried. She signaled to Arthur Stanton, who frowned at her, glanced at Josh, and then rushed across the room.

"Bryan never got to California," Beth told him.

"What?"

Josh lifted his head, forced himself to recount the facts. "He phoned the people he was supposed to be visiting, told them his plans had changed. Jesus, Art, I don't know where my son is."

"Okay, okay. Calm down. Did he board the flight?"

Josh looked at Beth, shook his head. "I don't know. We dropped him at the airport. God, I should have stayed, seen him off. Damn security. I should have insisted."

"This isn't your fault, Josh," Beth said. She looked to Arthur. "You can find out, can't you? That way at least we'll know where to start looking."

"I can find out. Five minutes. I need the flight info."

Josh looked down at the notepad on the table beside the phone, where he'd scrawled the flight information when he'd ordered the ticket. He tore off the page and handed it to Arthur. Art took it, pulled a cell phone from his pocket and walked away while punching numbers.

"He didn't want to go," Josh said softly. "He threw a fit about it, and then all of a sudden, he changed his mind."

"If he called them, Josh, he must have been all right."

"We don't know that."

She closed her eyes, and Josh knew she was as afraid for his son as he was.

Arthur was coming back, Chief Frankie at his side, her eyes worried. "He never boarded the flight," Arthur said. "Which means your son is probably still here in town, Joshua."

"Yeah," Josh murmured. "And so is Mordecai Young."

"It's not a big place. We'll find him."

"Get me a photograph," Frankie said. "We'll get flyers made immediately." Then she turned to the people still gathered in the room. "People, can I have your attention? We have a situation here. And we could sure use your help."

Beth looked out the window. "Oh, God," she whispered. "It's starting to snow."

Bryan's mind was working overtime. Just when the sound of the lunatic's friendly voice had him ready to bolt, he stopped himself, gripped Dawn's arm and stopped her, too. "Don't run, Dawn."

"Are you crazy?"

He shook his head. "I think that's what he wants us to do."

She frowned at him, but remained still—stiff, alert and terrified, but still. And poised to take flight at the slightest movement from Mordecai's direction.

"He can't see us any more than we can see him," Bryan whispered. "It's pitch-black in these woods. We can't even see each other unless we're standing as close as we are right now. The only way he can keep following us is by sound. We keep crashing through the forest, plowing into limbs and tripping over stumps. We've been making it easy for him."

"He knows we're here," she whispered. "He could be creeping closer, even now."

"Every time we stop, he stops, too. Then he calls out to us, tries to shake us up, get us running again, so he can hear where we are."

"But we can't just sit here and wait for him."

"We're not going to. We're gonna move, but we're gonna be so quiet, the bastard can't follow us. Okay?"

She stared at him, her eyes wide in the darkness, but she nodded. "Okay."

He pushed himself upright, off the tree where he'd stopped to rest, looked around. He could see a distance of about three feet in any direction. No farther. He picked a direction, not angling up and left as he'd been doing, but instead veering sharply to the right. He walked, placing his feet lightly, carefully. Dawn did the same.

"Bryan, where are you?" Mordecai called. "Come on, you can't hide from me forever."

Wanna bet, you sick bastard? Bryan stepped again, slowly, carefully. He made no sound, and Dawn was as quiet as he was—maybe even a little quieter. He heard nothing to indicate that Mordecai was following. So he kept going.

He told himself not to feel overconfident, not to underestimate the guy. Hell, if Bryan could move silently

through the woods, Mordecai probably could, as well.
And then there were his voices and spirit guides, who,
according to Dawn, were not all in his head and were
sometimes deadly accurate.

God, even if he outmaneuvered the loon, he was still in
more than a little trouble. He had no idea where the hell
he was. He knew the way back was downhill, but this
mountain felt as wide as it was tall, and he could go downhill and still end up miles away from his goal.

It was dark. And now that they were walking, virtually
tiptoeing through the woods instead of running, it was getting colder and colder. The air chilled his nose and face. His
hands were cold, and he wished for a pair of gloves. The
breath in his lungs was icy, and he exhaled thick clouds of
steam and wondered if they were visible from very far
away.

"Bryyy-annn. I'm still following you."

Bryan closed his eyes and swore in a harsh whisper. It
wasn't working; the bastard was still keeping up.

Dawn was going to freeze before long. Hell, out here
overnight, they both might. Then he glimpsed a pair of
headlights moving along a road far below. He nudged
Dawn. "Look. Look down there."

She looked, saw what he saw, nodded. "So?"

"Listen to me, Dawn. I have a plan."

She looked at him. "I hope it's better than the last one."

He nodded. "It is, but you're not going to like it. You
saw the car, the way it moved around the base of this hill.
If you go down, you're gonna hit that road, and from there
you can find your way to help. Get hold of my dad, tell
him what's going on."

He spoke emphatically, but in whispers. He was terrified this wouldn't work, but he vowed he wouldn't go far
until he was sure it had.

"You think I'm going to leave you out here all alone?" She shook her head firmly. "No way, Bry."

"You have to. If we don't get some help, we're either going to freeze to death or he's going to catch us. One of us has to go for help."

"Why don't we both go?"

"Because he would follow. And he might catch us before we made it down there."

"So you want me to go alone and just leave you here?"

He nodded.

"It won't work. He's just as likely to follow me."

"No, he won't, because I'm gonna hide you so well a rabbit couldn't find you, and then I'm gonna make so much noise crashing off in the opposite direction that he'll be sure to follow me. Once I get a ways out, I'll stop, listen for him. If he's not still on my trail, I'll come right back, in case he's on to you. But if he does follow me, I'll keep leading him upward. Once you're sure he's long gone, you head down toward that road. Mark the spot where you come out of the woods, so you can tell them where to start looking. Okay?"

She blinked at him.

"Dawn, you've gotta get me some help. I'm the one he's after. He doesn't care that you're out here. Please, do this."

"You think I don't know what you're doing? This is a typical guy stunt. Protect the helpless female, lead the bad guy away and send her scurrying for help."

He put a hand on her cheek. "If he caught up to us and something happened to you...I don't know what I'd do."

Her lips trembled, though she tried to look angry. "Macho garbage."

"I can handle this if I don't have to worry about you, Dawn. And I can move faster on my own."

"Liar."

He sighed, not sure what to do. The next thing he knew, he was leaning closer, kissing her, wrapping his arms around her and holding her against him. He tasted salt, knew she was crying. When he lifted his head away, he cupped her neck in his hand, his face close to hers, and whispered, "We can't handle him alone, Dawn. We need help. It's not macho to admit that, but I don't have a choice here. I need you to get word to my father. I'm counting on it."

She sniffed, nodded. "All right." Bryan heard footsteps in the distance, then crunching of underbrush. Still many yards away, though. "Come on, it's now or never. He'll be close enough to hear what we're doing soon. Get under this pile of deadfall. I'll cover you up and then lead him away."

She let him lead her. He crouched down, lifting fallen limbs and briars enough so that she could crawl underneath. She couldn't get all the way inside, but enough. He lowered the brush again, rearranged some of the limbs on top, then added some more from the ground nearby.

"Don't move until you're sure he's gone. Even if it takes a while. If he doesn't follow me, I'll come back. Okay?"

"Be safe, Bryan. Be careful. I'll be fast."

"Don't be fast. Quiet's more important. At least till you get down there a ways."

"All right." She sniffled. "God, I hate this."

"I do, too. I'm going now."

"Bye, Bryan."

"See you later, Dawn."

"We're going to find him." Beth had said it a dozen times in the past couple of hours. But if she couldn't convince herself it was true, she didn't suppose she had much hope of convincing Josh.

"I can't stand this waiting." He was pacing the floor. He'd pushed his hands through his hair so many times it was sticking up all over, and she swore there were worry lines etched into his brow that hadn't been there before.

"I don't like it, either." She sent a resentful glance toward the living room where Arthur Stanton had commandeered her phone lines as well as his own cell phone and a computer he must have had in his car. "He has troops on the way, he tells me. And he says it as if it ought to give me cause for celebration."

"It should," Josh said. "You'll have a lot more protection."

"Yeah. Let's not forget what happened to me the last time government troops came to the rescue. One of them put a bullet in my gut."

She saw him turn away quickly, thought he had winced at her words, reminded herself he was the one going through hell right now, not her. She moved toward him, slid her hands up his back and curled them over his shoulders. "But it'll be good when they get here, because it'll be that many more people looking for Bryan."

He sighed. "I want to be out looking for him myself."

"So do I. We'll go, just as soon as we have some idea where to look. Whether that government watchdog in there likes it or not."

He nodded. "We should have something soon. It was nice of that guy who owns the print shop to run off all those flyers for us."

"Stanley Kipp," she said. "One of Maude's many friends. So were all the others who showed up here tonight. By now they've got the town papered in those flyers, and have spread the word far and wide that he's missing."

"We got a hit," Arthur said, slamming down the telephone. He came across the room to where Joshua and Beth were alternately pacing and sitting. "Bryan spent last night at a motel outside town." He licked his lips and averted his eyes.

"What else? What aren't you telling me?" Joshua asked, reading his face.

Arthur sighed. "Josh, uh, he wasn't alone."

Josh's brows went up.

"Oh, hell. The girl," Beth said softly.

Josh swung his gaze to her, looking astounded. "What girl?"

"I didn't know what to tell you. There was a...an article of girls' clothing...on his bedroom floor the other day. I had a feeling he'd struck up a romance with one of the local girls."

"He had a girl—in his bedroom?"

"Josh, he's seventeen."

Josh gaped at her, then stared at Arthur. "This girl was with him in the motel?"

"Apparently, yes. But they were in a room with two beds, Josh."

"Oh, well, *that's* reassuring. Here I am scared to death he's been abducted by an insane murderer, and he's holed up in a cheap motel with some—"

"*Let me in, Goddammit!*"

The shrill cry came from the front porch. It was a girl's voice. And one Beth knew as well as she knew her own.

20

Beth went rigid at the sound of that cry, then surged to the front door ahead of the men, both of whom were telling her to wait, and yanked it open. The police officer Frankie had stationed on the porch had his hands on the outer arms of a girl who was struggling to break free.

"Let her go!" Beth's voice came out firm and deep, a tone of command so powerful it startled her. The cop turned to look over his shoulder at her, and the girl stopped struggling and looked up at her, her eyes desperate and damp. Straggles of blond hair had escaped the knit cap she wore, and there were leaves and bits of berry briar tangled in them and clinging to the hat. Her face was scratched and smeared with mud. So were the front of her coat, the knees and bottoms of her jeans, her shoes. And her hands...

She tore free of the cop and flung herself into Beth's arms.

"You know this girl, Ms. Slocum?"

Beth nodded, holding her daughter close, stroking her back. "Dawny, my God, what's happened to you?"

"Dawn?" Joshua repeated the name, and Beth caught his eye and nodded once, then tried to focus on the broken words that punctuated Dawn's sobs and gulps.

Mordecai and *forest* and *Bryan*.

Beth gripped her shoulders and stared down at her

face. "Slow down, take a breath and tell me what happened."

Dawn sniffled, nodded jerkily and wiped the back of one muddy hand across her face, smearing more mud there. "Mordecai is after Bryan."

"You know where Bryan is?" Josh shouted.

"I know where he was. I—I didn't want to leave him. He made me come for help. I can show you."

Josh gripped her arm. "Let's go."

"Joshua, for God's sake," Beth said. "Look at her. She's half-frozen, wet through, scratched and bruised and God knows what else. She needs—"

"No." Dawn put a hand on Beth's shoulder. "No, we have to go now. I'm fine."

"We can take my car," Arthur Stanton said, pulling out his key ring, aiming it and hitting a button. The car came to life in the driveway, headlights flashing on, engine humming softly.

"I'll take mine, too, and use the radio to call for more help," Frankie Parker said.

The others who had gathered in the house were already thundering down the porch steps, shouting about getting search parties organized and who had ATVs that could be used as they got into their vehicles.

Dawn was shivering, her hand like a block of ice when she closed it around Beth's and tugged her toward the waiting vehicles.

"Wait." Beth pulled free and ran back inside, yanking her coat and Josh's from the closet, and a blanket from the back of the sofa, then rejoining Dawn outside. They jumped into the back seat of Arthur's car. Josh got into the front with Stanton.

As they pulled away, the chief followed. Beth held Dawn in her arms, stroking her shoulders, trying to comfort her as snow fell in the twin beams of the car's headlights.

"Here," Dawn said when they'd gone only a few yards. "Turn off onto that dirt road there. I walked along this thing for I don't know how long, looking for a house, a car, anything. But I marked the spot where I came out of the woods—it'll be on the right side."

"What did you use to mark it, Dawn?" Beth asked her.

"One of my socks. The other one is at the spot where I last saw Bryan."

"He was okay? When you last saw him?" Joshua asked.

Dawn nodded. "He was fine. And it was only a couple of hours ago."

Joshua sighed in relief, then lifted his head again, facing Dawn from the front seat. "You have to tell us what the hell has been going on. Have you been with Bryan ever since he supposedly left for California? Hiding out in a motel outside of town?"

Beth saw Dawn's eyes widen, and then they shot straight to hers. "It's not like it sounds. I swear we weren't—we didn't—it wasn't anything sexual."

"Well, then, what the hell was it?" Josh asked.

"Jesus, no wonder Bryan can't talk to you!"

"Dawn—" Beth warned.

"I'm sorry, but it's true. God, does he really think we would have risked our lives just for a chance to get laid?"

Josh's face registered shock at the frankness of her words, but Beth wasn't shocked at all. "Cut him some slack, Dawn," Beth said. "He's worried about his son. That's all."

Dawn relaxed back on the seat. "That's no reason to take it out on me." She faced Beth, addressing her, not Joshua. "Bry and I were in touch online. When Maude died, I got the feeling something was up, and then your house exploded, and I knew. Mom and Sean were out of town on a story, so I decided to come up here and make sure you were okay."

Beth closed her eyes. God, Julie didn't even know Dawn was here?

"Once I got here, I convinced Bry to hide me so you wouldn't go ratting me out or sending me home. He hid me out up in his room." She turned to Josh. "Where I slept on the bed, and he took the floor." She sent him a look that should have wilted him as she spoke, then turned her eyes right back to Beth's again. "And we started doing a little digging. We thought we had a good shot at helping find Mordecai, so when you all decided to send Bryan packing, we faked you out and checked into a motel." She looked up at Joshua. "A room with two beds."

"All right, all right. I'm sorry I offended you," Josh said. "But I still don't see what drove Mordecai to go after my son."

Dawn lowered her eyes. "He lost a daughter," she said. "Maybe he's looking for a replacement."

Beth felt her daughter's pain, and she saw the sympathy appear on Josh's face, as well, but before either of them could say anything, Dawn jerked her head up again. "Slow down, Mr. Stanton. It's up here somewhere."

Arthur slowed the car to a crawl, and everyone scanned the roadside for Dawn's marker as she went on. "Bryan and I staked out the funeral, and sure enough, Mordecai showed up. He was watching the two of you. We followed him when he left, found out where he was staying. But he spotted us, and we had to run for it. He recognized Bryan somehow. I don't even know how he knows him. I don't think he ever realized who I was." She paused there. "That's odd, don't you think? I mean, even if he didn't see me clearly, wouldn't that sixth sense of his or his guides or whatever have told him?"

"Honey, he's not right," Beth said. "Who knows why his mind or his senses work the way they do?"

"There it is. That's the spot where I came out of the woods!" Dawn thrust her arm between the two men in the front seat, pointing excitedly.

Arthur pulled over, and the headlights picked out the dirt-streaked white sock knotted around a low-hanging branch that stuck out over the road.

"What happened tonight, Dawn?" Joshua asked. He asked it gently, his expression no longer hostile.

"Bry and I were lurking outside Maude's house, waiting for you guys to leave so we could get in. I was going to look for Arthur Stanton's number, or maybe Lieutenant Jackson's, so we could phone someone and tell them where Mordecai was. I wasn't sure we could trust the local police, and if we told you or Beth, you'd have sent me back home and Bry off to California." She shrugged. "Though Bry did insist that if we couldn't find the number tonight, we had to come clean with you. Anyway, Mordecai walked up on us in the woods. We ran, he chased. After a while Bry hid me in some brush and ran off in the other direction." She lowered her head. "He led him away from me so I could come down here for help."

Josh nodded. "So he's up there?" As he spoke, he opened the car door, got out and stood staring at the rising, forested mountain. Snow was falling around him, big flakes of it drifting at a steadier rate than before.

Dawn opened her door and got out, as well. She pointed to a stream. "I found that stream and followed it down, so it would be easier to find my way back up. Follow it up a long ways. There's a spot where the slope levels off and the beavers dammed the stream up to make a tiny pond. When you get to that point, the stream veers right. You need to keep going straight up. About fifty yards, to the pile of deadfall where Bry hid me. I tied the other sock there to mark it. From there, Bry headed up, but at an angle off to the left." She pointed to illustrate.

Joshua nodded. Beth and Arthur had gotten out of the car to join them, and Frankie's squad car had pulled up behind them. "I'm going up," Josh said. "Arthur, you and the chief can organize the volunteers, form a search party. Maybe get us a helicopter out here."

"And someone ought to check out the house he was using," Arthur added.

Josh shot a hand to his arm. "I don't give a rat's ass about the house or about catching Mordecai, Arthur. I want every resource devoted to finding my son. Do you understand?"

He nodded. "After he's safe," he corrected himself.

Josh turned to Beth, and suddenly his face changed. It was as if he were suddenly torn. "Beth—"

"Don't even start with that protective bull, Josh. You have to go after your son. I'll join you in the search—just as soon as I get Dawn situated."

He thinned his lips, shot a look at Arthur Stanton. "Don't leave her alone. Not for one fucking minute. Keep her safe until I get back."

Arthur looked surprised. Then Josh snapped an arm around Beth's waist and pulled her to him, bent his head and kissed her hard. "Be safe, Beth."

"You, too," she whispered, cupping his face with her hand. "Find him, Josh."

He nodded, then turned and started up into the woods.

Beth watched him out of sight, then turned to Dawn. "Where is this house Mordecai was using?"

"That little town between Blackberry and Pineville."

"Pinedale," Beth corrected, then looked at Frankie. "She means Bonnie Brook."

"Yeah, that's it," Dawn said. "It's on the main road, one of a whole row of big Victorians all clustered together. Pretty."

"I know where that is," Chief Frankie said. "Which one is he in?"

"The one with the pink-and-green trim."

Frankie nodded. "I'll get one or two of my men on that. Just to watch it, in case Mordecai tries to go back there tonight."

"But Josh said—" Dawn began.

"Josh is upset," Beth interrupted. "If Mordecai gets Bryan, chances are that's where he would take him. Frankie's right—we have to cover it. And also, organize all the searchers we can get our hands on."

"I'm on that," Frankie said. She was already reaching into her car for the radio.

Beth put an arm around Dawn. "I'm going to take Dawn back to my house."

"Not alone you're not," Arthur said. He held open his car door. Beth got inside. Dawn followed, and Arthur Stanton drove them back to the onetime inn.

"There's a hot bath just about ready, Dawn." Beth handed her a steaming cup of cocoa. "Take this with you and go soak."

Dawn took the cocoa between her palms and took a sip, but she was shaking her head even before she swallowed it. "I just want to put on some dry clothes and head right back out. We have to look for Bryan."

Beth put a firm hand on her shoulder. "One teenager at risk is more than enough, Dawn. You're going to soak in that tub and drink your cocoa. And *I'm* going to contact your mother."

Dawn thrust out her lower lip. "She and Sean are in

D.C. Doing preelection reporting for News Four. They won't be back for another three days."

"And you have her number there?"

Dawn sighed, but nodded.

"Write it down for me before you get into the tub."

Sighing as if Beth were asking her to surrender a kidney, Dawn turned to the telephone stand and scribbled a number on the pad there. "Don't send her into a panic. Tell her I'm okay, but I'm damn well not leaving here until this is over."

"Dawn, don't be ridiculous. This doesn't involve you."

She lifted her eyes, locked them with Beth's. "He's my father. If it doesn't involve me, who the hell *does* it involve?"

Beth frowned at her daughter. "It's not your responsibility."

"I feel like it is. I feel like I have to see this through to the end. And I know you understand that, Beth, because I know it's how you feel, too."

Beth had to avert her eyes.

"If you send me home, I'll run away and come back the first chance I get." She sighed, turned and headed up the stairs. "Tell Mom I'll call her before bed. She'll want to know when she's going to get the chance to lecture me."

"I'll tell her."

Then she was out of sight. Beth heard the bathroom door close, sighed and went to the telephone. She understood all too well what Dawn was feeling, though she had to admit Dawn's feelings came as a surprise to her. She was too young to take on so much.

Sighing, she picked up the phone. This was not a call she looked forward to making.

Mordecai was furious when the guides called him off the hunt. "By God, why now? I'm so close!"

They're going to the house, Mordecai. You have business to take care of. Leave the boy. There will be another chance with him.

"Another twenty minutes," he snapped. "In another twenty minutes I can have the boy and be on the way out of here."

Searchers are fanning into the woods even now. If you're caught, Mordecai, your mission ends unfulfilled. You won't have brought Lizzie to her rightful end, and you won't have passed your gifts on to your heir. It will all have been for nothing.

"To hell with my mission! Jesus, I'm tired of it. I'm so tired of it all."

Suddenly Mordecai's head filled with a roar, like that of an avalanche, or the thundering floodwaters of biblical lore. So loud it was deafening. So powerful, it filled his skull with pressure that threatened to split it apart. He pressed his palms to his ears, his face twisting in agony, and dropped to his knees there in the forest.

Gradually the roar faded, leaving him with a pounding headache, his entire body trembling and weak. "I'm...sorry. Forgive me my pathetic human condition. I'll do as you say."

Go down, get to your vehicle and activate the counter measures you prepared for the house.

"And after that?"

We'll guide you. Trust in Spirit, Mordecai. Spirit knows.

Closing his eyes, still on his knees, Mordecai bowed his head. "Thy will be done."

Beth held her breath waiting. Then Julie picked up her cell with a brisk, "Julie Jones."

"Hi, Jewel. It's Lizzie."

There was a pause. Her friend was probably startled to hear from her, especially in D.C.

"Honey? What's wrong? Is everything okay?"

Beth drew a breath, let it out. "Dawny's here."

"What?"

"She got wind of what was happening here and came out. Apparently she's been lurking around for a few days now, and we didn't even know she was here."

She could almost see Julie's brow furrowing. "Something's happening there?"

"You mean it hasn't hit the wires yet?" Then again, she thought, it had only been a few hours since the paper ran her story. "She's safe, Jewel. She's upstairs now. Arthur Stanton is here, and by morning he'll have this place crawling with Feds."

"Is Mordecai there, Beth?"

Beth sighed. "Yeah. He's in town. But it's no secret. They know where he's been staying, and there's a team headed over there now to check his place out." She stopped there, but Julie was waiting for her to go on. "Stanton sent me another bodyguard. A decent one this time. His name is Joshua Kendall. Dawn and Joshua's son, Bryan, have been playing detective. Mordecai saw them, went after them, wound up chasing them through the woods."

"Oh, my God," Julie whispered. Beth could hear Sean's voice beyond her, asking what was wrong. "We're checking out," Julie told him. "Dawn's in trouble."

"She's fine, Julie. Bryan led Mordecai off in another direction and gave her time to slip away. She showed up at the door tonight, and that's the first I even knew she was in town."

"When I finish hugging her, I think I'll kill her," Julie said. Then, "Sean, do you have Lieutenant Jackson's number with you?"

"Jax?" Sean replied, his voice coming from very close to the phone. "Yeah, I've got it. Hold on."

Beth went on. "Bryan's still in the woods somewhere. Joshua's looking, and the police chief is forming search parties to go help. I'd be there, too, but…"

"But you don't dare leave Dawn."

"I don't want to leave her. And she won't leave me. Jewel, it's as if she feels like she has some kind of obligation to do something about Mordecai."

"Yeah, we've talked about it. You can't reason with her. I tried taking her for therapy after everything that happened last year, but that didn't help, either."

Beth sighed. "It's not right."

"I know. Look, we'll be there as soon as we can."

"It's not going to do any good. Look, either he's going to come after me, or he's going to leave town. Your being here only gives him a wider range of targets."

"We'll be there."

She heard Sean's voice but couldn't tell what he was saying. Julie said, "Hold on, hon," and covered the phone with her hand. Their voices were muffled. Then Julie's came back on the line. "It's not going to be as easy for us to get there as I thought. There's an ice storm here. Sleet and freezing rain. I didn't realize how bad it was, but Sean says the airports are canceling flights. Jesus, I hate this."

"It'll be all right."

"I'm calling Cassie Jackson. I don't know what she can do from Syracuse, but she's the best cop I know. And she has a vested interest in Dawn. And Mordecai."

"Have her call me. But meanwhile, don't worry, Jewel. I'm watching over her."

"Easier said than done. But I know you are. Can I talk to her?"

"She said she'd call you before bed. I've got her soaking in the tub right now."

"God, poor thing. Is she all right?"

"She got pretty cold, plenty wet, had a few scratches and bruises from stumbling through the forest in the dark, and I imagine she's exhausted, as well. Not to mention scared."

"She must have been terrified."

"Still is. For Bryan, I mean. She wanted to change clothes and go out looking, but I wouldn't let her."

"Yeah, well, if there's a window in that bathroom, you might want to nail it shut. If she *can* get out, she *will*."

A chill rippled over the nape of Beth's neck. "Don't worry," she assured Jewel. "I'm watching her like a hawk. She'll call you soon."

"Okay, honey. Take care."

"You, too." Beth hung up the phone. Then she hurried up the stairs, stopped at the bathroom door and knocked on it. "Dawn?"

No answer.

She pounded this time, then tried the knob. It was locked, but Dawn wasn't answering. Beth stood back and delivered a sharp kick to the door. The lock consisted of a small bolt that slid into a bracket on the frame. The bracket was held in the door casing by two screws, and her kick was stronger than the wood that held them. The door popped open, and Beth stared in at the bathtub brimming with water and the open window beyond it.

"Dammit."

Beth raced along the hall, checking bedrooms until she came to her own. Dawn wasn't there. "At least I know where to start looking," she whispered. "Be okay, Dawn."

Beth went to the window to fling it open. "Dawn! Dammit, Dawny, you wait for me or I'll kick your ass when I catch up!"

"What's going on?" Arthur Stanton's voice came from

behind her, and Beth turned to see him standing in the hallway.

"Dawn sneaked out to go looking for Bryan. I'm going after her." She yanked open a drawer, searching for the items she had managed to get unpacked. Tugged out two unmatched gloves and a knit hat. Then she grabbed her thickest surviving socks and pulled them on, as well, turned and headed down the stairs.

"You should stay put," Arthur said. "I've got men ten minutes out, I can send them as soon as they arrive."

"I'll leave a breadcrumb trail for them." She opened the closet door and found Maude's winter boots. She'd bought the hot name brand, long before they were the favored footwear of inner city youths. Probably five years old, barely worn and likely worth three times the purchase price at the moment. Leather on bottom, waterproof rubber on top, fleece lined and heavily laced.

She stomped her feet into them, jerked the laces tight and tied them, then grabbed Maude's parka off the hanger and put it on. She headed into the kitchen and opened the cupboard where Maude had kept emergency supplies. First aid kit, candles, flashlights, lanterns. She grabbed a flashlight and dashed out the back door and across the lawn, ignoring Arthur, who was chasing after her and shouting at her to wait.

She went to the edge of the woods, stopped and snapped on the light, looking around. Stanton was beside her within a second. "This is where she and Bryan first encountered Mordecai," she told him. "They took off running—that way, I think. She'll take the same path they did then, I imagine."

"Look, Beth, if I don't wait for my men, they're not going to know what to do when they get here, much less where everyone is."

"You got walkie-talkies?" she asked.

He frowned. "Yeah. In the car."

"Get me one. I'll go after Dawn. You wait here for your men and then come after us. We can stay connected by radio."

He nodded. "It's a good plan."

"I'll wait sixty seconds for that radio, Arthur," she said. "And then, if you're not back, I'll go without it."

Joshua trudged steadily through the darkness, up the steep hill, following the stream Dawn had pointed out. The dread in his belly grew with every step he took. It was so big now, he felt close to vomiting. But he couldn't let himself stop long enough.

God, if anything happened to Bryan...

He couldn't take it, that was all.

When he reached the place where the stream bed curved sharply right, at the beaver dam and the little pond, he went straight and began looking for Dawn's signal. He found it after walking a good distance—maybe close to the fifty yards the girl had estimated—thanks to the beam of his flashlight. He shone it around the ground, locating the pile of deadfall where Dawn had been hiding.

Hell of a man, his son was, hiding her and leading the maniac away. God damn, he better be all right.

From there, Dawn said Bryan had gone up the slope on an angle that veered to the left. Josh followed, but he disliked not having an exact idea of where his son was. Bryan could have changed direction at any time, and probably had, to try to lose Mordecai.

He had the most hollow, horrible feeling in the pit of his stomach. The temperature had dropped to a bone-numbing level, and the fluffy snowflakes had by now become a heavy snowfall. Just what they needed.

"Hold on, Bryan. I'm coming, I promise. Just hold on."

* * *

Bryan had hiked about as far as he figured he was capable of hiking. He was so damned cold his teeth kept starting to chatter, and he had to clamp his jaw hard against it, for fear the insane man would hear. He was shivering so hard he thought he'd strained some muscles. God, it was cold.

His fingers were numb and burning. His feet felt like heavy lead lumps as he pushed on, stomping over uneven ground, tripping more often than he had before, and landing harder. And yet every time he paused to catch his breath and strained his ears to listen, there were sounds. Snapping twigs, rustling brush, swaying limbs. Some of it might have been the wind or animals scurrying through the forest, but he couldn't be sure. One thing he did know: he couldn't go on much farther.

He had started scanning the forest for a place to hole up about the time the snow started falling. He estimated it had been maybe three hours since he'd sent Dawn for help. And the fact that he wasn't seeing any sign of help on the way made him worry about her. God, he hoped she'd made it back okay. Maybe it had been a mistake to send her off on her own. Maybe something had happened. She might be lost or hurt or…

He closed his eyes, and before he could prevent it, the thought rushed through his head that he wished his father were there. He reminded himself that he was angry at his father, that none of this would be happening if not for his father screwing everything up, just like he'd screwed up when he shot Beth in the first place.

Yeah, trying to do his job and eaten up with guilt ever since.

He'd screwed up again by taking on this job of protecting her without knowing all the facts.

Probably out of guilt again. Protect an innocent to make up for having killed one. Even though he really hadn't.

Screwed up even more by not telling her the truth.

Out of fear of losing her. Dawn's right about that. The idiot loves her and doesn't even know it.

And he screwed up even more than that by trying to send Bryan away when things got dangerous.

Yeah, to protect me.

He glimpsed a fallen tree up ahead. Its roots had pulled up from the ground when it toppled, and they formed a plate the size of a small flying saucer at its base. Bryan glanced behind him, then walked around to the underside of the upright root platter. A huge hollow in the ground marked the spot where the roots had once rested. White snowflakes were beginning to gather and stick on the blackened earth. Up close to the base, where the bottom of the root plate rose up from the ground, long, twisting tendrils tangled in thick masses.

Making his decision in that instant, Bryan crawled into the tangled mass. He sat on the cold, damp ground, his coat around him, drew his knees to his chest and wrapped his arms around them. He tugged his hood tighter around his head and bent his head to rest it against his knees.

And then he waited and he worried. He probably shouldn't have stopped. He really shouldn't rest for very long. He could easily freeze to death if he spent the night, so he would only rest for just a short while. Maybe give Mordecai time to move on past him in the darkness, and then he would get moving again. Keep his circulation going, keep his body temperature up.

He yawned. God, he was tired.

What if Mordecai found him? Did he really want to sit there and just wait for the man? Did he really think that lunatic wasn't going to see right through all this?

Maybe he should move now.

No. No, he had to wait. Wait it out. He had to rest, and

he wasn't going to find a better place than this. He was even starting to feel a little less cold than he had before.

God, he wished his father were there. He sure hoped Dawn had made it home okay. He hated to think she might be outside in the cold, in the dark, hiding out the way he was. So he just wouldn't think it. He would picture her safe and warm, instead. He would picture her rallying the troops to come after him.

Yeah. That was better. And her crazy bastard of an old man wasn't going to find him, either. His guides weren't going to tell him shit, because if a buggy fuck like Mordecai had spirit guides, then a decent human being like Bryan must have some, too, right? Maybe he couldn't hear them. Maybe they didn't impart secret information to him, but they must be out there. And if they were, then this would be a real good time for them to get active. Maybe toss some kind of a veil over his hiding place and outmaneuver the other guy's guides.

Yeah, right. Now *he* was thinking like the lunatic. He didn't believe in any of that crap.

He yawned again. It was hard to stay awake. At least he was far less cold than he had been before. How long had he been out here now? Six, seven hours? Maybe he was adjusting to it. Like when you went in swimming and the water felt cold at first, but then you got used to it, and it started feeling warmer. It must be like that.

He sighed and let his eyes fall closed. This was really much better than trudging through the woods and freezing. Just resting, just for a few minutes. He would feel a lot better later on.

21

—▶ ◀—

Josh heard motors rumbling and turned toward the sound to see a beam of light far in the distance but bouncing ever closer. It picked its way through the trees, and he moved cautiously toward it.

Then another light came behind the first one, bounding and jumping, the motor sounds growing louder. He took cover behind a tree and watched, until the light from the rear showed him the source of the light in the lead: an ATV. He realized that was what both vehicles must be and kept watching until the front one stopped. The rear vehicle pulled up beside it and stopped, as well, and then the motors went silent.

Voices rose, calling for Bryan. And then they called out for him, as well. "Joshua!"

Among them, he heard women's voices—Beth's voice.

Josh stepped out into the open and shouted back at them. "I'm here," he called, and trudged closer to where the vehicles waited. As soon as he stepped into the glow of the headlights, Beth ran toward him, and he caught her in his arms, amazed at the power of her embrace. How tightly she clutched him. How good it felt. How much he'd managed to miss her in spite of everything else. Or maybe because of it. Maybe he needed this woman to get through the crises in his life.

"Is there any sign of Bryan?" she asked, searching his face, her cheeks pink, eyes glistening.

"No, not yet. You shouldn't be out here, Beth, it's cold, and Dawn is—"

"Dawn is with us." She released her hold on him, so she could look him in the eye. "I can't keep her home, Josh. She sneaked out and took off to join the search the first time I turned my back. I went after her on foot, and then Frankie and Arthur caught up with us on the ATVs."

He looked past her to see Arthur Stanton on one of the four-wheelers. The man was sixty; it had to be a tough ride for him. On the other was Chief Frankie Parker, looking as comfortable as if she'd been born bounding through the woods on a four-wheeler. Dawn was riding behind her.

Frowning, Joshua slid an arm around Beth's shoulders and walked over to the waiting vehicles. "What's the situation?" he asked.

Arthur said, "We've got twenty locals with ATVs combing the woods. I split my men up among them. Other groups are searching on foot. One person in each group has a radio. A local hardware store owner brought us a bunch of extras for the civilians. We're coordinating on channel nine. What's the range on these things, Chief?"

He didn't address her as if he were doubtful of her skills or humoring her, but like one professional addressing another. A colleague.

"Five miles, give or take," Frankie said.

Josh focused on her. "Did you check out the house where Mordecai was staying?"

Frankie narrowed her eyes, and her face went tight.

"I insisted on it, Joshua," Beth said. "I know you said not to, but I thought Mordecai might try to take Bryan back there, if he had him."

"Cagey bastard was ready for that, though," Frankie said.

"What do you mean?"

"He torched the place. That house was engulfed before we ever got there. A neighbor had called it in, but the fire department couldn't do much but keep it from spreading to the surrounding houses. Burned to the ground. More than a century old, a landmark. It's still too hot to dig around, but I'm betting he had it rigged. Might have even set it off by remote control."

"Jesus."

"That's not entirely bad news," Arthur said. "If he torched the house, he likely didn't do it from up here on this mountain. He would have had to get closer. Probably gave up chasing after the boy hours ago."

"That's small comfort, Art. My son is still out here somewhere, and it's getting colder by the minute."

"We're going to find him." Arthur got off his ATV. "Take this one and go on. I'll catch a ride with the next machine to come by."

Joshua wasn't going to argue. He got on the four-wheeler, unsurprised when Beth climbed on behind him.

"Chief, you go with him. You know these woods better than any of us," Arthur added. "But don't go too fast, now, or he'll never be able to keep up." He leaned over Josh. "The way she rides that thing, I suspect she races them cross-country on her days off."

"You sure you'll be all right here, Art?" Joshua asked.

Arthur nodded, holding up his walkie-talkie. "I'll be fine. Beth's got a radio, and so has the chief. Contact me the minute you find Bryan."

Josh nodded, looked at the controls in front of him, turned the key and hit the start button. The machine roared to life. He kicked it into gear and started forward as Beth's arms tightened around his waist.

* * *

Bryan was dreaming. He knew he was dreaming, because he was warm and safe, and because his mom was there. And even though in some part of his mind he knew the past six months had happened—she had died, and he'd lost everything—it felt as if they hadn't. As if all of that were just a dream, and he was home in his own bed, and she was leaning over him, the way she used to do when he was smaller. Kissing his cheek and whispering, "Wake up, Bry. It's time for school."

He smiled a little. His mother hadn't woken him that way since fifth grade. As he got older, she'd started treating him older. She would open his door and call softly to him, and later still, she would just knock. But when he was little, this was always the routine. Her soft kiss on his cheek, her warm breath tickling his ear. "Come on, honey, wake up now. You don't want to be late."

Smiling, Bryan lifted his head, opened his eyes.

He wasn't in his own bed. He was in a dark forest. The damp ground had soaked through the bottom of his coat and his jeans. His arms were wrapped around his knees and covered in a light coating of snow. It was cold. He could see his breath.

And he could hear something. A dull, distant roar.

Bryan looked at his watch, but there wasn't enough light to tell the time, and it didn't have one of those light-up dials. He made a mental note to get one that did, then tried to clear his head and make a guess at how long he'd been sitting there, huddled under the mass of roots. A while, judging by the snow that now coated everything in the woods. An hour, at least, maybe more. Man, it was really coming down.

Was the madman still lurking out there somewhere?

The sounds of the motors grew louder. Then they

faded, maybe stopped, and he heard voices. People…calling his name.

Frowning, he sat up straighter, and the roots around him rustled as puffs of snow fell around him and down the collar of his coat.

In a moment the motors started up again.

God, that had sounded like…

"Dad?"

Hell. He couldn't stay here. Even if Mordecai Young was lurking out there somewhere, he had to risk it. He had to get the hell out of here.

He started to move, only to realize that movement brought pain. His muscles had tightened and cramped. Probably too long in his huddled position in the freezing temperature. He forced his legs to unbend, wincing at the throbbing in his knees but otherwise ignoring it.

Move, he commanded his limbs. And they did. It hurt, and it took a long time, but he managed to work himself free of his shelter, and by the time he was out and able to stand upright, the motors were louder, closer.

God, he thought, keep coming in this direction. Please.

Step by painful step, he began moving toward the motors. It seemed to take forever, but eventually he saw lights. No sound from behind him. He was almost afraid to think he'd given the bad guy the slip, but it was starting to seem as if he might have done just that.

The motors stopped, but the lights stayed on. Voices called his name again. He heard his father's. He heard Dawn's. He called back, but the only thing that came out was a hoarse croak. Swallowing, he cleared his throat and tried again with slightly more success. This time it was a squeak. And still he lumbered forward.

Finally he stepped into the beam of one of those lights.

"Bryan!"

"Hi, Dad." He sank to his knees.

And then his father was there, bending over him, lifting him up, talking so fast Bryan couldn't really follow the words. But his arms were around him, tight and hard, and in the headlights' glow, Bryan saw something he didn't think he had ever seen before. He saw his father cry.

Beth watched Josh turn with his son in his arms and carry him slowly toward the ATVs. In the twin beams of the headlights, the tears on his face glittered like diamonds. And that was the moment, Beth thought, when she realized that she didn't care what secret he was hiding: she loved him. The emotions swamping him…she knew them well. They were her own. She'd felt them, and she knew their depth.

She went to him, vaguely aware of Chief Frankie speaking rapidly into her radio, but she could do nothing to offer Josh any comfort. Their eyes met, though, and she knew that he saw the kindred emotions in her own. It was as if a dam broke, allowing his feelings to flood into her mind and hers into his, until the waters met and melded into one swirling pool.

"Oh, God, is he all right?" Dawn cried, rushing forward, breaking the spell.

"I don't know." He looked past her. "We have to get him down off this mountain."

"It can be done," Frankie said, joining them. "I've had to do it before, hunters have accidents up here all the time. Bring him here, Joshua."

Josh carried his son to the ATV, though it was difficult with Dawn in the way, hovering, touching Bryan's face, speaking to him. Frankie said, "Put him down on the seat. Here, let me help." She guided Bryan's leg over the seat, helped Josh ease him down. "There, let me hold on to him while you get settled in front of him."

Josh looked at her doubtfully.

"Go on."

Josh complied, and then Frankie leaned Bryan against his father's back. Bryan roused a little, lifting his head, looking around as if confused, his eyes unfocused.

"He'll never stay on," Josh said.

"I told you, I've done this before. Beth, come here, and get yourself on behind Bryan. It'll be tight, and you'll have to hold on for dear life, but he won't fall off."

Beth got on behind Bryan, her rear end barely on the seat. Josh shifted forward as far as he could, and Beth slid Bryan ahead, as well, then scooted closer, pinning the half-frozen teenager between her body and Josh's.

Chief Frankie took Beth's hands and guided them to the bars just below hip level on either side. "You hang on here."

"I should hold on to Bryan, shouldn't I?"

"Your body will hold him in place. You don't hold on, you'll be the one getting bounced off the back of this thing. It's not a smooth ride." She sighed. "I'd do it myself, but you're smaller and probably a little stronger." She winked. "Not much, but maybe a little. I'll lead the way. Dawn can still ride with me."

Beth nodded, holding on to the bars.

"Follow me," Chief Frankie said. Then she jumped on the other machine and started it up again.

Josh turned his head, looking back at Beth. "Ready?"

She nodded. "Let's get him home, Josh."

Dr. Granger might not have shown up if he hadn't been so fond of Maude. House calls were obsolete, even in small towns like Blackberry. But Beth knew this was different. Hell, the entire town had been rallying around her since the newspaper article had come out. She had beenMaude's dear friend, her heir, and apparently she had inherited more than just a house from the old woman. She'd inherited an entire community. Now Joshua and Bryan were included in the goodwill being sent her way, so the doctor had come, and was upstairs in the bedroom with Bryan now.

Arthur and two of his men were downstairs, pacing and talking. So were Chief Parker and a handful of her officers. They were handling all the locals. Folks had been coming by in groups ever since the search was called off and word spread that the missing boy had been found. The volunteers and others wanted to know if he was all right and, more than that, whether the evil man who'd destroyed two Blackberry homes and maybe murdered its most beloved citizen was still lurking somewhere.

Between them, the chief and Arthur were doing a good job of reassuring people, thanking them for their concern and sending them on their way.

Beth was grateful for their help. And grateful, too, for the food that had been contributed earlier, since it kept everyone well fed. That gave her more time to hover outside Bryan's door, worrying with his father and Dawn.

Dawn was doing double duty, worrying outside the door while speaking to her irate mother long distance. She'd just hung up when the bedroom door opened and the doctor came out.

He smiled at their expectant faces. "Bryan's suffering from exhaustion and exposure, but nothing's broken, and there's no frostbite. He's going to be fine."

Beth thought Josh might collapse in relief, and she moved closer to his side, slid an arm around his waist to offer her strength.

"I want you to keep the electric blanket on him. His body temperature is still low. If he feels stronger in a couple of hours and wants to, a warm bath would be all right, but not yet, and when you do, don't make it too hot. He's too weak right now."

"I washed the worst of the mud off him when we first got him home," Beth said. "We had to strip off his wet clothes and dress him in warm dry ones anyway."

"You did fine. The bath can wait till morning, if necessary. If he sleeps, don't wake him. Let him rest. Keep him warm. If he gets hungry, go with hot soup, hot tea, hot cocoa, that sort of thing."

Beth was nodding, making mental notes.

Josh said, "Are you sure there's no other damage?"

"Pretty sure," the doctor said. "But I'd still like to see him in my office just as soon as you can get him there. Call in the morning and make an appointment. I'll notify my secretary to make room whenever it's convenient for you. All right?"

"All right. Thank you, Doctor."

Dr. Granger nodded. "Go ahead, go in and see him."

When Dawn took a half step toward the door, Beth took her arm gently. "Let's let his dad have a few minutes with him first, hmm?"

Swallowing, looking impatient but understanding, Dawn nodded. "Sure."

Josh sent Beth a thank-you with his eyes and walked into the bedroom to be with his son. Sighing, Dawn turned to face Beth. "So what are the cops and the Feds doing about Mordecai?"

Beth glanced toward the stairs. "They seem to be of the opinion that he's taken off again."

Dawn's expressive blue eyes narrowed. "But you know better, right?"

Beth didn't answer. She didn't want to give Dawn any excuse to hang around here. As soon as morning came, she had to convince her that this was all over, and that it was time for her to go home.

"Beth, come on. You know him. Better than I do, better than anyone does. You know he won't give up until he's done whatever he came here to do."

Beth licked her lips. "He may have decided to withdraw until all the excitement dies down."

"Not when he thinks you're going back into hiding somewhere else."

Beth drew her brows together and shot Dawn a look.

"I saw the paper. Heard the cops going off about it and took a look for myself. You were trying to force him to make a move."

Beth shrugged. "Maybe I'm tired of hiding."

"He hasn't gone anywhere, Beth. He's out there, some-where, right now." She looked past Beth at some invisible point of nothingness. "I can feel it."

Heaving a sigh, Beth put a hand on Dawn's shoulder. "You never got your bath, did you?"

Dawn eyed her. "Changing the subject 'cause you can't argue and win?"

"Let's take a hot shower, hmm? You can use my bath-room and I'll use Josh's. We'll put on our thick socks and flannel nightgowns, and then we'll curl up by the fire downstairs with a pot of hot cocoa and some marshmal-lows, and we'll catch up."

Dawn swallowed hard. "I have to see Bryan."

"His dad's gonna be in there with him for a while. Be-sides, you don't want him to see you with berry briars in your hair and dirt on your face, do you?" As she asked the question, she reached out and plucked a stray twig from

Dawn's hair. "We can be clean, dry, warm and fortified with cocoa in a half hour, tops. What do you say?"

Sighing, Dawn nodded. "Okay."

Mordecai wrestled the old kerosene space heater down from the shelf on the wall, shook it and was amazed to hear sloshing in the bottom.

Why so surprised, Mordecai? Don't we always provide what you need? Don't we always sustain you?

He sighed, nodding. He had emergency gear in the car, of course. Sleeping bag, a couple of changes of clothes and a stash of MREs. No space heater. Plenty of C-4, wire leads, ignition switches, two types of timers. No more primer cord—he'd used it all up rigging the house to go up in flames. He smiled to himself as he recalled how neatly it had worked. The flick of a button had ignited the flammable cord. He'd run it along the baseboards, through every room of the house. One spark, and the flame flared and traveled like a Fourth of July sparkler along the cord, along the baseboards. It ignited the curtains of each and every window. It traveled behind every piece of furniture, setting off the upholstery. It set the carpet to burning, as well, and within the space of five minutes, the place became an inferno. By the time anyone outside saw flames and dialed 911, the house was already beyond saving.

Mordecai had made certain there would be nothing left but ash.

His guides had told him how.

Just as they always told him what needed to be done. They took care of him, and he felt guilty for doubting them so much lately. But he'd been so obedient for so long, and it seemed the more he did, the more demanding they became. He was running himself ragged and still it wasn't good enough for them. He was beginning to wonder if anything ever would be. He was tired.

He had left the car two miles away, well hidden, and had hiked here with the supplies he needed in a backpack. Now he took a waterproof tin of matches from that backpack, struck one to life and touched it to the wick of the old heater. It caught, and it lit, but as the flames spread, thick, foul-smelling black smoke billowed from the thing.

Waving his hands, Mordecai rushed to one of the shed's rear windows and struggled until he got it open. It faced away from the road, so it shouldn't draw any attention. There was a shelf beneath it, lined with old paint cans currently serving as containers for various items like screws, nuts, bolts, broken tools and unidentifiable bits of hardware.

He waited, because he knew he was supposed to. Eventually the old part of the heater's wick burned away and the smoke stopped spewing. He should have trimmed the wick first. Idiot. Still, it was working all right now.

He set to work making himself comfortable, clearing a space amid the clutter in the place. Hoes, rakes, no less than three old lawn mowers—one of them so old it didn't even have a motor, but was a push model—hand scythes, buckets and pails and watering pots of every imaginable shape and size. And that was just the beginning. The shed was full of garbage. The discarded remnants of a once full life. Like old bones rattling around in a crypt. But there was no life here anymore.

Or wouldn't be much longer.

When he had cleared a spot on the floor, he unrolled his sleeping bag there. He'd taken off his shoes near the rickety door, to avoid tracking snow inside. He moved them now, closer to the heater, so they would get dry. He set the backpack far away from the heat source, not wanting to be blown to bits before morning. But first he took out one of the MREs.

Meals Ready To Eat were a wonderful invention. He tore the top off the plastic bag, then added water from his stash. After opening the accompanying packet, he poured its contents into the bag, as well, and watched as the chemical reaction caused the water to boil, heating the food pack sealed inside.

In minutes his meal of beef stew was piping hot and ready to eat. He cleared off a shelf with a sweep of his arm, pulled up a five-gallon pail that had once held house paint and used it as a chair. He liked sitting by the side window. Enjoyed the view.

Hell, he didn't know why he had doubted his guides. This place was far more practical than the Victorian in Bonnie Brook anyway.

He ate his stew, looking out across the back lawn at the former Blackberry Inn. Beth's house. A lot of people were milling around in there now. Cops coming and going, cars parked outside. Several ATVs were lined up there, too, along with the pickup trucks that had brought them. And Stanton was there. But so were Mordecai's targets, both of them, under one roof, which made it extremely convenient.

Once again, the guides had been right.

Eventually the others would leave. Eventually Lizzie or Bryan or both would be left alone. Unguarded.

Lizzie wasn't going anywhere. She'd insinuated that she was leaving only as a ruse to force him to move more quickly. Before he was ready. And he'd almost fallen for it, too. But not now.

Mordecai was cozy, warm, well fed and sheltered.

He could wait.

22

— ← —

Bryan felt warmth. Heat surrounded him like a blanket, and it felt good. Soothing, comforting and then…confusing.

His head was clouded and fuzzy and it ached, but even with all that, he was sure he'd fallen asleep outside, huddled under a bunch of roots while the snow fell. He remembered being cold, and then just sleepy. He remembered thinking the snow would hide him even better than the roots alone. And that made him remember what he'd been hiding from—Mordecai.

He opened his eyes wide and sat up slightly, only to wince in pain.

His father leaned over him, hands on his shoulders. "Lie back now. Relax, Bry. You're okay."

Bryan sighed, every cell in his body flooding with relief to see his old man. He never would have expected to be this glad to see that face. In fact, he was so overwhelmed he had to close his eyes to hide the hot moisture that sprang into them.

"You're gonna be okay."

"What about Dawn?" he asked. It surprised him that his words seemed croaked rather than spoken. He rubbed his throat and tried to clear it.

"Dawn's fine. She's downstairs with Beth, waiting her turn to come in and see you." Josh took a pillow from the side of the bed near him, then eased Bryan's shoulders up and tucked it under him. After that he took a cup from the nightstand and held it out. "Tea," he said. "One of Maude's medicinals. It's probably cooling off by now."

Bryan took the tea, sipped it. It was good, spicy and sweet.

"Dawn told us what you and she have been up to, Bryan."

Oh, great. Here it comes, Bryan thought. He lowered the cup, shot his eyes to his father's, waited.

Josh sighed. "If you didn't want to go back to California, you should have just said so."

"I did say so, Dad. Remember?"

Josh licked his lips, lowered his eyes. "Still, this was…if you'd been honest with me—"

"Like you're being with Beth, you mean?"

"Bryan—"

"No, wait." Bryan thought addressing his father with sarcasm was getting to be automatic. "Actually, Dad, I think I finally get it—what you're doing, I mean. Because I've been kind of doing the same thing."

"How so?"

Bryan sighed. "I thought I could do some good, help nail Mordecai. And if I had to use deception to do it, I was willing to. It was worth it. That's exactly what you're doing with Beth. I understand it now."

Josh stared at him for a long moment. Then his hand moved to Bryan's hair, stroked it lovingly, tenderly, and Bryan found himself trying to remember when his father had touched him that way before.

"I almost lost you. My God, Bryan, what the hell am I doing here, anyway?"

Bryan frowned.

"Listen to me," Josh said. "I was wrong. You've been

right about this all along. I never should have kept the truth from Beth. All I've accomplished is that I've dug myself into a hole so deep, I don't know how to climb out. What happened to you and Dawn ought to be validation to you that you were right the first time around. There's nothing to gain by lying to the people you love."

Bryan blinked. "You...love Beth?"

"That's not what I said."

"Yeah, it is. Kind of."

Joshua shook his head, averted his eyes. "I can't believe I've screwed up as badly as I have with you, Bryan."

"You haven't—"

"Yes, I have. I know when I screw up. God knows I've done it before. I screwed up in my job and lost it. I screwed up with your mother and lost her. And you along with her. I've screwed up with Beth and don't know how to begin to fix it, and I screwed up so badly with you that you almost got killed over it." His eyes were damp when they locked onto Bryan's. "I don't know how I would have gone on if I'd lost you, son. You mean so much to me."

"I do?" Bryan had never thought his presence in his father's life was much more than an inconvenience. Oh, he knew his dad loved him—in his way. In the same way all fathers were obliged to love their offspring.

"I think I'd have died. You are the most important part of my life. More than the job, or the business, or this case, or Beth, or anything. I mean it. And I swear, I'm going to do better."

Bryan smiled a little, finished the warm tea and set the cup on the nightstand. "You didn't do too bad tonight, Dad. Hell, you found me in the middle of the woods. You brought me back."

Josh leaned over and hugged him hard. "Thank God."

When his father released him, Bryan felt odd. Different.

As if something he'd been missing had been returned to him before he had even been aware he'd been missing it.

"I think we're gonna be okay, Dad."

"I think so, too."

Nodding, Bryan drew a breath. He hadn't intended to mention this to his father, but now he decided to go ahead. "I think I—I think I saw Mom." He took a chance, looking at his father's eyes. They were wide, searching and eager. Not skeptical, not at all. Encouraged, Bryan went on. "I was sound asleep out there, so well hidden you never would have found me. I dreamed I was little again, and she was waking me up for school. She leaned over me, like she used to do, kissed my cheek." He swallowed hard. "That's what made me wake up. And that's when I heard the ATVs and crawled out of my cover."

Josh nodded very slowly, thoughtfully. "I'll bet it was her," he said. "I'll bet it was."

It made Bryan feel inexplicably elated that his father believed him, that he didn't ridicule him or try to explain away what felt like a genuine miracle.

Josh drew a breath, got to his feet. "I...should let Dawn come in. She's probably climbing the walls waiting."

"Yeah. I imagine she's worried sick."

Josh nodded. "Beth brought her back here after she showed us where to look for you, but she sneaked out to join the search." He thinned his lips, shook his head. "She's a lot like her mother, that one." He nodded at Bryan's quick look. "Yeah, she told us you knew about that. We didn't get off to the best start, but I think I like her."

"I'm glad."

Josh nodded and started toward the door.

"Dad?"

He turned back.

Bryan swallowed and forced the words to come. His father had reached out to him tonight, really opened up. He deserved reciprocation. Honesty. "When I was huddled out there in the cold, hiding from that maniac, all I kept thinking was, 'I wish Dad was here.'"

Josh smiled, and his eyes looked funny. "Seriously?"

"Yeah. I thought you'd want to know that."

"It means more to me than you could imagine, Bry."

Bryan nodded and knew it was true. "I love you, Dad."

"And I love you, Bryan. Good night."

"'Night."

And then his dad stepped out of the bedroom, into the hall and closed the door. Bryan lay back on his pillows. And for the first time since his mother's death, he thought he might really be all right. He might really be able to grow up and go to college and live a real life without her. Partly because he had his father—finally. And partly because he didn't really think he was entirely without her after all.

Josh bumped into Dawn in the hallway and sent her in to see Bryan. He found Beth in the kitchen. He didn't have to search for her; he just seemed to automatically know where she would be. She was standing with her back against the counter, sipping cocoa and looking pensive, and she didn't know he'd stepped in just yet. He paused for a moment to enjoy that; observing her, drinking her in when she wasn't on guard. She always seemed to be on guard around him, always holding something back, even when they made love. It felt as if she didn't quite trust him not to destroy her.

And why should she, given the size of the secret he was keeping?

She had on plaid flannel pajama bottoms. The top that went with them wasn't winter wear, a gray, tiny thing with thin straps, short enough to reveal an inch of midriff, clingy enough to make his mouth water. A heavy bathrobe was flung over the back of a chair nearby; he thought the warmth of the kitchen had made her take it off and gave silent thanks to the old furnace for hanging in there. They'd cranked it up for Bryan's sake. The fireplace was going, too, and judging from the mess on the counter and the mouthwatering aroma in the air, the oven was on.

Beth finally looked his way, caught him staring, smiled gently. "How's our boy doing?"

Josh couldn't quite put a name to the kind of feeling it gave him when she sent that smile his way. Comfort, maybe? Healing? It was magical, whatever he called it. "We just had the first real conversation we've had since his mother died."

"And?"

"And...it was good."

She pushed off from the counter, setting her cup aside and opening the oven. The aroma that wafted out made his mouth water. He saw the chocolate chip cookies, and his stomach rolled over in delight. "Yeah? You gonna give me any details?" She used a spatula to remove the cookies from the tray, laying them on a wire rack to cool. When she got to the final cookie, she carried it to the table, snatched up a napkin and set the cookie on it in front of him. "Cocoa or tea?"

"You don't need to wait on me."

"Sure I do. It's my turn." She pirouetted to the stove, turned on the heat under the teapot, then got out a clean cup and emptied a packet of cocoa mix into it.

Josh reached for the cookie, burned his fingers and promised his mouth it was coming soon. "He told me he loved me, Beth. I haven't heard him say that since he was eight years old."

"Oh, Josh."

When he looked at her, she had a hand pressed to her heart, and he knew she understood just how much the conversation had meant to him. Of course she knew. She met his eyes and told him so without a word; then she turned to the fridge and stretched up onto her tiptoes, reaching up on top for something.

He frowned, then, because her top stretched up, revealing more of her back, and he saw the long, linear scar that didn't belong with her smooth, taut skin. He'd never noticed it before—and as he thought about that, he knew why. The first time they'd slept together it had been in the dark, and the second time she'd kept her camisole on.

She came to earth with a bag of minimarshmallows in hand and caught him staring. "What's wrong?"

"I...just noticed the scar on your back."

"And winced 'cause it's so darn pretty?"

He made a face. "And winced at the thought of a bullet tearing through you."

"Oh." She dropped a handful of marshmallows into his cup, replaced the twist tie on the bag, then came closer to him and pulled up her shirt. She was looking down at her own middle, and one of her fingers absently touched a far smaller scar a few inches below her navel and slightly to the left. "This is where it went in. It really isn't very deadly looking, is it? Barely as big as a dime."

He put his hands on her hips, drew her closer and pressed his lips to the mark. His heart was breaking as he relived the moment, pulling the trigger, sending a searing hot piece of lead screaming through the air until it sank deep into this woman's abdomen, burning her and tearing her insides apart.

He sat back, drawing his lips away, but his eyes remained glued to the spot. Why had he pulled the damn trigger? Hell, he knew why. More than likely he'd seen a muzzle flash and shot at it. It had been too dark to fire at more than flashes in the night. But it didn't matter what he'd been shooting at—all that mattered was what he had hit.

"It went in here," she said, poking the scar with her forefinger tilted at an upward angle. "Then it went up and right, because they were shooting from below. I was upstairs, you see."

She drew a line with her finger, upward at an angle that crossed her belly button. "Tore my uterus to hell, in one side and out the other. Took out an ovary, nicked an artery. I was bleeding internally and didn't even know it." Her finger kept moving across her belly, around her waist to the scar on her back. "This is where they found the bullet. It hit a rib, fractured it, but that's what finally stopped it."

"God, Beth, I'm so sorry."

She shrugged. "Don't be silly. It's not like you had anything to do with it. Besides, I'm fine. Just so long as you're not the type to get all queasy over a few hard-won battle scars."

"Nothing about you makes me queasy." He ran his fingertips over the surgical scar. "I've been with you twice and never even noticed them. That's how deeply you affect me."

She smiled. "My effect on you isn't the whole reason you never noticed them," she said. "The little one on my front is barely noticeable, and I've been careful not to give you a good view of my unclothed back."

"You didn't want me to see the scar?"

"Shallow, isn't it?"

"No." He leaned closer and kissed the surgery scar, just as he had the entry wound scar. "You're not shallow. You're perfect."

"I'm so far from perfect it's laughable, Josh. And I wouldn't want to be. But thanks for saying so."

She was. She was the most perfect thing he'd ever seen. And he really didn't think that observation was based on guilt, or on the situation, or on his buying into his own cover story. She'd been forged in fire, yeah. Hurt, brought down low, only to rise up again, stronger than before. To him, that was perfection.

The teapot whistled. Beth turned to get it, poured steaming water into the cup, stirred and brought it to the table. He tried again with the cookie, cool enough now to eat, but hot enough that the chocolate chips were still melty. And the marshmallows in the cocoa were gooey and soft.

She returned to her work then, standing at the counter, spooning cookie dough from a bowl onto the cookie sheet. "I made up a room for Dawn. That means almost every room is full," she said softly. "The usable ones, anyway. It's almost like the inn is already up and running."

"Except that none of them are paying guests," he observed.

She shrugged. "I'm sure Arthur Stanton and his two cohorts would disagree. They'd say they're paying by risking their lives to protect me."

"You sound like you don't buy into that," Joshua said.

Beth shrugged. He couldn't see her face, her back was toward him as she worked. "I think Mordecai is the real reason they're all here. They want to catch him. Keeping me alive would be a bonus feather in their caps, but I don't think it's their priority. If they had to choose between capturing him or saving me, I think I'd be history." She looked over her shoulder at him, as if waiting for him to comment on that. "What do you think?"

"I think…you're a little too insightful for your own good."

"Then you agree with me."

He shrugged. "A few weeks ago, I wouldn't have. But

Arthur...he's not the man I thought he was. I'm not so sure about him anymore."

She slid the cookie sheet into the oven, reset the timer. "That wasn't really an answer."

He shrugged. "Doesn't matter if keeping you alive is their first priority, Beth. It's mine. And you can believe me when I tell you nobody will protect you the way I will."

She smiled slowly, moved closer to him, bent low and kissed his ear. "My hero."

"Hmm. Everyone gone to bed?" he asked.

"Everyone but Dawn. I'm sure she's still in with Bry."

"She'll sleep like a log. They both will tonight."

She lifted her brows. "What about Arthur and company?"

"I don't really care about them. Do you?"

"No."

"So is that the last batch of cookies?"

She smiled slowly. "Yeah. But you've been run ragged, up all night on no sleep, half-frozen—"

"I still have a pulse."

She leaned down, and he pressed his mouth to hers, tasted evidence that she'd been sampling her own cookies, thought about getting her upstairs to bed....

The doorbell rang.

Josh frowned, eyes popping open, mouth still on hers. She was frowning back at him. With a sigh, she pulled away. She looked tired, despite her cookie baking—which she was probably doing just to keep busy, he thought. To keep from thinking. To keep her fears at bay.

"Stay here and relax," he said. "Drink some cocoa. I'll go see who it is."

"You still have your gun with you?"

"Naturally." He glanced worriedly at the back door, the darkness beyond the glass. "Never mind. Come with me."

She shrugged but didn't argue. Instead she tossed her pot holders onto the counter and walked with him back through the house. He liked that she walked close to him, and that he didn't have to tell her not to line herself up with the door or a window. Then again, she'd been living under the looming threat of Mordecai Young for a long time. She probably knew more about caution than he ever would.

"Who's there?" he called.

"An old friend of Beth's. Sort of."

It was a woman's voice. Josh sent Beth a questioning look. She frowned at him, then approached the door. Josh didn't like that, so he pulled a gun, and moved around to one side, behind the door, then peered out the window there. "One woman. Blond. Alone." He gave Beth a nod. "I think it's okay."

Beth nodded, flipped the locks and pulled the door open just a little. Then she blinked and opened it wider. "Jax?"

The newcomer smiled, even while rubbing her arms. There was snow in her hair. "Long time no see. How are you, Elizabeth?"

"Fine. I mean…God, come in. What on earth are you doing here?"

The woman walked into the house and without glancing at Josh, said, "You can put it away. I'm no threat. Nice work, though." And she pushed the door closed behind her.

Josh frowned, already tucking his gun back into its holster. He reached behind the woman to lock the door again, sizing her up as he did. She was pretty but didn't seem to know it, or maybe she just didn't care. No makeup, long blond hair gathered in a careless ponytail that hung down her back, shapeless trousers over a pair of suede boots, all topped by a stereotypical cop's trench coat, dark gray. If he was reading her right, and he thought he was, she was deciding whether to hug Beth hello or just settle for a handshake. She opted for the handshake. Apparently the two hadn't been the hugging sort of friends.

Josh cleared his throat, and Beth looked at him quickly. "I'm sorry. I'm just so surprised—Joshua, this is Lieutenant Cassandra Jackson."

"Lieutenant?" He extended a hand.

She took it. "For now. Syracuse Police Department," she told him. "But you can call me Jax."

"You're bucking for a promotion," Beth said, smiling.

"Yeah, have been since you left. I was standing close enough to you that day in Virginia that they decided to give me some of the credit. I figure a bump up the ladder ought to come with it."

"You deserve it."

"I didn't do a damn thing." Jax glanced at Josh again. "What department are you with?"

He blinked, unprepared to answer.

"Fed?" she asked. "You're definitely law enforcement."

"No."

"Former, then. You don't look old enough to be retired."

"I've never been in law enforcement, Lieutenant Jackson."

She blinked, met his eyes, and he read them without even trying. They said she knew better but wouldn't push it, in case he had legitimate reasons for lying. Meanwhile, Beth was looking curiously from one of them to the other.

"Josh is a bodyguard," she explained.

"Private security consultant," he clarified.

"Smart move, hiring your own," Jax said with a nod. "You can't trust the Feds."

"I agree, but I didn't hire him. The government did."

Now Jax's frown was clearly disbelieving, and when she looked at him again, it was with suspicion in her eyes. She had to know the government had its own agencies and its own men, and rarely hired outsiders for this sort of thing.

"Jeez, take off your coat," Beth said. "Come on in and sit. Did you drive all the way up here?"

Jax walked farther into the house with Beth, but Josh felt her eyes on him, probing. She knew something wasn't right with his story. He decided to make nice, see if he could win her over, even though he sensed it would be a wasted effort. His gut told him this one was a good cop. Not easily fooled nor, he thought, put off the scent.

"So what brings you to Blackberry, Lieutenent?" he asked.

"Jax," she reminded him. "I had a call from Julie Jones. She filled me in, told me Dawn was up here."

Beth said, "I knew she was going to call you, but I thought you'd phone us, not drive all the way up here."

Jax shrugged. "Jewel sounded worried to death, but with the weather, she can't get up here for a couple of days, and she knows damn well the kid won't go home."

Beth nodded. "She's right. I told Dawn I was sending her home, and she promised she'd head back here at the first opportunity. I figure it's better to keep her here, where I can at least watch out for her until Julie can come and get her." She waved to the most comfortable chair in the living room, and Jax sat down.

"That's what Julie thought, too," she said. "I was in the middle of my vacation week, so I thought I'd take a drive up here. See if I could be of any help."

"That's incredibly generous of you," Beth said.

"Not really." Jax didn't relax in her chair. She sat upright, leaning slightly forward, feet evenly spaced and flat on the floor, elbows on her knees. "Julie said Young was up here. I've always wanted another shot at collaring the bastard." She glanced at Josh. "It would be a major bust."

"Are you looking to be the next chief?" Josh asked. "Or skipping straight to mayor?"

She shrugged. "My captain's retiring next year. I wouldn't mind that job. Who knows?"

He nodded. A good cop and an ambitious cop. Hell, it just got better and better, didn't it?

"Julie said you were turning this place into an inn," Jax observed.

"Re-turning it," Beth said. "It was an inn once, but it's been a while."

"I'd love to be your first paying guest."

Beth glanced at Josh, real regret in her eyes. "We aren't technically open for business yet," she began, "and right now, all the rooms are—"

"A mess," he interrupted. "But if you can give us twenty minutes, we can have a room ready for you."

Beth frowned at him, but he sent her a reassuring look. Hell, he wasn't planning to sleep alone tonight, anyway. It wouldn't take any time at all to move Beth's stuff into his room and change the bedding.

A bell pinged, and Beth jumped up. "That's my timer," she said. Then she smiled at Jax. "I'll be right back with warm, gooey chocolate chip cookies fresh from the oven, and a cup of hot cocoa for you. Then you can relax while we get your room ready, all right?"

"Sounds great."

Beth rushed off to the kitchen. Josh got up and started to follow, but the second Beth was out of earshot, Jax said, "So what is it you're keeping from her?"

He stopped, his back to the woman. "What do you mean?"

"Come on, I saw you take up position behind the door. The stance, the way you held your gun. I know a cop when I see one. You undercover?"

"Something like that."

"You can't tell me, huh?"

Sighing, he turned slowly. "Look, this is...sensitive. Her life's at stake. I can't risk anything making her skittish right now."

"Skittish?" She shook her head. "Young could single-handedly fill all ten slots in the Most Wanted list. She's way beyond skittish."

"Of him. Not of me."

She nodded, her eyes narrow and brimming with intelligence. "You need her to trust you."

"There's not a reason in the world why she shouldn't trust me. I'm on her side."

"So am I. Just so you know."

It was a warning. He heard it loud and clear.

23

Saturday

"It's almost…anticlimactic, isn't it?"

Beth was standing near the front door, watching the unmarked sedan roll away over the bare ribbon of road, carrying two of her house guests with it. Three days had passed since Bryan and Dawn's encounter with Mordecai in the forest. Three days, and no sign of the man. The press had descended on the town when the wire services picked up her story. She'd been interviewed a dozen times, in between overseeing Will Ahearn's work on the house. And then the press had left again. And still not a sign of Mordecai.

Josh stood behind her, his hands on her shoulders. God, she loved having him in her life. Close, reassuring, constant, dependable.

She trusted him, she realized. As much as she'd been determined to keep her guard up where he was concerned, he had worked his way around it, through it, beneath it. He was inside her now. In her heart, in her home, in her bed. She'd been in love with him for a while now. But the trust—that was new.

And a little scary.

"Anticlimactic in a very good way," he told her. "When you consider what the climax could have been."

She lowered her head. "I've been waiting a long time to finally face him down. To end this once and for all. Damn him. Three days, and not a sign he's within a hundred miles." The car carrying the two federal agents wound out of sight, and she turned as their boss, Arthur Stanton, came down the stairs.

Josh slipped an arm around her. Arthur stopped halfway across the room, set his suitcase on the floor and dropped a manila envelope on the coffee table.

"So you're leaving, too?" she asked. "I thought you were going to stay one more night?"

"I was, but we've just had a sighting of Young."

Her heart jumped, and she caught her breath. "Where?"

"Raleigh, North Carolina. He was at a Youth for Christ rally. Some of the cops working security there recognized him from the photo we've been circulating."

The photo. She shivered, because it was emblazoned into her mind. Arthur's people had taken an old photo of Mordecai, then used some sophisticated computer program to enhance it according to Bryan and Dawn's description of how he had looked when they'd seen him. She'd been devastated when one of her own students identified him as the same man who'd been substituting for her social studies teacher for a couple of days—a Mr. Abercrombie.

God, it gave Beth chills to think that Mordecai could so easily get close to innocent children.

There were several versions of the sketch floating around now, with various hairstyles, lengths and colors, with glasses and without them. Mordecai's piercing brown eyes, with their thick black lashes, never changed. Those eyes could look at once angelic and demon-possessed. They chilled her to the marrow, those eyes.

She sighed, blinking to clear the image from her mind. "What if it wasn't really him?" she asked.

Arthur smiled reassuringly. "This is the third sighting in the Raleigh-Durham area, Beth. And the witnesses are reliable."

"Almost too reliable," she muttered. "It's not like Mordecai to let himself be seen by police officers and county deputies," she said. "Not unless he wants to be seen."

"Don't think we haven't thought of that. But, Beth, we're leaving you in very good hands. And it's not as if you're going to be sitting here like a glowing neon target, after all."

"It's not?" She saw the look Arthur exchanged with Josh, and she frowned. "What haven't you told me?" she asked, looking up at Joshua.

"You haven't told her?" Arthur asked. Then he snatched up the envelope he'd set down, brought it to her and thrust it into her hands.

"What's this?" Beth asked.

"It's your new identity. We've got a place all picked out for you."

She lifted her brows. "Timbuktu?"

"Illinois. Right on Lake Michigan. You'll love it." He clapped a hand to Joshua's shoulder. "I'll check in every couple of hours. If there's anything the least bit odd—"

"I'll call. Don't worry, we'll be fine."

"Just get her settled in the new place, Josh. Don't waste any time."

Josh thinned his lips as Arthur nodded to her, then dashed out the door. Then she stared up at Joshua and said simply, "I'm not going."

"You have to go. Listen, it doesn't have to be permanent."

"No."

"We have a plan."

"A plan you didn't even bother to discuss with me."

"I told you we should have discussed it with her," Jax said. She was in the kitchen, where she'd been making herself a sandwich from the leftover ham Beth had baked for dinner. She had half the sandwich left, clutched in one hand, and she took another bite before going on. While chewing, she said, "It's really a great plan, Liz."

"I hate being called Liz."

"So you keep telling me." She nodded at Josh. "Tell her the plan." Then she took another bite.

"What plan?" Bryan asked, coming down the stairs from his room, Dawn at his elbow, as always. She'd barely taken her eyes off him since that night in the woods, even though Bryan was mostly recovered now.

"The plan." Josh drew a breath.

"Yes, Josh, the plan," Beth said.

He cleared his throat. "The plan is that I put you, Bryan and Dawn on a flight out of here. You'll be on hopscotching flights, and at a couple of the stops, you'll be changing names, so it would be impossible for anyone to trail you. Eventually, you wind up at O'Hare, where a van will be waiting to drive you to the new place. You don't use the final new identity until you're settled in there."

"And where will you be?"

"Julie Jones McKenzie and her husband Sean will meet you there, to take charge of Dawn."

"And I ask again, where will you be?"

"I'll be here."

"With me," Jax said. "Only I won't be me, I'll be you."

Beth blinked. "Come again?"

She moved closer, munching her sandwich and reached behind her to pull her long ponytail around with her free hand. She held it up.

Beth frowned. "It's darker. You changed your color—that's *my* color."

"To. A. Tee." Jax smiled. "I'm getting it cut this morning. Shoulder length, just like yours. And there's a bottle of peroxide upstairs waiting for you."

"Right. I'm going to bleach my hair."

"You're butterscotch. I'm platinum. When you leave here, honey, you are going to be platinum in a ponytail, wearing some of my clothes. And I'm gonna be a butterscotch babe."

"You're going to pretend to be me."

"Brilliant, isn't it?" Jax asked. "Josh came up with it."

"It really is a great plan," Bryan said.

Beth slid her eyes from his to Dawn's. Dawn rolled her eyes, shook her head. At least one person in the room got this.

"So I'm supposed to sneak off to safety and leave another woman to take my place on the receiving end of Mordecai's final vengeance."

"Not another woman," Jax said. "A cop. A trained police officer. This is my job."

"It's not your job, Jax," Beth told her. "It's no one's job. It's not a job at all, it's life. *My* life." She slapped the envelope against Joshua's chest and let go of it. He caught it as it slid toward the floor. "I'm not going anywhere. And if Mordecai is still in town and coming after me, then it's me who will be here waiting for him."

She turned and started for the stairs. "And if you guys keep trying to interfere with that, then I'll be waiting for him alone."

"Beth is right," Dawn said. She'd been sitting on the bottom step, but she got to her feet now. "Besides, no one knows him like she and I do. No one else can hope to outsmart him the way we can."

"There's no we in this, Dawny," Beth told her. "The second Julie can get here, you are outta here."

"But—"

"I almost died trying to save you from him—twice now. Do you really think I'm going to let you hang around here risking your neck? I'd have sent you home by now if I thought wild horses could keep you from rushing straight back here. But once your mom comes…"

Dawn flinched, maybe because it was so unusual for Beth to refer to Julie as her mother—but she was, Beth reminded herself: morally, ethically, even legally now. Not Beth, not anymore.

"Look, it doesn't really matter," Bryan said, getting to his feet. He slid one hand over Dawn's shoulder, squeezing her there. "Mordecai's long gone anyway. The whole town knows it. They're all planning for Maude's memorial service now that things have settled down."

Beth blinked, looking behind her to the bottom of the stairs, where the two teens stood. "But we decided to postpone that…."

Bryan nodded. "I know. Someone's supposed to call you about it tonight. Maude's friends and Reverend Baker all feel it should go on as scheduled."

She sighed deeply, lowering her head. "That's an even bigger reason for me to stick around," she said. "For Maude. I owe her this much."

Then she turned and moved on up the stairs.

Leaving.

She'd told the press she was leaving. Taking on a new name, a new identity, going back into hiding. But Lizzie wasn't going anywhere.

Mordecai had given up on waiting for her to be alone in the house. She would never be alone in the house. And she would never relax or let her guard down. It was almost as if she could…feel him there.

She should. They were connected, he and Lizzie—their souls were bound. He felt her life, her breath, her blood, twining and mingling with his own as he sat in silent meditation in the garden shed, and he was overcome with longing.

Selfish, he told himself. He mustn't give in, mustn't risk revealing his presence. Especially now. The servants of the Beast had gone. Government men were so easily led. These had been no different. Highly placed men with secrets they preferred stayed hidden made excellent witnesses, he had found. And three such men had reported seeing him far away from here. Far away from Lizzie.

God, but he wanted to go to her.

Go, then. Sate your hunger for her this once.

Mordecai's eyes opened as he slowly rose from the trancelike state. He lifted his head and saw that it was dark outside again. Had he been still so long, then? It had been midafternoon when he'd sunk down on the cold wood floor, folded his legs beneath him, closed his eyes. He started to rise, but his legs had been bent so long they didn't obey him, and he fell to his knees again, wincing in pain.

Damn, what he wouldn't give for a warm bed, a heated room for the night.

Soon.

Mordecai rose again, using a support beam to aid him. He'd grown hungry. Dinnertime had long since past. But now he had a greater hunger. And permission to assuage it. He wondered why his guides would allow him to risk discovery, but he had no doubt there were reasons. He moved to the shed's window, looked through it at the darkened house.

"She's not alone, though the government men have

left." He wiped impatiently at the dirt-streaked glass, then gave up and went to the door, pulled it open, stepped outside.

The house stood there. It was greatly improved now from its initial appearance. It had been repainted over the last three days. Missing shutters had been replaced and loose ones tightened. The porch no longer sagged in the middle. And the second-floor windows were shining clean and filled with clean curtains now, where before some of them had been streaked with dust and bare.

"The lady cop is there, still. The one from Syracuse," he whispered.

She sleeps.

"And the boy, and that girl who is with him. Is there some reason I've never seen her face?"

She is unimportant.

"And the man."

You hold the key to his demise. Go. Look upon your woman. We near the end of this journey, and time is short. And take your bag with you.

He blinked, looking back at the large black satchel inside the shed door, stored far from the kerosene heater. He could guess why they wanted him to take the bag with him, and he very nearly argued with them. Knowing he would be punished for that, he bit it back.

"The doors are locked," he said instead.

Go to the back. Climb the tree there. And don't think about questioning your instructions, Mordecai. Spirit knows far more than you do. Humble yourself and obey.

Mordecai sighed, but he didn't question. He didn't doubt. He took heart in the fact that the guides were telling him this journey was nearly over. He no longer cared so much how it ended. Taking up the bag, he closed the shed door and walked through the dying grass to the rear of the house. He went up to the maple tree that stood there and climbed it, though doing so was a challenge with the bag in one hand. As he made his way higher, he saw the wisdom of the guides, as he always did. An attic window stood within reach of a long, gnarled limb. He climbed out upon that limb, paying no attention to the way it gave under his weight, the way the tree groaned and cracked— no more than he paid to the cold of the night. The guides must be obeyed. If the limb broke and sent him to his death below, then there was a reason.

His palm pressed to the window, he tried to raise the sash, but it was locked. Something rattled, though, and he frowned, inspecting it more closely and seeing that the caulk around the windowpanes was old, crumbling. The glass didn't sit tightly, and a little manipulating of the loosest pane soon had it coming free.

Reaching through, he unlocked the sash, opened the window, then climbed inside, pulling his satchel in behind him. It was that easy.

Setting the satchel on the floor and leaving it there, Mordecai crept through the house. He didn't even need to ask which bedroom was hers. He felt her. He was drawn to her. Led to her. A magnet and steel.

The halls were pitch-black. Not a light had been left on, not in the entire house. So when he paused outside her bedroom door, gripped the knob, turned it slowly and pushed the door open, he saw nothing until the faint flickering glow from within caught his eye.

Candlelight.

It gleamed golden yellow, bathing her skin and the darker hands that slid over it.

Mordecai almost gasped aloud at the pain, as if a white-hot blade had slid neatly between his ribs. She was lying there, her arms and legs twined around the man, her hands pressing to his back, her eyes closed, lips parted, body writhing beneath him.

Damn her, he thought. Damn her for a lying whore.

His hand closed around the bone handle inside his boot. He drew the hunting knife out slowly, careful not to make a sound, and straightened again, with hatred and hurt burning his heart.

A single step forward. She moaned the other man's name as his hips snapped against her, impaling her, defiling her.

They would both die. Here. Now!

No.

Mordecai clenched his jaw. He would not obey, dammit. Not this time.

You will obey. She will die for her crimes, Mordecai, just as we have always insisted she must—even when you rebelled and pleaded for her life. She will die. At your hand. But not yet. Not today.

Tomorrow, though, you will bring her a taste of the pain she has brought to you this night. Tomorrow there is a blade you will thrust into her heart. Not the one in your hand—not at first. First, Mordecai, you will use the blade in your pocket.

He tightened his grip on the hunting knife, his fist clenching and unclenching almost like a spasm.

Put it away, Mordecai! And with the command came a blinding pain behind his eyes. He pressed a hand to his forehead, fast and hard.

"What was that?" Lizzie stopped moving, her voice a harsh whisper.

Mordecai backed into the pitch-black hall, pulling the door closed, not latching it, though, lest they hear. The pain faded. His body steadied, and he obeyed, bending to slide the knife back into his boot.

Now, take out the other blade. The one in your pocket.

Closing his eyes against his heartache, he thrust a hand into the pocket of the shirt he wore, and there he felt the folded scrap of paper. He took it out and remembered without needing to look at it. The newspaper clipping—the one showing that fornicator's face, identifying him as the ATF agent responsible for shooting Lizzie all those years ago.

He leaned back against a wall, tipped his head upward. "Is it time, then? Is it finally time to destroy her?"

It's time. You'll leave that paper for her—we'll tell you where. She'll find it tomorrow. For now, return to the attic and fetch the bag, for you have more work to do. Once she has lost her lover, she must lose everything else she holds dear. Indeed, your work this night will cost her more than even you know. She will be brought to her knees, Mordecai. She will welcome death when you bring it to her. She will beg you to end her pain.

"The house?" he asked softly.

Yes. First the lover, then the house. And something even more precious to her than that. Tomorrow.

"But tomorrow is the day of the memorial service. Half the town will be here."

Even better. Go now to the attic. Get the bag and begin your work. And, Mordecai, set the timer for twelve-thirty. Half past noon. Exactly.

Beth awoke in Joshua's arms to commotion already going on in the house. She lifted her head from his magnificent chest and looked up to see him smiling at her.

She frowned, only now noting the brightness of the morning sun through the windows. "God, what time is it?"

"Almost nine."

She blinked and felt her heart jerk into rapid motion. "Joshua, how could you let me oversleep? Today of all days!"

He stroked her hair. "Didn't have the heart to wake you. Beth—I want to talk to you."

"I don't have time for talking." She sat up in the bed, swinging her legs over the side, reaching for a robe. "Half the town will be here by noon. God, there's no way I'll be ready—we should have been up two hours ago!"

"Will you calm down?" He got up as well, going to her, clasping her shoulders to still her frantic motions. "Listen."

She frowned, but listened. From below she could hear movement; the entire house was in motion.

"Dawn's been giving orders for the past couple of hours already, and from the sounds of all the to-do, Jax and Bry are hopping to obey. You don't have a thing to worry about."

She met his eyes at that last line. "I have everything to worry about. And I think you know it."

He stared into her eyes. "I think he's gone, Beth. I really do. I think it's over."

"It will never be over. Not until one of us is dead."

"Jesus, Beth, can't you let it go? Just for a little while? I want to talk about—about us."

She smiled gently. "I'm in love with you. What more do you need to know?"

His breath stuttered out of him, and he stared into her eyes as if he couldn't look away. "It's not what I need to know, Beth. It's…what you need to know. About me."

An icy chill slid down her spine, robbing her of breath. "Don't—"

"I have to. It's waited far too long, and dammit, Beth, it's time."

She shook her head. Something like panic rose up in her throat, a feeling of certainty that she was about to have her heart torn from her chest. It battled with the tiny voice inside—the one whose trust he had won utterly—which told her to keep believing in him.

She turned her face up to his, searching the depths of his eyes. And she saw in them that whatever he meant to tell her was something he feared, something horrible. And then she closed her eyes.

"Do you love me?" she asked him.

His breath whispered against her forehead as he leaned closer. "I do."

"Then do this for me. Wait. Let me get through today, just today, Joshua. Let me focus on Maude today. On honoring her memory, on thanking this town, on saying goodbye to her. And then, tonight…tonight you can tell me this secret you've been keeping."

He frowned at her.

"I've known all along there was something," she said. "Tonight. All right?"

He cupped her cheek. "All right."

She nodded, then, turning, fled from him, from the room, and threw herself into the work, the preparations, as if the fate of the entire world depended on this day's success.

The morning flew by, and she found herself avoiding Joshua, even though she told herself it wasn't deliberate. There was so much to be done, that was all. They removed the living room furniture, and lined the room with tables and folding chairs. They pushed the dining room table to one side, and added other tables, and still more chairs when some local men in pickup trucks arrived to deliver them. They covered each table with a white linen cloth, brewed vats of coffee and stirred gallons of punch, set up the food the caterer brought.

Inch by inch, the buffet table was covered—trays of finger sandwiches, vegetables, crackers and cheese, pickles and olives, roasted meats, rolls and pastries, deviled eggs. Bowls containing every imaginable type of casserole and salad. Crock-Pots filled with meatballs, chicken wings, chili and stew. And they needed a second table just to hold the desserts.

People filed in, and at noon, when Reverend Baker took the podium to speak about Maude, the place was packed full.

"You've been going nonstop," Joshua said, sidling up beside her where she stood in the back of the room. "Thank God it's finally getting under way. If you kept going much longer I think you'd have dropped."

"Don't be silly. I'm fine."

"Yes," he said, "you are."

She smiled at him, but avoided his eyes by looking at her watch. "Reverend Baker's speech should take about twenty minutes."

"And then we line up for the food," he said. "I'm starved." He closed a hand around one of hers. "Beth, I—"

"God, look at that," she said. "No one brought out the dips. There are three bowls of it in the fridge. The caterer must have forgotten she put them there. Be right back."

"Beth—"

She tugged her hand from his and hurried through the crowd, into the kitchen. She felt his eyes on her, his will calling her back, but she ignored it and moved on.

In the kitchen, there were others. Women, being helpful, carrying one last round of food items into the other rooms, the dips among them. Beth hadn't come for the dip, anyway. She hadn't come for anything except solitude. She needed to be alone, to think. God, Joshua's secret had been plaguing her all day. She didn't want to lose him, and yet she was afraid—so very afraid.

The reason for her fear was the sheer power of what she had come to feel for him. It was all-encompassing. She'd never loved like this before—not even her teenage obsession with Mordecai had been this strong.

She let the other women go past her. They picked up the pace once they heard the boom of the minister's voice. Then she leaned against the back door, hand on the knob, forehead resting briefly on the cool glass. "I'm sorry, Maude," she whispered.

Beth opened the door and stepped outside.

It was cold, not bitter, but cold. Forty, despite the sun that beamed from a crystal-blue sky. The breeze carried an even deeper chill, and it blew stiffly over her face. She hugged her arms and felt her hair whipping. And yet the cold felt good. Bracing and brisk. It helped to clear her mind.

Nodding, affirming that this had been a good idea, despite the fact that she was missing a part of Maude's eulogy, she walked across the back lawn, just a little way, and then she stopped.

There, on the old maple tree, what was that? White, and flapping in the wind like the broken wing of a captive bird.

Frowning, she moved closer. Her heart iced over when she realized it was a sheet of paper, pinned to the tree trunk by the blade of a knife.

"Mordecai," she whispered, fear gripping her soul. Wide-eyed, she looked left and right, ahead and behind her. Then, drawing herself up straight, she moved a few steps closer, and reaching up, yanked the blade from the tree with her right hand and took the sheet of paper in her left.

And then she bent and stared at the clipping, at the photograph, at the headline, and she forgot her fear.

24

—————

The photo of Joshua wasn't grainy or out of focus. It was perfectly clear, even in gray scale. Oh, he was younger. The angles of his face softer than they were now, and there were no laugh lines around his eyes. But even if there had been any doubt in her mind, the caption was there to remove it. ATF Agent's Bullet Killed Unarmed Seventeen-Year-Old Girl in the Raid on Young Believers.

The article told her the rest.

He'd been there. Joshua had been there. He'd been a part of her worst nightmare. And lied about it. Beth didn't understand that. She scrubbed the hazing tears from her eyes with the fist that held the hunting knife. Her other hand, the one that clutched the article, was trembling so badly that she could hardly read. Her eyes raced over the lines all the same, and it felt as if she'd been kicked in the belly; it knocked the breath from her lungs. Her hands clenched, then went limp, the knife dropping to the ground, the article fluttering after.

"He shot me. Joshua is the man who shot me."

Her now empty hands pressed to her abdomen, she felt again the pain of the bullet ripping into her. Hot, deep, burning pain, every bit as real and crippling as the pain in her heart.

Joshua had shot her. His bullet had torn through her uterus, robbing her of any hope of bearing a child. Robbing her of the daughter she already had. Of the chance to raise her, to love her. To be her mother. To be anyone's mother. She'd been so wrong to think she could love him no matter what his secret was. She couldn't. She couldn't love the man who'd cost her Dawn.

She flashed back to the day she had first met him, recalling the way his face had changed when he'd looked at her. The surprise, the shock and recognition in his eyes.

"He knew…."

He knew who she was. And yet he'd lied, deceived her, all this time. And what about his alleged feelings for her? Were they just one more part of the lie? A means to an end? Was he trying to assuage his guilt or pay some kind of penance by protecting her now? By pretending to love her? Or did he really believe his feelings were anything more than an attack of conscience?

Did it matter? Either way, they were just as false.

Someone called her name. She heard it, coming from the kitchen, she thought. Shaking her head, brushing the tears from her cheeks, she ran away, crossing the back lawn and entering the shelter of the woods, stopping only when she was deep enough in the trees to be hidden from view.

She couldn't face anyone, not now. And God forgive her for missing Maude's service, but this was just…it was too much.

She wondered how long she could avoid seeing anyone, how much time she had to cower in the woods and try to pull herself together before she would have to paint a look of normalcy on her face. The minister would speak for twenty minutes. She wouldn't be missed by too many until he finished. She glanced at her watch. It was twelve fifteen.

"Hey, Beth? You out here?"

She turned back, looking toward the house from amid

the leafless trees of the forest. She saw Bryan standing in the open back door, looking across the lawn, and she knew he couldn't see her there. "Sorry," she whispered.

Then she turned away and followed the winding path through the woods all the way to the little pond and the stream that twisted and bubbled through the forest. She stopped there, taking a breath of the crisp apple air and wondering why the hell she hadn't come out here more often since Maude had died.

This had been the old woman's favorite spot. There was a park bench she'd bought at the local hardware store. Heavy, solid. She'd told Beth how she'd paid a local man thirty dollars to lug it out here and bolt it together, five years ago.

The wood was weathered, the iron blotched with green. But the bench was still solid. A few feet from it, a bird feeder hung from a limb, devoid of seed. Maude wouldn't like knowing that Beth had let the bird feeder run empty.

She sank onto the bench, lowered her head. "Why did I believe in him, Maudie? Why did I trust him? God, when did I forget how much it hurts to love a man who's not what he pretends to be? A man who lies and makes promises he never intends to keep? Didn't Mordecai teach me anything?"

Finally she dropped her head into her hands and wept.

"I never made you any promises I didn't intend to keep, Lizzie."

Sucking in a sharp breath, she jerked her head up so fast it hurt her neck. A man stepped into the tiny clearing, and she stared at him. Even as she did, he reached up to peel the thick shock of black hair from his head. Underneath, it was still clean shaven. Then he took the Coke-bottle-thick glasses from his face, and she met his eyes.

He'd always had the most beautiful eyes. Deep, velvety

brown, with paintbrush lashes. The goatee Dawn said he'd been sporting before was gone. But he hadn't shaved recently—three days' growth of beard shadowed his jaw. He smiled at her, just a little. "I never lied to you, Lizzie. I never betrayed you."

She rose from the bench, moving very slowly, her mind racing. She felt the lump of the handgun she wore underneath her sweater, wondered if she could manage to pull it out and aim it at him before he could kill her. She'd stopped carrying the little derringer and realized now that it would have been far easier to manipulate without notice.

"You betrayed me, though," he said. "Told me you loved me, then tried to put a bullet into my heart. Do you know how much that hurt me, Lizzie?" He shook his head slowly, then said, "Oh, but you do know how it feels, don't you? To have the person who says they love you, shoot you? That's what your boyfriend did to you."

"He's not—"

"Not what? Not your boyfriend?" He curled his lip. "Don't lie to me, Lizzie. I saw you last night. Saw you lying underneath that grunting pig. I saw you."

She swallowed hard, a voice in her head telling her this was it. This was the showdown she had always known would come. Only one of them was going to leave this little spot alive. "I don't have to answer to you, Mordecai. Not anymore."

"No. But you have to answer to God."

"And you don't?" She moved a step closer. It only instigated him into pulling a handgun from his waistband and pointing it at her. She stopped moving but kept talking. "You've killed people, Mordecai. You could have killed an innocent boy the other night, chasing him into the woods and then leaving him there to freeze."

"What's between the boy and me has nothing to do with you," he said.

She frowned. "There's nothing between you and Bryan, except in your own mind."

He shook his head. "You don't know. You never understood."

"I understand more than you know, Mordecai. I understand that you had a choice to make. A choice between a woman who loved you, a daughter you fathered, and the voices in your head. And you chose the voices."

"I chose God."

"You chose insanity!"

He looked furious but quickly calmed again. "You aren't humbled, even now, are you, Lizzie? The guides were right, all along. I've stripped you of damn near everything, and still you're blinded by your own pride."

She lowered her head. "You killed Maude, didn't you?"

"It was her time."

"If it was her time, she would have died in her sleep. Not lying on the floor, paralyzed and terrified and unable to draw a breath."

He averted his eyes. She was striking a nerve.

"It was a horrible death, Mordecai. She didn't deserve it. Maude was a good woman. A Christian woman."

"It was her time," he said again. "I was only God's tool."

She shook her head. "Don't you think it's a little vain of you to believe God couldn't have taken her life if that were what He wanted—that God needed a mortal to do His work for Him?"

He said nothing. She pushed on. "You destroyed my home. God gave me a new one. Would He have done that if it were truly His will that I be homeless?"

"You know nothing about the will of God."

She lowered her head. "What's God's will now, Mordecai? That I die? Why don't we put that to the test, hmm?" She looked upward. "You want me to die, God? Is it my time? Then take me. Here I am, just take me. You have the power."

"If you insist," Mordecai said, and he leveled the gun on her.

"Beth, where are you?"

Bryan stepped out the back door and let it bang shut behind him. He was sure he'd glimpsed her out there, but there was no sign of her now. He took a few steps, looking around, his nerves tingling a little, even though he told himself Mordecai Young was long gone. He supposed that night in the woods had scared him a lot more than he wanted to admit. He'd been jumpy as a cat ever since.

He scanned the trees. The woods out back had changed a lot in the past few days. They looked like a watercolor painting left out in the rain—all the color had run to the ground. Hardly any leaves remained on the brown, brittle branches, but they made a thick carpet on the ground.

Then he spotted something else on the ground and felt chills rise on his arms and the back of his neck. He moved closer, saw the knife lying on the grass. No blood on it, thank God. "Beth?"

Still no sign of her. Bending, he reached for the crumpled piece of paper that lay near the blade and smoothed it open. When he saw what it was, his heart seemed to skip a few beats. "Oh, no."

Bryan closed his eyes briefly, realizing now Beth knew the truth his father had been keeping from her all this time. He looked back toward the house, thinking he should go find his father, but then he thought he heard something. A voice, coming from the woods. Beth's voice.

Biting his lip, Bryan shoved the clipping into his pocket, snatched up the hunting knife and moved quietly into the trees. He followed the meandering path, and as he did, the voices came more clearly. Beth's voice, and then the one that sent shivers down his spine. The voice of Mordecai Young.

"God, I can't! I can't do it!" Mordecai cried.

Bryan thought his voice cracked a little. Then it came more calmly. "Yes, yes, I know. Thy will be done."

Bryan crept closer, moving so silently he couldn't even hear his own footsteps. He went still when he saw them; Beth standing with her back to the pond, and Mordecai, opposite her, his back to Bryan, pointing a gun at her.

"You can't just kill me, Mordecai. Not like this," Beth said.

She looked so scared, her face pale, her eyes wide and wet. Bryan stepped to one side, putting a tree between him and Mordecai, but keeping him in sight. His hand closed tighter around the knife. He was damned if he could stand here and let the maniac just shoot her.

"No, I can't," Mordecai said. "Not yet. Not until you realize there is nothing left for you—no one left for you but me." He sighed deeply. "Dammit, Lizzie, you never learned humility. Not with all I've done to teach you—show you."

"Teach me? Show me? Show me what, Mordecai? That you're a crazed killer intent on destroying my life?"

"Show you that you *have* no life. Not without God."

A look came over her face then. Bryan saw it change, saw her mind working, saw her thinking her way out of this. He relaxed his grip on the knife a little, hoping to God he wasn't going to have to use it.

"You're right, Mordecai. I…I've been so wrong. All this time." She lowered her eyes. "What can I do to make it up to you? What can I do to make it right with God?"

But Mordecai only laughed, a low, frighteningly soft sound that wasn't really a laugh at all. It made the hairs on the back of Bryan's neck stand up.

"Oh, that's very good, Lizzie. Almost convincing. But no, no, you haven't repented, not in your heart. Maybe when you've been brought so low you can't hold your head up anymore. Maybe when you've been stripped of everything."

She blinked slowly. "But I have been. I've lost my home, my best friend and the man I loved. What more can you take from me, Mordecai?"

"You'll go back to him. To that house and to him. I know you, Lizzie." He looked at his watch. "But in a few minutes, you'll understand what it means to be utterly without."

She frowned. "What do you mean? Mordecai, what have you done?"

"Nothing I haven't done before. I'm very good, you know. I was in that house of yours last night. And in a few minutes, it will be no more."

"Oh, my God," she whispered, her eyes going wider. "You've put some kind of bomb in the house."

"Now you're getting it."

She lunged forward, as if to rush past him, but he swung the gun he held, catching her in the jaw, snapping her head backward. She hit the ground hard.

Damn him! Bryan lifted the knife and stepped out from behind the tree, and in that instant, Beth's eyes met his. "No!" she cried.

Bryan froze.

Beth jerked her gaze back to Mordecai's. "No, Mordecai. That house is full of innocent people. Please, you have to let me go. Let me *get everyone out.* I have to go. *Now. And get everyone out.*"

Bryan heard her message, loud and clear. And he understood. He backed away slowly, then turned and hurried back through the woods. He raced across the lawn and through the back door, bursting into the kitchen and lunging through the dining room. "There's a bomb! Everyone out of the house!"

People shot to their feet, gaping at him.

"Outside! Everyone outside! Now!"

And then they burst into motion. All of them racing for the front door. It was a crush, people pushing, jostling, but still keeping it under control. After an initial hassle at the front door, Frankie started issuing orders, and they eased back and made their way outside single file.

Bryan joined them when there was a break in the line and began searching the crowd gathered on the front lawn for his father, for Dawn.

Chief Frankie gripped his arm. "Bryan, what in God's name is going on?"

"Mordecai Young. He's in the woods, he's got Beth, and he says there's a bomb in the house." He looked back toward the house. "God, where's my father?"

"Come on, Beth. I want you to see it when it goes. I want you to see what your unrepentant pride has wrought." Mordecai gripped her upper arm and jerked her to her feet.

She didn't fight him, because she needed desperately to get back to the house, to make sure everyone had gotten out. "When...when is this bomb going to go off?" she asked, running to keep up with him as he strode through the woods, still gripping her arm.

He smiled and looked at his watch. "Less than two minutes, Beth. And maybe then you'll be humbled before the power of almighty God."

They emerged from the woods and heard voices, loud, alarmed voices coming from the front lawn. "What's happening?" Mordecai asked someone who wasn't there.

Beth wrenched her arm free, jammed her elbow into his windpipe and ran around the house. But he chased her, and then he had her again, his arm snapping around her neck from behind. They were standing there on the front lawn, twenty feet from half the town, but concealed by one corner of the house. She could do nothing. Mordecai had her, his gun jammed against her temple.

And that was when she heard Bryan saying, "Where's my father?"

"Last time I saw him, he and Dawn were looking for Beth," someone said.

"They went upstairs," someone else said.

"Jesus, they're still inside!"

"No!" Beth cried, wrenching against Mordecai's imprisoning arm. "Joshua?" She no longer cared if he shot her, so she sprang into the open. "Dawny! God, no, Dawny!" Mordecai lunged after her, grabbing her again.

Everyone turned at her cry, seeing the situation, the man holding her, the gun pressed to her head. They went still and silent. Frankie held up a hand, keeping everyone calm, and Beth noted Jax at the edge of the crowd, working her way closer, one hand behind her back.

"Dawn?" Mordecai whispered close to her ear. "You mean the girl—the girl who's been with Bryan all this time—she's our Sunny?"

"You didn't know? Mordecai, you have to do something. Sunny, our Sunny, she's in that house!"

He looked at the sky. "That's why you wouldn't let me see her?" he asked. "How could you? How could you trick me into killing my own child?" As he said it, his imprisoning arm relaxed a little. Beth jerked free and ran for the house, but he came after her. She mounted the front steps, only to be yanked roughly back again. Mordecai flung her to the ground, and she landed hard, as he raced past her and through the front door.

"Beth, you have to get back!" Jax was beside her, lifting and tugging her backward, over the ground, and then Frankie was on her other side, dragging her away from the house, over the grass.

She pulled against their hands, scrambling to get to her feet, but just as she did, the entire world exploded in light and sound. The shock wave sent her flying backward, and she landed flat on her back on the ground. She couldn't hear, couldn't see, as she instinctively drew her arms and legs over her body against the rain of debris that pummeled and pounded her into the earth. And even when it stopped, she didn't want to get up again.

Mordecai had kept his promise. He'd taken everything. Everything. Maude, Joshua. *Dawn*.

"Beth!"

Jax was at her side, prying her arms away from her face. "Are you all right? God, look at your head. Lie still, hon. Lie still, help's on the way."

Beth blinked through tears, staring at the smoke and rubble that had been Maude's home. *Her* home. She shook off the hands that were on her, pushed herself upright, got to her feet, staggered a little. "Oh God, oh God. Joshua…" she whispered, and her heart told her what she should have known before. She still loved him—even learning what he'd done hadn't changed that. And now she'd lost him and—oh God, Dawny.

She heard Bryan calling for his father in a broken, choked voice, and knew someone must be holding him, too, or he would have been beside her right now, fighting to get in. There were bits of the house still standing amid the dust and smoke; unrecognizable walls, beams, part of the roof angled upward from the ground.

"Joshua?" she called. "Dawn?" She started forward, heard sirens in the distance. Some of the smoke cleared.

And then she saw something moving. Something...in the smoke and dust. Something rising, rubble tumbling off its back. A man's form.

"Joshua?"

It staggered forward a few steps. Just enough, and then he stood there, wobbling on his feet. Mordecai, his face streaked in dirt and soot, his head bleeding.

Beth lunged at him, shrieking, pummeling. Mordecai sank to his knees even as Jax and Frankie gripped her arms and dragged her off him. "You killed them! You bastard, you killed them!"

"Beth."

The voice came from beyond Mordecai, and she went still, stopped struggling against the arms that held her, and looked.

Another form rose from that same spot. The dust cleared a little more.

"Joshua?"

He came forward out of the smoke, carrying Dawn in his arms.

A cry was wrenched from her lungs. People rushed past her, easing Dawn from Joshua's arms, as she shouted, "I'm fine! Put me down, dammit!"

Others helped Josh out of the smoke, onto the lawn. Ambulances had arrived, and paramedics milled around Dawn, while others went past her and returned again with Mordecai on a stretcher, only to lower him to the ground farther from the danger. But Joshua only stood there, staring into Beth's eyes.

Bryan rushed by her, hurling himself into his father's

arms. "Are you okay, Dad? God, I thought I'd lost you. Like Mom. Dad, don't let that happen, okay? Please?"

"Never," he promised. "I'm okay, Bryan." He hugged his son, but his eyes remained on Beth. He was filthy, streaked in soot and dirt.

"What about Dawn?" Bryan turned, pulling his father's arm around his shoulders and starting toward the lawn, where the medics were gathered around Dawn. Beth turned, as well.

"She's going to be okay," Josh said. "She hurt her leg, couldn't walk." The two of them came closer to Beth, flanking her.

She felt odd, outside herself, as if she were a stranger watching everything.

"She's going to be okay, Beth," Josh said softly.

And even as he said it, she saw Dawn sitting up from amid the people around her. "It's just my ankle, that's all. I think I twisted it."

Relief flooded her. She felt Joshua's hands on her shoulders. "Mordecai threw himself on top of her and knocked me to the floor in the process, just before the house went up," Joshua said. "I think he may have saved her life. Hell, maybe both our lives."

"M-Mordecai?" She looked to where he lay, saw the medics frantically beginning CPR.

"Beth—Jesus, honey, your head—" Josh said.

She looked at him. "You...you were there. You were there. You shot me."

His face went lax.

"She knows, Dad. Mordecai had a clipping," Bryan said.

Josh gripped her shoulders. "Listen to me, Beth. I n-ver—ent oo—"

Beth frowned, because his words were no longer words

but broken vowel sounds and partial syllables. Gibberish. "Josh?"

He was searching her face, and his eyes narrowed. "—eth?"

Everything went dark, and she collapsed against him.

It was too much for his mind to process all at once, Josh thought as he caught Beth in his arms. Firefighters charging past him, blasting water onto the wreckage of the house...

Her house. Beth's house. God, it's gone.

Jax had taken charge big-time, and Josh thought Frankie was glad of the help. The woman had herded bystanders off the lawn into a solid group along the roadside. She and Chief Frankie seemed to be speaking to each of them, checking for injuries, giving them the okay to leave the scene.

His hand stroked Beth's hair, sliding to her throat, where he felt a strong, steady pulse beating against his fingertips.

Paramedics took hold of Beth, moving her off him. He let go, though he didn't want to, and let them lay her onto a stretcher. One belted straps around her and another checked her vital signs.

She has to be okay. She can't die, not after all this.

Bryan moved to his side, stood shoulder to shoulder with him, put a hand on his back as if to offer strength.

He's a man. He's not a boy anymore. He's grown up while I've been too busy to notice.

Dawn was pushing her way free of the medics that surrounded her, and Josh felt his son tense. She got to her feet, none too steadily, and her gaze swept the lawn, the wreckage, the bustle of people—then it stopped on the man who lay just behind Josh and Bryan, medics still surrounding him. At her stricken expression, Josh turned to follow her gaze.

Mordecai lay there. The medics had brought a portable defibrillator, and even as he looked on, they sent a jolt through the madman's chest. His body jumped. But there was no other visible reaction.

As Dawn made her way closer, limping badly, moving past Josh, Bryan went to her, but she held up a hand, and he stopped. She kept moving, her face transfixed.

They shocked Mordecai again. One of the medics yelled, "Wait—he's coming back."

Another said, "I'm getting a pulse."

Dawn pushed through them and dropped to her knees, and Josh couldn't help but move closer. He watched as she moved a trembling hand to the prone man's sooty face, touched his cheek.

Mordecai opened his eyes. He stared at her, strained to speak. "Sunny. My Sunny. I'm so sorry. I didn't know it was you. I didn't know.... I'd never hurt you, Sunny."

"You saved me," she whispered. "I'm all right."

He nodded. "It's time...for me to...go."

She had tears welling in her eyes. "I know," she told him.

"Do you...can you...?"

"I forgive you. Father."

The expression on the man's face changed from tortured to peaceful. "You're my next of kin," he told her. "Make them let me go."

She nodded. "I will."

His hand rose from the ground, closed around hers. "The guides were wrong, Sunny. About a lot of things. Especially about you. You were the one. It was you all along. All I have is yours, Sunny. My gift...use it more wisely than I did. And know I always loved you. Always will. Always..."

His eyes fell closed, and his hand seemed to clench hers fiercely for an instant. She gasped and looked down at where he gripped her, but then his hand went lax.

"I've lost the pulse!" one medic said as the machine beside Mordecai droned in a high-pitched, warbling tone.

"He's in v-fib. Give me the paddles."

"No." Dawn spoke loudly, firmly. "Let him go."

"But—"

"I'm his daughter. His only living relative, and I'm acting on his wishes. Don't shock him any more."

Josh was stunned at how she looked just then. Not at all like a young girl. She stood straighter, strong, chin up, face streaked and bruised, weight mostly on one leg, clothing dirty and torn, hair a mess. She was a strong woman— a woman claiming ownership of a decision no one should have to make.

He spoke. "She just gave you a legally binding DNR order. You have witnesses. Let the man go."

With a sigh, one of the medics reached out and flicked a switch, and the machine's now-steady tone stopped. Another covered Mordecai's face with a blanket. A sob was wrenched from Dawn's throat, and only then did she let Bryan fold her into his arms.

"Jesus, your hand," Bryan said. "It's on fire. Did you burn it?"

"No," she whispered, looking toward her father's sheet-draped form. "It's fine."

The next minute Josh realized they were bundling Beth into an ambulance.

Dawn noticed at the same time. "Is she all right?"

"She's going to be," Bryan said. "Go on, Dad. Ride in the ambulance with Beth. Dawn and I will follow in the pickup."

Josh glanced at the pickup truck, where it sat just out

of range of the explosion, safe, dusty, but unharmed; then he nodded, his gaze focusing again on Beth. Her skin was pale, her head lolling as they jostled her into the back of the ambulance.

"She'll be okay, Dad," Bryan said.

Again he nodded. "Tell Jax to leave the crowd control to Frankie and her men. She needs to secure the body." He nodded toward Young. "She shouldn't let it out of her sight until the Feds come to claim it."

Bryan nodded. "I'll tell her. Go on, Dad, I've got this."

Josh met his son's eyes. "I know you have. Thanks, Bry." Then he moved forward and climbed into the back of the ambulance, grateful for Jax and for Frankie Parker. Grateful for Bryan, too. But beyond all of that, he was afraid—terrified of losing Beth. Of all the things he'd ever lost in his life—and hell, he'd lost a lot of them—losing her or losing Bryan would surely bring him down. Those were losses from which he would never recover.

He sat beside the gurney, closed a hand around her limp one, leaned down close to her ear. "Be okay, Beth. Be okay for me."

25

━━◆━━

She was lying in a bed, unconscious and unable to wake up, and yet…aware.

The state was a familiar one. So familiar that for a time in her mind she wasn't certain there had ever been anything else.

But if there had been nothing else, then where was that yawning chasm that had once lived where her memory belonged? She knew who she was. She was Lizzie. She'd been at the Young Believers' Compound, and there had been a raid—and she'd been shot. But she'd gotten her precious baby out—given her to Jewel. And there was no one in the world she trusted the way she trusted Jewel.

And then she'd been in a hospital. She had known she was in a hospital by the smells and the sounds. The same as now. Antiseptic. Lysol. The soft steady beep of some kind of monitor. The hushed voices of those who came in to care for her. The occasional voice on a loudspeaker.

It seemed as if there had been something in between. Some break between the before and the now, a time when she had not been in this state. But it was gone now, vanished in the mists.

And then there was that voice again. The one that came so often that it was familiar by now. It was always accompanied by the touch of a warm, solid hand closing around hers. This time he also stroked her hair away from her fore-head, and he said, as he always did when he came, "I'm so sorry. I wish it had been me instead of you. If I could make this better, I would. I'm so sorry."

She knew he was sorry, whoever he was. She knew. God, he'd told her often enough.

"Beth, please come back to me. I don't want to lose you again, not again. I love you, Beth."

She frowned. Now *those* words were very different. He loved her? How could he love her? She didn't even know who he was. And why was he calling her Beth?

"Come on, honey. Dawn's worried sick about you, and Bryan's pacing a hole in the waiting room floor. Please wake up. Please?"

Dawn. Wait, that was Sunny's name now. And she was all grown-up. And just as smitten with Bryan as Beth herself was with his father. Joshua.

"Joshua," she whispered. And even as she said his name, the veils fell away and she remembered. She'd awakened from that coma so long ago. She'd lived an entire lifetime since then.

And yet the hand holding hers, and the voice speaking to her—they were the same.

"Joshua." She opened her eyes.

He smiled down at her. "Hey. It's about time. The doc-tors kept telling me you were going to be fine, but God…"

"You were there," she whispered.

He lowered his head. "I was going to tell you, Beth. I swear I was. I just—God, I couldn't bear the thought that you'd hate me for it. Yes, I was there. It was my bullet that destroyed your life all those years ago."

She held his gaze. "I know. But that's not what I meant."

"No?"

She shook her head slowly, as things became crystal

clear at long last. "You were there—in my hospital room. When I was in the coma."

He looked surprised. "I was, but how did you—"

"Your voice. I could hear you, Josh. I could feel you there. You were what kept me from giving up. That voice and the touch of your hand—you brought me back."

He swallowed hard; she watched his Adam's apple swell briefly. "I'd have kept coming, but they told me there was no hope. You'd be gone within a week, they said, and I had to move on." He shook his head slowly. "All this time, Beth, I thought you were dead. I thought I had killed you. When I saw you again, on Maude Bickham's front porch, I..."

He didn't finish. He didn't have to. She understood.

Her door had swung open while he'd been speaking, and Bryan and Dawn had come quietly into the room. Bryan spoke now. "Beth, my Dad has spent his life beating himself up for what he did to you. His guilt cost him his marriage, his job, the chance to raise me, and God only knows what else. He wanted to tell you—he did—but he was so afraid you'd bolt and maybe end up dead. He couldn't bear to be responsible for that—not again."

Josh turned to face his son. "Thank you, Bryan. But I think she needs to hear all this from me."

"I just wanted her to know," he said.

"Are you okay, Beth?" Dawn asked.

Beth nodded. Josh said, "She's okay now, but...I need a minute."

Dawn cast Beth an understanding smile, then put a hand on Bryan's arm. "I just wanted to see for myself," she said. "Come on, Bry. Let's give them some privacy."

The two teenagers backed out of the room. As they did, Josh turned, pushing a hand through his hair, sighing deeply. "I don't expect you to forgive me, Beth. Hell, I don't deserve your forgiveness. I let you lose everything—again."

"But I haven't lost everything."

Turning, he faced her. She sat up in the bed, and Josh quickly moved closer to prop her pillows behind her.

"The inn…" he began.

"Is just a building. Boards and nails and plaster and paint. Just a building. It doesn't matter. When it blew up—I thought, for one horrible instant that I really had lost everything, the things that really matter. I thought I'd lost the people I love more than anything I've ever loved or ever will. Dawny. And you."

He blinked down at her; then he sank onto the edge of her bed, as if his legs wouldn't hold him any longer. "You still love me—even knowing what I did to you?"

"I've loved you for a while now. You know that. The only thing that kept me uncertain was that I knew you were keeping secrets, my fear that they would destroy me. But now I know what you were keeping from me, Josh. And how much it's hurt you—it cost you as much as it cost me, that long-ago mistake. You lost your child, your life, just like I did."

He closed his eyes.

"All that's gone, and what's left is just this. I still love you. I'll always love you."

He gathered her very gently into his arms. "I can't believe it. I can't believe how damn lucky I am."

She slipped her arms around him, and when he turned his mouth to hers, she kissed him deeply.

When their lips parted and his eyes were roaming her face in something like wonder, he said, "Mordecai is dead. This nightmare you've been forced to live, Beth, it's over. You can live anywhere you want now, any way you want."

"I know."

"The inn is gone, but—"

"It's insured. Probably overinsured. Maude put the insurance policy in my name when she signed the place over to me. It was in that envelope full of legal papers her lawyer gave me. The premiums were paid through the end of the year."

He nodded. "So you can start over."

"I don't want to start over, Josh. I want to pick up right where we left off, you and I. Minus one big secret standing between us."

He smiled slowly. "I'm really glad to hear you say that. 'Cause I've been carrying something around with me for days now, and—" He sighed and pulled it out of his pocket. "Maude Bickham gave me this right after you and I met for the first time, on her porch. I think maybe she knew who I would ask to wear it. She must have seen it in the way I looked at you. Or the way you looked at me. Or…I don't know."

Beth gasped when he opened his hand and revealed Maude's antique diamond ring. The huge pear-shaped stone was surrounded by tiny, glittering emeralds and sapphires. "Oh, Josh."

"Marry me, Beth?"

She met his eyes, smiled slowly and nodded. "Yes."

Epilogue

—•—

"Our first guests are here," Joshua said, sliding his hands over Beth's shoulders as she wiped her hands on a kitchen towel and turned into his arms. "Great. I've got the chicken ready to go."

"And I've got the barbecue hot and waiting."

"Did you tell Bryan?"

"Bryan's already out in the driveway. He'll probably open their car door before they come to a complete stop."

"It's nice, they're both going to the same college this fall."

"Even nicer that it's an easy drive from here."

She smiled, and, turning, they walked arm in arm through their inn. They'd had it rebuilt as closely to the original structure as they could, and it still smelled of fresh paint and new lumber. It was furnished in antiques, and photos of Maude and her husband at various times of their lives had been donated by locals and hung in every room.

It had been costly, despite the insurance. But Josh had sold his condo in Manhattan, and that had brought in more than enough to make up the difference.

They walked out the front door, onto the porch and down the steps to where the newly painted sign swung in the summer breeze.

Maude Bickham's Blackberry Inn

Beth and Joshua Kendall, Proprietors.

Beth took a moment to relish the way reading that sign made her feel before heading down the sidewalk to join Bryan in greeting their first guests; Julie Jones McKenzie, her husband Sean, and the daughter she and Beth shared—with each other, and now with their husbands, and, the way things were looking, with Bryan. Dawn.

They were not a traditional family, Beth thought. But they were her family—all of them.

She had reclaimed the life she had lost in a misguided government raid long ago. And it was better than she had ever dreamed.